# THE BOYS WHO WOULDN'T GROW UP
## A NOVEL

# THE BOYS WHO WOULDN'T GROW UP
## A NOVEL

LAUREN B. MANGIAFORTE

The Bahnheur Press
2013

First Printing: 2013

ISBN: 978-1-304-99612-1

The Bahnheur Press
New York, NY 10029

www.laurenmangiaforte.com

U.S. trade bookstores and wholesalers: please email bahnheur@gmail.com.

For Ronny Riba:
The boy who will never grow up.
With eternal love and devotion.

# PART ONE

" 'Wendy,' Peter Pan continued, in a voice that no woman has ever yet been able to resist, 'Wendy, one girl is more use than twenty boys.' "

—J.M. Barrie, *Peter Pan*

# I. MAY

**THE SUN FLICKERED ABOVE THE NORTH** Sea, as it tended to do on spring mornings such as this one. As if not quite sure whether it was late in going to bed or early in rising, it teetered near the horizon—projecting spackled patches of soft, yawning light onto the enormous stone wall of the Castle that sat atop the cliffs. Everything was illuminated by the buzzing sun: the earthy sand, and the golden land, and the long green hairs of Scottish grass that fell over the cliffs' shoulders and down into the whirling, wash-pot sea below.

The grass shivered in its salty, icy bath, wishing the sun would hurry up and rise. Along the path that traced the cliffs, scruffy seagulls perched on lampposts laughed down at the grass in their customarily pert manner. Seeing the birds lose their balance as their rubbery claws gripped in vain at the slippery steel rusted with years of salty rain, the grass laughed back with chattering teeth.

This age-old exchange continued as tiny mice far below pounced from leaf to leaf, so light that no detection of their modest and urgent motions could be perceived from a human or bird perspective. They hurried between the Castle's brick and iron, weaving paths of trodden earth behind them in tangled yellow flowerbeds. Occasionally, they took the routes bequeathed to them by their furry ancestors, but more often they scurried in whatever direction they detected a discarded kebob or a Scottish flower. The mice were like that in those days—the mice were just like everyone else, easily swayed by their noses and stomachs.

The sandy beach was several dozens of yards—or metres, if that was your sort of thing—below the wall that surrounded the Castle. To access the sands, you had to struggle down steep, wide steps that wound down the cliffs' side like a curled spine. Keeping one's balance was a heroic feat to attempt in the damp Scottish weather, particularly when you had a bottle of wine in your hand, or a few drinks from the pub sloshing around in your stomach. No one could really say whether going down or climbing up was a more treacherous act, and no one ever really attempted to do either unless it was very early in the morning or very late at night.

During the warmer seasons, the beach was a popular gathering place for the students at the University, who exploited the townspeople and police's dislike for the hazardous steps as an excuse to do many things, among them: falling in love, breaking up, selling drugs, buying drugs, taking drugs, dancing, smoking, singing, crying, laughing, starting fires and putting them out, proclaiming God's goodness, cursing His unfairness, and, on several occasions, students even resorted to using the rocks to the west of the beach as a fatal place to fall from the Castle's high wall.

When someone did this, it was usually reported in the *St Albas Chronicle* as an accident. For one thing, the view from the Castle's wall was much more beautiful looking out rather than down, where stretches of volcanic rock had settled like crumpled, porous rags of a ruddy-brown color. But standing on the wall, looking toward the horizon, the calm rocking of the welcoming waves before you, joyous in the moonlight and sunlight alike, it seemed indecent to be anything but alive. Being there even made you feel you could fly, if you thought thoughts that were happy enough. So it wasn't a wonder that the locals thought it a cause for great concern, and an example of what was wrong with the privileged youth of St Albas, when anyone suggested by doing it that it might be possible to want to kill yourself in a place as beautiful as that.

On this particular morning, though, no one wanted to die. This wasn't just because everyone had been drinking since the sun went down last night. It was because this was May 1, and everyone wanted to run into the sea.

***

Two hours ago and as many streets away, a boy and a girl sat on a sofa. The sofa was the largest object in the cozy living room in the top floor of a building dating from the 17th century. The age of the building did not impress either of them; the girl was English, the boy Swiss, and they had seen their fair share of buildings from the 17th century. They had spent hours and days and years under this sloping ceiling, which had in a previous life covered an attic. Now, it was the boy's apartment, and he had brought his girlfriend to it after dinner. But dinner had been several long hours ago.

On the coffee table in front of the couch, two mugs of hot chocolate sat un-drunk, un-spiked, and getting colder every second. The boy felt sympathetic towards them.

"Are you sure you don't want to run into the sea with me?" he asked. His sneakers were still on his feet, though they had returned three hours previously. Over that amount of time the conversation had changed as little as his footwear.

"Quite sure."

"But you didn't do it first year, or second year…"

The girl turned to him.

"I said we could stay up all night if you wanted to, and it's already nearly three."

The boy sighed. He would probably never run into the sea.

"I don't want you to regret it, that's all. It's one of the things people do in St Albas. Everyone will be there. Peter, and me, and Simon too. And, you know, you don't have to drink."

Her eyes came to rest on his face.

"But you'll be drinking."

He reached for her hand, rested his head on her shoulder.

"I won't, if you don't want me to."

"Honestly?"

"Of course."

She directed her gaze to the wrinkle between his brows. His face looked tired. It hadn't when she'd met him. It was curious that someone so young could look so old. She thought it was funny that he wanted to run into the sea in the first place. For a moment, the boy was hopeful in his watching of her, thinking that she might actually be considering what he'd said, until she spoke again:

"We can sit and watch the sun rise here. Besides, the sea's still so cold this time of year. Nobody can ever find their things after they go in the water. Haven't you read the email they send us the day after with the lost and found?"

The boy nodded.

He was not, by nature, prone to fighting. And she was not prone to direct and honest proclamations of her feelings. So they both kept quiet, as they assumed was best in situations such as this, and indeed, in all situations. As it was the only thing moving in the room, they watched the steam rising fitfully from the hot chocolate.

Not being able to endure the stillness for long, the boy stood, picked up his mug from the table, and walked to the window, the floorboards crackling beneath his feet. At the age of twenty-one, keeping quiet was one thing; keeping still—another.

Beyond Sea Street and the Avenue, there was that sliver of the North Sea, a perfect sheet of silver, a mirror for the moon. On the street, people stood in bathrobes, bathing suits, and towels, shivering in the early, sunless chill. In their hands and purses, they carried bottles of wine and beer and monogrammed flasks full of liquor. There was even one industrious young man selling shots of Irish crème, which people poured into the styrofoam cups of coffee they had purchased from the charity stand of the University Christian Collective. The boy looked down at them enviously. He wanted madly, compulsively, to run into the sea with them, to drink with them in the street, to know their names and laugh loudly and put his arms around young male shoulders and his hands on young female waists.

The girl's mobile phone rang.

"Do you mind my answering?"

The boy nodded absently from the window.

*I suppose it's Peter*, she thought to herself.

She reached into the pocket of her heavy wool sweater, an effort that revealed an unnecessarily self-important iPhone. This had been purchased with the help of her father, at the Carphone Warehouse in Lancashire. The "Carphone" part was halfway to sounding antique. She liked that.

She put the answered phone to her ear.

"Hello."

"Hello," said Peter. "How are you, Catriona?"

"We're all right," she said. "What's the matter?"

"Wondering where you and Max are. Having quite a good night—party is mental."

At the window, Max listened carefully, though he did not realize that he was doing it. He listened to the creak of the floorboards, to the squeak of his sneakers as he shifted his weight, to the whoosh of infrequent cars and farm vehicles in the street below, to the echoing sound of drunken laughter as people scattered out of the way, to the music that boomed from a house party nearby. And he listened to his girlfriend as she spoke to her cousin.

"We're at home just now."

"Having fun, are we?"

"We're chatting to you."

"Max said he'd be here."

"Did he?"

"You said *you* would be here. I told my mother I invited you."

"I'm certain I appreciate it. But I'm afraid I won't be coming along and neither will Max."

"Tell him I say hello," said Max, reclaiming his seat.

"Did you hear? Max says hello."

"Hello from me, as well. Very well. Well done, Catriona. You win. I'll bugger off."

"Goodnight, Peter."

Catriona hung up and sat next to Max. She took his hand, stared straight ahead, and said, as though the room and everything in it was everything she had ever wanted:

"Now we're having fun."

Another street away, Peter turned his cell phone off and put it back in his pocket. Taking one more look at the relatively quiet end of Fair Street upon which he was standing, he rolled his head around his shoulders and picked his beer up from the top of the tartan-patterned mailbox where it had been resting and turned to walk back up to the house where the party was continuing on.

A wall of sound hit him as he opened the house's big, blue door and closed it quickly against the oppressive quiet of the street. It was a loud party and the best one among the many in town that celebrated the May Saving.

There they were: thirty, forty, 100 of them, all students at the University, making a tremendous amount of noise. Huddled in a kitchen, they drank and they talked and, occasionally, they went in pairs to the bathroom—sometimes to have sex, sometimes to get sick, sometimes to do lines of cocaine off the toilet. Which of the three usually depended on the size of their parents' incomes.

The party spilled from the house's insides and into the boxy backyard like a pile of undone sausage links. Music of unknown provenance blared from a source somewhere in the vicinity. People like these could always afford a new set of speakers when the current ones got trampled or rained on. Around the garden, kegs of beer sank into the slightly damp ground like oversized flowerpots.

Girls in stilettos also sank into the mud, happy to be drunk, for sinking into mud when sober made a dent in one's self-esteem and had a way of inducing crash diets. Now, carefree, they swayed and sank like stilted houses in a hurricane. Watching them was fun. Part of you hoped they would collapse.

There was someone ripping his t-shirt off to a pile of cheering undergraduates; several couples secluded in dark corners, their clothes astray and their tongues intertwined; there were even a few computer science students standing on the porch with their arms folded, their large plastic glasses reflecting the flickering light of the insect zapper.

Peter rejoined his flatmates at the kitchen table, where there was a drinking game in progress involving twenty pence coins and shot glasses. It appeared a few of the American students were attempting to teach their European and Asian counterparts the finer points of their drinking culture. Most of what the Americans knew about it had been learned on visits to see cousins and friends at UConn, UMass, UMich, you name it.

At the helm of this youthful madness was a guy by the name of Larry Liberatore, who was liked by almost everyone—with the exception of only the primmest British and French girls.

Larry was twenty-two years old and beefy with biceps that looked as if they had been stuffed with steaks that wiggled, uncomfortable and restless, under his skin. Though he had been raised on Long Island, he considered himself a New Yorker. The way he talked, you might think he spent his childhood stealing bubble gum from the Jewish deli down the street and swinging between tenement buildings on laundry lines, presumably while singing tunes from *Oliver!* In fact, his father was an orthodontist from Fort Wayne, Indiana, who married a girl from upstate. Having run a successful practice for many years of fitting braces and caps on the teeth of millionaires' children (an especially lucrative trade in July and August), his parents had now retired to Florida, considering it their right after raising two star quarterbacks and a cheerleader.

This was embarrassing to Larry, who wanted to be more than his high school football records. And that's why you had to give him some credit for coming to Europe instead of attending one of those big state schools out east where the athletic scholarships beckoned.

In spite of his straight, white teeth, one got a sense that there was something bold and unexpected waiting to emerge in him. Larry himself supposed this nascent quality to be courage, and so to a certain extent it was.

"Nah, nah, nah, nah, nah," he said to the South African girl beside him. "Now you gotta drink!"

She laughed.

"There you are," said Peter's roommate, Brett. "Is Catriona coming, then? I made sure to clean under my fingernails and scrub behind my ears."

"No, she's staying in with Max."

"Max is staying in with her, you mean. Poor devil," said Ashwin.

From their origins in the same hall of residence during first year, the trio of Peter, Brett, and Ashwin had been as predictable and solid as the middle section of a Sousa march. They had suffered and triumphed as a unit for three years in spite of the fact that they'd spent most of their time harassing one another. Peter was typically the straight man, with his straight English ways, hunting-jacket-green eyes, dark blond hair, and slightly crooked hairline. Ashwin was his trickster foil from the south of India: dark, handsome, with irresistibly large and impossibly innocent brown eyes that danced above a puckish smile. Brett, the Australian grandson of a mining baron, swung between them as it suited him, neither here nor there in his crisp, upper-class polo shirts and agreeable, moneyed face with its light blue gaze and dark, thick brows.

"My mum's going to give me such crap for this. 'Why don't you invite your cousin to join you? I think she's a bit out of sorts,' 'I know, mum, I do, but she—'"

"Just say it, man: your cousin is a bitch."

"Ashwin," said Brett, putting a firm, signet-ringed hand on his friend's slightly soft chest. "Not cool."

"Fine." Ashwin took a gulp of the beer in his hand. "But she is."

"At least you tried," said Brett to Peter, attempting to be helpful. "You can't get that girl to do anything she doesn't want to do. You know that, mate, and I'm sure your mum does too."

"How is that different in any way from what I just said?" asked Ashwin.

"You've cut right to the chase, haven't you," said Peter. "Calling my cousin a bitch. You've met her, what, three times?"

"Enough to know what she's like, between that and what you say about her."

"You've still got to have some manners."

Ashwin sighed. "Whatever, man. Sure. If it makes you happy."

"Thank you," said Peter.

"—All I'm saying is that if I ever have to sit through dinner with the two of them again, I am going to kill you in your sleep."

"Lay off him," said Brett.

"Thank you," said Peter once more.

"…But seriously, I will probably help Ashwin kill you if we have to eat with them again."

"Max isn't bad," said Peter, now on the defensive in two directions.

"No. He's a decent guy."

"And Catriona isn't—you know, *awful* or something. She hasn't got two heads."

"Look," said Ashwin, trying to keep his drink and himself upright, "she's never done anything to me. I just don't like that she's got you on call all the time."

Peter ignored Ashwin's last comment and said:

"I wouldn't worry about eating with them again. Catriona wasn't a fan of you lot, either. I can't imagine why—you're so charming."

Outside, a light rain had started. The stereo, wherever it was, played gallantly on. People cluttered themselves into every nook and cranny of the house, steaming like lobsters in the hot perspiration of many young bodies in a damp space all at once, folded together on doorsteps and couches.

One girl, who lived in the house, rushed from window to window, shutting and opening them as she saw fit, placing buckets and pans where the old ceiling lurched and dripped, and occasionally making small talk with the other drunks, including the most lurching, drippingly boozed of them all, her housemate: Caddy.

"Seriously, Julie," Caddy Faulkener said in her deep, raspy voice to the girl in the doorway of her upstairs bedroom, "just get that stuff tomorrow."

Caddy had been smoking since she was twelve. She was an indefinably wonderful creature out of New Orleans: white as a magnolia, raised with a careless gentility that couldn't be beaten away by the harsh coastal weather of a much more dour climate. By night, she glittered with a *joie de vivre* that was unique to her. At present, she combined her southern style and Continental sensibilities in a yellow Ralph Lauren polo and a tight, beaded mini skirt that hugged her wide-set hips passionately. She was puffing out the window with her umbrella in one hand and a mint julep in the other.

"Get out of the window," laughed Julie. "This isn't *Breakfast at Tiffany's*."

"Pah!" said Caddy, taking a drag and draining her drink. "Another successful night at our house."

She attempted to raise her hand to Julie in a high five and realized that both of them were otherwise occupied.

"I'll get you later," Julie said.

"You were getting awfully close to that Japanese dude last time I looked."

"It's May Saving. Shit happens."

"Crazy times, Julie," said Caddy in agreement, coming away from the window and stubbing her cigarette out on her mouse pad. "Crazy times."

"That they are."

Caddy sat on the bed in inebriated dreaminess, staring up at her poster of Toulouse-Lautrec's *At the Moulin Rouge* on the opposite wall.

"If I was in this painting, I'd be the lady in black back there."

This statement actually came out as: "Fi wasin this paining, I'd be th'lady in backablack there." Fortunately, Julie spoke the drunken dialect of Caddy-ese.

"Look at her, with those hands on her hips."

They giggled.

"Why don't you have a drink," said Caddy, messily mixing one for her using-whatever bottles of liquor had congregated on her bedside table. "You're not drunk enough to run into the North Sea. It's pretty cold, or so they say."

Julie knew from experience that one could never be too drunk for the Saving, and so she took the concoction and sat down on the mattress. Whatever it was supposed to be didn't taste half bad. She was not surprised. Caddy's bartending improvisations were the stuff of undergraduate lore.

"God," said Julie. "I hope this party never ends."

"It won't," said Caddy with conviction.

"We did a fucking amazing job."

"Don't we always?"

"Yeah, we do."

"Let's go downstairs."

"Okay."

"I want to kick Ashwin's ass at beer pong."

But the girls paused together for a moment, listening, conspiratorial. There was something exhilarating in hearing your own party going on below you. The stiller they became, the further away the booming of the music sounded, like it did in those scenes from old movies when people were under canon siege. Julie was happy that everyone was in such high spirits. They had not run out of alcohol, the police had not come, and as far as she knew, there was no one except Caddy smoking in the house. It was, as Caddy had said, another successful May Saving party, pulled off through the dual effort of their hostessing prowess—and the help of Caddy's father's wallet.

Julie swung her arms affectionately around her housemate.

"We have more friends than anyone."

"I saw how many. Downstairs."

"We're popular, Caddy."

"Are we?"

"The most."

They laughed.

It was then that a boy appeared in the box of light at the doorway, his shadow spreading onto Caddy's Persian rug. The girls looked toward him.

"Who's that?" Caddy asked the owner of the shadow.

"Larry's friend. We met downstairs, about an hour ago?"

Caddy gave no indication that she remembered and regarded the apparition with amusement.

"Huh. Welcome to our humble abode."

"Have you seen him? Larry?"

"Haven't seen 'im. Have you, Julie?" said Caddy.

"Last I saw, he was downstairs playing flippy cup."

Caddy, inspired by either the reminder that more alcohol was to be had or the opportunity to be a good hostess (her mother had raised her to be a lady), shimmied her way past the boy at the door. She tumbled along the hallway drunkenly like a sailor in a listing ship, vowing loudly that she would locate Larry at all costs.

"Hadn't you better follow her?" he asked Julie, in an accent she couldn't place.

"Oh no, she's a champ on those stairs."

Julie switched on Caddy's nightstand lamp, which made the shadow disappear and put a boy in its place.

Harry Ommar was dark-haired and dark-eyed. Tall and broad, he was always relying on women's assumptions of his size to get them into bed, although his height and jaw line were usually more than enough to accomplish those nefarious ends. Harry had always been a distressingly handsome boy, and in fact he had never looked like a child at all. The succession of nannies and tutors and music teachers who had raised him always went home and found, to some dissatisfaction, that their own boys would never be as genuinely, absorbingly handsome as the one they'd left behind in the bassinet or at the piano. It was an amused and flattered Harry, who, in high school, was accused of having affairs with two young teachers just recently out of university, and who, as an undergraduate himself, had actually wooed several female faculty members to the point of near-divorce.

His body had long since grown to match the manliness of his face, and women seemed to find Harry either brutish and crude, or brutish and maddeningly attractive. There was no middle ground. The arguments that transpired on the subject left groups of women (and sometimes men) bitterly entrenched against one another. One side inevitably cited his disrespect for women and his general apathy toward acceptable standards of sexual behavior. The other agreed wholeheartedly, but ended their consenting remarks with a rebuttal along the lines of "but have you seen him with his shirt off?"

There had been days during which Harry had had more affairs by sundown than many people have in all the evenings of their lives.

Some boys are just born the way Harry was: an emotional liability for any person drawn to his looks. Julie's side had been chosen for her the moment he appeared in the doorway, and she found herself thinking, rather reflexively, *I must have that one.* This rush of attraction had to it a potency she had never felt before.

"Harry Ommar," he said, finally introducing himself. "You live here as well?"

"Yep. I'm Julie."

She extended her hand. He shook it with his own rough-skinned one. She hoped he wouldn't speak again so that she might keep staring.

"Mind if I—" he said, indicating the vacated spot next to her on the bed.

"Nope."

He sat. The bed wobbled under his weight. Oh, but he smelled so good too.

"Is that booze up for the taking?"

"I think so."

"Fancy making me a drink?"

Under any other circumstances, Julie would have refused. In an alternate universe in which she was sober, she saw through the Humphrey Bogart act and was replying (*à la* Bacall) "make it yourself." But in this universe, the one where she had several gin and tonics coursing through her veins and a predilection for men of a certain height, it made sense to smile demurely and attempt to bartend over Caddy's 800-thread-count Egyptian cotton sheets.

"You're an American, aren't you?" he said.

"Yes."

"Where do you come from?" he asked, receiving his martini.

"Huh?" she said. She was picking an olive up from the floor. "Do you want this?"

"What?" He was distracted. Her breasts were falling out of her shirt. "No. Thanks. I was asking where you're from."

"Chicago."

"A beautiful city."

Only the truly well traveled had been to Chicago. Julie was impressed.

"You?"

"Lots of places."

She raised her eyebrows. A typical response of a Has when asked this question by a Has-Slightly-Less-in-the-Grand-Scheme-of-Things.

"You've heard that response before," he said. "Doesn't surprise me. St Albas is full of people like that."

"Yeah, people like you."

This made him smile.

"If that pretense is shot, I'm from London, for the most part," he said. "But my parents stay in Dubai more than half the year."

That explained a lot. The West Kensington, high-tea-and-high-times air about him. The suntan. The heavy five-o'clock-(in the morning)-shadow along his chin and cheeks. She imagined that it might have been his father who supplied the Ommar and the genes that went with it, and she imagined too that his mother must look like an old movie star and have an inflection to her voice that was romantic and chic.

"What brings you to St Albas? You're not a student, are you?"

"Oh no, I'm an old man. Graduated last year."

"From?"

"It's not usually considered polite to say."

"Harvard?"

"Yes."

Another one of those answers.

"And you're what—visiting?"

"A holiday."

"It's one of the world's most interesting places," said Julie, thinking immediately after having said it that he must have seen much more of the world than she had.

"It's different from Boston, that's certain. And London. And Dubai."

"And everywhere else."

He downed the rest of his drink and said:

"Do you enjoy St Albas?"

"I love it. Especially days like this. Days like this are the best ones. Parties, friends, running into the sea."

"Have you done the Saving before?"

"Every year," she said.

"Any advice for a newcomer?"

"If you're not drunk yet, you should get there quick."

"Don't worry, Larry's made sure of that."

"I'll bet. How do you know him?"

"Larry? We go a number of years back."

Julie wanted to know how far back. But by the lean in Harry's upper body, she could tell he was not in the mood for talking.

"You're interesting, Julie, do you know?"

"What?" she said, as he inched further into her personal space.

"Have you got a boyfriend, or someone?"

His face was close to hers. How this had come to pass was a question she could not answer. It usually shocked Julie Lovejoy when a boy wanted to kiss her who had never kissed her before. She was a perceptive girl when it came to many things, but the true feelings of boys (where they existed) were somewhat mysterious to her.

"What do you mean?"

"It's a 'yes' or 'no' question, really."

Nothing else was said or done that night because the light had begun to creep over the sea. In the yard, Julie heard the music growing lonelier as people ran into the road, heading toward the Avenue, the Castle, the beach.

Caddy had found Larry and was pulling him up the stairs. Harry leaned away, moving to the other side of the bed in just enough time for his offensive tactics to go undetected as the pair entered the room.

"Hey," Caddy said, "I found Larry."

He was standing next to her, just outside the room.

"I see you met Julie," said Larry.

"Yeah."

"Good. She's a good girl," he said. Julie heard a warning in his tone. "All set for the Saving?"

Having considered himself sufficiently found, Larry turned back on his heels, sweeping Caddy over his shoulder and carrying her down the stairs.

"May Saving!" they shouted in unison.

Harry followed them wordlessly, taking a bottle of liquor with him. He smiled at Julie as he turned the corner into the hallway.

Julie sat alone. In a moment, someone would realize she wasn't actually around, and that someone would probably be Peter.

In the dark without anyone else in the room, Julie felt an eerie premonition that she should enjoy this May Saving as if it were the last, that perhaps this time next year she would not find it all so amusing and charming. Maybe she would think it boring. Possibly she would think her friends boring. The thought that she could find these fascinating people from all around the world boring made her feel slightly ashamed and irritated at her future self.

Still, at the May Savings that had preceded this one, she hadn't taken a moment to herself. She had danced and gotten vividly intoxicated, and she and Caddy had stripped down to their bras and danced on their coffee table. She had kissed lots of boys. She had gone into the sea without her clothes on, surrounded by hundreds of people doing the same. But now, she found herself oddly enjoying this moment of solitude.

Julie shook off her thoughts and looked out the window. The rain had stopped.

Her face was like a jack-o-lantern now, as it always was: simple of expression, readable from far away. From her huge, exaggerated eyes there came a brightness that cast shadows over the triangular nose and competed for attention with the square teeth in her half-moon smile.

She sighed. The eye-fire flickered, and then it rose.

In a few moments, she would be contrite and merry with the rest of them, submerged and twisting in the icy waters of the North Sea.

Max sat, warm and dry on the sofa, staring at the inside of his right elbow.

Catriona had gone to bed.

# II. SUMMER IN ST ALBAS

**"THREE STREETS." THAT'S HOW EVERYONE DESCRIBED** it, but actually it was four. Perhaps people thought of it that way—and said it that way—because most of the actual living was done on only three.

As you know, St Albas was a little town on the sea in Scotland. What you don't know yet—though maybe some of you do—was that it was almost one thousand years old. It had therefore witnessed every human folly and triumph ever to happen under the sun. If the cobblestones and spires could talk, they would tell you that human nature never changed under any circumstance, no matter what the regime. And St Albas had seen more than its share of regimes, starting with the Church. In fact, the town as it was today never would have existed without the man who brought a bone from Saint Peter's thigh to the shores of St Albas's chilly pagan cliffs with the intention of building a great cathedral there. Eventually, the man would be a saint for his troubles, and eventually there would indeed be a cathedral, and eventually the cathedral would be sacrificed to the fires of the Reformation. That was how the story went.

The story always skipped the part about why the pragmatic people of St Albas agreed to help the man build his elaborate cathedral in the first place. Probably because the reasons are assumed to be righteous, virtuous, and sanctimonious—therefore unceasingly boring and not worth the telling. Even if one were to tell this supposedly pious version of the story of the cathedral's raising, it would be difficult to believe that the ancient St Albans could have been so mesmerized by a few dried-up bones that they found braving the windy, cold Scottish days and nights worthwhile. Not just for years or decades—but for *centuries*—as they built brick by brick, stone by stone, a church.

The motivation was actually human, selfish, and mundane. Because they have never been anything but a group of resilient realists, the native, medieval townspeople of St Albas wanted a warm place to dry their feet and listen to music and hear stories. So whipped, day by day by their dirty, wet surroundings—the fishermen in their boats on the spiky North Sea, the farmers tilling their crops and chasing hairy cows in their fields, the women scrubbing floors free of the water and the dirt and the shit their fishermen and farmers dragged into the house—mass was a fantastic excuse for escaping the toil of earthly life. But they needed a place to do it.

Imagine the sight of the cathedral, completed. Perhaps the vision is merely grand to your mind, accustomed as it probably is to electricity, heat, television, and extravagant hotel lobbies. But 600, 700, 800 years ago, the cathedral was nothing short of magnificent, especially to the ones who inherited the space from the generations who had labored tooth and nail to build it.

But try harder. Imagine the oak brought from the storied forests of Perth and Dunsinane, lording at the entryway, the religious figures carved into them perspiring with the heat of their holiness in the daily, nightly rain.

Imagine the arched ceiling—isn't that enough to make you believe in God? Up to heaven, the stone ran in spirals and angles, among angels and gargoyles. A simple cough, a laugh, a note sung in praise, they all whirled like leaves in reverse motion, defying gravity, balloons floating to the peaks and valleys of the roof.

Imagine the stained glass. The tragic, flat faces of Mary, Jesus, Joseph, and the rest of the cast, all there, but in spectacular colors not usually seen in this part of the world except in the tiny flowers of May. Even teenagers sat still in church, just looking, feasting their eyes on the stories in the windows.

Imagine the choir, singing in Latin. The only voices heard at home being mother's over dinner or father's over a pint—did the children harshly judge their parents' hummings in comparison to the distinguished tunes they heard at mass?

It was certainly warmer in the glowing church than anywhere else in town. Though the public house could compete as far as coziness was concerned, and though going to mass and going to the pub were liable to burn the same hole in a man's pocket, even the drunkest drunk must have known in his soul which was worth his silver.

Today, the cathedral was a ruin. The beautiful colors had burnt with it, and only two remained: brown and green—brown for the mud and the surviving stones it had stained, green for the grass. And the green was only in the summer. Most of the year, the grounds were a muddy pit of graves, an embarrassment to the town's Catholics and a minor point of eternal, unspoken superiority among the Protestants. Tourists from Everywhere stumbled around with their cameras, taking photos that could never accurately convey the decrepit majesty of the remaining structures. The cathedral ruins were notoriously un-photogenic, built, as well as destroyed, it seemed, to demand respect.

Though the cathedral spent three quarters of the year in this sad and slovenly state, the ground was lush and firm in the summer. Off-duty students loved to use the headstones as chair backs as they read for pleasure or to lie in the sun with their heads and hands in each other's laps on the crumbling stone altar, unaware (except for the occasional humanities student) that they read and loved just ten feet above St Albas alumni who had no doubt done the same.

From the outer wall, which had been constructed over time as a fortress to protect against Viking invasion, one could see the dark blue North Sea glimmering and pacified through the functioning, but hopefully unwarranted, bayonet holes.

The cathedral held its everlasting court at the point at which the four streets converged. To the north, running immediately along the sea, was the Avenue, which spanned the distance from the Castle to the Ancient Links. Paved with bricks, it might as well have been lined with books or horseshit, for this was also the street on which many of the University buildings stood. Six or seven Victorian mansions had been converted into buildings housing the various academic faculties. Views from the upper-story classrooms made the term "breathtaking" very literal, and first years had a habit of changing majors based upon a department's location. It was unknowable just how many students had lost marks or, in the early days of the University, had been hit on the back of the head, for daydreaming while gazing at the sparkling water. Nowadays, the picture in the windows not only revealed water, sky, rocky beaches, and the Castle but also traces of the modern. In the distance, oil rigs poked out against the smooth horizon.

The president's home was on the Avenue. Usually, it housed an old, white, English Protestant man with a wife and two children—one who inevitably went to Oxford, the other to Cambridge, as the president reminded the student body in his speeches that St Albas afforded pupils the best education money could buy. These days in St Albas, though, the person who lived there was a woman. In addition to this highly suspect character flaw, she was also a Catholic and an American. No one was sure as to how she had gotten the job (several of the old, male deans surmised the Devil's work in it), but the Catholics and the Americans and the women—they were sure happy about it.

Of course there was the library, an awful structure dating from the 1970s. In a cold, nauseous shade of beige concrete, it sat, battered mercilessly by the sea's salty gales. (The wind was rightly offended by the architecture.) Far too small for the eight thousand students who claimed they would have used it if there were enough desks, the three thousand who actually studied there were not only mentally unbreakable but physically strong. There was simply not enough air for the weak of heart, lung, or stomach. After being inside for five minutes, a person felt she had the disagreeable choice of choking on her own vomit, sweating to death, or braving the Scottish weather. It was best not to go in the first place.

At the end of the Avenue was the Ancient Links, one of the oldest golf courses in the world. How big it was exactly, the townspeople and students didn't know and didn't care unless they were playing it, exhausted, and inevitably longing to be sitting in a pub instead. The rich men who came from all over the world to play there took an awful gamble when they booked their tee times six months in advance—there was never a guarantee as to the weather's level of awfulness. Luckily for them, there was always money for another trip, along with a tastefully appointed room waiting at the Ancient Links Hotel, a swanky place full of faux Art Deco pieces, expensive whisky, and voices redolent of family wealth.

The most famous section of the course was a large, rectangular field, perhaps a half-mile long. Even under the snow, this part of the Links remained cocky with bright, healthy grass. Throughout the year, a little stone bridge could be seen hovering above a slender brook that wound its way down to the sea. From anywhere in the vicinity, you could see the long stretch of peachy beach known as Flat Sands.

North of the beach, up and through the Ancient Links, past the "Careful—Golf in Progress!" sign, and up the deliciously named "Granny Butters Wynd," you would find yourself on Sea Street. Townspeople, students, and tourists up from their beds and breakfasts mingled here each day.

In January, wealthy students butted heads over flats on Sea Street in a form of tribal warfare. The only thing stopping their parents from building high-rises there was the St Albas Historical Society, which strictly monitored the town's buildings, threatening legal action (in reality) and pitchforks (if necessary) in order to protect the crumbling brick façades from the evils of unchecked modernization. Given the competitive nature of housing on swanky Sea Street, parents had been known to argue over who would purchase a house for their daughter or son and their closest friends to live in. These bitter debates were meant to establish social ties. Of course, more alliances were ended than cemented in the process.

Not having to fret over mundane things such as rent, the students who lived on Sea Street spent their money on shiny things like dining sets, canopied beds, and chocolate fountains. They left their windows unlatched and their doors unlocked. When the sea's wintry gales pounded the panes and rattled the glass and slipped through the sills, they put the heat on as long and as high as they wanted. And when they had stuffed their wardrobes just as full of clothes as they could, and when their walls were filled with framed Banksy prints (and more than a few originals), and when their refrigerators were packed to the limit with champagne from Champagne and vodka from Russia and whisky from the Highlands, they would throw away a cashmere sweater or two in order to make room for stashes of pot, cocaine, and ecstasy. Institutionalized and inherited council housing meant that the people dealing the drugs and buying the drugs sometimes lived in the same building. This was ideal for both parties and good for the local economy.

Church Street was the farthest from the sea. While the Catholic church on the Avenue overlooked Flat Sands, the Protestant churches had been constructed farther away, in the newer, not-*as*-medieval part of town. The prim Victorian façades, the tree that was reputed to have been planted by Mary Queen of Scots, and the ice

cream parlor—busy even when the sun hadn't shone in weeks—
made this a popular place for walking and people watching as well
as living one's own unexamined life. Above the various kilt stores
and art galleries, the student residents of Church Street made tea
perpetually and wished that just a glint of sunshine might touch the
flowerboxes in their windows. Only the wealthiest students lived in
the old, crooked stone houses on Sea Street, while the merely rich
converged in the strict, mid-19th century townhomes on Church.

Between Sea and Church Street was Fair Street. People had been
coming here for hundreds of years to buy essentially the same
things: sweets, meats, spirits, pints, and all other forms of small-
town entertainment. The street's cobbled bricks, once replete with
horses and asses, were now congested with cars and the asses in
them. (Asses because you could walk every street in St Albas in
under an hour.) The stones lining the street were smooth in the
places where all the cars turned and rough in the places where only
seagulls landed.

Given the relatively tall buildings, there was only one point in
every rare, cloudless day during which Fair Street was completely
bathed in sunlight. At noon, there was a mocking hint of the slightly
warmer Continental climate just across England and the Channel.
This was the moment when sales of cherry tomatoes increased
exponentially, when orders of espresso were at their highest outside
the morning caffeine rush. This was the moment when the
Americans reminded themselves that they came to this little swath
of Scotland along the coast of the frigid North Sea for a reason:
they were still in Europe, a fact that Fair Street helped them to
remember with its used book stores full of dust and pound coins,
the bakery straight out of a 1950s Rodgers and Hammerstein
musical, the liquor shop where French wine was hardly considered
imported. Only the Starbucks on the corner and the North Face
jackets on their backs reminded them that America existed at all.

Town was quiet in the summer. The yearlong residents cherished
short lines in the single grocery store and the reclamation of their
pubs. But, come August, in a flood of Land Rover SUVs, Ray-
Bans, and nervous argyle, the students returned. While being in St
Albas during the summer was liable to give you the accurate
impression that you were in a comfortable Scottish town where
locals said "hiya" to one another and to you, the start of the autumn

term made both students and townspeople claustrophobic and contemptuous of one another. Instead of taking comfort in the existence of the vast fields to the north, or the hills to the west that looked like a gorgeous fat lady lying on her side, or the bright blue sea to the east, the residents of St Albas felt trapped, castaways on a tiny island with too many other goddamned people.

On this microcosm of an island, Catriona and Julie lived and walked, unaware in the collectively imagined St Albas chaos that they were pieces on a checkerboard. The number of moves in so small a town were finite.

Its inhabitants had always proved to St Albas that no, human nature never changed. It was only ever a matter of time before it didn't change again.

# III. SEPTEMBER

**SHE HAD A FACE LIKE A** hatbox. Or maybe it was more like a clock, with the way her nose ticked around her face when she saw something she didn't agree with, which was almost all the time. Her hair was short, cut specifically to the chin in descending waves of chestnut feather that made her look like an owl—and perhaps her face was also flat like that, with small eyes and fine feather brows that flared towards her temples. She had the look and the haircut of a person who paints her fingernails at an appointed time every week, who never dares enough to chip them. As they say, her life was all like that.

Even as a child she was keen to please her parents and to obey their rules. When her father told her to switch her lights off, she turned them off first and put down her book second, knowing exactly where it would fit in the space she left empty on the nightstand. Not once did her mother have to ask twice that she get out of bed for school: Catriona Darlington-Welland often woke her mother up in the mornings, having made breakfast for herself and packed her schoolbag on her own. She was the sort of girl who taught herself to tie her own shoes from a picture book on the subject. She progressed from a tricycle to training wheels to two wheels with no cuts, scrapes, or helpful pushes. In her entire life, she had never met a bike, checkbook, or kitchen scale she couldn't balance. Catriona seemed to have been born to do things right.

She had been head girl at the country school for young ladies she attended prior to university. Appointed, actually, because she was considered to be such a good example for the younger students, and because she was not friendly enough with girls her own age to have a moral problem with being a tattletale. Eager for answers, she always believed the first one she was told by parent or priest or teacher and held on to it like the end of the string of the world's most important kite.

Young Catriona was also curious about the natural world and what or Who made it. She saw the order in it—the hours that turned into days, and the days that turned into weeks—and found this admirable. She enjoyed long walks on the Lancashire moors, cataloguing the shapes of leaves and the lengths of caterpillars in her head, wondering why the sky was blue. At the local library next to the post office on the short high street of Axbury Town, she checked out all the books on stars and about planets. Often, these occupied the empty space on the nightstand after she was told to switch her light out.

She loved to teach her brother George about the moors and the leaves and the caterpillars and the sky's color, and to read all the planet books to him when she came home from school. They had adventures together, when he was old enough. They made tents with the cushions in the living room. They explored the woods near the house together, and when their cousin Peter came up from Surrey, the play was better than ever because the boys could pretend that they were wild orphans and that Catriona was their mother. Their real mothers let them pretend unattended outside, until the day that George fell from a tree and broke his leg. Catriona could still see the bone breaking through the skin. Afterward, her mother had scolded her for days, and Catriona hadn't blamed her. Finally, she was sat down for a talking to:

"It's an important job to be the eldest," her mother had said.

"Yes, mummy."

"It's your job to make sure your younger brother is safe. Do you understand?"

"What about when he's all grown up?"

"Boys don't ever grow up, my darling," her mother replied. "Not ever."

And so, Catriona had accepted it as fact that boys never grew up because her mother was not a liar.

Catriona's love of the outdoors ended, abruptly, with George being taken from her, from them all, on her watch. She had been so young to see it. Peter had been so young to see it. And George had been so young to die. There were no more games after that. The photos of George came down, and Catriona noticed that her mother didn't call her "darling" any more.

And so Catriona began to paint—abandoning her stars and planets and moors for pictures of them. Pictures were safer. No one could get shot by a hunter in a picture, especially not by accident. No one could bleed that much from a canvas. It was true that Catriona was skittish with the brush, but, as she grew, she felt she must distinguish herself somehow, must somehow make up for things, and she thought this was the best way. If her parents couldn't have a son anymore, they should have a daughter that was the best girl possible.

When it came time for the discussion of where she should attend university, Catriona had done so well on her A-levels that her parents suggested that perhaps Oxford or Cambridge might suit. But she ruled them out, privately and unemotionally, on the grounds that it would be slightly easier to get high marks at St Albas and that it would be easy to find a husband there that her parents would like—everyone knew that St Albas had the richest, most athletic students. And a whole half of them were boys. Besides, she could study painting, and be near Peter, and that would all do quite nicely.

After a term of finding studio art to be unsuited and wasteful (her newly mediocre marks didn't help either), she switched to art history. She was more comfortable among facts. The professors and color periodicals would determine her tastes. And oh! What a lovely, feminine occupation it would make.

And so, in preparation for her life as a lady of leisure, with a gallery or perhaps some business to do in a local museum, she spent her university days crediting and debiting works of art, happily purchasing textbooks with full reproductions of the all-important art canon, and turning it, somehow, into numbers. (And by now it should be obvious that she used Post-it notes always to mark her place, thinking it rude to dog-ear the corners.) Never again did she put paint to canvas; the most art she ever did was to drape pashminas around her cardigans, or to wear sleek, sculpted earrings and bracelets—because the fashion magazines prescribed them.

All of this is not to say that people did not enjoy her company. Or at least a few people found her tolerable, though to most others these people were considered too proper to be much fun. In St Albas, there was a social line of demarcation between those who followed the rules and those who followed tradition. Some of the wildest students in town were its most traditional, the most nostalgic for the glory days of all kinds of social orders: sexual, economic, academic. But Catriona was a rule-follower. And so, for the most part, were the friends she made, content to stay at home playing Scrabble and gossiping about nothing on their Friday nights, getting dressed up for a single cocktail at one of the posh bars on Saturdays. Catriona disapproved of them all for one reason or another but called on them for companionship when Max was out of town or as a group with which to attend balls and polo matches, which Max loathed. They ate equal amounts of cupcakes, Catriona's acquaintances, all through the week. The ones that looked like birds stayed birdlike no matter how many they ate with breakfast, with lunch, for dessert, and with tea. And there was always an excuse for tea in that place.

But Catriona Darlington-Welland was not bird-like like a flamingo; she was bird-like like an owl. While her face was thin, and stretched—at times it looked as if there was not enough skin there, or that what there was did not appear thick enough—her trunk was brick-shaped and soft in what were deemed the wrong places. Folds of skin slithered over one another when she sat, no matter what she wore. Her breasts were small and uneven, and she tried not to look at them when she could help it. And so Catriona was always wary of how many cupcakes she consumed. She thought of throwing them up each time she ate them, but that would ruin her voice, which she needed for singing in church on Sundays.

She went to mass at the Catholic church on the Avenue. Catriona came from a proud, long line of English Catholics. Although she was even descended from Sir Robert Constable, who had stood up to Henry VIII's break with the Church and been hanged for it, her family was not rebellious in nature. It was simply not in either the Welland or Darlington DNA to approve of change. In fact, it was a miracle of sorts that they hadn't resisted the conversion to Christianity in the first place, given their propensity for believing themselves to be everlastingly right about everything.

The church was an old stone building, the predecessor of which had been completed in just enough time to be torched in the Reformation. It was young, as far as St Albas was concerned. Some defiant Scotsman had rebuilt it on the cliffs in 1883, facing the part of Flat Sands that looked down upon what was once a popular bathing site. The large, wrought-iron crucifix on top of the church still wept down on bathers, but only Christ's crown of thorns could now be seen from the Sands: luxury row houses had been built in the Lord's airspace, snapped up at what was rumored with both pride and disgust to be the most expensive real estate in the United Kingdom outside London.

The church had a roof that leaked shingles and rainwater when the weather was wet, an event as frequent as Catriona's judgmental observances. On numerous occasions, the parish bulletin proclaimed the necessity of walking under umbrellas upon exiting the building: one old man after another was put in the hospital after pieces of slate had fallen from above. The building was in perpetual need of repairs and replacements, but mostly the parishioners spent their extra Sunday money on fudge doughnuts at Smith and MacFarlane's bakery. Sometimes they stopped to talk to Father Tom, and in the springtime most people would take a moment to admire the work Mrs. Leslie had done in the front garden. For hours she would slave on her arthritic knees, planting tulips and lilies and roses, rubbing the excess dirt on the washcloths she had fashioned from old cassocks. She never seemed to stop mumbling about the Garden of Eden and flaming swords. When it was too rainy to work, she would sit in the vestry, looking out the tiny window that faced the sea. People said it was because she was lonely, but no one ever actually asked her.

This was the Catholic church that Catriona attended without fail every Sunday, provided she was in St Albas. While on other nights of the week she afforded Max the right of staying with her, she usually limited both intimacy and sleepovers to every other evening but Saturday. This served a dual function, in that her sins of the flesh might have time to fade before mass, and also that she would not have to argue wordlessly with Max, the humanist, about the Church. And so without ideological impediments, she woke up early on Sunday, never turning her alarm to snooze or flipping her pillow over to the cool side for a few extra moments of sleep. Still tucked in with the duvet snuggly fitted around her body in the exact position in which she'd fallen asleep, she took ten seconds to open her eyes and direct them towards the calendar that rested on her bookshelf. When they had focused on the day at hand, she closed her eyes once more, said a prayer, and folded the blankets neatly away from her (these, unlike the pages of books, were acceptable to dog-ear). After stepping out of bed and into the clean slippers she laid out each night before going to sleep, she then showered, brushed her teeth and her hair, and got dressed. She was old-fashioned when it came to eating before receiving the Eucharist, and so out the door it was on an empty stomach with £20 tithe and an umbrella.

On this particular Sunday, Catriona arrived several minutes earlier than usual in order to pray in peace. The summer had been a difficult one, sitting at home in Lancashire for the most part, moving around the empty house, avoiding her mother all day. She felt as if she'd hardly talked to Max at all, and the last time she had seen him had been in Switzerland, over a month ago. Besides all that, the fact that Max had not come to see her in England over the summer deeply troubled her, and she was beginning to obsess about it. She needed to forgive him this negligence—if that was even what it was—before he arrived back in town, which he was set to do late this morning.

The church was empty. Her heels clicked softly, like pennies into a waterless well, as she walked toward the altar on the cold marble floor. She knelt before the crucifix, bringing her fingertips together in perfect alignment: the way she had always been taught was the proper gesture for prayer. Her spine bent and her chin rolled down to her chest, her folded hands rising to her lips. Silently, she tried to pray.

*Please, God. Help me to forgive Max.*

Try as she might, she could not bring herself to picture him in a black tuxedo with a white rose in the buttonhole, waiting for her at the end of this, or any, aisle. Each time she tried to envision him speaking the holy vows, he became mute. It made her recall a time when, as a child, she had tried to sweep the shadow of her hairs from the kitchen floor.

Hearing other people in the space behind her, families filling the old wooden pews with body heat, children's coloring books, and purses, she made a pressured cross over her forehead, torso, and shoulders. Trying to look consoled but coming off as rather smug, she took a seat among the rest of the parishioners, removed her coat, and opened her hymnal to the very first page.

In front of her sat a family. *What a treat*, she thought. *Thank you,*

*God, how wonderful to see a real live family, with a mother and a father and a daughter and a son. Thou shalt not covet, thou shalt not covet, but why am I covetous?* She said a prayer for George.

The music began from the organ, belting out of the brass pipes as if the player had a series of horns from God's own car laid out in front of him in a variety of pitches. The overwhelming sounds were comforting, forcing all her thoughts away. The vibrations of the lower notes produced warmth in her stomach and neck. She wished she could carry the resonances around with her in a little bottle for when she felt alone.

Down the center aisle came a pair of altar boys with crosses, incense, and other tools of their trade. Like the women, they were silent during the mass, except for when their high-pitched voices could make them useful in the production of praising sounds. Father Tom, the parish priest, followed behind them, privately thinking that it was something of a shame that the Church had banned castrati at the end of the 19th century. Everything must be sacrificed to praise the Lord.

Before Father Tom came Simon, a seminarian-to-be and theology student at St Albas. For the last three years' worth of Sundays, he had tried to focus on Jesus's pained, metal eyes when he walked down the center aisle but always seemed to picture Catriona instead. This happened not only at mass but whenever he saw or thought of her; the right hand did not seem to know what the left was doing. Still, that he wanted to be a priest was true. That he thought the Church ought to reinstate the Latin mass was true. That he tried very hard to believe lust a grave and serious sin of mind and body alike was also true. But Simon McLean was also a twenty-two-year-old man, and while he devoted himself primarily to developing his genuine and inherent yearning to be with God, he spent a significant amount of time avoiding the growing longing that Catriona incited within him—especially today. He had not seen her in months.

The summer holiday was difficult; he missed her there each weekend—dependable, hymnal on her knee, her brown, silky hair skimming the top of her soft, beige cardigan as she bent her head in prayer. He knew how it looked because he watched all the heads in the church bobbing up and down during the mass. Unseen by Father Tom, who always kept to the front of the altar, Simon could watch her all he wanted. He was the only man in the entire church praying for a long sermon, an extra chorus in the *Kyrie*, just so he might have a few more minutes to look—or try not to look—at her. Simon often found himself enjoying church because it afforded him time to think. And he thought maybe that was part of the reason God, in His infinite wisdom, had prescribed the weekly ritual. Even if it was a small sin to think about Catriona, it probably stopped him from acting on his feelings, which might have been a greater sin.

Catriona, for her part, never suspected that she had captured her friend's attentions. It just wasn't possible in her world. She had a boyfriend. If someone was looking at her from the altar, she suspected it was Father Tom, who she believed possessed the ability to perceive any wanderings of mind his parishioners experienced during his performance. Whatever report was being drawn up on her this particular morning and sent to heaven was not liable to be a flattering one, as she found herself more concerned with her earthly problems than her soul.

*Ite, missa est.* "Go now, this mass is ended." The final words from Father Tom's lips ending the mass caught her like a fish hooked through the throat. She hadn't been able to forgive Max at all. And now here she was, in the sea of people pushing and shoving to get out of church before anyone else, as if Father Tom had not just been talking about Loving Your Neighbor for the last hour and fifteen minutes.

Simon stood beside Father Tom after mass, learning how to fold his hands, and at what height to hold them, and memorizing the names of all the little old ladies who wanted a chat. One day, somewhere, this job would be his: trusted confidant of his spiritual community, overseer of births, marriages, deaths, and all sacraments in between. It was easy to imagine himself in the thick of things; he was the eldest of eight children. True to stereotype, this made him the reliable, sociable sort. His parents, who were also very smart and very kind, were publically, extraordinarily proud that their eldest was choosing a life in the Church. Though neither of them were too religious, at least not by the standards through which religious people judge other religious people, they thought that Simon's happiness would make them happy. And, as far as grandchildren were concerned, there were seven other children—among them three exceedingly pretty girls—who would likely provide those bundles of joy for their parents. But having clearly enjoyed their marriage in all its forms (the eight children being evidence of this), they occasionally wondered if perhaps Simon didn't know what he was going to miss. His father secretly hoped that his son would sort it out, at least once, while he was still in university, and not at the prestigious seminary in Rome at which Simon hoped to proceed with his studies after the end of his university course.

Even more so than his father, Simon was painfully aware of the sacrifices he would have to make. Catriona, beautiful Catriona, was a weekly reminder of them. But she had also been the impetus for the necessity to sacrifice.

They had met in first year at the garden party organized by the parish for all new Catholic university students. On the very spot in which he now stood, he had first seen her in her cream dress, had asked her where she was from, had recognized her as the girl who lived across from him in hall. Catriona was the admirable, honorable sort of girl he had always pictured himself with, and Simon was a straight-laced boy full of purpose, someone she could bring home to her parents, whom she could present to the family.

What had gone wrong there, he did not know. Somehow, one Saturday morning, he had seen Max in the hallway, emerging from Catriona's room in his pajamas, scratching his messy mop of hair. They had nodded at each other, both rather embarrassed though neither yet knew that Simon was going to be a priest. It was a decision he had made after Catriona had mentioned she was in love with Max.

"Good morning," she said to him today. On this crisp September afternoon, she was wearing a snug sweater of caramel cotton, a woolen skirt, and a pair of black heels. Simon dared to imagine what else—perhaps some underwear with something pink on it.

The two embraced politely.

"How was your summer?" Simon asked.

"Quite good, thank you. Got to ride a bit."

"And your parents?"

"They're doing very well at Axbury."

"Did you get to the Continent at all?"

"Yes, I visited Max. It was brilliant."

Max's mother had pretended for all of these brilliant days that she did not speak any English, which was much less English than she had spoken the first time she'd met her son's girlfriend. In fact,

Catriona noticed that Max's mother spoke less English every time she came to visit.

"Max came to Axbury?"

"Not this summer," she replied and changed the subject to something more pleasant than both missing Max and not forgiving him entirely. "How are you, then? Just returned? You look well. Did your hair get redder over the summer?"

Catriona had always liked his red hair.

"Lighter, I think."

"Maybe it is."

Simon smiled and was happy she had noticed.

"I came back last weekend. The weather has been superb."

"Today's a lovely day."

They stood for a moment in the sunny evidence, knowing from experience that it wouldn't last but another few weeks.

"I'd better be off. It's just me in the house soon."

"Is Miss Morgan leaving you all alone?"

"Such a negligent flatmate," said Catriona, with a small, genuine smile that was just for Simon.

"Where's she off to?"

"Spain, for a few months. And I need all the help unpacking I can get. So many of my things are still at Max's too. So much going on before classes begin. We'll see one another properly soon, all right? I have tickets to the polo. We should watch."

Simon nodded and returned to Father Tom. It was hard to say goodbye so soon after seeing her again when she had been such a long time away from him.

Catriona walked down Cracks Wynd, the passage between Sea Street and the Avenue, with the high walls and the iron gate to the University's quad. In it, one felt like a mouse in a maze. Carefully, she selected the stones on which to step, perfectly balancing herself in spite of her high-heeled shoes and the uneven bricks that made up the path. While she did so, she thought of Simon. Had she asked enough after him and his summer? She should have thought to inquire as to his grandmother's health. But perhaps he would have brought it up himself if he wished to discuss it. Wasn't it odd that Simon should wait for her after mass like that? But no. Had he? Had he been, in fact, waiting for her? He *had* stepped away to speak with her...

Her thoughts were interrupted, for, across the street, she saw Max. His suitcase trailed behind him. He did not see her, and she did not attempt to be seen.

It was to her great distress to discover, however, that the results of this momentary distraction in seeing Max were so profoundly tainted with evil. For when Catriona looked down on the spot at which she had stopped, she found her feet on the dreaded stones of WM.

The WM was a set of initials laid in stone in front of the entrance to an ancient, well-kept square of grass—the University's only quadrangle. Here, just before the Reformation spread throughout Europe, a university student named William MacGregor was burned at the stake for spreading Luther's doctrines in the Catholic town. For six hours, he cooked in extreme agony and then death, watched by his professors, classmates, and the clergy. As a sign of respect, St Albas students always walked around, rather than on, the spot where he had died. Over the years, this tradition had a certain amount of folklore built up around it. The current incarnation of these legends dictated participation in the May Saving as the penance for stepping on MacGregor's inlaid initials. Those who did not comply faced the traditional threat of failing to graduate. Step on the WM and you could be certain that the ghost of MacGregor would be sure to put insurmountable obstacles in your way.

Though Catriona felt that William MacGregor may have deserved to be burned alive for being such a troublemaker, and though she thought herself above participating in such superstitious nonsense, she was filled with dread. In three years, she had managed to avoid stepping here. Thanks to Max, that was all over. Determined that nothing else was allowed to go wrong for the rest of the day, she crossed the street. She would welcome Max home later.

When she had unlocked the front door of her house and taken a left into the living room, a surprise awaited her. It was the town cat, Barrie, who sat, tail swinging gently like a pendulum, on the couch. The window was open. The flower vase she had unpacked before church lay smashed on the floor. The ginger creature looked at her unabashedly.

"Get out!" she screeched.

Barrie, who was not accustomed to being treated like a common criminal, hissed in her direction. She lunged at the sofa, handbag flaring at him. Barrie jumped lithely down, strutted across the floor, and went back through the window once again. When he had gone, Catriona shut the window and went immediately to the kitchen for the rag and broom.

There was a note on the refrigerator from her roommate:

> Fetching my man from the airport! Eeee!
> Sorry about the living room — will help tidy
> before I leave for Spain. Promise.

Catriona had forgotten that things would be different this year, with this absolute plague of a boyfriend hanging about. The housemate neglect had already begun, and for what? That disrespectful, brutish idiot from London or America or wherever he was from.

*Oh, well,* she sighed. *Some people just don't know how to choose a proper boyfriend*—and swept away in the living room until a small bead of sweat dribbled down her forehead. She scoured the room's corners for remnants of glass. The pieces collected in an unassembled mosaic in the dustbin, reflecting the colors of the floor, ceiling, wall, and even Catriona herself.

For a brief moment, she held one in her hand, considering its jagged merits. But no. She could wait.

When she had thrown them all away, neatly stacked in a brown paper bag, she went upstairs to her room.

There, she began to unpack her important things.

# IV.

THAT EVENING, MAX WAS HOLDING A rotting wooden ladder for his flatmate, Fern, who had once again braved the attic, where they kept their things over the summer.

"Pass me up the torch," she said, in the brogue of Scotland's northwest.

"You want the handheld or your hardhat with the light on it?"

"Haven't unpacked the hardhat yet. But the torch is in the loo closet."

Max found it there.

"Got it."

A striking and lovely face appeared in the ceiling. It was literally weathered from years of camping and being rained on, but also, in the truest sense, naturally beautiful. Fern's was a face made of clear, caramel eyes and smooth, stony cheeks and a wry, strong smile that pronounced its owner's character. You could tell things had happened to Fern MacLeod, and that she had borne it all with a healthy sense of the absurd.

"Ta," she said when he handed up the light. Max was glad to hear her say it, to be back in Scotland with his best friend.

"Ta-welcome," he said. She sighed good-naturedly and rolled her eyes at his joke.

He watched her disappear into the attic with a whoosh of her extraordinarily thick brown ponytail.

"See anything? Have we been robbed?"

"What the fuck. *Max...*"

"Yes?"

"Every damn summer."

"What?"

"What the bloody hell are Catriona's things doing here?"

"Oh, yeah, sorry, I forgot to ask…"

"You forget to ask every summer if it's all right for her to keep her things here too."

"I'm sorry, Fern."

"My God. You didn't have time, all summer, to get rid of her? Too busy pouring cups of coffee in Parliament, were you?"

"I'm sorry."

This was an annual conversation. Max could recite it backwards. He was trying to think how it ended when Fern said:

"That's just fine. I found my things. *All the way back here*. Good to know that geology training is good for something."

Ah, it ended with the geology joke.

Fern had been only half-right about pouring the cups of coffee in Parliament. Max had indeed worked in Bern as an assistant to one of his father's friends, a member of Switzerland's National Council, as he had done for the last two summers away from St Albas. But he hadn't poured coffee. His days were spent buried in the business of researching policies and assisting in strategy: reading and thinking and writing and recommending. It had been intellectually challenging work, and Max had enjoyed it greatly. He had spent long hours in the office and at the library, far past the time when the other assistants had gone out to the bars or to sit by the river with their boyfriends and girlfriends and all manner of lovers and friends. Other than a trip home to Zurich to visit his parents and to see Catriona, who had come down from England, he had not spoken much to anyone. His parents, who he thought understood his neglect but who both missed him dearly in spite of being busy and important people themselves, were used to their only child's disregard and knew it wasn't malicious. Catriona was another story, though Max never thought to think of how upset she'd be that he hadn't been as attentive this summer as in years past.

Max had never lived life with his feet on the ground. He had no idea what, in fact, the ground felt like. Perhaps this was an apt metaphor given the fact that he was born to parents already in their mid-forties; born into a family without siblings or cousins; born into a family with people who only wanted to carry him around rather than pushing him or wrestling with him or hurting him. They proceeded to carry him around as a baby, to coddle him as a child, to give him every advantage as a young man. He had not learned to put one foot in front of the other out of necessity but rather out of the noble desire to at least try walking himself.

Max was the heir to several upper-middle class fortunes, from his grandparents, from his parents' childless brothers and sisters. While many of the wealthy students in St Albas were left to be raised by nannies and tutors, Max's parents and his relatives had managed to spoil him and smother him with money and praise. Their silent expectations were as real to Max as their unconditional love. He was eager not to disappoint—so eager, in fact, that he often forgot to love them and worried instead about making them proud. And there was a lot to live up to. Max's father was the chairman of the Political Science Department in one of Zurich's finest universities and the editor of one of Europe's more liberal magazines for high-thinking people, and his mother was an art dealer to some of the richest people in the world.

He was lucky he had been born with a good brain, especially because you could never say of Max that he had a good head on his shoulders. In fact people said he lived with his head in the clouds, but really Max's head *was* the clouds. He was well above six feet tall, with wispy, blond hair and a mind full of thoughts that were wispy too. It was not difficult to believe him to be innocent, for he looked it always. His eyebrows were shaped in an upward slant that gave him the effect of soft, perpetual inquiry; the look of one who sees the world as a tourist, as a kindly befuddled doctor looking at a patient for whom he has many possible diagnoses but no treatments. Beneath the brows sat two almond-shaped, droopy eyes of blue, an enormous nose, and lips through which a line ran that was parallel to a well-drawn chin. The sweetness of his face made it possible to automatically endow him with good characteristics that he did not possess, and he had relied on this genetic luck his entire life without ever knowing it at all.

But Fern was never one to give credit for good character where it wasn't due. At the moment, her own face emerged again on the ceiling in a grimace of disapproval.

"I can't do any more of this just now, Max. Shall we have a pint?"

"That sounds good. But—"

"No buts this year. It's our last go-round. I'm calling the shots, not that lassie of yours." She paused, for dramatic effect. "And we are having a celebratory pint."

"What for?"

"Well," she said, mounting the ladder to climb down it, "how about making it this far, for one thing?"

She jumped off the ladder's last two steps, wiped her thin, dusty hands on her thin, dusty jeans and headed to the kitchen. Max followed obediently—her giant golden retriever. Taking two pint glasses from a cardboard box and then removing the now-crisp newspapers from around them, she rinsed them in the sink. Max opened the refrigerator to see that Fern had already stocked up on beverages.

"You haven't even bought bread yet."

"Excuse me for being the best flatmate in the world and wanting to toast your homecoming. And hey—beer's carbs too."

"You have a point."

"Two points."

He opened one of the large glass bottles and poured evenly between them.

"Cheers," he said, "to the best flatmate in the world."

"To fourth year."

Their glasses clinked.

The doorbell rang as Max lifted his to his lips.

"You've got to be joking," said Fern.

"I'm sorry," he said, desperately. "I haven't seen her since July."

But he had. Out of the corner of his eye, this afternoon. She was wearing what he assumed were her church clothes, not that he had ever seen them in person. Not being in the mood to withstand the up-and-down criticism of his clothing and his general existence he was sure to face if he said hello, he had continued down the street praying that she was still praying and therefore wouldn't notice him across the way.

Max told himself he had missed Catriona during the summer in Bern. He missed having someone there to listen to his thoughts on politics and philosophy and to proofread his essays. She was such a gifted proofreader and never missed any tiny error. He missed having dinner with her every night, eating the food she'd cooked. He missed having socks that were clean and sheets that smelled fresh. He even missed being able to lie shoulder to shoulder next to her in bed because her perfume smelled like lavender and helped him to fall asleep. Catriona had always brought Max comfort, had always made it so easy for him to spend time in his mind because the little details of being a person were all taken care of.

"Are you listening? Max?"

"Yeah, sorry."

"Just give me your beer. I'm going to need two if she's still going to be here when I come out of my room in half an hour."

"I'm sorry," he pleaded, as she went toward her room. "What do you want me to do?"

"Get. Rid of her," she said, closing the door. "Forever."

"I love her," said Max to the door.

"Sure you do," said Fern from behind it.

Catriona rang the bell again.

"Coming," he said.

He unlocked the door and opened it.

Well, there she is.

He felt a slight sense of relief. The first seeing of the year was over. And Catriona looked more relaxed than usual—perhaps mass was extra holy today or whatever you called it when it was really good.

She wrapped her arms around him tightly.

"Hello, darling," she said, breathless. "Hello, hello!"

He rested his arms around her shoulders, holding his own hands. She put her cheek against his heart, taking a few deep breaths.

"I missed you," she said.

She extended her mouth up to his. Their lips met briefly. Max was glad to see her, glad that someone wanted to kiss him and make him believe he was handsome.

"I missed you too."

"How was your flight?"

She moved away from him and sat down on that sofa, patting the place next to her. The sun was setting in the window. Bright, golden rays were layered on top of dark, transparent rainclouds. The stretch of sea through the buildings gleamed in patches of golden water where the sun broke through.

"Good," he said, sitting obediently. It occurred to him vaguely to remember that it was because of Catriona that he had spent May Saving in this very spot. Then he remembered how right she had probably been about the water being cold and not being able to find your clothes.

"Is Fern home?"

The sound of video game explosions from Fern's room answered her question.

"Was church good?"

"It was. I saw Simon."

That explained why she was happy. Simon did that to her. Max was always thankful for it.

"Oh Max," said Catriona as she laid her head on his shoulder. "We're going to have a wonderful year. Can you believe how quickly the time has gone by? Fourth year."

"Yes. Fourth year."

In spite of how much time had passed, not much had changed. It might as well still be first year; he was still sitting next to Catriona on some sofa. But it occurred to Max that they wouldn't be in St Albas next year. They would have to grow up, to make grown-up decisions about where to go and whether to be together. Max had never gotten the feeling that Catriona believed being together was a question at all. She believed they would be married. She had implied it on several occasions in the past, most memorably this summer in Zurich.

"Don't they look happy?" she had said, as they strolled by the lake beneath the Alps. It was a hot day, but cool under the thick boughs of the trees around the water.

A bride and groom were having their wedding photos taken near the harbor. They walked along ecstatically, smiling and embracing as the photographer directed them.

"They do," he said.

"Doesn't it make you happy to see?"

"Yes."

"They are so in love. They look like they've been together for years."

He nodded.

"That's what people do," she said.

She had stopped walking.

"They're older than we are, though. I mean, they have to be at least thirty."

"I guess so."

But Max could tell she was hurt deeply. He hadn't said enough.

"Though, it is the next step, isn't it," he said.

He smiled at her, squeezed her hand. A small amount of encouragement couldn't do any harm. It couldn't even be called a lie. There was no reason on earth why she shouldn't think it was the next step, if it made her happy, if it made her feel at peace, if it made her stop talking about it.

"Who knows," he said, "that might be us pretty soon."

This seemed to satisfy her, and they completed the rest of the walk home without any unpleasantness. Max had long learned that as long as Catriona felt the future was secure, he could count on a peaceable existence with her. Max had never minded it before—the flowers, then the lunch, then the dinner, then the necklace with the sterling silver heart, then the golden necklace with the three freshwater pearls. The ones that caught the sunset in her neck. The ever steeper proof of his love. His logical mind he couldn't blame her for wanting more and more, to follow their relationship through to the conclusion she thought was natural and right.

Besides, there was no reason to rock the boat yet, either way. The end of the year was a long, long way off, and he was, after all, content enough to be with Catriona on the sofa.

"I think you're right," he said. "It's going to be a wonderful year."

She smiled and walked to the kitchen, where she put the kettle to boil, thinking she really should have said something about how much she'd wished he'd come to visit her over the summer.

But Max thought it was going to be a wonderful year.

And there was no harm in him thinking she really thought that too.

# V.

JULIE SAT IN THE FIRST CLASS of the semester. It was in the Victorian mansion they had renamed Bard House after sending the old furnishings along to a museum in London and fitting the previously lived-in bedrooms and living rooms and dining rooms with desks and projector screens. Bard House was located across from the Castle on the Avenue. Here, students in the School of English and their overactive imaginations were treated to panoramas of the sea, which, today, was thrashing erratically in a grimy, gray mix. *The lobster traps must be rattling open against the sea floor below*, thought Julie. Perhaps some crustaceans would be spared another day. The rain beat persistently at the windows and the wind rattled the locked shutters as the lecturer went on in a deep baritone about *To the Lighthouse*.

She had never been a great student, intelligent though she was. Her grades had always been just above ordinary, and she had no gift for studying in long stretches like so many of her peers. But Julie felt the nagging suspicion that still she knew more than the ones who spent their nights and weekends hugging their anthologies. It was her essay that had gotten her into St Albas, probably. That, and the need for American tuition to properly fund the University.

Julie was ever of the opinion that one could learn more about life by following Virginia Woolf's advice: experience both life and books, rather than just the books. Though she did not condone people drowning themselves in rivers, she often thought back to Woolf's observations about her own life and let them guide her thinking. She was easily led by dead authors. Whatever fictions she was currently reading and liking often dictated her perspectives on the nonfictional world around her. And so it was doubly funny to Julie how all these poor suckers should be furiously scribbling notes from the lecturer's mouth on their pieces of A4 paper when the real lessons were in the text of the novel and in those waves, just visible outside, that broke against the Scottish coast.

The rain continued to dive onto the window. In the Castle's visitor center, the old, bald man who was working there looked out across the street, apparently bored of the views the tourists paid several pounds, and what felt like dozens of dollars, to see.

Julie tapped her pen gently on the desk, thinking of the unpacked suitcases and boxes waiting in her room. She wished she was cuddled there in the middle of the bed, in the little valley two years' worth of previous sittings and sleepings had created in the rickety mattress, watching *Gone with the Wind*. She thought of the party she would go to tonight, she thought of what she would wear, and how many of the boys would be there, and which ones. The summer had been, by Julie's standards, slow and sleepy at home in America, at least in terms of her social life, and she was ready to wrest as much social life as she could out of her final year in Scotland. And she did not classify her education under the heading of "life."

The sudden sensation that ennui lay ahead hit her as it had during May Saving. Perhaps St Albas would become a routine, and it terrified her to think so. She had been excited to return to school during the summer. Everyone at home in America thought it was so romantic, and she too had thought so while away from it all: the Castle, the sea, and the cathedral, the thrill of seeing, daily, Flat Sands spread out before her like an immaculate lace-and-sea-foam tablecloth. There were the handsome, wealthy boys and the clever, beautiful girls, and there were balls, and high tea, and fashion shows, and displays of wealth disguised as displays of generosity. For her family, it was exciting too. They had pictures of the Highlands and Edinburgh Castle in their minds and on their coffee tables—Julie had brought quite a few large, glossy photo books home. They asked her questions about what was Great Britain and what was the United Kingdom and how were they different. Somehow, even the mediocrities of British statehood were deemed mysterious and exotic. But sitting at her desk in the School of English, the whole, familiar shebang seemed anything but.

"I see it's time to go," said Professor Harris, a genial man in his early forties with lanky legs, a preference for tweed, and one eyebrow that was completely white. "Thank you for a most excellent first lecture, all."

Julie packed her bag slowly as the others rushed out of the room to the library, to home, to the next lecture. She noticed she had written only the words "Woolf lecture" at the top of her page.

"Such an attentive start to the year," said Professor Harris to Julie, glancing at her notes, or lack thereof.

"You know how much I love lectures."

"Almost as much as you love writing papers, unfortunately. Though, thankfully, you've gotten better in your old age, Miss Lovejoy."

"How was your summer?"

Professor Harris had always been her favorite, and, for reasons neither of them could, or would try, to account for, she had always been his. When she had come into the room today, even his tweed had looked pleased. The only reason Julie had settled on an English degree had been due to his encouragement. She had tried anthropology courses and history and briefly flirted with languages. She had always been good at anything that involved people and understanding them, though she was only academic enough to squeak by at St Albas. Harris seemed to be the only British professor in the University who saw any value in such a student, and this had been the reason that he had recruited her for his department during second year.

"It was splendid. Went down outside of London to stay with the wife's parents. Many pitchers of Pimms were had."

"And you wrote?"

"And I wrote," he said. "And you?"

"I read a lot. America. Working in the city."

"They haven't gone and talked you into law school, have they?"

"No," she said. "Don't worry."

"Write any?"

"Some. Some bits and pieces."

"Thought about your dissertation?"

Julie pursed her lips.

"Not very much."

"Don't be in a nasty mood, protégé. I'll skip the lecture on potential. I'll walk you to Fair Street; I'm homeward bound as well."

When they reached the first floor foyer, Harris picked out their umbrellas from the cast-iron stand that stood above the rust spots it had created. Handing Julie's over, he threw open the well-oiled door. Just because the literati enjoyed onomatopoeia in their poems didn't mean they liked it in their hinges.

Julie opened her umbrella. It was the clear, plastic one with the pink polka dots on it. It made her look like she was walking around in one half of a spotted eggshell.

They passed through Bard House's back garden, which was soaking wet. The weight of the rain and the lift of the wind made all the leaves shiver. The whole garden, white and purple with heather and thistle, was so damp that it seemed to be taking shallow breaths of salty air.

"Nice to be back, is it?"

"It's a beautiful place," said Julie. "It's home. And I'm happy to see my friends."

"And favourite professors?"

"And favorite professors."

"You'll be quite surprised as to how quickly this year flies by."

"Probably."

"Julie," he said, putting a hand on her arm and stopping her in the narrow path to Sea Street, "it's going to go by. Are you listening?"

"Yes. I don't want to talk about potential. You promised. Please."

"It's not about potential. It's just time to consider how you'll prepare yourself."

"I'm thinking about it," she said, looking past his right shoulder. "I'm getting my degree, aren't I?"

"And?"

"Professor, and what?"

"What are you going to do with it, Julie? It's an English degree."

"You're the one who told me to get it!"

"Because I knew it would suit you. And it does. You'd be a wonderful journalist or a teacher or a starving artist. But what do *you* want to do with it?"

"I'm going to join the traveling circus, that's what."

Professor Harris quirked an eyebrow and began walking briskly. Julie followed.

"I'm not really going to," she said. "I'm sorry. You're right."

"I know," he said, turning around to face her.

"I'm figuring it out."

"I'm not asking you to think about forever, Julie. Just the next five or ten years. Just the next year, even. All right?"

"All right," she said.

"Good," said Professor Harris. "Good."

They were standing on Sea Street, where students in their emerald academic gowns darted in and out of cafés and houses.

"Now," he said, "why don't you go home and think some more about it? It's not an end to the fun. Or the selfishness. It's just a different type of selfishness."

"I'll think about it."

"And I don't just mean classes. Get outside your comfort zone. Didn't you do a couple of plays in first year? And why not write some more articles for the *Martyr*?"

"I'll think about it. I promise."

When Professor Harris had disappeared around a corner, however, she went down the street to Florians Bottle Shop. It was a short walk, mostly past houses that looked the same as hers, perhaps with the odd red or yellow door, or a crack-wrinkled staircase lined with flowerpots. It took a minute at most, unless there was ice on the uneven cobblestones. Though the walk was wet, it was pleasant for the fresh air and the sound of the rainwater rushing through the gutters.

Julie crossed the threshold of Florians, pushing the heavy glass door inward. The wooden floorboards drooped under the rainy-day filth as she shook her boots haphazardly over the soaked doormat and placed her umbrella in the bucket near the entrance. For a few moments, she browsed the bottles of wine. They hovered and rattled exquisitely in their gold and ruby tones on the beechwood shelves as Julie trod past. New Zealand, France, California. They provided an itinerary she would like to follow, especially if it meant days of sunshine and getting to taste them all. She tried to remind herself of all the adventure she was supposedly having here in Scotland. And, in the spirit of embracing her geographical reality, she left the wines and turned to browse the large selection of whisky on display near the front window. In a way, the romantically dreary backdrop of Church Street provided the perfect advertising scheme for the waiting malts, which ranged in price from twenty quid to hundreds of pounds.

As she picked up a bottle of Glenfiddich for examination and held it up to the indoor light, the door of the shop opened. Through it, there came a boy with a raincoat on. Julie stared at the boy as he shook the water off of himself the way a Labrador does after a swim—pleasantly, unfazed, joyful in doing what he is meant to do.

Feeling her looking, he glanced in Julie's direction, taking in the strange position of the whisky above her head. He wondered what exactly this girl was looking for in the bottle. Clearly she had no experience in selecting a whisky. He was right, for after he had crossed the shop to the wines, she had abandoned the endeavor and was asking for a bottle of gin and two six packs of Budweiser at the till.

After she was done paying and was standing in the street again, she walked home with a purpose other than reading *To the Lighthouse* or thinking about the future. Exhilarated. The sun was coming out. Professor Harris and his lectures of any kind could not have been further from her mind.

The boy in Florians looked familiar. This was because he had sat with her on the bed at the May Saving party. He had almost kissed her, perhaps had almost kissed her.

It was Harry Ommar, back in town.

***

"It's so good to see you," everyone proclaimed, whether it was good or not.

The first party of the semester had begun. The theme of the night lived somewhere between Greek life in ancient Athens and Greek life in college—a haphazard mix of bed-sheet togas and makeshift fig leafs. As ever, Ashwin played host alongside Brett and Peter; both tolerated or enthusiastically encouraged his antics with varying amounts of amusement as the evening railed and derailed.

The trio's flat was located a mile or two outside the town center, in a complex of apartments that had been built by the University in the late 1990s to accommodate fourth-year students. Though St Albas grew quickly rural on the road that led away from town, the Residences MacDuff were still within the thin boundaries of civilization. Some of the wealthiest students liked to live there rather than on Sea Street because living there was an excellent excuse—not that one was needed—for driving their Range Rovers and Jaguars too fast around the curves into town. Life in RMac, as it was affectionately called, also provided distance from the elderly townspeople who were liable to shut down student parties before midnight. Indeed, the police usually considered it too much of a hassle to have to drive anywhere, so RMac had a reputation for housing epic parties that was unmatched by any other location in or out of town.

What the apartments lacked in historical character, they made up for in shameless breakability. That is to say, the University had built the flats and furnished them using the cheapest possible materials. This was a trait of particular value at times such as this, when Ashwin had begun relieving the kitchen walls of their cabinetry.

"Ashwin, what are you doing?" said Julie, walking into the kitchen with Caddy.

"We need firewood for the beach."

"Oh, let me help you," said Larry, nodding hello to the girls as he went.

"You may be a pain sometimes, Caddy," said Julie, "but at least you don't rip out our kitchen cabinets."

Peter walked into the kitchen, which was steadily filling with people. He surveyed the crowd in his flat. Here was Julie in her blue toga, talking with Caddy and now Margot, the German girl who studied English and sounded like Ingrid Bergman. Next to her there was Neve, a Scot with bright red hair, and shit—what was her name? Well, that other girl. He could never remember. And then there was pretty Ruth, with the long black hair that reminded him of his own girlfriend, who was at another university down in England. Hearing a peculiar tearing noise to his left, he turned to see Ashwin and Larry hard at work. Larry had climbed onto the kitchen counter. People were being asked to stand back.

"You all right paying for that?" he said to Ashwin.

"Just cool it, man," was the response he received. Peter opened the refrigerator and, finding several lukewarm beers there, chose a Stella Artois and headed over to Julie's side with an extra one in hand. Margot and Caddy had gone to the coffee table to mix cocktails.

Julie took the beer from Peter, thankful and relieved to be with her closest male friend once more. It was the kind of friendship that required no greeting. Things were simply picked up where they were left off. But tonight, surrounded by all the people she had half-forgotten in the long Chicago summer full of heat and barbecues and working in the city and at the mall, Julie was even more glad of Peter than she usually was upon returning to St Albas. He was familiar—he was practically family. Every time she saw him one or two brain cells would errantly wonder why she didn't just get involved with Peter, who had all the traits you wanted in a boy: kindness, and loyalty, and a sense of humor (wry though it was). Then she remembered how much he could demand of her, and the brain cells agreed and moved on to other thoughts of other boys.

Princes and counts convened in the apartment, from countries she hadn't previously realized had things such as princes and counts. They were all dressed in their fathers' clothing: the starched, button-down Ralph Lauren shirts in an array of colors, the oh-so-bourgeois Brooks Brothers trousers, the startlingly transparent displays of timepiece wealth that one must never comment on. Julie remembered with embarrassment the first night in St Albas. She had told a Swedish noble how much she liked his Mont Blanc watch. He had not spoken to her since.

Peter, though, had been lovely from the first, had been kin from the first. Julie had always spoken openly with him, or at least felt she could if she wanted to.

"How are you, then? Impressed with Ashwin's antics?"

"As always," said Peter.

"How were classes?"

"Not bad. Modern history is going to be grand. And you?"

"It's all Harris, pretty much. Should be all right."

"Have you thought about next year at all?"

Julie took a long sip of her drink.

"Are you and Harris conferencing in or what? We just got here," said Julie.

"The time is going to fly."

"…And the coach will turn back into a pumpkin?"

Peter shrugged. "Something like that."

Julie pouted. "Give me some time to settle in. I don't have a job waiting for me, or unlimited cash reserves, or gold mines, like you guys. It's not that easy."

"I don't have gold mines," said Peter.

"Your father does really well for himself."

"I'm upper-upper-middle class, Julie. Not so different from you."

"I don't even know why we're talking about this, Peter. Let's just have a good time."

"Fine, fine," said Peter, putting an arm around her and squeezing the back of her neck affectionately with his hand. "You're right for now. I'll lay off."

Julie smiled.

Watching Julie and Peter from across the room, red-headed Neve said, "I think they're doing it."

"No way," said Margot. "You also thought Harry and Hermione would hook up, didn't you?"

"Just wait until Julie gets desperate enough. That's all I'm saying. It's been ages since she had a boyfriend."

"Okay," consented Margot with a grin. "Maybe you're right."

"What are you bitches talking about?" inquired Caddy.

"Julie and Peter."

"That's such a boring conversation. Let's gossip about someone else and not waste our precious time there. Julie would tell us if she were banging Peter. And even if she didn't, we'd know. She's a terrible liar."

Margot scanned the room with her enormous blue eyes, which eventually landed on Harry Ommar. "*Hello*, sir. Fresh meat: do either of you know who that guy is over in the corner with Larry?"

Their heads turned in Harry Ommar's direction.

"No," said Neve.

"Wasn't he there at May Saving?" offered Caddy.

"You're right," Neve said. "He tried to come on to me."

"He is really handsome though, isn't he," said Margot with a mischievous grin.

"You think so?" Neve looked at her friend skeptically. "He's a bit of a prick, I think."

"Maybe. But from a purely physical standpoint—"

The old debate about Harry had started again for the thousandth time. And meanwhile, his presence had not gone unnoticed by Julie. While she was eager to see Peter and to hear how the glorious summer in Surrey had been, she was more eager to be noticed by Mr. Ommar. So far she had been unsuccessful.

"Are you paying any attention to me whatever?" said Peter.

"Moan, moan, moan," said Julie.

"What's going on?"

"Nothing."

"Good God," he said. "Stop fussing with your toga."

"I'm not."

"Is this about a *boy*?" he asked, putting what Julie considered to be an irritating amount of emphasis on the final word of the phrase.

"No."

"Liar. It's about that chap over there in the blue toga."

"Well done, you."

"Why don't you pop over there?"

"Because I want him to pop over to me."

Peter had long been the sounding board for all sorts of similar games and tricks. Though he had ample experience dealing with the fallouts that followed Julie's mostly disastrous forays into romance, the beginnings were always much more treacherous to navigate than the endings. How serious she was about anyone was difficult to gauge. She seemed to latch onto people because she found them either useful or attractive, and it usually ended in one of two ways: with Julie doubting her own worth or the worth of the entire other half of the human race.

"Who is he?" asked Peter.

"His name is Harry Ommar. I met him at May Saving."

"Did anything happen?"

"Not really, no."

Peter could be relatively certain this meant that Julie had spent her summer in American suburbia daydreaming of Harry and his foreign charms.

"He looks like a bit of an idiot."

"I'm an adult. I can make my own choices."

"Your own bad choices, maybe."

"Don't frown. People will think you're jealous."

Peter rolled his eyes.

"Christ, look what Ashwin's got up to."

Ashwin had evidently become exhausted with the effort of ripping the furniture to pieces and had abandoned the idea of a beach bonfire in favor of a game of beer pong.

"Let's go play. Come on. You're my partner," said Julie.

Peter found the game childish, and so he declined Julie's offer and sat in the background, keeping an eye on Harry, trying to judge him. Since he made no attempts to be nearer to Julie, Peter relaxed.

Julie, on the other hand, was turning disgruntled for the same reason. She had recruited Brett for her partner and had put considerable effort into touching him unnecessarily at every opportunity in order to be noticed. She had cheered loudly when they'd scored and had generally gone to great lengths to look as if she was the most exuberant, fun-loving, and adorable girl alive. It was after a third victory at beer pong and around the dangerous time of two o'clock in the morning that they quit the game and drunkenly made their way to the sofa. Julie hoped that Harry could see her as she leaned familiarly into her friend's arm.

They had dated for six or seven months during their first year in St Albas. Julie had been attracted to Brett for his laid-back disposition—and the Australian accent hadn't hurt. Brett had been drawn to Julie's outgoing nature and free spirit. It was something of a tale as old as time, that way. They had shared some wonderful moments—a trip to his parents' lodge in the Highlands, Julie's first yachting trip in the Dalmatian Coast, a necklace from Cartier for Christmas. While she had been dazzled by the trips and the gifts, it did not take long to realize how little they meant and how carelessly they were given—and how young Brett was to be the giver. She was an accessory to the good times, not the center of them, not a necessity for his happiness, and it simply wasn't enough.

But theirs had been the politest, cleanest breakup in the world, mutually initiated and agreed upon. Julie had even tried to give the necklace back, and Brett had said:

"You wouldn't return it to a friend, would you?"

And just like that, they had returned to the friendship they had started several months previously.

"I heard about your summer in London. How did it go?"

Julie felt herself screaming over the music and through the cloud of sweat and hormones in the small living room.

"You want to go?" Brett yelled back. "You know, I'll take you sometime. We can go to the Tate. You would love what they have on at the moment. Anything you want."

"I wasn't—okay. Yeah, let's have a jaunt to London."

"Yeah."

"Be like old times," he said.

"Ha," said Julie.

"We could pretend we never broke up."

"We could pretend that right now," Julie said. "Who needs London?"

"Yeah," said Brett, defiantly, his Aussie accent sounding more attractive to Julie by the moment, and he recognized this by the way she smiled. "Why haven't you dated anyone?"

"What do you mean? I've dated."

"No one seriously," said Brett. "There are guys everywhere."

"There are boys, yeah."

"Should we go to my room?" asked Brett, putting a hand on her leg. Julie warmed to the idea of Brett, of kissing him familiarly and sleeping with him familiarly. The physical things had never been the problem.

"Okay," she said, smiling. Brett stood and took her hand. Julie noticed how many people were pouring into and out of the room. So many young, gorgeous people. So much music and alcohol and perfume. It was a genuinely good first party of the year. She allowed Brett to lead her out. As they turned into the hallway, Harry Ommar's figure came into view. He nodded to Brett as they passed, and his deep brown eyes came to rest on Julie's green ones. A smile split his lips. It was a genuine one. It was then that Julie felt nauseatingly sick.

"Brett," she said, her eyes on Harry, "I need the bathroom." She ran down the hallway, Brett close behind her. She went into his room, locked the door, and began throwing up in huge heaves all over his white porcelain toilet. Her face felt hot. Brett knocked at the door.

"Let me in, Jay."

"No," she said. That's when the gray patterns between the white tiles faded to black, along with everything else. The last thing she heard was Ashwin's made-up lyrics to a popular tune, echoing shrill in the hallway like the song of a Siren.

***

The next morning Julie woke up in a pair of Peter's shorts and a t-shirt. She was lying on the sofa with a splitting headache, listening to the ducks quacking in protest at the rising of the sun. Peter entered the kitchen shortly thereafter in a pair of boxers and a hoodie. Julie looked at his hairy, Englishman's legs and determined she did not like to think of them as the usual occupants of the shorts. However, they did seem to provide evidence as to why several underfunded colonies were able to become independent of their colonial oppressor.

"Good, you're still alive," he said. Peter sat down on a stool at the counter, assessing her discombobulated state with superiority.

"Not exactly the ideal morning greeting. But thanks for the pajamas."

"I'm not going to let you lie half naked on Brett's bathroom floor, am I?"

"What happened?"

"You didn't have what one might call a respectable end to the night. Brett broke into his bathroom and dragged you out into the hallway. Where I found you taking off your sick-soaked shirt."

"How did I get into these clothes?"

Peter shrugged.

"Oh, no. *Gross.*"

"Right. Because you covered in chunder is my idea of inescapable sexual seduction. It was out of the goodness of my heart and the strength of my gag reflex that you're clothed and on that sofa rather than lying naked in the hallway, so please don't flatter yourself. Now, Lady Lovejoy, you spectacular mess: would you like some breakfast?"

"Yeah."

"Don't beg me, now."

"Please, Peter, can I have some breakfast?"

"But of course. Egg on toast and cheese?"

"Sure."

"Shall I put children's telly on?"

"Sure."

Ashwin entered the kitchen, apparently high even after sleeping for a few hours. Either that or he had taken to smoking before breakfast as well as before every other meal of the day.

"Good morning, Julie," he said, filling a glass of water at the sink with pain in his voice.

"Hi, Ashwin."

"Has anyone seen Brett today?"

"No," answered Julie shortly.

Peter brought the toast and a large glass of orange juice to the sofa, where the three of them sat in silence for a moment, watching a short episode of a claymation children's show whose main characters seemed to be a police officer, a cow, and a mailman.

"Good God," said Peter, looking out the window. "You will never believe this."

"Those cow spots, they're coming after me," said Ashwin.

"You're high. Have a look, Julie."

She leaned over, pulling the curtains open.

"No way."

Brett and Ruth, the girl with the long black hair, were talking in the parking lot. Ruth was wearing her clothes from the night before. They kissed goodbye.

"Don't be jealous," said Peter.

"I'm not jealous. I'm embarrassed," said Julie. "I'm leaving."

And so by the time Brett came back inside Julie had slipped out the back door of the flat with her purse after tossing her other belongings into Peter's room.

"Hail the conquering hero," said Peter in slight disapproval.

"Stop it, mate," said Brett. "And before you ask, Ashwin, nothing worth detailing happened."

"I could have told you that," said Ashwin. "Clingy too, right? Were you born yesterday, man? She just broke up with her boyfriend."

"You're high," said Brett.

"But so very wise."

Brett sighed.

"I didn't know they broke up."

Ashwin appeared to reassess his friend's mental health, looking him deep in the eyes and then saying:

"Even Peter knew that. And he doesn't know shit."

"True," confirmed Peter. "Margot told me last night when I asked her to give me the run-down of summer gossip."

"Fuck."

Something buzzed in Brett's pocket.

"What?"

"I just got a text: 'Call me later.' Fuck. Me."

For a moment, the trio resembled three birds on a wire.

"Wow," said Ashwin. "She loves you! Good work. Exactly what a guy wants at the start of his fourth year!"

"I don't want to talk about it. Let's smoke," said Brett.

"I thought you'd never ask," said Ashwin.

"Peter?"

"Do I ever smoke with you guys?"

"Nope."

"Have at it. I'm going to tidy up a bit of this crap."

"Leave it, man. The maid's coming tomorrow."

It had always perplexed Ashwin and Brett that Peter kind of liked to clean up after parties himself. It helped to clear his head, to go over the evening's events. But Ashwin's father owned every single Indian railroad north of Mumbai. Brett's mother was heiress to that Australian mining fortune, his father a multi-millionaire in his own right, having started a tech company in his garage with some friends from McGill. Ashwin drove a BMW and Brett wore an expensive, crested ring. Neither of them had ever cleaned a thing in their lives.

"I got it," said Peter.

"All right, you weird-ass," said Ashwin. "Come on, Brett."

***

In flats across St Albas, students were waking up in one another's arms and beds and clothing, on one another's couches and some in suites at the Ancient Links Hotel after staying too late at the bar there. Many of them would claim that the previous night's activities had been a mistake—would claim it over tense coffees or terse text messages. And many would be lying. Many a plotted conquest and many a hoped-for hookup had come to fruition on the first party-heavy night of term. A summer's worth of wishes had been blissfully fulfilled throughout the bleary early morning hours.

In one such flat, the one he shared with his old friend Harry Ommar, Larry Liberatore slept on. A girl named Anastasia Zolotov was awake in his arms. Though she could tell that his bed sheets had not been washed since his arrival back in Scotland (do boys ever adjust to being away from their mothers?), the boy smell that emanated from them was cozy and familiar. She curled her tiny frame along his. Larry stretched and rolled over as she did.

Anastasia sat up in bed with a head that ached. She bent over enough to take her phone out of her purse to check the time. She opened her compact and gazed into its mirror approvingly as she admired her fine, smooth, black hair that hung to her chin. Her olive-shaped eyes did not look as rested as her plump, flushed cheeks or delicate collarbones, but that was all right. Larry wouldn't see them.

The American was in perfect comfort, having satiated himself to sleep. When he woke up, he would be ready, probably, for more. But she would put on her jeans and walk home. It was embarrassing to wake up next to someone who wasn't your type. Anastasia liked Larry well enough—he was kind, and the sex had been good. But he was American, and not very refined, and not quite wealthy enough for her liking. Anastasia had a fortune of her own and preferred to add another to it.

And so, Larry awoke to find Anastasia gone. It made him sad because he had never been with such an exotic girl. The sex had been good, and he liked the kinds of things she talked about.

But now there was no indication that she had been there at all. The imprint she made on the bed was too light, as if all she was capable of leaving behind was a trail of fairy dust.

# VI. OCTOBER

**THE HISTORY DEPARTMENT'S LIBRARY HAD LOTS** of big chairs and lots of big paintings of dead people. Dead men, to be exact. But being that they were both boys, neither of the room's present occupants seemed to mind or notice. They sat in the history department not because either of them studied history, but because the library was rarely used. Therefore, it was an ideal place to have a cup of tea and a private chat.

People considered private spaces to be a rare commodity in St Albas: many a social suicide had been committed due to the naïve, first-year belief that one's friends and enemies alike did not have eyes and ears in every café, restaurant, study space, and pub in town. Wiser students' heads swiveled habitually over teas, cakes, and pints, anticipating the possibility of overheard gossip. ("Did you know that Kim is sleeping with Bradley, who is engaged to Vaanika? Yeah, she won't have sex with him until they're married.")

Everyone was willing to talk and listen about everyone else, though everyone was also farcically outraged when a rumor about them had run through the mill and back. Only a small percent of the rumors ever heard floating around in that little town where true. Usually the more outrageous the rumor, the more inclined everyone was to believe it.

But on occasion, in the right setting and with the right timing, one stood the chance of hearing something quite true.

The figures conversing at present in the library were not the type to participate in petty gossip. Their interests lay elsewhere, perhaps too far Elsewhere for their own social good. Philosophy and religion do not often make polite table talk, which is why both Max and Simon were always glad to sit at a table together.

Simon had arrived there first, for the walk from the rectory was short. He settled into his favorite chair. It had been a long time

since he had seen his friend Max. He wondered whether or not the
summer had changed him, even though it hadn't changed Catriona.
As he waited, he laced his fingers together and apart. He unpacked a
thermos full of hot tea, a package of biscuits, and two paper cups.
However rudimentary this mockery of high tea might be, he was
sure it would relieve any tension that might arise. Simon was
English and had therefore been raised on the expectation that
shared tea cured all ills.

The reason for the tea today had to do with what had happened
earlier in the week, when Simon had realized that he must tell Max
how he felt for Catriona. He had been to the polo match with her.

"Thank you for coming," Catriona had said at the polo field.
"Max is terribly sorry he couldn't make it."

"No bother."

"He's been busy. Studying so hard already. You have to admire him."

She was smoothing a checkered blanket out before them.

"But my mother bought us tickets to the charity polo match, and
I'm so glad I didn't have to waste the other."

She stretched the blanket out on each of its four sides, trying to
resist the urge to do so again and again until it was positively flat.

"Have a seat," she insisted, squatting to the ground herself,
arranging her limbs and her tight tweed jacket. "I'm sorry it's
uncomfortable."

Simon could not be more comfortable than he was, sitting beside
Catriona.

He had had a feeling this would be the last fine, summery day of
the year. The polo grounds were still green, as were the little leaves
on the trees beyond the field. "Thankful" couldn't even begin to
describe his feelings, as he watched Catriona tuck her hair behind
her ear, and the horses trotted out to the center of the field with his
classmates astride.

*Yahs*, they were called: instead of "yes," or "yeah," they said
"yah." They didn't ever hear or say "no," so the naming was easy.
They were the students who majored in accounting and economics,
who were too elite to mix with foreigners (including, obviously, the
Scottish). Simon could tell how much Catriona admired them. It
was encouraging that she tried not to show it. The affluent English
boys with their thick cotton sporting shirts and their thick sporting
thoroughbreds. Because he loved Catriona, Simon could not see

that her admiration was envy, an envy strong enough to cut off the flow of blood to her brain. It gripped Catriona when she looked at the polo boys' girlfriends, with their long, thin legs that they wrapped in tartan trousers. The girls were chic in clothes that would have made Catriona look dowdy and round. My God, but they were thin. Their arms were long and thin. Their legs were long and thin. They were so thin. And their breasts were so perfect. Perfect like their shining long hair. Why couldn't she be thin and big-breasted and shiny-haired like them?

"I should have learnt polo," said Simon.

Catriona smiled away from the thinness and said:

"You would have been good."

"Most likely. I am a superb sportsman."

Catriona giggled.

"You are. The wind-surfing priest. What a sight."

"Well, I'm not a priest yet."

Though her face was in profile, he could see her brows wrinkling.

"No, not yet. But soon."

"Maybe. But maybe not."

Simon was startled that he'd said it. Let alone to Catriona. But he loved her. And if he could be with her, if there was any way, what was the sense in pretending he wanted to be a priest for another moment? Max wasn't like the polo-playing boys, either. If he'd had a chance and won Catriona, why hadn't it been him, Simon? Why couldn't it still be?

"Don't joke, Simon."

"I'm not."

"You have always wanted to be a priest."

"Not always."

"Since first year, at least," she said.

"That isn't true. And even if it were. Now, I don't know if it's right."

"It's right."

"I don't know if it is, though," said Simon. "Sometimes I think it's not right for me."

She turned to look him dead in the face, discovering through the quiet care in his voice that he'd been looking at her.

"What are you doing?" she asked, a little nervous.

"Watching the polo," he said.

*I love you more than anything,* was what he wanted to say.

Bringing his mind back to the task at hand in the library, he wondered if Max was the sort of person who would hit him. He doubted it. Max was a diplomat. He liked to turn things over in his mind, to look at a situation from all sides, not to settle hastily on anything. And besides, even if he became inclined to violence, he felt sure a subconscious desire to keep the scalding tea in its cup would prevent Max from doing so. Max adored good tea.

"Hello," said Max, as he opened the door.

"Hello."

Simon stood. He was relieved to see that his friend was certainly not any taller or handsomer than he had been in May.

The two shook hands warmly. Max clapped his hand on Simon's shoulder.

"It's great to see you, man," said Max, in earnest.

"You too. Sit, sit."

Max laughed to himself over nothing as he took the chair beside Simon. Eager to deploy the tea to its defensive location in both their cups, Simon poured.

"How was your holiday?" he asked Max.

"Fine, yeah."

"Catriona came down to Zurich?"

"She did." Max shifted his weight in the chair. "I didn't get up to England, or I would have looked you up."

*Of course not*, thought Simon. *You wanker.*

"No bother," he said, instead.

"What did you get up to?"

"Rome, for a month. I've just heard. That's where I'm to continue in seminary."

"Congratulations."

"Thank you."

"I know that's what you wanted."

Then the library turned quiet. Max, who did not usually notice these types of things, wondered why Simon had become so stiff there in his chair. He hadn't drunk any of the tea. He thought about making a joke: "Simon, is the tea poisoned?"... "Thoroughly un-English not to drink the tea, old chap."

The seconds crumbled on in succession, turning as stale as the markers in the cathedral's cemetery plot. There had never been a silence like this in the whole of their long acquaintance—an acquaintance that had had its many thoughtful silences in this room, in these chairs. He was used to civilized arguments and knew what Simon's face looked like when he should give him a chance to think, when he was forming an opinion further before speaking. But that was not what this was. The proverbial English Stiff Upper Lip was on display in a line the likes of which he had never seen, not even on Catriona. Simon was not thinking, he was being. So Max didn't speak. And kept not speaking.

After a moment of prayer that seemed much shorter to him than to Max, Simon said:

"You're probably not going to like what I have to say."

"What?"

"I want to apologize."

"For what?"

"Just—Max. Listen. It's about Catriona."

The only other person who had ever mentioned Catriona to him in this tense tone was his mother, who routinely asked in as kind a voice as possible if things were all right and left her son to his own judgments of his girlfriend. Max's father believed that eventually he would come to his senses on the subject of the English girl who tried too hard. But his mother, a nonbeliever, thought she would rather see herself damned before she let Max waste more of his youth not living it. And so, each time Catriona had come to Zurich, the visit was subtly less pleasant than the one before. But Max was one to take the path of least resistance (he had read Thoreau at an impressionable age) and couldn't imagine rescinding or avoiding the assumed, long-standing invitation for Catriona's visits in the same manner that he now avoided going to visit her family.

"Max?" said Simon. "Are you listening?"

"I'm sorry. I'm listening."

"Right. This isn't easy."

Max clasped his hands together, orbiting them around one another, almost in real time.

"I don't understand, Simon."

"Max, I love Catriona."

"You what?"

"I love her."

"Her?"

"Yes. Catriona. I'm sorry Max, but I do."

"Oh," said Max, raising his eyebrows. He caught himself wondering how Simon could possibly love Catriona. Simon could do better. He quickly calculated that this was not a flattering commentary on his own choices and broke the new silence with a half-serious question:

"You know you're going to be a priest, right?"

"I just wanted you to know."

"Now I do."

"Now you know."

"Wow."

"I didn't mean to take you by surprise."

Max shook his head, brushing off the apology.

"Can I ask—how long has this been a thing?"

"Since first year."

"First year."

"Yeah. When we lived all together."

"And you didn't want to tell anyone about this back then?"

"You were going together. I didn't have a lot of time."

"You had months. I was with Clara."

"But then, Catriona, Max. Right after. The day after."

"Was it that quick?"

"Yes. You'd never noticed Catriona before. I know you didn't. But then all the sudden you two were constantly together."

"I noticed her."

"You didn't."

Then before Max's eyes, the last three years came clicking back like slides in a projecting machine. Max saw himself coming out of Catriona's room early one morning, and there was Simon. There he was at his first Martyrs Monday, powdered head to foot in flour, standing next to Catriona, and there was Simon. There was the day he had gone to Dunglen to choose Catriona's Christmas gift. Not knowing what she liked, he had brought Simon. A thousand other recollections vied for recognition, their hands in the air. He was startled to realize that they were just below the surface of what was happening now, in the present moment. The memory machine jammed, and he was back again in the library.

"You're right. It happened fast. I'm sorry," said Max. And he was truly sorry, for a reason that was not quite clear to him. He suspected it had something to do with the fact that the entire situation with Catriona had always felt out of his hands.

Or maybe it was empathy. Max knew how it felt to desire someone and be unable to have her. There had been that girl before Catriona, in the first few weeks of first year, as he had just reminded Simon. A study abroad student, an American, a girl looking to replace the boyfriend she'd left on the Upper East Side. She had been older, beautiful, temperamental, self-destructive, addicted to cocaine. Max found her romantic. Perhaps for no other reason than to increase her own legend, she had gone home to New York secretly, in the middle of the night no less, and it was only the following morning that Max had become aware of Catriona's existence. Simon was right.

"It's not your fault. And it's all right. But I wanted you to know."

"She's my girlfriend, though. I can't help that."

"I know."

"I mean, I love her."

"I don't want you to think I would ever—"

"I wouldn't think that."

He looked at Simon with harmless eyes, lifting them onto him kindly.

"You aren't upset?"

"No," said Max. And he wasn't.

They talked about several other things that afternoon. Boys can be like that.

But for the rest of the day, neither could quite shake the inconvenient thought that, though the truth had come out, it didn't make such a difference. Max was shocked to discover, over and over in the repetition of the memories that played and played for the rest of the day, that he had, somehow, known about Simon's feelings all along. And it was even more jarring to discover that he didn't care, hadn't cared. So really, how was he supposed to respond to this? Scream at Simon? Hit him? It didn't seem, hadn't seemed, worth the trouble. Not because he knew Simon would never lay a hand on, near, or around Catriona in any way that he wouldn't in front of Max himself. Or because he knew Catriona would never allow such a blatant breach of the rules. It wasn't worth the trouble because nothing would change. The fact was, Max was all right with Catriona. He liked her. The last three years had been filled with her, and studying, and they had been productive.

Then there was a spark; perhaps things would change if Simon told Catriona. Perhaps she would rather be with him. Perhaps that would be better for her—Simon was the type of boy who would want to get married right away, if he wasn't going to be a priest.

Max had never concerned himself with thinking about what kinds of people should and shouldn't be together. Being with Catriona served its purpose. And, he was quick to tell himself, it made him happy. Besides, call it what you might and admit what you would, there could be no hope that Simon would tell her anyway, or that Catriona would ever allow anyone to deviate from the course she had set for the three of them. What good could come of rocking the boat, especially when doing it might end in loneliness, in a lack of routine that could very possibly negatively affect his studies right when they mattered the most?

When Max arrived at Catriona's, he felt himself appraising her, wondering what exactly it was one saw in Catriona Darlington-Welland. When she opened her front door to him, he had stood there for several seconds, wide-eyed, with his head cocked to the side.

***

Simon kicked through puddles left from the morning rain. How could he have been so dense as to have thought confessing his love for Catriona to Max would make anything better? It hadn't. The result was that he knew for sure what he had suspected for years: Max was deceiving himself. He did not love Catriona, not really. A man in love couldn't sit there, hear those things, and apologize with such sincerity. Simon considered himself an optimist concerning human nature, but he doubted virtue extended as far as all that. Stupid, stupid. To have thought it could have changed anything.

And as he reached the corner where the rectory sat sunk in the evening light, he shook off the water that had collected on his shoes with a strong, even kick. The droplets fell onto the slippery sidewalk in tiny spots of gold—the sun was bathed in its own setting.

How could Max not appreciate her in the way she deserved? The intolerableness of what he now knew was mere liking and not love made him feel as if he would have been justified to punch Max in the face. To be able to fall asleep with those soft arms over his, to have the privilege of waking up on the other side of this incredible seaside sunset and see her deep, sloped chin under the sheet and never to appreciate it. The idiot. He hated Max.

But on further inspection of his feelings that evening, after dinner with Father Tom and two freshers who were interested in the priesthood, after digesting and talking while looking out the bay windows downstairs, where Flat Sands was wet with what looked to be mercury, and finally, under the loving glare of the crucifix across from his bed, he realized it was just a pitiable arrangement for all of them. He tried not to take comfort in the fact that all three parties involved were miserable, in their varying degrees of awareness, of which he assumed rightly that his was the keenest. He was sure he could make Catriona perfectly happy, and it made him sad to think that she wasn't in the first place.

But instead of feeling angry, he took refuge in knowing that God had a plan. And in the plan, he had done his part, which was to do the right and honest thing. And that had meant letting Max know, and that was one of the things that made him a boy who could be worthy of a girl like Catriona.

So he did not hate Max. He loved him; particularly for the kindness and even temper he had shown in such a ridiculous situation. Really, credit must be given where it was due. When he laid his head on the crisp, cool pillowcase that Mrs. Leslie had ironed for him, he prayed for Max, with whom the secret was most assuredly safe, though he could not say why.

Still, in the dark, his thoughts turned to Catriona.

He had promised himself he would never touch her but only because it seemed an impossible thing.

# VII.

THE DJ AT THE SHARK LOUNGE was a man dressed in women's clothes. Mostly women's clothes, anyway; he did wear a black leather hat reminiscent of a police officer's. Other than that, it was a tight leather corset with pink ribbons on the sides and stockings with bows at the knees and a pink and purple tartan skirt. The student population loved him in, and for, his strangeness. They, of course, never saw him driving away from the club by the early-rising Scottish sun, cruising at the speed limit down Sea Street in his very sensible mid-sized Toyota sedan. Even the very heterosexual male yahs (who were always quick to remind you of how *very* heterosexual they were) were on a first-name basis with him. Everyone was. He played good music, he made just enough small talk, he took requests, and he didn't judge the occasion of the occasional dance floor make out.

When Julie and her friends arrived at the club, a twiggy girl was making a fuss outside its doors. She was wearing a tight black dress that would have scandalized her grandmother and four-inch heels that would have made her mother proud. (The prince was at St Albas, it was good of her daughter to make an effort.) She had long, hair-dye-ad locks in the shade of champagne. By the smell of her hair, dress, and handbag, she was only a half pint away from champagne kissing the toilet. The bouncers, two burly men from Glasgow who rotated from bar to bar each night, were not letting her in.

"But it's so UNFAIR!" she was screaming.

"Listen, we've told you: you've made enough trouble, and you're not to come back."

"But it's unfair!"

Peter detested the club but had been dragged there against his will.

"This is why I don't go to the club," he said to Julie.

He was as calm as a safari guide pointing out an elephant as he gestured toward the screaming girl.

"You'll have fun once you're in."

"That's what she said!"

"Thanks, Ashwin."

Ashwin was already on his fifth gin and tonic of the night. Before coming into town from their apartment, Brett had poured him a generous portion of gin in a wine glass. Handing it to Ashwin, he had said, "There you go buddy. Have some water." Julie had finished it herself, wanting Ashwin to make it through the night on his feet rather than his face. Now she was feeling the consequences.

The stick figure girl was still screaming.

"This is rubbish," said Neve, whose birthday it was. She pulled her red hair into a bundle at the nape of her neck, twisting it into a long, lovely rope. "I'm going to speak to this guy." Believing herself to be the only person in the group from the middle or lower classes, she felt she could at least contribute her Scottishness and affinity with fellow Glaswegians to the success of her birthday night out, if not her father's credit card. And anyway, credit cards and cash were too commonly tossed about to be considered valuable objects of bribery where bouncers in St Albas were concerned. A far more pleasing and persuasive inducement was the lilt of a Scottish woman's voice.

The charm worked. Two by two, Neve's large birthday party descended a narrow, black, rubbery set of stairs, which had accumulated several interesting objects in the course of the evening: a leather glove, a £50 note (which Brett picked up and put in his wallet), nail clippers, and several condoms of different types that had obviously been too clumsily exchanged. Possibly by the yah fresher men who were eager to get rather involved with their female classmates and had not yet learned that being the possessor of Extra Texture Strawberry Bliss was not necessarily the way to woo them.

"Need one?" said Peter to Caddy, pointing to the mess.

"No," said Caddy. She chuckled. "But I think maybe Julie will, if she's more successful tonight with the boys than she has been so far this term."

"Shut. Up," said Julie.

"Why?"

"It's nothing, just," she looked at Caddy, who was still drunkenly chuckling. "Just stop."

"I can't help it. You tell me everything. When will you learn?"

"Now I'm interested," said Peter.

"That's wonderful, Peter," said Julie. "But you were interested before."

"Just tell me it's not that one from—"

But Neve had opened one of the enormous, swinging doors that stood at the entrance of the basement club, and the noise drowned out Peter's sense. Neve's indescribably elegant flatmate, Helen, led the group into the chaos, her pastel blouse now dyed with twirling colors in the ever-changing patterns of neon light emanating from the dance floor. The rest of the group followed suit. In this room you had the feeling of being underwater, perhaps of being on a coral reef. Entire groups of people morphed into one another like schools of fish, pairing and tripling and singling one another out for conversation or drinks or other youthful transactions.

There was a long, sleek bar in an L formation close to the wall. On Saturday nights such as this one, there worked behind it three bartenders: two young blonde women and a young man, all three of them from the University of Dunglen, who traveled one hour for a five-hour shift serving cocktails to their wealthier counterparts across St Albas Bay. The tips, and, on occasion, the phone numbers left on bedside tables on Sunday mornings, made it worth their while.

The second area of the bar, inhabited by shiny, tightly sewn white leather couches, seemed to be made exclusively for the purpose of indiscreet grabbing and kissing. By morning, it would be a veritable lost and found of umbrellas, iPods, car keys, and tubes of lipstick. Girls in St Albas still wore it, and lost it, as though it were the 1950s. The couches glowed in the neon lights, and under the lights and on the couches the occupants of this room often felt submerged enough in the sea of people to do whatever they felt they shouldn't on land.

The dance floor resembled the one John Travolta danced on in *Saturday Night Fever* and needed no other description other than to say Peter claimed that it made him feel ill.

After shuffling off to the coat check, which was, as always, so thickly perfumed with every scent from the luxury counters of Harrods and Neiman's and KaDeWe that the local teenager inside should have been wearing a gas mask, Julie followed Peter and Caddy to the bar. Caddy promptly ordered two gin and tonics and a pint of beer, which were gratefully received. As they tussled their way back through the crowd, Caddy became entangled with a good-looking young man in a kilt. Peter used the opportunity to edge nearer to Julie. Standing in the center of the madness, he said, loudly:

"I love this place."

"You hate it."

"So what was Caddy tossing you about for?"

"None of your business."

"Come on."

"Not telling."

"Well, my trousers are vibrating."

"Your what?"

"My—oh, never mind. You are drunk." He reached into his pocket, pulling out the phone and showing the screen to Julie. "Catriona. Got to take it."

And so she was left alone. Everyone had scattered by now: to the dance floor, to the outdoor patio for a cigarette, to the bathroom. Out of the corner of her eye, she spotted Ashwin, tumbling around the dance floor, making friends.

Brett stood with a beer in his hand, relieved that he had not seen Ruth—whom he had been vigilantly avoiding since their one night of cuddling together. Across the room there was Julie. He thought perhaps he might go talk to her, but on second thought, no. No reason to stir things up when their friendship had gone back to normal, even after the throwing up and the yelling and the narrowly avoided ex-sex. She looked content enough; the sight of Ashwin spinning around always made for quality entertainment, and he was happy to see her happy. Even in the simplest way. He had always admired Julie's flair for the dramatic and her sense of humor. He took a sip of his beer. There were other girls besides Julie and Ruth. He allowed his mind to wander. Here was Neve, with her red hair and green eyes, and her crooked nose that somehow endeared her to him. But maybe that was just her boobs. Yeah, that was it. The boobs. And elegant Helen—what would it be like to get in on that?

His mental conquests, however, were interrupted at present by the stab of a stiletto into his boat shoes.

"Fuck," he said.

"Oh my God! Brett. Sorry," said the girl named Anastasia.

"Sorry about the language," he yelled.

"No worry." She was wearing a triangular sweater that exposed the flat bottoms of her stomach and sides. How on Earth would one tempt or trick her out of it, he wondered. "Going for a cigarette. Come?"

He nodded as she took him by the hand, leading him through the crowd, down the hallway past the bathrooms, and out the door.

"Good to have some fresh air, right?" She fumbled through her purse for her cigarettes. Finding them, she smiled.

"Yeah, definitely," he smiled back at her, offering a light.

"Aren't you aware that smoking kills," said a voice from behind them.

"Hello, Harry," said Brett. "Good to see you again."

Harry Ommar shook hands with Brett, who, having a businessman father, returned the gesture vigorously.

"And Anastasia Zolotov. Good to see you," said Harry.

"Good to see you."

"So," said Harry, "Larry and I just arrived. The redhead's birthday, is it?"

"It's Neve's birthday," said Anastasia.

"You've all just arrived then," said Harry.

"Yes."

This was good news. It meant Julie. Finally. Almost certainly. Harry felt his blood pressure rising. This game had gone on long enough. He had held out because girls liked the mystery of a man who didn't talk to them when they thought he should. He would speak to her tonight, he would set it all in motion. He stubbed out the cigarette he had been smoking, throwing it to the ground though it was only half finished. He had what he needed from it. "I think I'm done here. See you."

He walked confidently through the hallway, where he passed his roommate.

"Just saw Anastasia, mate," he said. "She's on to Brett. I'd hurry."

"Shit," said Larry.

"Patio," said Harry, nodding in that general direction. His friend clapped him on the shoulder at they changed places in the narrow corridor.

By then it was midnight. The temperature in the club had reached what would be its highest point. As Harry opened the door at the bottom of the stairs, Peter was saying goodnight to Julie.

"I have to go," he bellowed. "I'll call you in the morning."

"You just came back in. What gives?" she yelled back. "Is it that girlfriend of yours in Warwickshire? What's-her-name?"

"You know her name. And it wasn't. It was Catriona, remember?"

Julie smiled.

"What's the matter with her now?"

"Nothing."

Julie rolled her eyes. "Psh."

"Don't, Julie."

"Okay, okay. Brunch tomorrow?" She made the phone sign as soberly as possible, putting her thumb and pinky finger on her jaw and ear, respectively.

He nodded, and off he went, bumping into Harry as he did.

"Hey," said the latter.

"Sorry."

Peter watched as the bottom three quarters of Harry Ommar disappeared into the crowd. He traced the dot of pitch-black hair as it floated toward the dance floor, where Julie had rejoined their friends. He saw from the barely perceptible swish of curly golden locks that she had turned to say hello to him.

"What an ass," he mumbled. He was not entirely sure whether he meant Julie or Harry. All he knew was that this was bound to be his mess to clean up. He took a deep breath at the bottom of the stairs, bounding up them and into the cold night air.

Catriona had what she labeled "stomach flu," and he must get to the store before it shut to buy some antacid. Why Max couldn't do this for her, or why she wouldn't let him, he knew too well. The start of term was always difficult for her. And so was the end of the summer, with the memories of George. She needed Peter, and he would be there for her.

Julie had been dancing with Neve, Margot, and Helen. The tranny DJ was playing no shortage of Michael Jackson's hits, which was met with elation by the drunken mob on the dance floor.

Neve was having a good time. Both she and Helen had tied their hair into knots on top of their heads in a matador style. Helen had tiny pearls of sweat at the top of her forehead. As usual, she had attracted a grad student in glasses, and, more unusually, she was being swung around the dance floor with a coy smile on her face. In a corner, a barely-upright Ashwin was whispering friendly secrets, no doubt a hilarious commentary on something or another, into Margot's ear.

Julie felt someone tall behind her, pressing into her back. She turned to find that Harry was the perpetrator.

"Hi," she said, smiling up at him. She was convinced she must appear much more attractive at the angle by which he looked at her—a good foot of height difference that disguised the soft fullness of her cheeks and made her eyes look even larger than they were.

"Hi," he said, smiling too. "Do you have a drink?"

"No," she said, and followed him to the bar as Neve watched with crossed arms.

"What the fuck," she said in her Glaswegian. "I hate that guy, and I couldn't even tell you why."

"I know," said Helen. "I don't care for him either."

They exchanged hopeless glances and continued dancing. At the bar Harry ordered two vodka tonics.

"So," he said.

"So," she said.

"It's been a while."

"Yeah. How was your summer?"

"Good. Capri. It was hot."

"Nice. I haven't been," said Julie.

"You'll go," said Harry. "You seem like you're the adventurous sort."

"I am."

"How was the rest of the toga party? Did you survive?"

"Barely," said Julie.

"I like a girl who can't hold her liquor."

"Oh, come on."

"I'm serious. You must be fun."

"That's what they say," she said with a warm smile that made several physical and emotional entities in Harry stir.

"What did you get up to?" he said. "Over the summer?"

"Traveled the world. Made tons of returns on my investments. You know, returns and portfolios and dividends. Did some modeling," she said.

Harry laughed.

"Sounds productive. What's a dividend?"

"Fucked if I know," said Julie with a laugh.

The lights flashed. Last call. Tranny DJ announced that the bar was closing to drunken moans of malcontent.

"Good thing I finished this quick," she said with a thumbs-up sign, turning away from Harry to put her drink on the bar. "It's really nice to see you, but I think it's time to go."

"Hey," he said, putting his arm around her waist. "Larry and I are in for drunk food after this. Come."

Julie considered for a moment. Perhaps she should cash in some favors with Neve and Helen and Margot and Caddy and pressure them into fried food with Larry and Harry.

"I wouldn't come, other than it's drunk food," she said playfully.

"You can ignore me."

"I will."

"Meet you outside."

Harry disappeared into the hallway and out onto the patio, where Anastasia was sitting between Brett and Larry. Unhappy to have stumbled on what was potentially a very awkward, triangular situation, he thought about turning around to find Julie without mentioning his plans to his flatmate.

"Ready to go, guy?" said Larry, before Harry could escape.

"Some of us were thinking the chippy if you're game."

"Wonderful," said Anastasia, anxious to prolong what was probably a decision-making process. The sex or the money: it was a classic St Albas-girl dilemma, though any practiced observer could tell Brett and his signet ring had the edge.

Back on the dance floor, Julie fought her way through the crowd to Neve and Helen.

"I already know what you're going to ask," slurred Neve. "And the answer is no, I will not have fish and chips with people I hate on my birthday."

"Come on. They're funny. It's just Larry and his new flatmate, Harry."

"Julie," said Helen kindly in her pan-British accent, "they're dreadful."

"I know. I get why you would think that. But Larry's my people, and Harry is so hot. Neve, do you mind if I leave?"

Neve shook her drunken head.

"Any idea where Caddy and Margot are?"

"Gone home."

Julie nodded and kissed them both goodnight. Up the stairs she went, finding herself standing in the cold night air, newly chilly with the fall. There she joined Harry and the others. Brett offered her his jacket, which Julie took as a friendly gesture, and one of reconciliation after their near-hookup at the toga party. She did not know he had done it in an effort to make Anastasia jealous.

Having promptly acquired their greasy foods of choice—Julie always ordered a deep-fried haggis—the group huddled in a corner of the crowded chip shop. Run by Pakistanis, the Domain was nowhere near as majestic as its name would suggest. It was in fact a big, square room divided in equal parts into a kitchen and a waiting area by nothing more than a waist-high, grease-stained, glass counter. The level of hygiene practiced on both sides was not something the patrons or employees would have been proud of in the light of day, but since no one in the place was ever sober, no one seemed to mind.

Julie and Harry huddled close against a radiator. Nearby, Anastasia, Larry, and Brett were playing out their own strange soap opera.

"That whole *ménage a trois* is strange, right?" said Harry. "It's not just me?"

"Yeah," said Julie, swaying on her feet. "It's strange."

"Watch yourself," he said, putting an arm around her.

"Are you getting fresh with me?"

"No. Definitely not. Let's sleep together."

"No," she said.

"Not even in an hour?"

"No," she said.

"Why not?"

"Because you won't respect me then. And I like you."

"How do you know I don't like you, Julie?"

"Because boys are the worst."

Harry laughed.

"If you won't sleep with me, will you at least have lunch with me?"

"Lunch?"

"If it's not too much trouble. If you would be so kind as to come off your pedestal to eat with a plebeian such as myself."

"Yeah, okay."

"Can I get your number?"

"Facebook me," she said.

Harry looked abashedly around for someone to share his astonishment.

"Julie, I don't know if you're aware. I don't ask for phone numbers. Ever."

Julie's eyebrows raised themselves into her forehead. "Wow.

You'd better hope I don't remember that tomorrow."

"Right, then. I'll friend you. Kids today. No sense of courtship."

"You know my last name, don't you? Lovejoy."

"Right."

"I'm tired," she noticed, throwing her haggis away. "Will you take me home?"

Harry started:

"I thought you—"

"To my home, I mean. And you go to your home. At least tonight that's how we do it."

Before Harry could agree, Larry emerged at his side.

"I went outside to send a text," he said to Harry. "When I came back, they were gone. Goddamn it. Why, man? I really—I thought she—"

"Be a man," said Harry.

"You're right. And we should get this one home," said Larry, indicating Julie.

"Mind if we put you in a cab?" Harry asked.

"No, it's fine, I'll walk."

"Julie, no. You're taking a cab," said Larry. "Come on. I'm not letting you walk."

This was of course done just for the sake of chivalry and friendship. St Albas was the safest place there could be to walk alone at night, between its size and the number of CCTV cameras per capita.

She let Larry put her in a cab because she knew it would make him happy. He was a nice boy. When he was out of sight, she had the driver pull over and let her out. She paid him or thought she remembered paying him. And before she knew it, Julie was stumbling down Church Street alone, just as she'd wanted. Only a few other people were to be seen, most of them just as drunk as she by her own drunk assessment. She took her phone out of the pocket of her coat and dialed Peter.

"Peter?" she said, when he answered. "I'm lost."

"No, you aren't." He hadn't been to sleep yet. Reclined and keeping watch on Catriona's sofa, he had been waiting for this call. "Tell me what you see around you. I'll help you to get home."

# VIII.

**IT WASN'T ALL PARTIES IN ST ALBAS.** Or at least, not entirely.

One week in October, there was a career fair for the supposed benefit of fourth years. Seminars and lectures were canceled for the afternoon under the loosely enforced condition that all graduating students attend. Most everyone, from the biologists to the financiers to the history students, gathered their resumes and adopted affected styles of dress and manner in order to appear as attractive candidates for the well-paid positions of which they suspected themselves to be deserving.

Those who would likely be working for their parents or inheriting large amounts of independent wealth were the most excited of all at the prospect of the career fair. It was something of a joke. Ashwin had even proposed an eventually vetoed pregame.

After making the rounds at all the tables, Ashwin, Brett, and Peter returned home. Each was projecting an air of smugness greater than the last. Ashwin and Brett because they had nothing to worry about: they would work for their fathers as their fathers' fathers had. They would have a pretty wife, two children, and perhaps a mistress on the side. They would love and provide for all of these people because they were genuinely nice fellows. Peter was smug because he knew better than to suppose his life would improve much through the gaining of things such as financial assets and children and mistresses with hands outstretched for said assets.

"I'm going for my PhD anyway," he said. "But it is cool to be offered an interview on the spot, isn't it?"

"Good for you, man," said Ashwin, who was already heading to the fridge for a beer. "But can't your father hook you up with something?"

Peter's father could. A successful executive in a banking firm in London, he more than could; he had been trying for years. Peter had always obliged him during summer holidays from school, taking banking internships and going along to the city with his father to see how to turn a pound into two pounds fifty. This was not a magic that eluded Peter. He was a natural at finance.

"He could get me something. But doing something else? Getting my PhD? Studying history? That's cool."

"That is pretty cool," said Brett, finding the remote under a pile of video game boxes. "You mind if I put the BBC on? My Dad wants me to start keeping track of the company's stock."

"What's the symbol?"

"MIC. Like 'Michaelson.' "

"Like *Brett* Michaelson?"

"Yes," said Brett. "Why is that funny?"

Ashwin had gone into conniptions.

"I can't believe you have a stock symbol, man. That's so lame."

"If you had one, Ashwin, it'd be ASSwin, or something."

"Burn," said Peter evenly.

***

Max and Fern staggered down Church Street, their arms bending under the weight of the pamphlets, binders, and free pens they had been gifted.

"I thought it was fucking brilliant," Fern said cheerfully. "I got, like, offers, mate. From Exxon. My CV is in there with everyone else's. I think it's brilliant."

"You're going to make more money than any of us; I hope you know that."

"Fucking right I am."

Fern was the most rare of species, as far as the taxonomy of St Albas was concerned. Being Scottish, she was one of the smallest ethnic minorities. She was also a minority among the Scottish, being from the Highlands. She had not attended that fancy high school in Edinburgh. She did not go down to London on the weekends to buy on Bond Street the same things she could buy on Princes Street. She had spent her childhood on the beach with her brother and sister, fishing their dinner out of the sea. How she had come to be at St Albas, Fern didn't know, but she was the only one. No one doubted her quick intelligence and furious desire to do well. To do well meant not only studying hard enough to keep her substantial scholarship every term, but meant working full time in the pub back home during all the University holidays and coming back to St

Albas only at the last moment. All of this, she did without complaint. And on top of it all, she never whined that her wealthier peers got to go to balls and not work hard and never had to worry about making rent. Max had initially tried to pay more rent than her for their flat, and Fern hadn't spoken to him for days when she'd found out.

Max had always been inspired by her insistence upon not half-assing anything and wished he could be more like her when it came to being independent, when it came to being capable.

"You deserve it."

"I only spend every night up to my arse in petrol."

Max grinned.

"Bugger off. Petrology. You know what I mean."

The two progressed up two flights of stairs to their flat. Fern flung the door open. Max threw himself down on the black leather couch, stretching his legs in front of him. Fern went into the kitchen. He reached for the remote and switched on the television. By virtue of instinct after his summers in parliament, he flipped the channel to the BBC.

"I didn't see Catriona there," said Fern.

"No. I don't think she went."

"Catriona! Naughty, *naughty*. What's she going to do? Pop out some kiddies and lie with her feet up on the sofa? I pity the poor laddie who gets roped into that."

Max cast a firm look at his flatmate through the wall.

"We know how you feel about her. And I'm pretty sure she gets closer every day to figuring it out."

"So sensitive. Can it be you love her after all?"

This irritated Max. Of course he loved Catriona, in his way. Or in his way of loving her, in particular. Since his discussion with Simon, he had thought about it more. There were admirable qualities about Catriona. She was, for instance, loyal. She was a good student. She was always considerate, making his bed and never reprimanding him for spending too much time in the library. She set her mind to things. So, fine—it was true she wasn't the most beautiful girl he'd ever seen. There was nothing dramatic or overtly enticing about her. But Clara had been a knockout, and look how that had ended. When girls were attractive they tended to know it and make you miserable about it. That's why Catriona had been such an easy choice. Why she was an easy choice still. Not *easy*, that was the wrong way to think about it, but—

Fern sat down next to Max, staring into him. He ignored her, truly lost in his own mind. Then she sprang back up again.

"Tea?" she asked.

"Sure," he replied, turning his mind off as best he could and looking emptily at the television.

The lead story of the day was the presidential election in America. Everyone on the BBC was rather nervous about it. A crazy woman was on the ballot.

"It's not that she's a woman," said Max. "Just look at her. Anyone can tell she's incompetent. Insane."

"I don't believe she's a woman, actually. Anatomically."

"No kidding."

"Anyway, she's an atrocity, isn't she?" said Fern, coming back with two piping hot cups. "I mean, she's, well, nuts. One seventy-something-year-old heartbeat from the presidency. Hope the Americans pull something good off. I'd be handing in my passport."

Max nodded in agreement.

"And now to New York, for the financial news," said the newscaster, an attractive brunette woman of indiscernible racial origin.

"This'll be boring," said Fern, as she grabbed the remote. "Want to see what else is on?"

Max nodded in agreement, as he always did.

In the year that followed, some St Albas students would return home to smaller homes than the ones they'd left. A few people's parents went to prison. Substantial savings were tapped into, boats were sold and so were vacation homes and so were pieces of jewelry and art. If only because their parents thought that having children at St Albas could fortify the social ties that kept all that money in the cozy confines of the St Albas-attending class, everyone carried on largely in the way they were accustomed to carrying on.

And that included Max, who didn't carry on at all.

*** 

"Holy fuck," said Julie, who was sitting on her bed with her laptop. "Caddy!"

"What," said Caddy, across the hall.

"You see the markets? This isn't good," she said, pointing to a little box on the screen with a red arrow running diagonally down its middle. "I don't know anything about it, but it's not good."

"Wow," yelled Caddy. "I'm glad my portfolio is diversified. What about yours?"

"Hilarious," said Julie. "So funny."

"I love you," said Caddy.

\*\*\*

Catriona was spending the afternoon baking a cake with Simon while Max was at the careers fair. This activity, domestic and cozy though it was, was wholly appropriate in her mind. It was the daylight hours, after all. Peter had reminded her that the start of the year at St Albas always made her ill, and though she had not admitted it to him when he had arrived with her antacid, he was right. It was important to live, to do things that did not make her unhappy. Even during the hard time of the year, when she thought about making good marks to make up for George. And this year, the pressures that came with the term starting included making sure her parents would have a son again. Even if it wasn't the one they wanted, exactly. Even if it was Max, whom they thought was a socialist pseudo-atheist. And who *was* a bit of a socialist pseudo-atheist. But, he had money and an evident interest in dating her and a top degree from St Albas on the horizon. What more could they ask for at this late stage of her university years? What more could she ask for?

Anyway, it made her happy to be with Simon.

"I hope my father's business will be all right."

"I think the sheeping business is fairly stable. Especially on the scale your father's involved in."

"Like the priesthood," she said. "It's stable."

She was happy to have made a little joke.

"I just hope Max will be all right," she said.

"I wouldn't worry."

"I don't."

"His mother has to have some pretty valuable art, if nothing else."

Simon had said it light-heartedly but realized immediately that it sounded crass. Before he could say so, Catriona said gravely:

"It's a beautiful collection."

Catriona very much admired and coveted Max's mother's collection, even though she wished there wasn't quite so much Kandinsky in it.

"I'm sure."

"Anyway, his situation seems comfortable," said Catriona.

"Situation" was the politest term for "net worth" in St Albas. Catriona blushed to hear herself say it out loud.

"I wouldn't worry. Max is a smart fellow," said Simon. It made him sick to think that Catriona would think about Max's money or his mother's art collection.

For a long time thereafter, he maintained his silence as he watched Catriona's hands in the act of baking. He thought and watched and listened to the poofs of air popping under her smooth knuckles below the sound of the Bach on the radio.

Simon had no idea of Max's financial situation in its specifics, at least not in the same way one usually got an idea about other people's economic status in St Albas, which was just by looking at them or observing their smallest behaviors. Max was generous occasionally, picking up dinner or coffee or tickets to a film, but he never spent extravagantly. Indeed, he rarely spent at all. His clothes were always slightly on the shabby side, and his favorite tweed had been purchased at the charity shop, despite Catriona's gentle protestations. The appearance of two very put-together and well-dressed parents at Max's door during parents' weekend in first year had muddled Simon's perceptions of where Max came from, of what kind of family it was that he had back in Zurich.

Simon changed the subject to one he knew Catriona loved to discuss, her flatmate.

"Where is Vera, again?"

"Barcelona."

"Really."

"For a few months. She'd doing some sort of design exchange."

"Good for her."

Catriona's brows lifted in tandem.

"I don't understand it, to be honest. Why she's there."

"Hmm? Not enjoying it?"

"She's enjoying it, all right."

"But?"

"But," Catriona said, mixing some eggs into the sugar and flour mix she had sifted with care, "her boyfriend's just come here, to be with her as she finishes her degree. Which is odd in the first place because I thought he didn't want anything except—well, except sex.

But this! Perhaps he's serious." She sighed. "I don't trust him, Simon. I don't even trust the idea of him. I never have. I suppose he's doing a master's degree, and that's all well and good, and a good enough reason for being in St Albas. But now, Vera's gone I don't know what he is doing with himself here. He isn't a very nice boy."

# IX.

**HARRY OMMAR HAD ACTUALLY CALLED—ON** the telephone. Nothing he could have done would have been more shocking to Julie, who had not received a phone call from a boy asking her on a date since high school, since the times before texting. Since the days of yore, since the Stone Age, when relationships began with voice-on-voice-contact, with talking rather than typing. It made her slightly suspicious that he should call on the phone. It also made her giddy.

Harry was becoming an integral part of the group. He was no longer "Larry's friend" or "the master's student" or "that hot guy." He was "Harry," and he was now invited to parties, nights out, lunches, rounds of golf on the Links, and shooting north of town. Julie was delighted at the chance to look at him, though during social occasions in which the girls were present he had appeared no more interested in her than in any of the others. Frustrating though it was, she still felt the deep conviction that he had a role to play in her future—if only the future of the next few months. Standing next to him at the bar in the student union and exchanging hellos could make her weak in the knees. And so had hearing his baritone on the phone.

"Where did you get my number?" she asked.

"Larry. Walked right down the hall and asked him for it."

"Effort. He's the gatekeeper, you know."

"I know. I told him I needed help learning to read."

"I bet you do, Harvard. I'll see what I can do. So, what's up?"

"I was just seeing about that lunch you promised me."

"I don't remember promising anything."

"At the Domain. With the greasy chips. You know...civilized, sober conversation. You said we could have some, over food, during the daytime."

"Hmm. I may recall something along those lines."

"How does next week look for you?"

Julie searched her mental calendar. It was a mess. She could never quite keep the boxes numbered, ordered, and scribbled on in her head.

"I need to find my planner."

Julie did not own a planner.

"I don't know you well, Julie, but I know you well enough to know you probably don't have a planner."

"I do!"

"How about this afternoon? How about just sod it and sod the mind games, and let's have lunch together today."

Julie considered this. There was a lot of reading to do, and there was a meeting with Professor Harris for which she had not prepared, that she would probably not prepare for under any circumstances. At least not to the extent he would be expecting. It made her feel slightly nauseous to think about letting him down. Making her feel yet more guilty, George Eliot's *Middlemarch* stared forlornly at her from her desk, its thick spine begging to be held in her cushiony palms rather than stuck to the hard wood. But she was not planning on reading it before she absolutely had to, and even then it would probably come down to the Sparknotes, the Wikipedia page, and a couple of JSTOR articles.

Of course, the prospect of saying "yes" would allow Harry to conclude that she was overeager. That was what her grandmother, and Caddy, and all her friends would say, if they weren't discouraging her from going on a date with a boy like Harry Ommar in the first place.

But Julie was a little more adventurous than that. Besides, she wanted Harry. And when Julie really wanted something, she threw the considerable force of her enthusiasm behind it. School was boring, and Harry was exciting. It was a simple equation, and *Middlemarch* didn't stand a chance against it.

"Mr. Ommar," she said, "I accept. Where should I meet you?"

"The Grape. Three o'clock."

"See you there."

She hung up, in awe that in addition to calling, he had chosen a time and place. That was a thing boys usually didn't do.

Julie took her time getting ready, as *Middlemarch* developed lower back stiffness. As she straightened her hair, she read the newspaper.

The *St Albas Chronicle* was a local rag of below-average usefulness in terms of discerning important events in the world, the United Kingdom, or the east coast of Scotland. Its more relevant, recent lead stories, for instance, had included a full-sized picture of the largest lobster to be caught in St Albas Bay in the last twenty years. The fisherman and the fishmonger shook hands in front of a storefront, as the confused lobster stared, possibly already dead, into space. The *Chronicle* was absurd, but that was the reason Julie loved it. This tiny section of the world, for all its strange habits, was still an interesting place after all. Things like the ill-fated, freakishly-large crustacean helped her to remember why she had given up admission to a school back home and accepted a place in this strange world instead. It was a relief to see.

One of the most colorful sections of the slim paper was the horoscopes. These were written, without the least hint of irony, by a medieval studies student, though only her celestial name, Illusia Heavenbelt, appeared in the paper. The short biography below the daily horoscopes stated that she had trained at the Astrology Academy of East Wales, and that she was completing a PhD on witches in St Albas. This described only one very mousy and unimpressive sorceress that Julie had met in the English department on several occasions. Although she often saw this mundane and terrestrial being walking the streets in white sneakers and patched jeans, Julie still read the stars with amusement. Today, the only advice she was given happened to be the following:

Tell no one what you are doing.

With Harry and all, this seemed apt advice. The last thing she needed was a lecture on how no boy who was that good-looking could possibly have good intentions as well. And so, when she finally descended the stairs, Julie avoided waking Caddy, who was asleep on the couch, watching television, and snoring with admirable clarity.

Out the door she went, striding down Fair Street and all its attendant, familiar sights: the outdoor staircases with the flowerpots, the blue street signs with their institutional white letters, the shingles that dripped and dropped droplets even in the sun. She breathed in the cool, moist air, imagining it spreading through her veins, meeting the buzzing heat in her blood that had to do with the anticipation of seeing Harry Ommar.

Harry was already in the downstairs café. The *Financial Times* rested on his knee like a napkin meant to catch money, and it did not fall when he shuffled his large feet in their large leather loafers. It looked as if some of his father's holdings might take a small hit, but Harry was largely unconcerned. Little other than a full nuclear holocaust could dislodge his financial standing. And so his computer glowed on the table, open to ESPN.com. The Patriots would probably lose this weekend, that's what the columnists said. They were playing the Green Bay Packers. Harry resented this notion, having become a fan of the Patriots at Harvard. He did not think much of Julie's imminent arrival until the bell over the door rang.

He turned his cell phone off and put it in his pocket, shut his computer down. Just in case.

And while many boys in St Albas would have stood at the entrance of one of their female friends, Harry sat. Julie mistook this for a sign of actual equality.

"Julie," he said, kissing her once on each cheek.

"Hello," she said, alert to the prickly stubble there.

"Have a seat. Glad you could join me."

"We'll see about that," she said with an airy smile.

"I'm flattered you were able to clear your busy schedule."

"No worries. It's my pleasure."

"It will be, I promise."

"Just don't bore me, okay?"

Harry smiled.

"You have an aversion to boredom I take it? What kinds of boredom are you prone to, Miss Lovejoy?"

"What are you going to eat?" she asked, avoiding the mischief in his gaze for the moment.

"Considering the bacon roll. I'm a bit hung-over, you see."

"The Scottish swear by them. I see you've learned a lot since you've been here."

"What are you having, Julie?"

She furrowed her brow, pulling the menu from between the salt and pepper shakers.

Harry watched her watching the menu. He liked her, was pleased by her. Her hair was straight today. He could see down her shirt again, like at May Saving. He wanted to see more. As much as he could, really. Now was the time to explore. He would much rather do impetuous things with possibly exhilarating outcomes than do nothing and simply wonder what the outcome might have been. So, she didn't want to be bored. A girl like that should never be bored. He could fix that. He could fix that easily.

Harry said:

"Would you care to drive to Edinburgh, Julie?"

"Edinburgh?"

"Scotland's capital. Have you heard?"

"Yes," she said. "Don't tease. We can't go to Edinburgh."

"Why not? I have a car."

"It's Wednesday."

"Edinburgh exists most days of the week."

"Harry, we're having lunch here, in St Albas. I agreed to it on a narrow margin, and I think you're pushing your luck, dragging me down to Edinburgh."

"Julie, think about it. Princes Street? The castle?"

"We have a castle here. Don't tease. Come on, let's order."

"You come on. I'll take you to dinner. How about the Sorcerer?"

Julie's face split into a grin. She loved the Sorcerer.

"I love the Sorcerer," she said.

"Almost as much as you don't like me?"

"Almost."

"Let's go then."

"Really?"

"Really."

Harry put a big bill on the table for the half-drunk coffee in front of him and placed his hand low on Julie's back as he guided her through the door, up the steps, and into his car.

***

By the time they had reached Edinburgh in Harry's car, the castle was closing along with the shops on Princes Street. Julie was as happy as she could have been, watching the sun setting behind the magnificent mound of volcanic rock with the sprawling, clinging castle atop it outlined against the golds and yellows of the sunset. She cherished Edinburgh's castle, a mighty fortress, and one that had changed dramatically throughout its reign over the city that expanded or contracted below it, depending on bubonic plagues, tribal warfare, coronations and elections, stock values, and livestock prices.

The ride through the Scottish countryside had been anything but boring. Harry took the curves too fast, but in such a way that he could hear the excitement in Julie's pleas for him to slow down edging out her slight worry that she had a car crash coming to her as punishment for enjoying a Wednesday night so thoroughly. They had stopped off in a small village for tablet and crisps to tide them over until dinner, but were both fantastically hungry as Harry pulled the car over and handed the keys to the Sorcerer's parking attendant.

"I'm starving," said Harry.

"Me too."

"Shall we?"

To her surprise, Harry offered her his arm. And again to her surprise, she took it without thinking about what it might mean, other than that it felt like Harry must be spending time with some weights.

The Sorcerer was unapologetically lush in its way of heavy drapes and sexy, stuffed-full leather chair backs, and spectacular views of the castle. Sitting in the depths of the old restaurant and gazing up through the below-ground windows, the castle looked even more imposing and grandfatherly than it did from the street. The candelabra, heavy with sculptures made of last night's wax, were being lit by waiters and waitresses in smart scarlet shirts as Harry led Julie to the best table in her favorite dining room.

After a spectacular bottle of wine had been ordered and salads and soups had been consumed, Julie said:

"Mr. Ommar, well done. My favorite restaurant in the world, on an evening when I should be at home reading a novel."

He shrugged.

"I don't mean to flatter myself, and I know you wouldn't let me if I tried, but I'll venture to say this is better than some dusty Victorian book."

"Between you and me and the Cabernet, you're right."

"Do you know why?"

"Why?"

"This is real life, Julie."

"St Albas is real life."

"You think so?"

Julie nodded defensively.

"Yeah."

"How?"

"What do you mean, 'how'? I've lived there for almost four years. I think I would know."

"But how would you know if it was real life like I'm talking about, if you never knew real life yet?"

"I guess I wouldn't. But still."

"St Albas is a game. A very amusing set of little games. I'll give you that."

Julie frowned and wanted to speak, but Harry cut her to the chase.

"I love St Albas. Don't get me wrong. And put that pout away, I'm not insulting your town. I like it a lot. I love it. But when you see real life, you should know it. And if you don't know it, it's up to me to tell you."

"Maybe this isn't real enough. And it's not up to you to do anything."

"No?"

"No."

He laughed, watched her taking another sip of her wine, noticing the insides of her lips getting redder and redder. Julie smiled.

"I have an idea," said Harry.

"What's that?"

"Let's talk about me, for a change. I'm tired of talking about you."

"What do you want me to know about you," said Julie.

"Whatever you want."

One waiter brought their entrées, while three more arranged their plates and knives and table-things to accommodate Harry's roast loin of Cairngorm venison and Julie's breast of duck.

"I remember you said at May Saving that you were just visiting St Albas," Julie said after a few heavenly bites.

"I was. But I was also thinking about the master's program. Getting a better feel for the town."

"Had you been to St Albas before?"

"Yes."

"Even though it's not real?"

"You're merciless," he said and put a big hand on her knee, rubbing it back and forth a few times before returning to his meal.

"So you came for your master's."

"Yes. Finance. You know that."

"But why St Albas and not, you know, Oxford or Cambridge?"

"I have some good friends up here."

"Like Larry?"

"Like Larry. It really is odd that we didn't run into each other sooner."

"I always say: it's a small, small private school world after all."

He really liked that one.

"We were bound to meet," he said.

"You think so?" she said.

"Yes."

"I think so too."

Harry cut into his meal.

"I have a question for you," he said. "When we're out, why don't you ever talk to me?"

"I don't know what you mean."

"I mean you can say 'hello, Harry,' instead of avoiding me like the plague."

"I'm flattered that you mind it when I don't talk to you. But that's not what I'm doing. I want to talk to you."

"You do?"

"I mean, I drove down to Edinburgh with you. So yes. I want to talk to you. But you know how people talk. And I don't want to look any certain way."

"I'm just saying, you should talk to me. If you're not too enthralled with that Peter Manfrenjensenden or whatever he's bloody called."

"I am not enthralled with Peter," she said.

Harry Ommar smiled. This was excellent news.

Dinner was ended in high spirits. Then there was another fast ride through the countryside that did not yet end in a kiss.

# X. NOVEMBER

**THERE WERE LOTS OF TRADITIONS IN** St Albas. Not because it was a particularly interesting place (do not be fooled by the many books that have been written on it and in it) but, more likely, because it was a particularly old one. One of the longer standing of these rituals was Martyrs Weekend.

Though it was meant to honor all of the Catholic and the Protestant persuasion alike who had given their lives for their faith over the course of the town and the University's tumultuous and sometimes-bloody religious history, the festival was really an excuse for all of the second, third, and fourth years to indoctrinate and inebriate the newest arrivals. Light humiliation was traditionally passed down and practiced in honor of this day with a measure of seriousness from generation to generation in another curious St Albas subset of tradition: academic families.

Joining an academic family in St. Albas was often wrongly likened to rushing a fraternity or sorority in America. The process of getting into an academic family was much less formal and much more gentlemanly, though what happened at initiation sometimes wasn't. There were no parties, sign up sheets, or phone calls from grandmothers who were influential Chi Omega alumnae. As a first year, you were invited into a family by luck and trying to force it was the worst thing a fresher could do. To get in, you were either tapped by a third or fourth year that wanted a brother for her oodles of academic daughters or you were noticed by a second year that wanted you as a sibling and asked his or her parents to adopt you. Or you were, quite simply, cool. In this system, the wealthy, the rich, and the upper-middle class mingled comfortably, enjoying family barbeques, tea parties, and pub nights throughout the year. Perhaps the idea of a fake family was so appealing to St Albas students because they were so far away from their real ones, many of which were horrifically dysfunctional to begin with.

Martyrs Weekend involved academic parents boozing their children up badly, dressing them in costumes, and parading them around town carrying large and/or stolen objects. Only the boozing up part resembled normal collegiate behavior. The costumes, well— they were weird. These ran the gamut from live nativity scenes walking unevenly, to seven Marilyn Monroes of both genders flashing their shaved legs, to groups of Teenage Mutant Ninja Turtles stumbling down Sea Street. As for the large and/or more-than-likely-stolen objects, they were weirder still. The local constabulary asked annually, nicely, fruitlessly, for students to please not uproot garden gnomes, hoist boats out of the harbor, or steal worktables from the library. Each year, this request was boisterously denied. All the police could do was watch, as the weirdest part of it all happened: the culmination of all the drinking and the dressing up and the carrying. The flour fight on the quad, an ignominious parade of sloth, drunkenness and general vice.

Julie and Peter discussed their first Martyrs Weekend as they made their way down Sea Street with their own academic brood.

"And we were dressed as mimes by our academic mum, remember," said Peter.

"And we both hated mimes."

"And we both hate mimes, Julie. Present tense."

"That was the beginning of a beautiful friendship," said Julie.

"What?" said Peter, over the rising noise of the crowd as it made its way to the quad's blocky main gate.

"I said, 'I think that was the beginning of a beautiful friendship.' "

"Yeah, right," said Peter, smiling. "Worked out well for you, didn't it?"

"You love me," said Julie.

"I know, I know," said Peter.

Julie was being carried by four of her and Peter's new academic children, known today as John, Paul, George, and Ringo. Yoko, the only girl, a leggy blonde from California, cowered behind them, wondering what she had done to deserve the slightly politically incorrect makeup and a ratty, tangled, black wig. Julie, however, was enjoying the festivities, sitting in a chair of gilt and red plush that she and Peter had borrowed from the University Chapel.

It was a cold day and gray, but as always with St Albas student events, everyone partaking was, for the most part, too drunk to care. They didn't care, even, that the local and national media were there with their cameras. The festivities made for an excellent photograph, a good article on the wasted youths of Scotland's Best University, a great article on how the generation was taking the last vestiges of decency with it, and in good time too. Those Mayans might be right about the world ending, and let's hope so, what with the recession and globalization and interracial marriages and what's next! The police were lined up too, halfheartedly attempting to control the chaos.

On any other day, the quad was an almost-sacred space, not to be walked on, touched, or breathed on incorrectly. It acted as a holy doormat of sorts to the 500-year-old University Chapel. One man's entire job in life was to keep the quad lawn manicured. He got excited when they took new brochure photos with people standing in front of it—it was good to see one's work in print. Today was the one day that he did not come in to work. He would spend the next 364 days attempting to get the lawn back to the state he had left it in before Martyrs Weekend.

Julie was glad it was Martyrs Weekend. She had a difficult week, academically speaking. The Harris meeting for which she hadn't prepared had not ended well:

"Come in," he'd said, opening his office door for her.

Harris had the choicest office in the School of English. It looked out across the Castle ruins, offering a bird's eye view of the courtyard as well as the sea. A half-circle window was the favorite landing place of seagulls and doves, and it resembled an underwater porthole on days when the rain came in luxurious, curtained layers. He had outfitted the room with the requisite bookcases and hardcover volumes, with cheap prints of the places he had traveled as a young man, and later, with his wife. There was a low seat that ran the length of the window, and it was covered with a thick set of cushions. It was here that he invited Julie to sit, as he poured her a cup of tea.

"Should I cut to the chase?"

"My essay?"

"Your essay. Your essay, your essay."

He handed her the tea with one hand and the essay with the other. Julie set the tea down on the windowsill and flipped the paper over. She blanched.

"Seriously? It was better than that."

"It wasn't."

"I tried."

"You're better than this, Julie. This isn't good work, and you know that."

"It is good."

"It could be much better."

"Ugh."

"I want you to do well. I want you to be prepared for life after St Albas. For the real world. We've discussed this. I can't be easy on you."

"You've been easy on me for three years."

"I hope you enjoyed them."

"Seriously?"

"Seriously," he said and took a long sip of his tea. "That's all, Miss Lovejoy."

Sitting on what amounted to a throne, talking with Peter as she was carried through the streets, she couldn't help but think that Professor Harris was wrong, just as Harry had been. This was real life, or there was no real life. Real life as Harris imagined it was his mousy wife and their silly little house and their silly little evenings at home together talking about things that only people without a foothold in reality or sense of adventure talked about.

As for her, she wouldn't be boring and stuffy and completely grown up. She would enjoy her last Martyrs Weekend in St Albas. She would enjoy her friends and the flour fight. She would go to a rowdy party on the beach below the Castle tonight. Which meant Harry would be there, which meant it would be fun to get ready to go out because she was going out with a purpose, which would mean she could stand with him against the wall with a beer in her hand in the flickering flames, flirting and feeling him tall and close and electric next to her. And next weekend, there would be the November Ball—which she planned to look stunning at. If her ball gown didn't seal the deal with Harry, she didn't know what would.

"What are you thinking about up there," said Peter.

"Nothing," said Julie.

"Liar," said Peter.

***

Martyrs Monday was a tradition, along with the wearing of

academic gowns, in which Catriona was an enthusiastic participant. This was primarily because she and Max had adopted children together as third years, and again in their fourth. It gave her a sense of stability to hear people calling them "mum" and "dad." She suspected Max enjoyed Martyrs Monday as much, though perhaps because it was one of the few events per a year at which she blatantly ignored the fact that he was drinking.

"Do you think everyone is having a nice time?" she asked Max, as she refilled a few bowls of crisps in his kitchen.

"I think so," he said.

*It could be more fun, though,* he thought.

Max remembered his first Martyrs Monday, when he had met his new academic sister with the snarky sense of humor and one of the keenest bullshit radars of anyone he'd ever known. Fern had kept Max upright on the walk to the flour fight despite the fact that she was half his size. He thought fondly of that day, and it had occurred to him every year since that there might well be a parallel universe in which he was at a messy, loud apartment someplace drinking beers with Fern and his old academic family.

"Max," said Catriona, who must have been talking.

"Sorry?"

"That girl—the new one—Ashley…"

"What about her?"

"She seems rather rude, doesn't she? I'm not being unreasonable. I wish she would have contributed to the party. All the others brought something."

"She didn't know, I guess. I'm not sure she has very much money."

"She seems to have spent an awful lot on that makeup she's got on."

"I don't know."

"She's loud, don't you think?"

"I think she's nice. She's friendly with the other kids."

"Friendly with that bottle of vodka."

"Maybe, but let's give her a break. Okay? The party is wonderful."

Catriona smiled vaguely.

"Really," said Max. "You have done a wonderful job. Everyone is having a nice time."

"All right," she said, shaking the crumbs from the bottom of the bag into the large plastic bowls she had bought for Max's flat two years ago on this exact date.

Max put his arms around her.

"Don't worry so much. Just relax. Come here."

He kissed her on the mouth, brushed a hand through her hair. Catriona nestled into his chest for a moment, still clutching the bowl.

"I love you," he said.

"I love you too," she said. "I'm sorry for being anxious."

"Don't apologize."

"Okay."

"I love you."

"I love you too."

Back in the living room, Catriona surveyed their family. It had grown to eight children. Not bad. Mostly, they were art students that Catriona had recruited from the Oil Painting Enthusiasts Society with a few that Max had reeled in from the Moral Philosophy Department. They mingled easily with Simon's academic brood, which had been folded into the clan.

Catriona felt a sense of ease as she watched Simon talking to the loud girl. He was always such a gentleman. He always knew what to say to people. Funny, that he could be so intelligent and outgoing at once. She admired him greatly for it.

Simon turned his head to find her looking at him.

"Having fun?" she asked, crossing to him.

"Yes," he said. "You've done a splendid job."

Catriona glowed. Simon was such a nice young man.

"Thank you."

The clock tower across the street chimed the hour.

"I guess it's time," she said.

"We'd better get them dressed," agreed Simon.

"Excuse me," Catriona said, in the biggest voice she possessed. "Um, everyone, excuse me, attention please..."

"Excuse me," said Simon in priestly tones, then, the room went still. "I think our hostess has something to say."

"Yes. Thank you. If the freshers would please head down the hall to the bedrooms, there are bags with your costumes in them. They are clearly labeled with your names and surnames..."

The drunken crowd was moving towards the back, not bothering too much to listen to the rest of her instructions.

"Boys in the first room on your left," she called after them. "Girls, on your right."

# XI.

**ST ALBAS STUDENTS COULD BE ACCUSED OF** a great many things, but they could never be accused of putting on a shabby party. As a rule, they weren't capable of it.

The November ball was held on the estate of a now-defunct farm several miles away from St Albas. Cainland House, despite its somewhat cryptic Biblical name, was the favorite venue for the University's riotous fêtes. The cavernous barn had been converted into a large, heated reception hall. Students liked it because it was especially noisy when full, given the hard wooden floors that made dancing in high heels and slippery-bottomed dress shoes a fun and a slightly precarious activity. In the midst of their rustic surroundings, everyone felt even more gloriously overdressed than they already were.

Though several balls were held on the premises each year, from the Clay Pigeon Shooting Club's Bowtie Ball to the University-sponsored Graduation Ball, the most popular event at Cainland was the November Ball. For the occasion, the barn's highest rafters were straddled with tons of decorations: glass stars of silver and gold hanging by fishing wire in order to disguise the fact that they were as prone to gravity as anything else, lush green bushes of hairy holly and berries of red, twinkling fairy lights that never showed up in photographs exactly as magically as they appeared to a girl who had a bottle of champagne in her system. Dozens of rectangular tables stood draped in red and green, determined to shape the destinies of those at them via the seating arrangements they imposed. At the center of each table, a spilling arrangement of sweet-smelling oranges, cinnamon sticks, and pinecones surrounded a many-armed candelabrum with candles that burned away in traces of wispy black smoke. The freshers liked to put these out with their fingertips at the end of the night; not surprisingly, the local hospital saw an increase in injuries related to open flames during this time of year.

Having consumed several beers each before their arrival, anyone who had come from the Ashwin-sponsored pre-party was in a cheery mood. The night was chilly, but then of course everyone was thankful for the flasks full of whisky tucked in their handbags, kilt socks, and tuxedo trousers. On the half-hour bus ride to Cainland alone, Brett and Anastasia, now a regular item, had drunk an entire flask themselves. Their faces were furiously spinning together on the coach bus. Ashwin and Margot, also fairly intoxicated, threw bits and pieces of paper at their heads. This juvenile behavior seemed only to fuel the fire. Larry did his best not to notice for the hundredth time that Anastasia had chosen Brett, and Julie was trying her best not to notice that Brett threw occasional glances at her between kissing Anastasia. Ruth sat next to Julie, staring forward, disappointed, with her folded hands resting on a lap of folded purple silk.

"He's being rude," said Ruth. "You shouldn't pay him any attention."

"Yeah, he's a good guy. But he can be childish."

"That's a nice way to put it."

Julie realized that Ruth was comforting Julie about Brett to comfort herself. While Julie had mostly brushed aside her drunken antics with Brett at the year's first party, it was clear that Ruth had not. It was funny how different girls could be in reacting to boys and their insensitivity. Julie said:

"You shouldn't pay attention, either."

"I just don't understand it, Julie," Ruth said, her dark eyes opening innocently on her friend's. "You know Brett and I aren't close, but I thought he had at least some respect for me. Or my feelings. I don't know. When we woke up in the morning, he was holding my hand. He told me I looked beautiful. He kissed me goodbye. He even told me he'd call. But he was lying. Maybe I'm being naïve. I just don't understand how someone can spend the night in the same bed as you and then never call again."

Julie wondered what Ruth had expected.

"I don't understand, either," she said.

"It's just sad to me. It's sad that I should expect to be disappointed with him, rather than being surprised if he disappoints me."

"That's boys for you," said Julie. "Honestly."

*You'll get used to it*, she thought.

"It's just sad. I guess he's not winning any awards for maturity any time soon. It makes me miss Clark. Clark would never do this to anyone."

Julie nodded, though she had no idea whether Clark would or wouldn't.

No matter if you were a virgin, or not, or stood somewhere in between the two, there was no making sense of boys, thought Julie. There was never any telling whether they would do the things they said they would. As she looked out the window at nothing, her mind turned to her own set of boy-related mysteries.

She had been warm with Harry at the bonfire party on the beach after Martyrs weekend, and he had been warm back. Peter had done his best to interfere, leaving Julie's side only to prevent Ashwin from lighting himself on fire and to walk a drunken Margot to Julie and Caddy's nearby house to put her to bed on the sofa. But the twenty minutes of conversation his absence had afforded had been welcome by both parties, and no amount of Peter's presence could have prevented the looks they had exchanged across the beach throughout the night, over the music from Larry's guitar and the traces of heated breaths mixing with the bonfire's ashes in the curving patterns of cigarette smoke.

With her gown and its neckline in mind, Julie had asked him if he would be coming to the ball.

"The ball?"

"The one everyone's talking about. The November Ball."

"Not sure," he said. "Possibly."

Julie rolled her eyes.

"Come on. Next Saturday."

"If I'm back in time."

"Back in time?"

"I'm taking a short trip."

Julie refrained from asking where. Asking where boys were going showed them that you cared, and if you showed them that you cared, there was absolutely no chance that they would ever care about you.

"Well, I'll be looking very good."

"I'm sure you will. Maybe I'd better stay at home in any case. That might be too much for my heart to handle."

"I worry very little about your heart," she said with a smile.

"Because I don't have one?"

"Exactly."

As Julie stared at the back of Peter's head in the seat in front of her, she felt a sense of peace. If Harry didn't show at all, she would have someone to dance with. There were so many advantages to having a boy for a best friend.

At the back of the same bus, Catriona and Max sat in silence. Catriona was wearing a boxy satin dress of bronze, with black satin gloves on. And there was Max, mismatched with his girlfriend in his tweed jacket, light blue shirt, and red bow tie, mildly miserable and trying not to complain out loud.

He had successfully avoided most student balls in St Albas, finding the company bad and the pseudo-philanthropic justification for having a ball worse. Max always tried to give other people the benefit of the doubt (this was the side effect of studying universal morality obsessively but living as a relativist), but it had occurred to him more than once over the course of the last four years that he had perhaps chosen one of the world's more difficult locales in which to achieve a mindset of acceptance towards mankind. Balls, he felt, brought out the worst pretension in his contemporaries: events marketed as benefitting charity where people ended up donating a total of £10 after all the costs of food and drink and music were paid out of their £100 tickets. Perhaps these events stimulated the local economy, he thought, but they did little to help the actual starving children in Africa (or wherever they were) that made all the sons and daughters of the Influential People feel good while conducting themselves in the most ostentatious way possible. At least, his slight disgust gave him something to think about other than how much longer he had to be out in public in his dress shoes.

To make matters worse, they were with Catriona's circle of acquaintances tonight. Among their muted beige and pink dresses and black velvet heels, Max couldn't have felt more claustrophobic if he were in the center of a flock of flamingos. Catriona's studied smile spread across her face whenever one of them spoke. It had the effect of making one feel as though someone behind her was pressing a gun into her back, threatening to pull the trigger if she released her mouth from the stress of performing sweetness.

In the hurried, polite movements that brought them all into the hall and out of the cold looking like a crowd of dressed-up sheep, Julie had lost sight of Peter. Though perhaps it assisted her in distancing herself from the rumors that were always flying errantly around that the two were a covert couple, she was annoyed that her social life raft had drifted away for any amount of time, let alone so early in the evening. When she spotted him in the crowd, he was standing next to a tall blond boy who looked familiar and next to what was an unmistakably English girl—Catriona, Peter's cousin. Julie recognized her from the street and from the family photo in Peter's room. So this must be her boyfriend, shuffling his feet, standing next to her—tall and blond. Younger, maybe. Cute. Julie had always liked blonds. Especially tall blonds with lots of hair. He had to be Scandinavian. Or German, maybe. Austrian.

Catriona's tiny eyes darted around, experiencing the uncomfortable sensation that her boy was being looked at. Before Catriona could find the eyes on Max, Margot was pulling Julie's arm around and away. She had already made some friends of the male persuasion and was introducing them to Julie. And to see Margot in that bright blue ball gown, with her huge, baby-doll eyes, you wouldn't be surprised that they listened quite attentively.

"Don't you just love balls," Margot said happily, adjusting the gossamer-y wrap on her round shoulders. "Isn't it wonderful? Everyone is so beautiful. So young and beautiful."

Julie had to smile and agree that they were, as Peter made his way back to her side.

"Hey, thought I lost you."

"Just saying hello to Catriona and Max."

"Did you invite them to come have a drink with us?"

"Yes."

"Well?"

"You know my cousin doesn't drink like that."

"Would it kill her to meet me, though?"

"Julie."

"You introduced her *and* her boyfriend to Brett and Ashwin."

"That was dinner. It was tame. And even that was almost a disaster. No one had fun, I promise you."

"She can't be that bad if she's related to you."

"She's not. She can be lovely."

"I like lovely."

"But you would probably hate her."

"I know I tease you about being her babysitter and all that, but I mean, come on. I'm friends with several quiet, proper people."

"Name one. Name one quiet, proper person you're friends with."

"Ruth."

"Ruth is quieter and *more* proper than the rest of our friends. There's a difference."

"I can talk to anyone. Give me some credit. And he looks normal enough."

Max's looking Normal Enough was one of the reasons he did not want to introduce him to Julie, on the off chance that any feelings developed either way. Boys were quick to develop feelings for Julie, when they had the inclination, and Peter knew that most boys were susceptible to liking her, if only because they saw her general enthusiasm for other people in her eyes when they looked at her. Max seemed especially prone to admiration and praise (Peter suspected this was how Catriona had hooked him in the first place), and her cousin had no intention of letting Catriona's heart be broken. The stakes were far too high.

And no good could come of introducing Catriona to Julie anyway. She had her own suspicions of Peter and Julie and had voiced them repeatedly throughout the years. She had told him it wasn't proper for a boy with a girlfriend to be such good friends with a single girl. Peter had nodded and gone on being good friends anyway.

Even besides all of that, Peter liked to keep his worlds apart. Julie was a part of his most joyful world. As close as they were, she did not know that he had seen his cousin, his other best friend, shot in the chest as a child. Julie had a deep heart, and Peter didn't want to fill it with any amount of sadness or worry for him.

Peter had always invited Catriona to come out with his friends. It would do her good, and his mother had asked him to. In first and second year, he had even hoped she might show up to something, might have drink or two, might enjoy herself, might be young.

Now his invitations came of habit, and her declining them did too. He mostly just asked her so that she realized, in some unspoken way, that he was keeping an eye on her. Peter rarely saw Catriona unless he was sleeping on her sofa during one of her "sick" spells or picking her up to drive down to England, which was to say he rarely saw her unless it was to do his duty. To pick up the slack where Max wasn't doing his because Catriona wouldn't let him. Because, quite possibly, Max might not rise to the occasion even if he did identify her sickness or know about George or care enough to notice the small cuts on the tops and backs of her legs.

"Catriona is different from you. You wouldn't get on. That's a reflection on neither of you, but it's how things are. All right? Care to leave it at that?"

"Okay, okay. Jesus. Fine. I'm sorry."

"No bother."

"I really am."

"I know you are," he said, pulling his vest down at the waist.

"Let's have a good time."

"I'm quite ready to," he said.

"Me too."

"Grand."

"But why won't she like me?"

Peter looked to a God he didn't believe in for patience, and said:

"This is your last question, Juliana Lovejoy."

"You know I hate that. No one has called me that in years."

"—Juliana, my dear friend: Catriona is my family. I'm afraid I can't do anything about it, unless you have a time machine and a grim fascination with my Aunt Harriet and Uncle Chauncey's reproductive habits."

Julie confirmed that she had neither of those things.

"I like you both," he said.

"I like you okay," said Julie. "But you didn't answer my question."

There was someone walking by with a tray of sparkling champagne. Peter took two glasses and changed the subject.

***

A short while later, after coats and seating cards had both been checked, dinner was served. And boy, was it ever served. It was so well served you wanted to pinch yourself. Impeccable waiters in crisp, white shirts and tartan vests served up thick, opulent cuts of game and goose. Being already in the ball gowns in which they so wanted to fit, even the girls in the room ate their fill—the alcohol helped to impede inhibitions of many a type. When the complementary champagne and wine ran out, smug arguments over who wanted to pay for another bottle or bottles rang through the hall. At other universities, men would have wagged something other than their wallets at each other to prove their masculine virility. But in St Albas, the alpha male was the one with the longest credit card bill.

Through dinner, a jazz quartet played. The lights that hung in suspense on the ceiling quivered in helpless shimmers across the saxophone's tremoring bell of gold. Heeled feet tapped, plates clanked, loud conversations bred laughter that giggled and gave way to snorting as glasses of whisky and wine were refilled. This had been a barn at one point, and other than the music it sounded like one still.

After dinner had been so carefully laid out and then made to disappear, there were fireworks across the hills at Cainland. They illuminated the countryside, disturbing the sleeping sheep at non-defunct farms and bringing awe to the eyes of the highly educated assortment of drunks who had converged on the broad gravel drive to watch. These were not amateur fireworks; someone had hired a professional company to design and execute the show.

Max, full from dinner, enjoyed the fireworks and thought less about the African children after all. It helped that he had run into one of his academic sons in the men's room.

"Qiang," he'd said. "Do you have a flask?"

The first year had nodded drowsily.

"Two."

"I really, really need a drink."

"Is Catriona being—"

"I need one."

"Understood."

Max had downed half the alcohol in one fell swoop, thanked his son for his loyalty, and put a £50 note in his palm before returning to dinner with the flask. His resentment of his peers had been on the decline since. My God, they looked like they were having fun. They looked so close to one another. He began to envy them, with an ache in his chest and a potent loneliness that could not be fixed by reminding himself that Catriona was here too. He wished that he were here with Fern, and then he wished for more of Qiang's whisky: Fern was his best friend in St Albas, but she was still only one person.

Julie was huddled next to Helen and Neve, both in tight, black dresses with bows in their hair. Between Helen's white skin and Neve's red hair, they looked like the two queens out of a deck of cards. The three kept warm among the rest of them: Ashwin and Caddy stood arm-in-arm, Brett and Anastasia's hands disappeared into one another's clothing, Margot's hand was around Larry's waist, which was around Ruth's shoulders, and Peter cradled his cell phone gently next to his ear, trying to speak to his girlfriend through the crackling of the fireworks. From afar, Catriona watched her cousin and his friends. And through the crowd, Simon had spotted her watching.

He had come with the Windsurfing Society, a ragtag group that was difficult to define by the typical social laws of St Albas, being of heterogeneous social backgrounds. Riding on the frigid waves of the North Sea and secluded in the pubs afterward, the potheads and future priests of the world enjoyed one another's company. Their one commonality being their sense of adventure: they even ventured out together occasionally at events such as the November Ball where the rest of the student body was free to marvel at their friendship. Presently, Simon excused himself from them and strode over to Max, Catriona, and the gaggle of girls around them.

Max smiled when he saw Simon, and Catriona smiled when she saw Max smile for the first honest time that night. Simon shook Max's hand and gave Catriona a small hug in which body contact was cautiously avoided out of English propriety and Catholic guilt alike.

"How are you?" he said. He was looking at Catriona, directly into her eyes. He wanted to tell her just how beautiful she looked with her hair swept up tightly into a bun, how much justice the dress did her, how thrilling the outline of a curvy leg swelling through the material was when he stood a short distance away. But he asked the simple question and hoped that Max had told her instead.

"I'm fine," said Max. "It's good to get out of the flat sometimes."

"And good to get out of the library, in your case," said Simon.

"You know me too well."

"We're having a nice time," said Catriona. "Dinner was quite good. Are you enjoying yourself?"

"I am. Very much so. Can't wait for the dancing."

"And you don't even smell of alcohol," she said. "Some of the boys here don't know how to have a nice evening without."

"I've had some wine," said Simon. "Don't give me so much credit."

Max pretended not to hear the comment about the booze, removed the flask from his suit jacket, and took a sip. He could hear Fern practically cheering from home, where she stayed because she couldn't afford balls, and she wouldn't let Max pay.

"I think everyone's going inside," he said, wiping his mouth to Catriona's silent horror. "Would you like some, Simon?"

Simon shook his head.

The fireworks had stopped.

Inside, another band had installed itself in the place of the jazz quartet; this one did covers of Sinatra and Snoop Dogg and every pop artist in between. Rounds and rounds and merry-go-rounds of drinks were ordered. The cocktail waiters and bartenders were beginning to look the worse for wear: sweat began to spread under their cotton shirts; drinks were spilled and cleaned up hastily or not at all. The previously pristine students were also becoming increasingly ragged while remaining impossibly chic. The dry-cleaning bill from the ball's finery would amount to the yearly salary of a full professor.

Julie was enjoying herself, and whether it was despite or because of the fact that she was alone she did not waste time pondering. She danced with Peter and Ashwin and a spectacularly intoxicated Caddy, who had shown up in a limousine just before the fireworks display. She had been home in New Orleans for the weekend at her grandmother's funeral and had come straight from the airport in Edinburgh to make it to the November Ball.

"My darling," said Caddy, "you are looking hot."

"So are you. Doing okay?"

"Grandma would have wanted me here, partying. All of us here, partying. Partying for Grandma, ya'll," she shouted to a group of strangers who raised their glasses in response. "Need a drink?"

A few more of Caddy's vodka tonics later, and Julie was on her way to the ladies' room to have a sit on the sofa when she saw something that interested her. Its name was Harry, and, in her delirium, it appeared to be walking toward her through the large door in the main hall's entryway.

"Good evening, Miss Lovejoy," he said. He pulled her into his chest. Her cheek rested against it thankfully. This was better than any stupid sofa in any stupid ladies room. His herringbone jacket was cold and smelled of cigar smoke. Julie's arms were exactly the right length to extend around his waist. She stayed there for a moment, breathing deeply.

"You came," she said. "How was your silly trip?"

"Silly," he said. "I want to dance with you."

"I want to dance with you. I wanted to dance with you all night."

"I didn't know I'd be so missed," he said. Julie heard a tender tone in his voice. "Are you a little drunk?"

She showed him via a closed-lipped smile that this was undoubtedly the case.

"Uh-huh."

"I'm not. Not yet. Let's get a drink for me, and then we can dance."

"In front of everyone?"

Harry did not answer but took her gently by the elbow and guided her back to the crowded room with the dance floor. In a moment, they were standing in front of the bar.

"Will you get me a glass of red wine?"

"I think you've had enough."

"Oh, come on. It's Vonember Ball! Only happens once a year, like I told you."

"Right. I'll get you a glass if you promise not to chunder all over the floor or my suit."

She considered the offer.

"I can't promise that."

"Right. Better make it apple juice then."

"I've never heard such a big man say 'apple juice.' "

After Harry had acquired the drinks, he walked Julie over to a dim corner of the room near the dancing. Julie spotted faces she recognized whirling past, including the blond boy who danced clumsily with Catriona.

Harry did his best to make conversation but was having a rather difficult time given the neckline of Julie's red dress, a sweetheart cut with off-the-shoulder sleeves that showcased her décolletage in a way not even a Dutch master could have improved. The hair she had tried too hard to straighten into ruler-drawn lines was falling in waves around her shoulders. Small bits of perspiration gathered at her brow, just below her widow's peak, and between her breasts. Her cheeks were pale and her eyes were very green, drawn out by the smoky black makeup she had applied with reckless abandon before the bathroom mirror.

He was thankful when Julie said:

"When do you think we'll go home together?"

He looked at her with respect for her directness and without words in return.

"Tonight?" she said. "Do you think tonight?"

"What do you think?"

"I'm not sure yet. I think if you dance with me it would help."

"Still making up your mind?"

"It takes more than dinner in Edinburgh and a couple of friendly conversations."

"It does?"

"I'm a lady."

"And what a lady you are," he said.

*You're a girl*, he thought.

Harry led her to dance. He tried to remember that he mustn't overstep his bounds, not in this huge room with all these people watching. It was so hard, though. Hard because there were inching feelings, ones he was starting to have for Julie, who didn't seem to care to do anything ever but have a good time. He loved that about her. He thought she could probably fly to the moon if she thought it was an amusing enough place to go.

But there was no need to make things harder for himself or for Julie or for any of them. Though each person in their social circle was wrapped up in his or her own drama for the evening, it was good to dance with one of the other girls every few songs. He could pay attention to Julie, as long as he also paid some to Anastasia and Helen and Caddy and Margot. These things, things like the game he played with Julie, were best won in secret—quietly. He felt the thrill more acutely that way anyhow. He must be patient and discreet, and certainly not paranoid, although he felt Peter's eyes tracing his every move, counting the moments he spent with Julie, tallying them up.

At midnight, Julie whispered up to him:

"I decided."

"Yes?"

"I want to go home with you."

"You do?"

"Yeah."

This made him bold, and he took this statement as permission to touch her on the sly for the next two hours.

After the dancing was done and the band was packing up and the waiters and the caterers had headaches that would last for days, long lines began to form outside the coat check. Julie had gone with Caddy to the ladies room as Harry waited on his herringbone.

"It's just one coat coming up for you, yeah?" said a voice behind him.

Harry looked over his shoulder to find Peter and turned to fully face him.

"Yes. One."

He held up a finger in the illustration.

"I've got Julie's ticket right here. So you don't need to worry about it."

"Good. Wouldn't want her to be cold."

"You can worry about yourself."

"Good to know."

"I don't like you," said Peter.

"I know you don't," said Harry.

He gave his ticket to the boy at the counter, retrieved his overcoat, and said:

"Goodnight."

Then he walked toward the buses and opened his phone to find a message from Julie:

Find me before you get on bus.

To which he responded:

Already on a bus. Meet you in front of yours.

Upon arriving home, Julie said a hasty goodnight to Caddy. She went into her room and shut the door. She took her red dress off and put on a matching set of underwear and bra. She dabbed perfume unevenly beneath her breasts and under her jaw. Over it all, she wore a silk slip and a raincoat (*I'll give him "real life,"* she thought) and went quietly into the dark hallway after hearing Caddy's door click close.

"Where you going?" said Caddy, who was sitting in front of the stairs with her arms folded. "Oh, wait, don't tell me because I already know: Harry Ommar's bedroom. Bad life choices, Julie. I'm tellin' you."

"I am not going there. And I don't like the accusation. Nor do I like you huddled in the shadows, spying on me, you're like Gollum, this is crazy…"

"Riddle me this, Sherlock: If you're not going to Harry Ommar's, then why has he been touching your ass all night?"

"How do you come up with this stuff?"

"I'm telling you, Julie. This dude is bad news."

"You like him just as much as I do."

"Duh. He's hot. And he's fun to drink with. But I wouldn't want to get involved with him. God knows what kind of diseases are crawling around in those trousers of his."

"You're just jealous."

"Wrong."

"I didn't mean that. I just really like him."

"Fine. But I'm just stating for the record that this is a dumb thing. This isn't a thing. This is real dumb."

"Okay. Can I go?"

"You sure can."

Caddy sighed and moved aside.

Julie stumbled down the stairs, threw the front door open and closed, and walked into the street. There was Harry Ommar, waiting.

He intercepted her into his arms, pushed her back into the neighbor's garden wall, and kissed her. When she had a moment to speak, she said:

"Thank God."

The next morning, she woke up beside Harry in the flat he shared with Larry. He had slept facing away from her with the palms of his hands pressed together between his legs. His dark head lay between, rather than on, the pillows.

Julie wondered: what does a person say when she wakes up next to someone she has not shared a bed with before? "Did you sleep well?" "Fancy seeing you here?" "I didn't know you snored." "I love you." She had never figured it out. Of course, it wasn't often that she allowed herself permission to do something like this. Normally, she was extremely discerning. But there was something about her and Harry that was unavoidable, biologically destined. Her reactions to him were chemical. And judging by the events that had taken place in the small hours of the morning, something (it was probably not the God she was raised on) had blessed and legitimized the situation. Without moving, Julie could tell that her legs and arms and everything else were sore.

She let herself be for a moment. It was Saturday morning, after all. She thought about whether or not she should want to be there when he woke up. After a moment, he stirred.

"Good morning," he said.

That was a good one. Julie wished she'd thought of it.

"Hi."

"Can you roll over and look at me please?"

She obliged him.

"Hello."

"Hello."

"How did you sleep?" she asked.

"Fine. You snore."

"Well at least I don't giggle in my sleep."

"I don't *giggle*."

"You did giggle."

She burrowed into the pillows. He pulled her against him, kissed her neck.

"Would you care for some breakfast?" he mumbled.

Whether this offer was designed to keep her from going home or to get her there quicker, she could not tell. It forced the question, either way. So, instead of listening to her head, she listened to her stomach, which was nauseous from the night of drinking. She couldn't bear choking down something that resembled one of Peter's cheese toasties, made with love though she knew they were.

"No thanks. I'm going to get going."

"Are you sure? I'm not talking about cheese toasties, you realize. I'm talking about eggs Benedict, muffins, fresh orange juice, bacon, crepes…"

"Honestly, thanks. But you know Caddy. She might be worried—"

"Or angry," he said. "She figured it out, right?"

"Well, yeah."

"She's smart."

"And besides, if I'm honest, I don't want to run into Larry in the hallway."

"Why?"

Julie thought about it.

"I want to have a secret for a little while."

"That's pretty hot. Is it a secret if Caddy knows?"

"She won't tell. She likes secrets too."

"I wouldn't worry about Larry, anyway. I don't think he came home last night."

"Oh."

"I don't know why he's stuck on that Anastasia. He seems pretty bent on sleeping around until he forgets."

"Poor guy," said Julie.

*Americans are taken in by what's different*, she thought. *People do crazy things in foreign countries, with foreign people.*

"Stay," said Harry. "I'll run out and get the newspaper. We can do the crossword."

She couldn't help smiling as he stood up and pulled on his trousers. Finding a t-shirt on top of the dirty clothes pile, he put it on without ceremony. Then he searched his tuxedo for his wallet, and, having found it with a certifying pat, kissed her on the mouth. Harry winked as he closed the door to his room.

And so she was left alone. She thought momentarily of scouring the area for information about the still-mysterious being that was Harry. She decided against it. Harry's bed was soft, big, and warm. She stretched like a cat underneath the blankets. She dozed. When she awoke fifteen minutes later, she looked around the room. It was a fairly typical lair for a boy of Harry's age: a poster of Marilyn Monroe, change scattered everywhere, piles of notebooks, a guitar gathering dust in the corner, golf clubs with fresh grass on the ends. Above the messy desk that acted primarily as a place to keep his iPod and speakers, there was a wipe board. Here was Harry's to-do list:

~~Rent~~
Oil change
~~Nov. Ball ticket~~
Tee time w/Larry?
Read *Economist*
Vera

Before she could wonder what the last one meant, who she was, and how serious they were, Harry was coming up the stairs. She rolled over, pretending to be asleep once more. He opened the door loudly. She didn't stir. He snuck back out without saying anything, after setting what turned out to be a batch of daffodils on the bedside table.

She smiled at the flowers and listened to him making breakfast. He whistled while he worked. Finally, he came up the stairs with a tray full of food, a newspaper folded to the crossword section, and two newly sharpened pencils.

"Breakfast," he said.

Julie sat up. Harry put the tray on the bedside table and got back in with her. He moved his arm so there was a hole for her at his side. They kissed. He unfolded the newspaper.

"I like this better than car rides or balls," she said. "Or dinner." She yawned.

"I know I do," he said.

He squeezed the hip on which his hand rested. Julie thought for a moment about how nice it would be to fall in love with Harry. How nice it would feel to have it to think about, instead of thinking about things that weren't so nice, like leaving St Albas or St Albas becoming boring. And it wasn't boring with Harry around. It wasn't going to be boring with a handsome Middle Eastern billionaire, Harvard-graduate lover. The only restlessness she was determined to feel was the restlessness between one kiss and the next.

Still, she heard Professor Harris in her head, talking about real life and how it was coming.

But this, whatever it was with Harry, *was* real life. Right here, in St Albas because Harry had said being with him was real life. Julie thought with satisfaction that they had both been a little right that night in Edinburgh. But not Professor Harris.

Harry cleared his throat.

"One across: 'Eliot novel town/Eliot town novel.' "

She grabbed his arm, and lowered the newspaper along with it.

"Let's do that later."

Their legs were rubbing slowly against one another, and breakfast was quickly forgotten.

# XII.

**PETER WALKED THROUGH CATRIONA'S FRONT GARDEN.** At the very end, he was greeted by a dumpy doormat that grew slightly more unsightly with every rain in which it was drowned. "Welcome," it read, but one was not inclined to believe it. Peter imagined it frustrated Catriona to have such little sway over the Scottish weather and its effect on doormats. He bumped his fist against the door in a passionless way. He was very hung over from the ball, it was absolutely freezing, and the sun had decided to come out. The drive south would not be very pleasant, he thought. The light would come in through the driver's side window.

"Come in," said Catriona.

"Good morning."

"Morning," she said, kissing him hastily on the cheek.

"That's more like it."

"Are you wanting some tea, then? I'm finishing mine just now. I expected you earlier."

"Sorry I'm late. No tea."

"All right, then," she said, heading to the kitchen. "My bag is in the living room."

Peter walked in that direction, sneering at the large, unintentionally comic portrait of an English bulldog holding a grouse in its teeth that hung in the hall. Each step on the hardwood floor put his head in agony. He should never, ever listen to Ashwin again. He had gone so far as to set a reminder in his phone for next Friday at nine o'clock in the evening *Never, ever listen to Ashwin. It sounds like fun, but it isn't.* He wondered if Future Peter would heed his words of caution.

"Hello," said Max, who was reading on the sofa.

"Good morning," said Peter.

Peter had always liked Max as an individual. He even thought that they might be friends, if Catriona let anyone really be friends with Max. But he did not entirely approve of him as a boyfriend for Catriona, who he felt needed someone more like her. Someone more conservative, someone slightly more outgoing than herself, someone she would trust enough to tell about George, someone who would make her warm and bring out the small, genuine smile that Peter missed. The one she'd had when she'd still loved the outdoors: when she'd still been impossibly sweet and unstoppably curious.

Peter knew too that Catriona was unflappable in her desire to marry Max. And Peter thought that if marrying Max would keep her from going off the deep end, he was in favor of it. Though it hurt him to think it, he knew his cousin was, to an extent, damaged. And he felt that if someone wanted to marry her, she should marry him. If that's what she thought would make her content. Few things in life, after all, were perfect.

"What's that you're reading?" he asked Max, to keep from getting too sentimental or too introspective.

"*Hallo!*"

"Insufferably stupid magazine."

"It is. But I'm learning a lot about the Princess Royal's taste in china."

Peter shuffled over to Max.

"What a lovely cultural experience for you," he said, clutching his forehead. "Oh, *God*, Max."

"Hung over?" said Max.

"Yes," said Peter. "Did you have a good time at the ball?"

"Not as good as you," he said. "But good."

"At least you escaped a hangover."

Max had not escaped a hangover.

"Yeah."

"Are you tagging along, then?"

"Down to Lancashire? No."

He avoided Peter's eyes.

"Too much work. I've got a hell of a course load this semester."

"I see," said Peter.

*You son-of-a-bitch*, he thought.

"I'm presenting a paper next week at the philosophy department forum."

"Interesting."

Catriona emerged in the hallway, staring at her bag and the two boys in her life with great annoyance.

"If you've got my bag in the car, I'm ready."

Not knowing for sure if she was speaking to him or to Max, Peter crossed to the fireplace to pick up the little, immaculately clean flesh-colored weekend bag of scratchless leather.

"Max, we're leaving."

"Oh, right."

He was thinking of the ball as he flipped through *Hallo!* He wondered what everyone else who had been there was doing this morning. Probably several people had gone home with a different person than they had gone home with last year. Friends were probably waking up hungover on couches in other people's living rooms, stripped down to their underwear and a t-shirt borrowed from the person in the house with the nearest dresser. They were probably going to order bacon sandwiches together.

At the sound of Catriona's voice Max stood, put his wallet in his pocket, and met her in the hall, where he gave her a kiss on the cheek. She didn't like kissing on the mouth when he had not yet brushed his teeth. Max put on his shoes. They walked out the door.

Peter had already started the car as Catriona checked the lock on the door several times, pulling it, pulling it, and pulling it again. When she was convinced of its integrity for the thousandth, two-thousandth, three-thousandth time, she followed Max to the car. Max waited on the sidewalk as she got in next to Peter.

"Drive safe," he said to them.

"Goodbye," said Catriona. "Have a nice weekend."

"See you. Love you."

As they pulled away, Max felt a sense of relief, a twinge of freedom. He told himself it was because now he would be able to concentrate on his work completely. But when he got home and found a note on the kitchen table reminding him that Fern was climbing some rocks somewhere over the weekend, a pang of loneliness touched him in the stomach. Max didn't like to be alone when he didn't have a choice in the matter.

In the front seat of his car, Peter shuffled through the radio, attempting to find a diplomatic solution to his and Catriona's vastly divergent musical tastes.

"For goodness's sake," said Catriona, sitting up even straighter in her seat. "Just choose one, won't you?"

"I'm sorry," he said. "They're all going out of range."

It was true. The countryside was enveloping them on all sides, in a stationery-store-variety of fields and birds. The motorway, a thick black inky line, lay ahead of them. The static on the radio overwhelmed Peter. Finally, he switched it off.

"We'll just chat then, shall we?"

"Must we?"

"Yes. Tell me all about how your semester is coming along."

"You know very well how," she said, directing her attention out her window. Each cow she spotted seemed to have less hair than the one before. "It's quite the same as always."

"How is Max?"

"I know what you're wanting to ask."

"He's not coming this weekend. I suppose grandmother and Aunt Harriet will be asking questions about it."

"What on earth can you be insinuating?"

"Only that they might think he isn't very serious. That's all."

"Don't be ridiculous," she said flatly. "Mother and grandmother know that Max and I are going to be married."

"How do they know that?"

"Because I've told them."

"Does Max know he's asking you?"

"Peter," she said sharply. "I suggest we talk about something else."

"I'm sorry for being anxious about you," he said. "When the slightest thing can make you so different from your usual self. And Max not making you happy is not a slight thing."

"I don't want to talk about that."

"We have to talk about it sometime."

"He is making me happy, though."

"He is?"

"I don't want to talk about it now."

"I'm sorry. Fine. On the way back north, then. Promise me."

"I'm doing all right with that all, if that's what you mean."

Peter took a deep breath.

"I don't have to ask you to show me, do I?"

"No. And I'm wearing tights anyway."

"What about with the eating?"

"It's all right."

"What about your flu a few weeks ago?"

Catriona's body turned toward the window.

"I was sick."

"You were sick."

Peter stared down the road.

"Right. You were sick."

"Yes."

"Catriona," he said. "You're getting worse."

"I'm not."

"You are," he said.

Catriona looked back at him with eyes that were angry and sad.

"It's my last year of university too," she said in a small voice.

"It's a hard time for everyone. It's a big change."

"What am I going to do?"

"What do you mean?"

"I don't know what's going to happen next year, do I?"

Peter glanced at Catriona.

"You'll—well. You'll do whatever you please."

"Exactly. I don't know where I'll be or what I'll do."

"Move to London. Work in a gallery."

"That's not what I want," she said.

"What can I do to make you feel better?"

"Nothing."

"There has to be something."

"I want Max to ask me to marry him," she said. "All right? I don't think you can make that happen. And I doubt you even want it to happen. Will you leave me alone, now?"

"Will that make you happy?"

"It would," she said. "It really would. Now please be quiet."

"I just want you to be happy, Catriona," he said.

Catriona said nothing.

"I want what's best for you," he said.

*I miss the girl you used to be*, he thought.

*I miss George too*, he thought.

Catriona stayed quiet.

The first time Peter had seen her do it had been in the Cotswolds, where their grandparents kept a holiday cottage. The holidays hadn't been quite holiday-ish since George, but for a year or so after there was a proper English attempt at keeping calm and carrying on; so, they had gone to the Cotswolds in spite of it all. On top of being a pair instead of a trio now and on top of the agony of missing George, Catriona and Peter were dealing with the awkwardness of being a teenaged boy and girl. The mutual knowledge that they would never be equals any more made all things more difficult. Catriona stopped fishing. Peter refused to play games. A fine line of demarcation had assembled itself between them. It broke both their hearts a little.

The second day they'd arrived, he'd found her sitting by herself in the gazebo by the lake. He snuck up behind her in the bushes of cattail. She had been crying. Her shoulders were slumped in a defeated posture. He watched as she pulled a little paring knife from the pocket of her sweater. She lay out on her back, stretching her right leg toward the sky. With a trembling movement, he saw her move the blade across the skin on the back of her knee. He saw the scarlet blood trickle up her thigh, saw her take the piece of kitchen roll and blot it away with water from the lake. There were no food wrappers or traces of vomit. Those would start a few years' worth of family holidays later.

"Catriona," he said.

She turned to find him there. She looked as if she'd seen a ghost. She looked like she'd seen George.

"Peter," she said. "I can't help it. I miss him so much."

"I do too."

"I'm so lonely, at home."

"I'm sorry."

"It's all my fault. I can't undo it. You can't undo anything, ever."

"Nothing could have changed it," Peter said, repeating something his mother had told him hundreds of times.

"I could have changed it," she said. "It should have been me. I should be dead."

"That's not true."

That long ago day Catriona had cried, and Peter had held her.

"Don't tell on me. Promise."

"I promise."

From then on, they had hardly ever talked about George. And Peter had never talked to anyone about all the things Catriona did to make herself feel better.

As the motorway raced beneath him, he came to realize that he must take matters into his own hands. If it would make Catriona happy to marry Max, he had to do everything in his power to facilitate it.

*But what if it doesn't work? What if Max doesn't ask her?* said a voice in his head.

*Then I'll be there, like I've always been,* he said back. *Then at least we'll know. And Catriona can try to get on with her life.*

*You think she's really capable of that?* said the voice.

Peter didn't answer.

That evening, he asked their grandmother if he might have her mother's diamond ring. She thought it was meant for Peter's girlfriend and promised not to say a thing about it to the rest of the family.

Peter was pleased that it was so Victorian. Catriona would love the design.

***

When they returned to town, Peter went to Max's flat and gave him the ring.

"You love my cousin, don't you?" he said.

"Yes," said Max.

"She wants you to marry her."

"I know."

"Do you want to marry her?"

Max had always hated confrontations. He hated disappointing people. And he liked Peter. So he said:

"Someday."

"Make it soon," said Peter, and he handed the box to Max with a frown. "End of this term. Early next. All right?"

"All right," said Max.

# XIII.

**FOR A UNIVERSITY WITH SO MANY** homosexuals, it was a great waste of energy, if not necessarily talent, that it did not house an actual drama department. But the students, of their own initiative, more than made up for it. Several societies were dedicated to bringing theatre, or its look-alike, to St Albas: the Tip of a Tap Society, which provided musical theatre and sent up a poorly sung and acted rendition of *Rent* every few years; the Opera Society, whose shows were widely thought to be executed with professionalism purely because of the subject matter; the Not-So-Royal Shakespeare Company, which never stooped to playing the texts in the time and place the author intended them for; the Gilbert & Sullivan Society, as essential to a rich-kid university as a rowing team, polo matches, and Pimms; and the St Edmunds Hall Players: unruly, undisciplined, perpetually lazy, and drastically overfunded—the bastard child of the other theatre societies and by far the most beloved.

After his weekend alone with his books and his surprising conversation with Peter, Max had decided to direct a play. Anything he could do to not think about the ring was a good thing. And he had not thought about it as much as one might believe. Max was a master of mental compartmentalization. In addition, he told himself that directing would be something good to have on his *curriculum vitae*—leadership skills and all of that. Of course, he also supposed it would be nice to socialize. After the ball, it had become more apparent that he was missing out on something that all of his peers gleefully took for granted. To have an excuse to meet some new people in his fourth year and to experience more of St Albas as others experienced it (that would mostly meet with Catriona's approval) would be good.

That he knew so little about directing a play did not bother Max. He had seen several St Edmunds Hall productions—Fern was involved as a stage manager—so it was clear that no one was expecting much. He attended a general meeting of the society with Fern by his side, and pitched the president and the vice president the idea of producing *Vojtech*, a classical play of Bohemian origin. He read a few pages, accompanied by Fern, and these few pages were enough to convince the society that the material was twisted enough to make good St Eds material. Max had the job. Pleased with himself, he mentioned the small victory to Catriona one night, as they sat reading in her living room.

She was in a large sweater and her golden-framed glasses—a studied "I don't care how I look while I'm studying, or at least that's what I want you to think" look. At the coffee table, she was bent slightly over a gigantic book of Monet, which was open to some haystacks.

"I'm going to direct the St Eds play," he said.

"Hmm?"

"I'm going to direct the St Eds play."

"You are?"

"Yeah. Fern helped me pitch it, and they said yes."

"Why?" she asked.

"Why am I directing it?"

"Yes. You've never directed anything."

"It'll be fun."

"You only have—what—a month to prepare? When is it?"

"December 16th."

"I suppose this means you'll rehearse a lot."

"Yeah."

"You don't think you'll be too busy?"

"No."

"Congratulations, then," she said. "I'm sure it'll be interesting."

She returned to her reading without further comment.

He was happy, anyway. He printed fliers and posted them around town, in the coffee houses and churches and in the library's foyer, announcing auditions. It was one of these that Julie noticed as she sat sipping tea with Margot after a lecture in Pier House, a nautically-themed café with ridiculously ornate cupcakes on Sea Street.

"*Vojtech*," she said. "Auditions."

"Oh, you should do it. It's a good play," said Margot, who was always eager to see her friends make fools of themselves, especially on stage. She knew Julie to be a good target and had been egging on her performances since first year.

"Is it a German playwright?"

"Czech. Twisted stuff but good."

"What's it about?"

"It's about a man who wants to know the future, and so he asks a witch to show it to him. When she does, he sees that it's awful, but he's so indecisive that he can't bring himself to change it."

"Huh." Julie said and looked more carefully at the flier. "Tonight's first auditions. I think I'll go."

"It'll be good for you. You love acting."

"This is true," she said. "Let's eat another cupcake, and then I have to go get ready."

Julie felt a rush as she walked home. She loved being on stage, and auditions were her favorite part of the process. Getting to play so many parts was always fun.

The diversion would be good for her because things with Harry had been—interesting. After their lovely breakfast, after all that had happened the night before it, after all the weeks of flirtation, he had asked her to lunch the next day and acted as if he didn't remember a thing. They sat there, doing the crossword, smiling at each other and talking, but not a word was said on the subject of the way their relationship to one another had fundamentally changed.

Julie had the horrible, terrible thought that perhaps Harry didn't feel that it *had* changed, even though he succeeded in bringing her home after lunch twice and after a night at the pubs once. In his room the next morning, she noticed that the wipe board on the wall no longer said "Vera." Perhaps they had broken up. Perhaps he didn't want Julie to know. She tried very hard not to think about it, but the truth was Julie felt that Harry owed her something, though she couldn't have told him what.

So, she had asked in bed, as the sun came up:

"You do remember what happened at November Ball, right?"

"Yes."

"And what seems to keep happening?"

"Of course I do," he said.

"Then why don't we talk about it?"

"Julie," he said, lowering his voice. "What's to talk about?"

"I don't know."

"I think we're communicating just fine."

"I don't mean like that."

"I know you don't," he said and kissed her forehead. "Let me ask: is there a reason to ruin what we have by talking about it?"

"How would that ruin it?"

"I'm only suggesting we enjoy it. Can you enjoy it without talking about it?"

"I can try."

"Is it that hard?" he said, putting a hand on her cheek.

"No," she said.

"I want it to be you and me, in here. If we start talking, and labeling, and all of that—it's a slippery slope until we start telling other people, and then the whole town knows, and then it's not our secret."

"Caddy knows. And now Larry knows."

"It's because you're loud, Julie."

"You're loud. And I saw him in the hallway last night."

"Neither of them will say anything. That's what housemates and best friends, for that matter, are for. Now, should we keep talking, or get back to enjoying one another's company?"

She had smiled and agreed that they should get back to the enjoying.

But the auditions would help. She needed to be someone else, another character, to compartmentalize herself. She read halfheartedly through the afternoon, and, after eating a chicken breast for dinner, brushed her hair, put on a skirt, and walked down the street to the Noble Theatre.

The Noble was the University's way of trying to disguise its general lack of interest in supporting the performing arts. It only existed because an alumnus of the University had made a generous donation upon his death, stipulating in his will that the sum be used to finance an arts venue for student productions. And so, when the small printing press near the library went out of business, the University purchased the property and fitted it with what it assumed were all the traditional theatre trappings: seats, some lights, sound equipment.

The space's inconvenient shape was marketed to the students as an exciting challenge for them to conquer using the analytical skills the University had no doubt instilled within them. Blocking in the

L-shaped stage space was a nightmare, and the audience had difficulty seeing all the action no matter which seat they were seated in. But the students had a hard time asking their wealthy parents for money for something as silly as a theatre, and so they were, for once, thankful for something they had been given and loved the Noble despite its limitations. There was a power in a place like this—one that was meant solely for expressing themselves in an original, meaningful way.

Or producing *Rent*. Whichever.

Max sat in the front row of the Noble's audience with an empty legal pad in front of him. Fern, who had agreed to stage-manage, sat next to him, scribbling away furiously as people auditioned. Max's pad of paper remained blank, except for some proficient doodles he made at the bottom of the page. He had no idea what one wrote on an audition form. He concocted an elaborate system of smiley faces to describe his like or dislike of a person's performance. He vacillated between interest and boredom. He wanted a cigarette and thought about that instead.

Julie stood in the hallway, filling out an audition form, as she had done several dozen times before in her life. Picking up the audition monologue and reading through it once (it was better not to overdo it), she sat in line and waited for her turn to present whatever it might be that was going to come out of her mouth when the time came along. And so the time came. She was called.

She walked into the dark room. There were a few lights illuminating the stage area. In the front row of the audience sat a slouchy boy with blond hair, sitting next to a skinny girl with long, brown hair. The boy sat up when he saw her. He was half-lit. Younger maybe. Cute. Austrian, maybe, or German. He looked familiar.

"I'm Max," he said. "And this is Fern."

"Julie."

"Whenever you're ready."

Julie began.

***

The next day, Max was lying on his stomach on Catriona's bed, his laptop spread out in front of him. She sat at her desk, puzzling over a different kind of Mackintosh. It was the chilly sort of autumn evening that reminded you with a smack that winter was on its way, and in only a few short turns of the earth. The full moon illuminated each tile on the sloped roofs of Church Street. Catriona counted them deliberately.

Max's computer made a little beeping noise.

"Done," he said. "Cast list is off."

"Excellent news," she said. "Are you happy with who you chose?"

"I didn't have a whole lot of choice. But it should be a good show. Or St. Ed's good."

"I know it will be. You'll have to let me know if I can help. Perhaps I can attend a rehearsal."

"Once we get going. I'll be too nervous if you come right away."

"All right."

"Aren't you proud?"

"Of course I am. I'm always proud of you."

Max climbed down from the bed, which was high even for him. He crossed over to the desk at the window and draped his arms loosely about Catriona's neck and chest. He kissed her ear.

"Are you all right?"

"Of course. Why wouldn't I be?"

Across town, Julie checked her email. An email from mw5@st-albas.ac.uk had appeared in her inbox with the title line "*Vojtech* cast list." Here it was. She clicked it open, and there was her name next to the role of "Witch."

*Awesome*, she thought to herself. *I'm going to be a witch.*

"Caddy," she shouted. "I'm going to be a witch!"

"*Going* to be?" said the voice from downstairs.

# XIV.

**THE FASHION SHOW WAS HELD IN** the Ancient Links Hotel. This, like November Ball, was a big, old deal. For years, it had taken place in the spring, but once the committee had recognized the potential for wearing furs and hats and winter accessories on top of all the gowns, a vote was held to move it to late November. The committee was made up of five girls, all of them as thin and pale as the cigarettes they smoked as replacements for food, as well as one completely un-ironic, straight third-year male whose father ran a fashion house on the Continent. His name was Franz Sweinsmach, and, in his words, he didn't make fashion—he bought fashion.

*The Stroll* was taken seriously by the first, second, and third years, who were still attempting to establish their ranks in their social circles. They spent an obscene amount of what some of them still referred to as "pocket money" to purchase gowns, shoes, and suits for the occasion. A popular destination for the upper echelons of St Albas society during this time of year was Paris, though many went as far as Asia over the summer in an attempt to find something no one else would be wearing. The safe bets—Versace, Miu Miu, Prada, Temperley, McQueen—they were all on display, sounding like an Ellis Island roll call and looking as far from it as was possible. But the truly fashionable showed up in labels no one had ever heard of. The more obscure the designer and the more elegant the fabric, the better. For the social climbers, much of the evening was spent saying bullshit things like, "Oh, Boxy Mouse, yes, I saw her spring/summer show and it was fab!"

This was the only fashion show in the world where people dressed as if they were going to the Oscars. Many of the student-designed collections on the runway were significantly less formal than the fashions in the crowd on either side. That was St Albas for you.

Julie had always borrowed Caddy's dress from the year before. They were a bit loose at the waist, but that was always easily fixed by a few stitches from the little Turkish woman on Redfriars Street. Caddy was in the habit of having her clothes taken in and given to Julie. Julie had protested that it was too much in first year, but Caddy had been just as quick to remind Julie that without her help she would not have survived life past the Fresher's Week vodka bar in their hall of residence. From then on, Julie held her tongue in remembrance of nights spent holding Caddy's hair away from the toilet bowl and wore the clothes without further ado.

And her reward tonight was a canary yellow gown of silk—just your average Oscar de la Renta—or, in her case, Oscar de la Rental. It was more Caddy's color than hers, and the garnet necklace was definitely more Caddy's than hers. *In fact*, thought Julie, *the only things I'm wearing that I managed to purchase are my underwear and my shoes. Ana that's only because they're not visible to the naked eye.*

This was just another example of how one knew how to be what Julie and her sister always referred to as "Fake Rich." It was an art that could launch a person into worlds that they never knew existed. Employing an air of Fake Richness was a tactically noble counterpoint to, say, Manon Lescaut's, the upper-middle class girl's way of getting into powerful circles without having to marry into them. Why this was a talent Julie had, or where she had acquired it, she did not know. It was not something she had polished or cultivated, either before coming to St Albas or during her time there. She simply knew which things she should and should not talk about, care about, and buy. The best passport into social circles where people played polo and wore crocodile shoes was wearing the crocodile-and-polo-logoed shirts of the men who wore the crocodile shoes and played polo. That and acting like you belonged there in the first place.

The rest was their assumptions and her omissions. She could afford St Albas on a mix of student loans, and the fact that she worked hard during her summers at home, bustling into and out of the city, working both at the mall and as a lackey at her mother's legal firm, something she described as an internship. Internships and family businesses; these things her fellow St Albas students understood and appreciated.

She was not the only one who had learned the art—Neve had

mastered it too. Her sheer lack of caring what people thought about her gave an impression of wealth, and the force of her personality and good looks alone had gotten her into this world of champagne paid for by the boys she went to school with and ball gowns paid for by golfers who were just passing through.

And so, although the clothes were hand-me-downs, Julie felt comfortable in them, as she did with her friends. She was lucky she had found a group who did not care that she could rarely pick up the tab for everyone. Not all people in St Albas were like that. Most of her friends had more money than God and would still never say anything about her second-hand gown—other than, perhaps, how beautiful she looked in it.

On cue, Ashwin kissed her hand. This was the one event a year for which he was sober. He said that when he was old and infirm, he wanted to remember what gorgeous women he had gone to university with.

"Julie. Stunning."

"You too. I love the tie."

It had sunglasses all over it.

"It's Nilgiris."

"Is that an Indian designer?"

"No. It's an Indian supermarket chain. Cost me £2."

He helped her into the cab.

"No limo this year?" said Margot wryly behind her. "Brett, has your mother chosen a new favorite child among your brothers?"

Brett's mother had always ordered a limo to the fashion show, but Ashwin's decision to rent it to a couple of second years during last year's event had ended the tradition. The driver had taken them to Loch Ness.

"Isn't Harry coming?" Julie asked Larry when they had all piled in.

"Yeah," said Larry, not meeting her eyes. "He's coming later. I thought he would have said so."

"No."

"It's kind of a big day."

Julie thought she heard an extra meaning in that but didn't want to press him in front of all the other eyes and ears in the cab.

"Let's go then."

The driver heard her and pulled out of the driveway in front of the boys' building. The radio was going. Champagne was being popped. Anastasia was passing around little pills, and Neve was rolling down the windows. Long hairs were whipping like ribbons in the wind because the only thing more St Albas than a long ball gown was long, messy locks, undone.

At the front entrance to the Ancient Links Hotel, Julie watched happily as her friends stepped out of the vehicle behind her.

*And here,* she said to herself, *is Helen Donaldson, in a frothy pink creation by Elie Saab. What wonderful movement! What fine tailoring!*

They came out, each and each, the heels of their heels complementing the beautiful colors from their waists to their hems. She was proud to be among them.

"What are you staring for, missus?" said Neve.

"You look beautiful."

"Thanks, love. You too. Just promise me one thing—don't ask me where I got this dress."

"Okay."

"Let's just say it's from Harvey Nicks."

"It's nice."

"Let's just say, I have a new boyfriend."

"Well, it's a fantastic dress."

"She's got a golfer," said Margot loudly.

"Shut it, you old slag," said Neve and kissed her. "She's right though, it is a golfer."

The Ancient Links Hotel's Hall of Laurels was dimly lit and incredibly sexy. Sheer red scarves had been thrown over lamps. Large, drippy candelabra were emitting smoky Neroli oil above Swarovski crystal. The program explained helpfully that the décor was meant to "reawaken the fascination with Italian sensuality that characterized the English imperial era." In the distant corners of her mind in which she considered herself a student of the back and inside covers of the literary works of this period, she found this theme dubious in historical accuracy. In an Edwardian script, the word "stroll" was outlined in chalk over a banner of black lace and hung over the runway. Someone had chosen some pretty choice Italian ceramic tile to cover the runway.

Of course, one mustn't forget that *The Stroll* was a charity event to raise money for children affected by wars, and other similar misfortunes, in Africa.

At the bar there were Bellinis, bottles of Prosecco, and a cocktail that had been especially created for the event by Lucinda Jones, celebrity bartender to those wealthy enough to be known only among celebrities. Her "Piccadilly Pomodoro" was a mix of McClelland's Scotch and fresh squeezed tomato juice—with bitters and a slice of lemon. It was hard to smile while you drank it, but that was all right because smiling wasn't necessarily stylish.

Julie drank as a distraction against texting Harry to ask where he was and as an insanity defense if the distraction should fail. She wanted him here, next to her, talking to her, entertaining her. Even if they hadn't discussed their relationship, or whatever the hell it was, they had talked in bed about all other things. About childhood pets and favorite siblings and where they would like to travel—with vague references to going to some of the wheres together.

Julie liked to think of him as her boyfriend, even without the definition of what she was to him. At first, she had told herself that he only wanted her body and that a dinner in Edinburgh was a means to that end. That much had been certain, and she had accepted it because there would always be Peter, or someone like him, in her life. A man she could be close to and talk about actual things with and ask advice of and know she was loved by. Their deep friendship had always outlasted the physical ones, and so it was smart to take advantage of the physical while she could—even at the slight expense of her friendship with Peter.

But it did not feel that way now. She did not care so much that Peter was not at the fashion show, which he loved as much as the club and about which he had said, "after the November Ball, I don't care if I see another ball gown just as long as I live." She wanted Harry here to talk to, not Peter. Harry was charming and thought she was amusing. Peter could be so critical.

Soon, she was sitting at the table with a pout on her face, forming a buffer zone between Larry and Brett and Anastasia, who were making eyes at one another. Everyone was inevitably paired up by this time in the year. Caddy was even sitting at a different table, with some large boy in a white suit, who was captain of the rowing team. She waved to Julie across the room. Margot was sitting next to one of her handsome German friends, whom she claimed she was not interested in but whose arm she would not stop touching. Helen's charms were working effortlessly to ensnare a waiter, who probably liked the vines of black lace crawling up her arms in the form of some very luxurious gloves. The mint green sheath she wore only enhanced her muse-like charm. A drunken Neve and a sober Ashwin were joking with one another in exactly the same way as when the tables were turned. Julie felt alone.

The champagne ended. Before Brett could raise his DeBeers-cuffed wrist to ask for more, the emcee began with a brief announcement about how proud everyone should feel for contributing to such a worthy cause, without stating exactly what the cause was. Everyone clapped proudly. The lights went down, the DJ started the pounding club music, and the girl-like skeletons strutted down the runway, clothed most heavily in light. Their hipbones clicked up and down as they strutted past.

Julie's head wobbled with the ended champagne. Across the runway, the prince sat with his friends, drunk on the importance of their suits and the quality of their whisky. Next to them sat the skeletons that were too wealthy and well bred for this sort of mundane strutting across the stage. The prince sat still in his chair, looking a bit bored, until some girl in a meshy, see-through dress walked past on the runway, her long brown hair the only biological voluptuousness of which one could speak in the entire show. Julie saw his eyes light up. He sat straighter. She envied the girl, whoever she was. Not because of the prince. Lord knew they came a dime a dozen in St Albas. But because of the way he looked at her as she walked back down the runway.

When the intermission came, Julie was properly drunk. Having watched her pout from across the room for the entire first half, Caddy excused herself from her date and took her roommate by the arm.

"Would you like to come to the ladies room?" she asked.

"I want another drink first."

"I don't think so. Have some water."

She handed Julie a glass from the nearest table.

"That," said Julie, pouring its contents to the floor, "is what I think of your water."

"Bathroom. Let's go."

A moment later, they were in an unmemorable, if very expensive, bathroom stall. Caddy was turned away as Julie sat on the toilet with her elbows on her knees and her head in her hands.

"I just think everyone deserves to know."

"No. They don't."

"He can't just get away with this! We are sleeping together. He has to acknowledge it!"

"This isn't the time."

"You always think you know it all."

"When have I ever been wrong?"

"Where is he? He should be here."

"I'm sorry."

"He loves me, Caddy. I know he does."

"Julie," said Caddy, "I don't think you're thinking about this the right way."

"He does love me."

Julie lifted her face from her hands.

"No matter what you do," Caddy said, "don't talk about it with the others."

"Don't you think he loves me?"

"Not the time. Not the time to talk about this. Understand me? Nod. Nod that you understand."

Julie dropped her head in her lap.

"He will come or not," said Caddy. "And when or if he does, I'm guessing it won't be with a declaration of public affection. You need to live with that. So please, don't do anything stupid. If you like him, you need to cool it, honey. If you push him tonight, in front of everyone, you're not going to look good."

"You don't know everything. You don't hear us talk in the morning."

The bathroom attendant, a slightly overweight local with frizzy brown hair and bright purple glasses said through the door:

"Darling, make sure you're keeping your self-respect, that's all your friend is saying."

"She's right," said Caddy.

"Self-respect," murmured Julie.

"You ready to get back out there?"

"Yeah."

"You can do it without doing something stupid?"

"Uh-huh."

"Good."

Back at the table, before the second half, Brett proposed a toast. Ashwin, as usual, took the spotlight.

"This is my favorite night of the year," he said to the circle of crystal glasses. "I can't believe it's our last one. I hope we meet for the rest of our lives, guys. I hope we will always remember being here at St Albas together. I love you. Cheers."

"Guys, I'm sleeping with Harry," said Julie as the rest of them drank.

Several jaws dropped onto the red lace tablecloths. Helen looked at Julie with pity that read as chic on her soft face. Larry spit his champagne back into its glass, not so much because of the information that had just come from Julie's mouth, nor of the boldness with which she said it—but because Harry himself was standing behind her. To the absolute relief of the entire table, the lights dimmed and the show began once more. Harry sat down next to Julie in the blackout. When the lights on the runway came up, there he was, wearing a black tuxedo. His shoulders made a perfect triangle down to his waist. Julie looked around the table with dread and then pride. Harry kissed her on the mouth in full view of everyone in the room.

"Sorry I'm late," he said loudly.

He put one arm around the back of her chair and, with the other, pulled her chair much closer to his. There was never a second in the next hour during which he was not touching her, brushing her hair back into place with his hand, kissing her on the neck, rubbing her knee, whispering in her ear.

"You're so beautiful. You should be in the show."

"You think so?" she said through the alcohol.

"They should give you your own show."

"*You* should be in it. So handsome. You should be in it."

"You are so charming when you're tipsy, Julie."

"You're so charming always."

Harry kissed her hand.

At the end of the show, it was customary for the female models to sell themselves on dates to the boys with the most money in the room. Julie was always vaguely disgusted by this tradition and had succeeded in not watching it every year by striking up a dramatic conversation with the boy nearest her. This year, it wasn't difficult to identify target or subject matter.

"Harry," she said, nestling into his breast pocket, "you're not mad at me for telling, are you?"

"No. I realized something today, actually. About you."

Julie beamed.

"What is it?"

"Ladies and gents," said the emcee on the stage, a quiet drop of mystery in his voice, "we have with us tonight a very special guest indeed. She would like to present herself in the auction. Ladies and gentlemen, the chairwoman of two past *Strolls*, Vera Morgan."

Julie's stomach plummeted as this creature, several inches taller and several dress sizes smaller than she, entered the runway and walked to the end. She was in a tight pair of light, washed-out jeans and simple white cotton t-shirt that stretched across perfectly proportioned size B breasts. The wipe board in Harry's room corroborated the evident shock on his face. This was Vera. The Vera. And now she knew: his Vera.

Julie did not wait to hear the winning bid, a stunning £600 sum from Harry. Nor did she see the loving embrace this thin girl gave him, nor did she hear Harry's happy, "You sneak! What a surprise!" Not looking anyone in the face, she ran out of the room as fast as she could in the opposite direction without stopping, which eventually led her outside through a security door. Its alarm began wailing as Larry entered the patio behind her.

"Larry," she cried. "Make that thing stop."

He looked helplessly at her.

"I don't know how to fix it without breaking it."

A server from the hotel made her way to the scene.

"You really can't be out here," she said.

Larry shuffled around in his pocket and handed her a £20 note. It meant more to Julie, knowing he or someone within the last two generations of his family had earned it by working as opposed to inheriting.

"Have a good evening," said the server, and she closed the door.

A stretch of green, the Ancient Links lawn lay before them. In the distance, under the quarter-lit moon, the hairy bulk of grass before Flat Sands was quivering kindly in the wind that combed it. The lights of St Albas were mostly out.

"It's going to be all right," Larry said.

"I'm the queen of being wrong about things. That is like the one thing I'm good at. Where's the career for that, huh? I should do it. Really. Professionally. It would be a great move. Jesus Christ. Why am I so stupid?"

"Listen, we should have told you earlier. He should have told you earlier. I should have told you about her. I thought you knew. She wanted me to help surprise him. Coming home early and all."

Larry looked at Julie looking out at nothing. He wished he knew what to say to make her feel better. He thought he would want someone to be honest with him. So he said:

"This girl—they're together. I mean, really together."

This did not have quite the effect on Julie he had thought. Her eyes were blank when she lifted them to his face and no anger was in them. A little choked laugh escaped her throat.

"I sort of suspected about the girlfriend," she said, explaining her reaction. "Who is she?"

"Her name is Vera."

"That's kind of the one thing I knew."

"She's from London."

"London?"

"Our fathers have all been friends since business school."

"How long have they been…?"

Larry took a deep breath, in and out.

"It's been about ten years, I guess. They went to boarding school together."

"Ten years?"

She laughed. She shook her head.

"I'm sorry for being such a shitty friend," said Larry. "For not telling you sooner. I thought you knew. I really did."

He hadn't wanted to be the one to tell her outright.

"It's okay," she said.

"I know how it feels," he said. "I really do."

"I'm sorry."

"Anastasia looked really pretty tonight, didn't she?"

"She's beautiful, Larry."

For a moment, they stood there, assessing one another with respect.

"It's kind of a shitty place," she said. "Isn't it? The people and their money. Boarding schools and fashion shows. I always thought I came from a privileged background. Until I came here."

"I know," said Larry.

"It's not what I thought it would be. And now it's almost over. This isn't what I thought college would be."

"No," he said emphatically, putting his arm around her and turning his head out toward the Links. "It's better. It really is. Look towards town. There's an ocean down there, Julie. Don't tell me this isn't better than some lame school in the suburbs."

# XV.

**THE CHRISTMAS LIGHTS WERE BEING TURNED** on that night. It was the final day of the St Albas Festival. The Festival had been held at this same time of year for the last 200 rotations of the Earth around the Sun, and the townspeople and students upheld the traditions that went along with it with befitting pageantry and tomfoolery. On the first day there was an enormous parade, sponsored by the Ann Anderson Society.

The Society had been around for the last 150 years. Comprised of about forty students, its stated purpose was to promote St Albas's history and keep its sacred traditions. Its members were the sons from the wealthiest and the most influential families at the University. Between eight and twelve new members were elected every year from several dozen applicants. All of these young men vied for their place through partaking in a series of secret contests, interviews, and meetings. The most private aspects of one's life, including a sexual history and the size of one's trust fund, along with one's tolerance for alcohol and other drugs, were revealed and tested during this time. When elected to the club, one's duties were much less imposing. A member might have to occasionally vote on a string quartet or for which charity to donate the proceeds from a ball, but other than getting to wear an obnoxiously embroidered vest with a seal about town that let everyone else know how important you and your father were, the day-to-day involvement of any member was minimal.

And on this special day, the members of the Society, along with several dozens of St Albas's handpicked elite, were dressed as famous characters from the town's history. Everyone came out to watch. There you stood, hot cider or mulled wine in hand, seeing everyone from Benjamin Franklin to Mary Queen of Scots to Saint

Alba himself pass by on horseback and on foot. The horses were giants, healthy and athletic, but easy to ride despite their daunting appearance. It had been years since anyone had been thrown: the only people normally invited to participate were rich enough to know how to handle one well.

This year there were even more people than usual at the parade. Particularly, first-year girls. The prince was rumored to be participating, playing the part of one of his royal ancestors. This wasn't exactly the case: while his brother rebelled by going as Stalin at fancy dress parties, the elder and less controversial prince subverted his status in a much friendlier way. He was playing Bonnie Prince Charlie. The Scottish didn't mind him so much, and the first-year girls were giddy.

After the parade, there were bagpipes and several venues for ceilidh dancing. The pubs stayed open later than usual to accommodate the revelers. Parties in the streets erupted noisily. Breaking into the cathedral ruins and trying to conjure ghosts or scare one another was a popular activity among the drunken students.

However, the one thing at the Festival that brought the town and gown together, like nothing else would for the rest of the year, was the switching on of the Christmas lights. These had been strung between all the buildings on Fair Street. In the square that had a fountain in the summer, St Albas's semblance of traffic was stopped from sundown onward. Though the lights appeared to be switched on by the mayor's wife, who held a box of wood with a big red button in the center up on the platform, they were actually controlled by the electric company, which sent a representative to connect the lights at the appointed time. The whole thing was fairly inaccurate, as the person who turned the actual switch couldn't see when the mayor's wife pressed her button. Embarrassing moments had resulted from this arrangement in the past, but it added an extra element of suspense. Of course, to the intoxicated and the children, which were most of the crowd, it was all the same.

The mayor of St Albas gave a speech that no one could hear but that everyone listened to. It was a shame it was inaudible; the mayor took his duty as the keeper of town lore to be sacrosanct.

On this night, Catriona and Max were walking down Sea Street with Simon and Fern. Though Simon and Fern got along famously, the predictable, mutual dislike between Fern and Catriona had recently reached a peak. Catriona had backhandedly accused Fern of pilfering a pink scarf she had lost, or at least that's what it sounded like to Fern.

"Max," she had demanded after her accuser had gone home, "you've got to get a grip on that lassie of yours. She's fucking mental."

Max thought of how mental Fern would be herself if she ever found out about the ring and reminded himself to find a better hiding place for it.

"She's not crazy," he said. "She's just particular about things."

"I don't even wear pink. You know this. I know this. She knows it. And she should be quite happy I don't strangle her with it when I do find it somewhere stupid."

Max was silent.

"All I'm saying is man up, mate."

"And what?"

"How about, stand up for me and tell Catriona I would never take it?"

Max was silent again.

"You could also just break up with her."

"I'm not doing that."

"Why not?"

"I love her."

"You love her, do you?"

"Yeah. And it's our last year in St Albas anyway."

"Meaning?"

"Meaning, you'll never have to deal with her again after May."

Fern sighed and said:

"I'm not looking forward to going out with her this weekend."

"It'll be fun. Simon is coming."

"And I like Simon well enough, mate. I do. But I'm going for you, not for him—and certainly not for that Catriona Darlington-Whatnot."

"Thank you."

Max was genuine about the thanks he had given, and thankful that the two were at least managing to ignore one another. Sure enough, Catriona had forgotten that she'd left the scarf in her other handbag, where it would appear neatly folded two days after she'd broached the subject with Fern. She would not mention this fact to

Max and would not wear the scarf out since.

Among the rest of the town waiting for the lights, Simon and Catriona were happily looking into shop windows together as Max and Fern strolled ahead.

For all her hot-headedness, Fern was an astute observer. She could immediately, and accurately, discern what was really happening, unspoken, between people. Because of this, Simon's feelings for Catriona were absolutely transparent to her. He looked in the window. Then at Catriona. Then in the window. Then at Catriona. How obvious could he be? She thought about telling Max. But, by how comfortable Max seemed to be around each of them, she guessed he knew. He didn't flinch when Simon pulled Catriona aside to show her a painting that was hanging in a gallery window. He didn't say a word when Simon brushed a snowflake off her shoulder. Max wasn't exactly going to duel someone to the death over Catriona. Fern had known this for years.

After the lights had been turned on, successfully synchronized this one time for what would most likely be the next ten years, Catriona excused herself and Max from the rest of the festivities with a harsh look from Fern, who decided to stay out with Simon and have a pint. When they had reached Catriona's house and taken off their coats, she asked:

"Would you like to spend the night?"

"Of course," he said. He pulled her to him by her hips.

"I do love you, Max."

"I love you too."

He gave her a kiss.

They followed their usual bedtime routine. They brushed their teeth. Catriona took her pills. Max got a glass of water. Catriona got undressed, with the lights out. As they sometimes did when they spent the night together, they had sex with the lights out. Catriona was always careful that Max shouldn't see the little cuts. She was lucky her boyfriend was not the type of boy who noticed things.

Then they talked with the lights out, still. Max held Catriona in his arms.

"When are you going home for Christmas?" she asked.

"I don't know. Probably around the 20th."

"We'd love to have you in Lancashire, Max."

She remembered Peter's words in the car about doubting Max's seriousness, and her chin became a little more set in its space. She wondered with embarrassment that she'd shared so much with Peter about her need to marry Max.

Max braced himself before speaking.

"I don't think it's going to work out this year."

Coming down to Lancashire was something Max had learned to avoid at all costs. Catriona's family made him uncomfortable, to say the very least. Her mother was what Catriona might be in thirty years: namely, a frigid housewife stuck in Lancashire with a frigid husband and a child who was, for all Max could tell, stuck between wanting her mother's approval and being scared of her at every waking moment.

This predestined continuity was not surprising: convention was the most prized object in the world of the Darlington home. Academic excellence, respect for one's mother and father, a slight, proper, conservative racism, and faith in God via Catholic means were their only requirements for a peaceable existence. For Max, being in this system felt like being a loaned Picasso in a museum full of Monets. He stuck out. The thought that these people might become his legal relatives if he and Catriona stayed together repulsed him. He hated their silly house and their silly Bichon. He hated her conniving, paranoid, and obsessive mother, her daft and glacial father. He hated the tiny, dumpy village in the middle of nowhere where they lived in the nicest house, thinking themselves better than everyone. The worst part was that they probably were, only because no one worth knowing would ever move to or live in Axbury Town. He felt sorry for Catriona, growing up in a place like that, locked in nightly, trapped upstairs. It was really no wonder she was the way she was.

Catriona had once told him that her mother felt he was a bad influence on her. Max hoped it was true.

"We've been seeing one another for three years now, and I don't think it too much to ask for you to come and spend some time over the holiday in Axbury."

She was surprised at her own boldness.

"They aren't my family yet."

"I know," she said. "But one day we will be."

Max sighed.

"You're right."

"I just wish you would."

"You know I love you. Don't worry so much, yeah?"

For a moment, they were quiet. Max looked out the window. Catriona spoke in a small voice:

"Why don't I come visit you, then?"

"What, in Zurich?"

"Yes."

"Catriona, you know it doesn't work like that. We travel a lot."

"But don't you think it would be nice for everyone to meet me?"

"My parents have met you."

"I know. But don't you think everyone else should? You have met everyone I know at home. My whole family."

"It is important. Just not this Christmas. Maybe over the summer, yeah?"

"If you say so," she said. "If you could just think about how it looks, Max. If you could think about it, I would be happy."

"I will. Goodnight."

Catriona put the problem in a box full of arguments inside her head. In there, they fought, causing such a ruckus that, at times, it was difficult to lay still. Max hadn't come to visit over the summer, and her mother had commented that it might mean that Max's intentions were not serious ones, just as Peter had said. It was a sign of seriousness to spend Christmas with your girlfriend, especially if she was coming to a foreign country to see your family or if you were going to a foreign country to see hers instead of being with your parents at home. So, it was a sign of unseriousness to do the opposite. And that was what Max was doing. Catriona did not look forward to all parts of Christmas in Lancashire, and she did not love coming to Zurich, but she did love the holiday and all its traditions—wanted to share them with Max, wanted Max to want to share them with her.

Max turned over. He did not want to go to Lancashire. Now it was not only what she expected, but also what her family expected—and it was more than just going to Lancashire for Christmas. She and Peter both were insisting on their being together. Forever. Not in some abstract way, but in a way that would merge assets, in a way where there would be no way out unless it involved a divorce or a death. There would be no excuse. The thought of being locked in with Catriona in life as her husband

and in death as the body next to hers in the ground was not an entirely pleasant one. He couldn't be a husband. He hadn't even gotten to be a boy. He thought in a panicked way of the May Saving, how he hadn't done it.

But Max could no more imagine actually marrying Catriona than he could imagine breaking up with her. Max hated making big decisions and feared them more than anything in the world. That was, perhaps, why he trusted and loved books more than he did people. No matter how much you agreed or disagreed with a book or the ideas in it, you could close it when you wanted and think about it until you were blue in the face and there would be no consequences. There was always a way out with a book. Books didn't get upset with you when you paused to think or put them back on the shelf and never picked them up again. But he had noticed that people were not like that.

If only there was a way to make her feel like they were moving forward without having to move forward, actually. To bookmark Catriona. To commit and therefore make her happy, without really committing, so that the rest of the year could go smoothly. So that he could get high marks and please his parents. There must be a way around it that would leave him the option to commit if he wanted to, later. Or not. Probably not. But maybe.

*You could* ask *her to marry you,* said a voice in his head that did not sound like his own. *You have a ring. That might keep her happy for the rest of the year, until you are both gone from St Albas. Until you are far away, starting your master's degree. Then you could just take it back.*

Catriona watched the gaslights in the street, unchanging on their question-mark posts, as they glowed in the street. When she was sure Max was asleep, she would take a trip to the bathroom to throw up her dinner. She would take a little paring knife from her drawer, just to relieve the stress.

# XVI.

**MAKE-BELIEVE WAS THE THING JULIE WAS** best at in life, and she loved to tell stories—so naturally, Julie had always loved to act. Her younger siblings, cousins, and neighbors had, as children, all come under the iron hammer of her direction, had played the villain to her princess and the princess to her villain. Thus, it was no surprise that Julie, in her current incarnation as a St Albas student, still thought of her life as a play and of her friends and relatives and professors as her supporting cast. Creating her own reality, one that was more interesting than the routine and ordinariness that she lived in most of the time, helped to form the buoyant personality that drew others to her. It was why her supporting cast was so large.

All that being said, there was a reason she didn't typically get into bed with the student theatre companies of St Albas. The theatre societies were full of enormous egos with little talent to match. Most of her peers had only started acting or directing in high school or, worse, at St Albas and still had a childish naiveté about theatre that annoyed Julie, who had been on the stage for most of her life.

But Margot's encouragement had inspired her to audition, and she was grateful that she had. Professor Harris's advice to participate in some student societies at the start of the year resurfaced in her mind. Now that she didn't have Harry to distract her, she was finding Professor Harris's advice more apt and his classes just a bit more pertinent too.

She was excited to start rehearsals, with a small cast comprised of people she had never met before. It was always interesting to meet new people in St Albas. You never knew what prime minister or prince's child you might encounter on any given day of the week.

It was bitterly cold as she arrived at the Noble Theater. She knotted her scarf tighter, feeling the hard scratch of the wool at her throat and thinking it reminded her of the hard scratch of Harry's beard. She frowned. She shouldn't think about Harry's beard.

She rested against the building, folding her arms out in front of her. She looked at her phone a few times. Perhaps she'd made a mistake with the rehearsal time. Just as she had become irritated enough to go back home, Max emerged on the path before her.

"Hello," he said. "Julie, right?"

"Yeah, hi."

"Max," he said and put out his hand.

They shook hands through their thick gloves.

"Hi," said Julie. "How are you?"

"Good, good. Good that you're early."

"I am? I thought there must be something."

"Oh—the email said seven thirty."

"I guess it did. I checked the doors, they're locked."

"You're in luck. I have keys."

He jingled them in front of her face with a grin and felt an overwhelming self-loathing at his awkwardness immediately thereafter. He opened the double set of glass doors, and, in a moment, they were standing in the chilly, narrow foyer. Max found the lights. Julie opened the door to the theatre space and crossed the cold, black floor to the piano bench in the far corner of the room, where she sat to take off her many layers. Max took a seat in the audience, removing his own scarf and coat and watching Julie out of the corner of his eye. She was a pretty girl.

"It's so cold out," said Julie, to ease the silence.

"I know," he said. "Really cold."

"And cloudy," she offered. He was a cute boy, but good God—he should think of something to say.

"Tons of clouds."

"It's cloudy here."

"Lots of cirrus clouds today."

He laughed nervously and wished he could think of something to say. He was tired. It had been a long day. He had needed to go down to give a paper at a political theory conference at the university in Edinburgh. Then he had taken the nauseating bus ride back to St Albas to have dinner with Catriona and her housemate Vera and her boyfriend called Harry—with whom he had quickly determined there could be no conversation that was not shallow in nature. The only thing that had kept him from losing his mind completely as the girls gossiped, and as Harry sat shoveling Catriona's much-labored-over leg of lamb into his mouth was the knowledge that he could escape to rehearsal. There was a deadline. There was a way out. There was an excuse.

And being in this room with Julie did relax him, did give him peace for the only time that day. Even if he couldn't think of anything to say. He'd been anxious to see her since auditions. When she had stood there in the middle of the floor, making the Witch's speech, he had felt a knowledge of her settling lightly over him like a clean, cotton nightgown. Dread and happiness and a teasing anticipation fluttered around his head like fairies. He wanted to grab her hand and fly around the room. She looked like she could use a flight around the room too.

Though she'd been energetic in her reading at auditions, there was a sadness that concerned him now, and it was in her eyes. Her curls hung limp, and she looked tired in the way he looked tired when he saw himself in the mirror. He wondered what had happened to make such a pretty girl so sad. A part of him hoped that if the source of the sadness had a Y-chromosome, that it was being severely punished for its meanness.

"Did you have a good day?" he said.

"I did. Yeah. It was all right."

"Really?"

"Did I really have a good day?"

"Yeah," he said.

"You really want to know?"

"Yeah."

"It wasn't a good day at all," said Julie. "I was looking forward to rehearsal."

"I can respect that," said Max. "I had a terrible day."

"A *terrible* day? Wow."

"The worst," he said, raising his hands to the gods in which he did not believe. "And I'm not even trying to one-up you."

"Oh, is that how this works?" said Julie. "I see."

"I'm making it up to you. For talking about the clouds."

"We've all been there."

"I don't get out much, Julie. You'll find that out quickly."

He was sort of funny, wasn't he? And nice. She reminded herself that most boys seemed nice when you met them. But there was something about this Max. He was sweet looking, with his fluffy hair and big nose and the towering height that would no doubt make him look graceful and wise when he was old. You could tell he would never hurt someone on purpose. Or you thought you could tell, which was more than you could say of most people even once you got to know them.

*Fucking Harry. Fucking Vera. Fuck. Fuck. Fuck,* Julie thought.

"Do you want to work on your scene?" he asked. "We have time."

"I would love that."

"Come have a seat next to me, and we'll look at the text."

When the rest of the cast came in fifteen minutes later, they were sitting close together in the audience, in a deep discussion about the play that was punctuated by laughter. Julie hadn't really smiled since *The Stroll.*

She was one of those girls who just didn't see the point in bringing out her best smile unless she was really happy.

\*\*\*

After rehearsal that night, she met Peter in the Midway pub for a pint.

"Hello," she said, kissing him on the cheek.

"Hello," he replied as she threw her heavy, winter coat over his head. "Look who's back from the dead."

"I know, right?"

"I'll hand it to you, Julie, you know how to bounce back and forth between melancholy and happiness better than anyone."

"I'm usually happy. I don't bounce often."

"That's true. But still. When you do."

Peter had been her first phone call the morning after the fashion show disaster. Though she hadn't admitted to him that she'd been sleeping with Harry, Peter had, of course, known all along, had predicted the affair's demise. He had come from his apartment into town to take her to breakfast and to have a long walk and talk with her in the hills surrounding St Albas. He had listened to her cry and berate herself for stupidity and berate Harry for his betrayal and still he had never once said the words "I told you so"—a fact Julie neither noticed nor appreciated. Peter was used to it and was simply content now to see Julie smiling her old smile. He loved to see her happy and hated to see her sad. It was as simple as that.

He said:

"To what pleasure do I owe this unexpectedly pleasurable company?"

"Just happy."

"Something must account for that."

"I can't just be happy?"

"That's the trouble with you. No. You can't just."

"I think I met someone, Pete. I really do."

"Oh no. No. No. No."

"But Peter."

"I am not doing this again," he said, slapping his hand on the table. "No way. You. You cannot do this to me."

She cocked her head to the side with a grin on it, put a hand on his cheek.

"Who's my best friend?"

"Ugh," he moaned. "Who is it now? What boy are you going to allow to ruin our lives for six weeks this time?"

"He's directing the play I'm in."

"What a cliché."

"I know I haven't known him long, but he's handsome, and funny, and he actually seems like he isn't a jerk."

"Uh-huh. Does he have a girlfriend? Supermodel or otherwise?"

"I don't know," she said. "But I think he would have mentioned her, right? Guys like to do that."

"Not all of them. Can we remember that not all of them like to immediately mention their girlfriends, and that sometimes you find out from a wipe board that they exist, and then you are eventually humiliated in front of hundreds of people."

"I guess I deserve that."

"If he's a St Albas student, you might guess that it's a terrible idea."

"What's that supposed to mean?"

"We graduate in half a year. Wait to find some real men. Move to Chicago or London or wherever you want to go, and date someone who isn't a boy."

"I don't want to talk about next year. Not until next semester."

Peter rubbed his eyebrows with his fingers.

"Not until next semester when it's too late."

"It won't be."

"Thinking about who you're going to be with doesn't make it all right not to think about who you're going to be or what you're going to do. It's a distraction."

"But he has a good heart, this one. I really think so. It's not a distraction either."

"How do you know?"

"I don't know it. I feel it."

"Did something happen with him yet? Have you...?"

"No. Nothing like that. We just talked tonight before rehearsal. It felt nice."

"One conversation. It felt nice," said Peter.

"Yes."

"What is this lucky fellow's name?"

"Max Wilke."

"Oh Julie," said Peter, his head sinking onto the bar. "Are you joking?"

"What?"

"Do you remember my cousin, Catriona?"

"Yes," she said, a sick feeling growing in her stomach. "What?"

"Do you remember what her boyfriend's name is?"

"Shit," she said, her heart completely sunk into her back. "Can we forget everything I just said?"

"I think we'd better," said Peter.

"You won't say anything to Catriona or to Max?"

"Don't be ridiculous," he said, imagining the major drama that would ensue if he breathed a word in this direction. It was then he began to put the pieces together: Julie had slept with Harry. Harry was dating Vera. Vera was living with Catriona. He racked his brain: did Julie have a way of finding out that Vera and Catriona were friends? Might Vera tell Catriona that Julie was the perpetrator, leaving him exposed to long lectures on propriety? He could only hope that Vera's circle was too elite and that Catriona's was too insular for that news to travel. He had no way of proving that he hadn't known about Vera. He must hope Julie would believe him if she did find out. But what could he have done to stop her from sleeping with Harry even if he had *known* known and not just suspected?

This was the way one's mind had to work in order to sidestep social landmines in St Albas. Preparing for every possible fallout scenario and understanding the near-scientifically accurate rumblings of earthquakes in one's social circle required logic and a stockpile of excuses.

And that was before he even thought about the ring. He

remembered how Julie had a way of getting under people's skin, of making boys like Max feel like men. And she would be in close quarters with Max for a few weeks…

He could see that Julie was sad again, and it made him sad. Still, the appeal to reason had to be made if she had any chance of a happy finish at St Albas. If any of them had a chance of a happy finish at St Albas.

"Please, Julie, for my sake, I beg you—leave it alone. For once, just leave it alone."

"I will, Peter. You're right. I promise."

"You're enough on your own, you know. You really, really are."

"I don't know."

"I know," he said. "But I'm telling you, it's time to think about next year. No one else is going to solve it."

"Okay."

"That's my girl," he said. "Are you hungry?"

She stayed behind for another drink after Peter had gone home for a phone date with his girlfriend in Warwickshire. Even the bartenders, strangely maternal in their aprons, avoided her. As if the sadness smelt, and it was contagious.

# XVII. DECEMBER

**A FEW WEEKS LATER, MAX PUT** on a new tie for opening (and, incidentally, closing) night. It wasn't exactly new, but it was new to him. He'd purchased it at the charity shop that afternoon in a rare burst of enthusiasm for material things. While usually it took a mandate from Catriona or his mother to make Max even consider shopping, if he did it on his own it was a result of both necessity and impulse. Max always waited until the very last moment of a decision to actually act upon it.

Standing in front of Catriona's mirror, he realized he had no idea how to tie it. Not wishing to disturb her as she put her makeup on (it always made him nervous to watch girls sticking things near their eyes), he made several clumsy and ultimately frustrating attempts at doing it himself.

"Fuck. *Fuck.* Do you know how to do this?"

"Yes," she said, continuing to apply her mascara with her mouth shut. She didn't like responding in a positive manner to such foul language.

"Can you help me?"

Catriona put down the makeup. She had always liked to help her father tie his ties in the mornings before church. She took both ends in her hands, wrapping them around one another:

"Fatty over thinny, fatty round again, fatty through the keyhole, fatty down the drain," she recited.

"That's not very nice," said Max playfully.

"It helps me remember," she said, zipping herself into her dress and walking away. It was a trick that Catriona could pull off that would have left other women in a heap on the floor. "Would you like me to wait for you after, or shall I go straight to your flat?"

"If you could run by the grocery store for snacks and things, and then to mine, I would really appreciate it."

"Of course. Did you remember to put some tickets aside?"

"Yes."

"Good. I told Simon he could have the other one, if that's all right."

"Perfect. I'm glad you won't have to watch alone," he said.

Max was done dressing himself.

"How do I look?" he asked, with open arms.

"Good," said Catriona, who always spoke objectively on the matter. "It's getting late. You'd better go. I'll see you after."

On the way to the theatre, Max ran through a mental checklist. He had too little experience to know whether he had done everything he should, having had no experience at all of an event such as opening night. In his pocket, there were the house keys and his phone, which jockeyed against one another jovially as he strode toward the Noble. He hoped that was all he needed. It was all out of his hands now anyway. That much he realized. Fern would take care of it all. She had been at the theatre since the morning, putting final touches on the lighting and the set and making him promise not to come by.

"You'll only get in the way," she'd said. "I love you, but you're a great oaf."

A girl cut in front of him on the sidewalk a few feet ahead. Her hair bounced wildly as she walked buoyantly down the street. He wondered what the curls trapped under her green knit hat were thinking. He recognized the ringlets immediately, and they looked less sad than they had in rehearsal. Perhaps they were happy since it was opening night.

Max had hardly spoken to Julie throughout the rehearsal process, except for their first conversation together in the Noble before the rest of the cast had arrived. The time when she had touched him on the arm after he made her laugh as they sat next to each other in the empty audience. He had gone to the next rehearsal a little early, hoping that she would be there early too. And he had gone to the rehearsal after that a little early. And the next and the next. He began to go early even though she didn't, not because he thought she would, but because he hoped it.

He found in his wanderings of mind during those dark, frigid weeks that Julie seemed to keep appearing in it, and that it was pleasant and warm when she did. She appeared as he read Kant and Arendt. She appeared as he thought about just war and welfare and The Rights of Nations. He would go along, studying away, and suddenly there was Julie in his imagination, lovely and kind and funny and full of all good qualities that she may not even possess. It didn't matter if Catriona was sitting next to him or if she was across the street. Catriona had never existed in his head like this. She had only ever existed before his eyes.

And anyway, it didn't matter. Julie arrived with the rest of the cast for each of their rehearsals and did not look him in the eye when she did. She seemed to make a point of not speaking with him or anyone else. It was silly to think that someone like Julie would ever be interested in him, anyway, he had thought. But her silence only seemed to intrigue him more.

Max felt a desire for Julie and could not define it further than that. It was not a grand, sweeping desire because grand and sweeping desires were brave in a way that Max was not. But he felt the desire to make a space for her under his arm, to which she could always return if she wanted to be there. Even if he didn't know much about her.

Walking down Sea Street to the Noble at present, he was undecided as to whether or not to catch up with her, to try to have a moment alone, to see if it made a difference in her demeanor. But good God was he nervous to talk to her, now that they hadn't talked. He had spent so many hours thinking of her, of wondering about her. Action seemed impossible.

If Max had been a more intuitive boy, he would have realized that his friend Simon would have been one to understand, and perhaps this kind of realization would have caused him to act and to change all their futures for the better. But he wasn't, and he didn't.

In the time it took him to think about intercepting her or not, Julie had already entered the stage door and was fighting her way through the busying hall.

He passed her wordlessly at her table as he entered the brightly lit dressing room. He caught her flushed face in the mirror as she sat and thought with dread that tonight might be his last chance to—

*To what?* Said the voice in his head. *To what? Sweep Julie Lovejoy off her feet? What, with your incredible charm? Your confidence? Your devastating, good looks?*

*I don't know,* thought Max.

*Exactly,* said the voice.

The lights had been turned on above the mirrors. The actors

stood in front of them, painting their faces and talking energetically to one another, though they always kept their eyes on themselves. A particularly voluptuous actress powdered her bosom. The skinny, Scottish leading man said "hello" to Max very warmly, knowing that this was his first opening. The radio had been turned to the classical station, where *Rhapsody in Blue* was cranked up absurdly, sounding slightly square as it was being played by an orchestra from London.

Julie took off her coat, a motion that revealed the stretchy, black top and tight, dark leggings that formed the basis of her Witch costume. It was not so complicated: she had to only smear some makeup the color of clovers on her cheeks, put on a ratty, white wig that had been recently relieved of its job of collecting mothballs, and throw an elaborate quilted shawl around her midsection. The rest of the transformation was left to her own discretion and to the whims of the character she had nursed into being. Having no interest in chatting with the rest of the cast, whom she considered nice enough but whom she had to ignore if she was going to ignore Max, she applied her makeup efficiently and walked back into the hallway with *Mrs. Dalloway* in her hand, headed for the stage.

The stage was dark and bare: that's how Max had wanted it. The curtains hung limp and thick like slices of heavy prosciutto. Out there, the boards creaked because of nothing, perhaps doing their own preparations, stretching and settling, anticipating the weight of performers and sets and props. A blue light, hung some twenty feet above the stage, spread hushed gloom through the air. Julie walked to the center of the stage, where she sat cross-legged, the book in her lap. The floor was cool beneath her. She ran her palms out behind her, reclining her entire body, staring up. There were all the heavy lights and wires, the things she had never understood. Where all the real tricks happened, ignited by the push of a technician's thumb against a button. Not unlike the mayor's wife at Christmastime, with the lights and all.

She could hear them in the dressing room. Someone had brought the *Avenue Q* soundtrack. It was all very typical.

She sighed, hugged *Mrs. Dalloway* to her chest. It had been a difficult couple of weeks. It had been a difficult end to the semester. But she guessed that she had to grow up sometime, and maybe growing up meant you no longer got the things you wanted. Maybe Peter was right: the serious future was coming. The fun ended. Was that what he'd meant? That the fun ended? That's what it felt like.

The universe was conspiring against her. First the nonsense with Harry, now the nonsense with her silly, stupid crush on Max. Besides all that, Professor Harris's disappointed stares during lecture were weighing on her heavily, diligent though she had been in making attempts in recent weeks to actually come prepared to class and to participate when she was there.

She had to push that man and those boys out of her mind for now. She just had to get through the performance. Then she would see her friends, and everything would all be all right. She inhaled deeply, feeling the book sink into her and rise up with her breath. That's when she heard the footsteps. They were long feet. Stubborn, gentle, anxious, leathery steps. The steps stopped. Julie sat up and found Max was there.

"Are you all right?" she asked.

"What!" Max jumped. "Holy shit!"

"I'm sorry. Didn't mean to scare you."

"No! No. No, I'm fine. Didn't see you there is all."

He was breathless, trying not to clutch the organ that beat erratically below his left lapel. Julie laughed in spite of herself. She put a hand on his shoe and shook it.

"It's going to be fine," she said. "It's ready for an audience. You've done a wonderful job."

"Really?"

"Really."

She grinned at him.

*What the hell,* she thought. *It's the last time I'll ever talk to you. I can smile.*

"Everyone will love it," she said.

He couldn't quite meet her gaze. This was because he was thinking again about that space under his arm, and Julie in it.

"Yeah. We'll see," he said, the nerves evident in his voice.

The curtain ruffled. Fern was there dressed in the same all-black clothing she had worn since the beginning of technical rehearsals earlier in the week, a fact that made her feel as though she had earned the right not to shower merely because she had to smell her own filth more than anyone else as she sat alone in the tech booth.

"Max, I'm about to open the house. Better get off the stage. Want to go tell your cast they'd better pipe down?"

Fern noticed Julie there, staring up at Max.

"You know, just forget it, mate. I'll do it."

She marched off into the hallway.

"Fern is the best," said Julie.

"We live together," said Max. "She's my best friend."

"She's been really helpful this week. I like her."

"She is cool."

They sat quietly for a moment.

"I think I'd better go rally the troops," said Max.

"I suppose that includes me."

"It does."

"I'll come with you," said Julie.

Max extended a hand to help her off of the floor.

***

Catriona and Simon met inside the foyer to collect the tickets Max had put aside for them. As one might imagine, Simon was rather looking forward to spending some time in the dark next to Catriona, so close that he could smell her perfume—close enough to touch her leg with his if he was brave enough to make the mistake. After exchanging pleasantries and getting their tickets, they entered the auditorium together. The curtain had already risen to reveal the blank stage and the blue light, and the lights in the audience were dimmed. They struggled into their seats in the awkward way of people who are trying to cut in a queue at airport security because they have spent rather too long having lunch before their flight.

By the time they found their seats, most of the audience was already absorbed in pre-performance chatter. Professors, townspeople, students—there they all were in their tweed and pearls, making believe that they were in a center of civilization about to see a proper show. Perhaps you couldn't blame them, and perhaps this was a more virtuous sort of entertainment than the fashion shows for Bangladesh and balls for AIDS orphans in that it did not purport itself to be anything more than what it was. Any misconceptions as to the purpose of the event or its contents were solely on the side of the participants, not the creators.

Many of Julie's friends had shown. Among them were Neve and Helen, absorbed in the dramaturgical notes and reading through them at the same rate; Ashwin and Caddy, complimenting one another on their mutual good taste because they had brought Julie the same bottle of champagne. Strangely, Ruth wasn't present though she had said she would be. And Brett and Anastasia were already in the Seychelles celebrating Christmas with his family. But Larry had come and was sitting beside Neve and Helen. Since he had taken care of Julie after the incident with Harry at the fashion show, they had decided that perhaps this hulking, American boy had more to him than what met the eye.

Most importantly, Peter sat proudly with the rest of them. A bunch of slightly wilting flowers he had run out for just as the florist closed lay at his feet. He spotted Catriona several rows ahead. He considered saying hello just as the lights faded to black completely.

It began.

Up in the tech booth, Max observed his hard work: the actors, the audience, everything that surrounded them. He was surprised to find that, though he was nervous, he was also very pleased. He had accomplished something of which he never would have thought himself capable. He had done something—not just thought of doing it. He always thought he had good taste in these sorts of things—that is, theatre, art, music. But piecing it together from nothing, making it actually *happen*, why, that was something. Lost in his own thoughts, he barely noticed when the lights came up for intermission.

"Hellooooo," said Fern. "Are you comin' down?"

"Nah," said Max. "I think I'll stay up here."

"Suit yourself," she said, clapping him on the shoulder. "Going to go refill my water and have a quick chat with the backstage crew. I hope you're happy with it. It looks quite good, doesn't it?"

He nodded. Fern descended the ladder out of the room, closing the trapdoor behind her. Now he was alone, watching them all. Catriona and Simon were standing together, talking. His feet were spread wide, belly turned toward her in a subconscious suggestion. Catriona stood with her pointed chin in the air, giving Simon the courtesy of a smile every now and again. The superiority suggested in those folded arms was upgraded to snobbery with every deepening of the folded creases in the elbows of her Burberry jacket. Peter made his way toward them, revealing the flowers below his chair. Max wondered who they were for; certainly, the vibrant selection of wildflowers was not for him. They must be for one of the girls in the cast. Didn't he have a girlfriend in Warwickshire? The dull roar of conversation came in waves at the glass windows before him, seeping in through the cracks and disrupting the quiet. He scarcely knew what was happening before Fern was squeezing behind him again, taking her seat at the switchboards and putting her headset on.

"Ready?" she said. "It's almost time."

"Right. Yeah, ready."

Fern reached for the walkie-talkie that she kept in the pocket of her worn-out jeans. She noticed the distraction in Max's face but did not mind it. What others thought of as aloofness in Max she had always known to be contemplation, amusement, or confusion.

The walkie-talkie beeped.

"We're all set up here. Is everyone in places?"

"Yes," said a voice on the other end.

The lights in the theatre dimmed. Catriona made a hushing noise. Soon, others were hushing too, and within twenty seconds the entire room had gone quiet like a fire with a wet blanket laid on top of it.

Backstage, Julie was standing in the wing from which she would make her entrance. She rolled her head back and forth a few times. She stretched her mouth, making a large, hallow "O" with her lips. She yawned. She could never decide whether it was better or worse to try and run through her lines immediately before going on stage. The intermission music faded. Through the cracks in the black drapes, she could see the audience: someone scratching her leg, someone turning her phone off, someone adjusting the flowers under his seat. Then, the lights came up, an eerie green.

Julie saw the set transform into something real: a foreign environment, a forest, in this case. Her gifts of over-imagination were so useful when she acted. She had rehearsed these very words and deeds in this space for many weeks leading up to this moment and hadn't felt it was quite as real as it would be during the actual performance, and now, here it was transformed. Whether the metamorphosis was more profound from her perspective or the audience's, she could not know. All she knew was that the gaze of the onlookers altered everything. There was a new urgency to get the make-believe right.

The light helped. It made the huge swaths of ragged fabric look more like a Black Forest swamp. So did the music, a composition of flutes that sounded like deadly birds and basses that croaked like bullfrogs. At the opposite side of the stage, a smoke machine gushed a mushy fog that choked Julie's senses. And so, when she entered into the audience's view, she became a witch:

*Vile creatures of the night,*
*Gather ye here to this monstrous glen!*
*Leave off the pursuit*
*Of thy beastly appetites:*
*Heed your mistress' bellowing summons.*
*Owl and mole,*
*Bear and hawk,*
*How passionately she beseeches you.*
*For, in this forest,*
*Under Venus' watch,*
*An avowal of love*
*Tonight must be stopp'd!*

In the audience, Catriona sat back in her seat. What an odd girl, up there on display. She looked familiar. She waved her hands around, perhaps rather too much. Still, she was scary, wasn't she? She stole a glance around her. No one was moving. Simon was leaning forward. The audience, it seemed, had heeded the Witch's call. Perhaps she had underestimated Max. The casting was really quite good.

\*\*\*

After the show was over, the actors, the tech crew, and the audience gathered in the Noble's narrow foyer. The actors were sweaty, the tech crew exhausted, and the audience ready for a drink after sitting through two hours of heavy drama performed by amateurs. In spite of all this, the unique elation that follows a show permeated the air.

Julie came into the crowd, her green makeup mostly, but not wholly, wiped from her face. She greeted her friends. Hearing their compliments made her surprisingly shy, and it was difficult to make her shy. There they were, standing around in a circle with their coats on. Several of them had their hands behind their backs, ready to display the cards, the flowers, the champagne.

"You were wonderful!"

"Love the makeup. Green is very you."

"Hey, Julie, we always knew you were a huge witch."

"Shut up, Ashwin. Jay, you were amazing."

"You stole the show."

"Can I have your autograph?"

Hugs and thanks were exchanged as quickly as shares in the stock market just a few months before and with as much apparent self-importance. People started to filter out of the foyer and into the chilly Scottish night, moving in flocks to the pubs. Peter, having given his congratulations to Max, crossed the room to Julie. He was relieved to see that she was not talking to Max.

"Well done. Another outstanding performance," he said, embracing her.

"Thank you."

"A small token of my audience-member appreciation."

He handed her the flowers. Julie's green-tinged face shuttled into an instant smile.

"Thanks!" she said, putting her arms around him tightly and kissing both of his cheeks. "I love them."

Across the room, Catriona watched as her cousin spoke to his friend. Who cared about the silly grocery store. That could be done in a moment, after she watched Peter with that girl, Julie. She had told Peter that it wasn't proper to have a girl friend like that. Not when he had a girlfriend. Clearly, he didn't care what she thought. In what might as well have been the light of day, Julie was openly warm and affectionate with Peter, smelling the flowers and extending them around the group. The blonde curls, the big eyes, the way she had kissed him on each cheek. Catriona pitied Peter's girlfriend in Warwickshire but reminded herself that at least Julie was expending her wiles on some other girl's boyfriend. It was every woman for her self, after all. There could be no teamwork or sense of solidarity, nor should there be. Not with so few quality husbands to claim. Which reminded her to remind Peter how important it was to find a loyal spouse, not a flighty one.

When she turned to say something to Max, he was gone.

He had recognized the flowers and had watched Julie and Peter embrace.

# XVIII.

**AFTER SEVERAL CELEBRATORY AND CONGRATULATORY DRINKS** with her admirers, Julie was tipsy and tired. As she walked along Fair Street past the pubs and shops, she imagined some book or article, half-read rather than unread, wallowing on her desk. It needed tending to. Professor Harris and his things needed tending to. For a moment, she considered going home, picking some dirty pajamas out of the hamper, turning her iPod on, and trying to sober up to do some work.

But her cell phone buzzed in her pocket, and she looked down to find a text from an unfamiliar number:

> You have to come to the cast party.
> No excuses. 5E Sea Street.

She took this as a sign from the gods that she should have more fun after all. So, she changed routes and soon ascended the stairs to Max's apartment on Sea Street, where he'd said the party would be.

Having arrived at the top landing with all her facial and dental assets intact, she took a moment to steady herself. The people inside were not used to party-time Julie. They didn't know much about her. But she felt it important to see Max—just one more time, just out of curiosity. At least that's what the center of gravity near her belly button told her. And so she resolved to let her hair down and be sociable. In her drunken mind, she thought Peter would forgive her anything. Certainly he would forgive her a short conversation with Max, and that was all this would probably lead to.

Her knuckles had hardly made a sound against the door when the top of Max's soft, blond hair appeared in the circular window above it. He opened the door, tilted himself into the gap there and, smiling at what he found, opened it wider.

"Julie Lovejoy, I presume? Come in."

He had had a bit too much drink. The red in his cheeks told her so.

"Thanks," she said.

She kicked her shoes off sloppily. Max noticed, liked it, and didn't move them to the side even though he knew it was bound to get on Catriona's nerves.

"Can I get you something to drink?"

"No, I'm here to sober up."

He looked at her skeptically.

"Are you sure? Because if you aren't sure, I will keep offering throughout the night."

"I'm sure."

"Whatever you say."

With this, Max turned into the kitchen. He was absolutely astonished that Julie had shown up and had shown up without Peter. He made a mental note to send happy thoughts to that girl in Warwickshire, who had most likely called him home. With this impediment removed, perhaps he could find a way to situate himself next to her without making it look like that was what he was doing or what he wanted. His last chance had turned into a second last chance. Now he couldn't screw it up.

Catriona was there by the window at the sink, pouring candies into the ugly plastic bowls that had been at Martyrs Monday too.

"You don't have to do that," Max said.

She didn't respond, except to smile. She hated it when Max drank. You could never tell what drunken people would do. They were hard to control.

"I'm going to go back in the other room if you don't need anything."

"Of course. It's wonderful."

In the living room, Julie was sitting next to Fern, and the two were laughing loudly. He couldn't help but think how different Julie and Catriona seemed. He wanted dearly to know, to be certain about, just how different.

He felt his heart deflate slightly as he reminded himself that she was Peter's friend. A close friend, by how it had looked. Maybe she even loved him, even though he had a girlfriend. Julie, so alternately warm and cold and hard to pinpoint, seemed like a girl who could love someone with a girlfriend. Who could have an affair. But Peter wasn't that sort of person.

*And neither are you,* said the voice.

*I'm not,* said Max to himself. *I could never do that. It wouldn't be right. I wouldn't want everyone to go around doing that, all the time. So neither should I.*

"I love Harrison Ford," Julie was saying to Fern. "I would kill for Harrison Ford."

"I know exactly what you mean. He is only the fittest man on the planet."

"I don't understand Luke Skywalker people."

"I know, right? How far up your arse does your head have to be for you to be a Luke Skywalker person?"

"They're all the same. And they're all Ashley Wilkes people."

"Exactly. And Mr. Bingley people."

"So true!"

Seeing Max hovering nearby, Fern pulled up a chair on Julie's side.

"Have a seat, mate," she called to him.

Julie nodded in agreement. As he came over, Max noticed with happy anticipation that Fern had succeeded in talking Julie into a glass of red wine. So he sat, and he listened to Julie, listened to her asking Fern questions about geology, about lighting design, about where she came from. Eventually, Fern stood. Her plan had worked. The text to Julie had been hers.

"That's enough about me. Max'll have to ask you about yourself while I go out for a cigarette."

"Don't leave," said Julie.

"I'll be right back," she said. "You're both intelligent individuals. You'll find something to talk about."

Julie sat there drunkenly, looking at Max. She had been doing this for weeks, and for weeks she had a near-perfect record of keeping her distance, but that was with the vital clarity of sobriety. Other than her transgressions tonight, she had been careful; she had been prepared. There was little exchanged between them but the hellos and goodbyes that made interacting with someone polite. But this situation, with the addition of wine, was too tempting. She should leave. Really, she should. She should tell him goodnight and leave.

But she opened her mouth instead.

"So, where are you from?" she asked. "I never know where you're from."

"Switzerland," he said.

"Where exactly?"

"Zurich."

"You know, I really couldn't tell. Your accent is weird."

"I did a year of high school in New York. That's where I got fluent. International school, lots of crazy accents."

"No kidding," she said, taking another gulp of wine.

"Makes sense, huh?"

"Yeah. Do you say 'dahling' instead of 'darling?' "

"Yes, dahling."

Her glass of wine was nearly empty. Julie couldn't help smiling to herself. She looked down into the shaded circles of red where the wine had been and did not speak.

Max could tell that she was on the verge of something, perhaps going home. It made him sad. He wished he could think of something else to say to make her stay and talk to him. Julie couldn't go home, he reminded himself. This was his second last chance. And she looked too beautiful to go home, even with the remainder of the green makeup creeping in the shadows of her cheeks, in the hollows of her eyes.

"You shouldn't go home yet," he said.

"It's getting late."

"I think you should stay and have fun."

"You do?"

"Yeah. I do."

Max had done two whole things in one day. He had directed a play and asked Julie to stay at his party. He was shocked at himself.

*Here he is, looking at me,* Julie thought. There was something about him that told her he had some kind of a role to play in her life, just like there had been with Harry. Something substantial. She'd thought the universe had put an end to that because of Peter and her love for him and because of Peter's love for Catriona and the explosive chain reactions these loves might set off when combined with the possibility of something between her and Max. But Max was asking her to stay. He did not want whatever was supposed to happen to never happen either.

But Julie too noticed Catriona standing there now plain as day in the doorway of the kitchen, speaking to no one, refilling the snacks like a dutiful, hired, minimum-wage employee. Not speaking to anyone, not since that other boy, the one with the bright red hair,

had left. There was something odd about Catriona. Maybe Peter
knew it. It wasn't apparent, perhaps, unless you paid attention to
people the way Julie did when she felt like it. Catriona had all the
right clothes. She had the Barbour jacket and the Hunters. She had
the shoulder-length hair and the clip that pulled it all into a faux-
Gibson Girl pouf. There was the long, prodding chin and the high
forehead. She had come from farmers, probably, gentleman farmers
and their fat, biscuit-privileged country wives. That much was
apparent in the big wrists, the sturdy ankles. The small eyes and the
large nose. She found herself judging Max rather harshly. What
could he have been thinking in dating someone like that? Someone
who stands in the kitchen, not talking to anyone?

Could they be happy, Catriona and Max? She indulged herself in
the wondering for a moment, and then did not indulge Catriona's
glare as she sat next to Max for the next hour. Other people came
and sat and talked to Max and Julie, but after ten minutes or so they
moved on. Perhaps they became aware that there could be
something starting here, something momentous, that they were not
an essential part of. They could smell it like the middle, low, and
finishing notes of the wine they were drinking.

As the length of their conversations increased and the bottle of
red between them became more and more deprived of its original
depths, Julie began to realize in full the ire with which she was being
stared at. Catriona hadn't moved. Now nearly statuesque, her
position in the doorway of the kitchen had remained unaltered. Julie
watched Catriona's figure, reflected in the window. Julie scanned the
room. The snack bowls were running low. But still, Catriona did not
move, for that purpose or any other. Julie began to feel less brave,
as if she were being marked. The owl eyes bore into the side of her
face.

Max, however, seemed oblivious, unbothered. If he could tell that
Catriona was seething, he couldn't or wouldn't show it. He sat there,
refilling the wine, asking her more about how she felt about theatre,
politics, art, the best kebobs to be found in St Albas, where she had
been on the Continent, which of those Virginia Woolf novels she
was reading next. He was delighted to be hosting a party, to be
hosting Julie.

And yet another hour later, when another half bottle of wine was
gone and echoes of future lectures on propriety from Peter began to

ring in her ears, Julie pronounced with profound delicacy her desire to use the ladies' room.

"Where is it?"

"Just back through there," he said, pointing toward the hallway. "First door on the left. Hurry back."

Julie stood carefully, tipsy as she was. Catriona's eyes followed Julie's movements with deliberate interest as she got up to pass the kitchen door. How someone dared to be that forward, she did not know. It had something to do with being American, she was sure.

And there Max sat, quite aware that Catriona was watching. He made eye contact with her, knowing she was miserable and humiliated, leaning against the doorframe as people squeezed past on their way to and from the bathroom. *He thinks he is so innocent,* thought Catriona. *He'll tell me I'm being too sensitive. And he's right, of course. It is my fault that much is for sure. I've eaten too many cupcakes. My waist is inching out again. I shouldn't eat. I am too fat already. Worthless. I can never do anything right.*

*But that isn't it. Max started dating me when I was even uglier than I am now. It's because I haven't told him what he needs to do. I haven't told him plainly what I expect from him. For too long,* she thought, *I have kept quiet. I have implied rather than told. And what has it got me?*

People had to get married. She must get married. Or else, what had it all been for? The makeup done not so much to imply womanhood but more so to imply potential as a wife, *that* was all in vain. A nice little wife with a nice little gallery of her own. If not, what had the Barbour jacket been for? The one that implied she was a bloom of the English countryside, who valued the land and gardens and horses and family values. Who wanted to sit in a garden and drink Pimms with her fingernail-painted pinkie out. Who would smile selectively at china patterns and the shapes of clouds, who would bear children and sit at home nursing them and being the wife to a respectable man.

And then, of course, there was the biggest gamble of all. She remembered the day as if it were this one. A sleepy, shivery, November afternoon. Most everyone had already gone home for the Autumn holidays. Peter had something to do—who remembered what—that had prevented him from driving back home to Lancashire with his cousin. She wondered what would have happened if the library hadn't been shut.

Max wasn't flying out until early the next morning. They had time to kill. She had already packed her suitcase. He never packed until the last minute. They had a beautiful day, walking along the coast, talking, seeing the flowers on the hill wither and die, the yellows turning to oranges and browns, the green turning to grey. With flushed cheeks and cold skin, they returned to her room. He put the kettle on.

"Would you like some tea? You look cold," he said.

"That sounds lovely," she said.

The kettle boiled. She seated herself on the bed.

Though they had known each other for only two months, they were very serious about their future together. Catriona knew this because they ate dinner together every night and sipped chamomile tea like this in the evenings, just like her parents did. They had done things she knew were wrong because Father Tom had referenced them in no uncertain terms. Still, the final thing had not been done. She was determined not to until they were married, even if it took years. Her mother had warned her all about buying cows and free milk and the diabolical intentions of young men.

Outside, the trees swayed in the wind, their branches gently tapping the elegant red brick building. Leaves twirled to and from the ground in natural arpeggio. Max turned around with two cups of tea. He gave one to her and put the other on the nightstand.

"I'll miss you when you're gone," he said, sitting on the bed and putting his arm around her lower back.

"You will?" she said.

"I wanted you to know before you go. I wanted to let you know I love you."

"What?" she said, clutching her tea and scalding her hands in the process.

"I love you."

No one had ever told her this before. She immediately wondered how he could think such a thing, how he could overlook so many flaws. Then it struck her: he didn't know. They had been together a month. He saw what she had wanted him to see: someone whose thoughts were in order, someone who hung her bras in the shower to drip dry and always made outlines for her papers before writing them. A feeling of dread slowly filled her from bottom to top, as if she had just been locked in a chamber where water was dripping.

She would drown to death, eventually, slowly. Someday, he might find out that she was not perfect. He might find out about George and it being her fault and the eating and the scars.

But he didn't have to. Not if she was careful…

As Max's hand took the teacup away and opened the front of her shirt and the front of her trousers; she tried her best to relax. *This is supposed to be enjoyable*, she thought. *If I'm going to break the rules, then I may as well try to find pleasure in it.* After all, hadn't she wanted this? She had wanted Max, at least. She had asserted herself after dinner in the dining hall, making a point to get up the courage to talk to him. She had found out his name and made sure to laugh at everything he said.

He was handsome, in his way: tall and blond with those big, blue eyes. He never overdressed, but that she could change. People liked him well enough. In the gossip-filled goings-on of the first month of first term, she had never heard a bad word spoken of him. Besides all that, he was studying finance or something. Economics or something. That she had heard. Vera Morgan, the only girl she had really befriended in St Albas, had found it out for her.

The next morning when Peter came for her, she wasn't a virgin any more. She hoped her mother, her aunt, her grandmother—she hoped none of them would be able to tell. The guilt was consuming.

And so now, having given him this gift, she must marry him. Catholic or not, he would stand at the front of the church and wait for her. There was no other way to do these things. These things had prices. He had wanted her virginity; he had got it. And now his job was to marry her and give her children and live in Lancashire or somewhere like it and very well be happy about it. He would bring her mother flowers on Mother's Day and call her father "Father."

Still, the sneaking suspicion that she was unworthy had never completely gone. Nor had her guilt about having slept with Max. She realized gradually that Max did not necessarily think people should only sleep with one person, and it made her frantic.

But try as she might, she could not let her inadequacy and guilt dictate her thoughts on Max entirely, especially when they told her that Max was trouble, that he should be punished, but that having her children and being her husband should not be thought of as this punishment. It was an honor. It should be. But why, then, didn't he think of it on his own? Why didn't he do anything to advance toward that inevitable future? Why didn't he come to Christmas in Lancashire or visit in the summer? The day of reckoning was coming. They would leave St Albas soon, and where would she go if she didn't know where he would go? How could she plan when he had no plans?

That things could turn out any other way than the way she anticipated was a complete shock. It was horrible to think of; it made her sick. What if he never proposed? What if he left her?

Simon would never do this to anyone.

When Julie had gone to the bathroom, Catriona moved toward Max.

"I think I'm going to leave," she said.

"Just have a seat," he said. "Talk with us."

"I'm a bit uncomfortable with everyone drunk."

"I'm not drunk. Just sit down. Please."

"No, thank you. I want to go home."

"What's the matter?"

"Please, tell me you're kidding."

"No," he said. "I'm not."

People were starting to notice the terseness in her manner. Even Max.

"I'm leaving," she said.

"At least let me walk you."

She turned around and strode angrily to the coat rack. Finding her Barbour, she put it on quickly and turned the door handle. She was outside on the landing before Max had time to get his shoes on properly. She started down the stairs, angrily stomping, not caring about her weight as it clopped around her knees. Max was in pursuit, taking the stairs in uneven sets of ones and twos and threes. He caught up with her on the sidewalk.

"What's the matter?" he asked, panting with the effort of chasing her. Never having experienced this kind of behavior from her outright, it unnerved him. "I thought you were having a good time."

They were walking down Sea Street at a steady pace. Her cheeks grew pale.

"A good time? You've neglected me the entire evening."

"I'm trying to be a good host."

"I'm sure you've convinced that girl that you are."

"Are you kidding me? She doesn't know anyone. I'm being polite. To your cousin's friend, by the way."

"Considering the fact that I'm rather sure she is trying to get to

Peter as well, her status as his 'friend' doesn't do much to calm my nerves."

"You are being completely unreasonable."

"Oh, that's me. 'Unreasonable.' When you sit next to another girl the entire evening, how is it you suggest I feel, Max?"

"I love you," he said, in the toneless voice of a mantra-sayer. "And if you don't know that by now, you're insane."

"I'm insane?"

"You're acting like it."

"If I'm insane, it's because you've made me insane."

"I've made you insane?"

"Yes?"

"How? How, Catriona?"

Catriona's eyes searched the air for answers. Finding none written clearly there, she said what was in her gut, messy and stinking and true:

"When are you going to ask me to marry you?"

Everything in the world paused.

"What?"

"Yes. When are you going to ask me?"

"I'm twenty-two years old, Catriona."

"You're not a child."

"I'm not old enough to get married yet."

"We'd wait. We would wait for a few years."

Max was silent. Catriona did not relent.

"I don't mean about the ring, necessarily. Though that would be nice. I just mean—when are we going to plan together? When are we going to talk about the future? Where are we going next year?"

"That's not a discussion for now."

"It's never a discussion for now, Max!"

"Wow."

"Make up your mind. Do you want me?"

"Yes."

"Forever?"

"Yes," Max said, and for the first time he began to realize it was a reflex.

Catriona shook her head.

"I wish you'd prove it. I'm going home."

"Good."

They were standing there in the still. A square of smooth pavement, a blank page of sorts, divided them. Her chest was heaving. Too much had been forced out all at once. She felt a sort of altitude sickness. Lightheaded, she sighed, but said nothing. Max looked at her with an amount of skepticism she had never seen before. This was not what he had pictured when he pictured an easy, quiet remainder of the year. What had gotten into her?

"I'll call you in the morning, then," he said without moving toward or away from her.

She nodded, folding her arms in front of her chest.

"Max," she said, quietly. "I'm sorry."

"It's okay. You're tired."

"I didn't mean to ruin your night. I know it's important to you."

Max looked up to the light coming from his living room window.

"You haven't. It's fine. But I have a house full of people," he said. He was coming toward her now. He kissed her on the forehead, where there was plenty of room. "I love you. I'll call you in the morning."

She nodded and headed toward Church Street alone.

***

Several hours later, Julie stood in Max's doorway. She was quite drunk on the wine. Everyone had gone some six or seven hours earlier—even Fern had excused herself to bed. She and Max had sat there on the hundred-year-old, creaking, cracking, wooden floorboards in his living room, eating bits of chocolate cake and finishing bottles of wine together. Though no one would have believed it, except perhaps for Fern, they talked and did nothing else the whole night through and into the morning too. Here it was, nearly nine o'clock in the morning.

Julie felt an extraordinary sadness as she put on her shoes. She wanted to take a broom to the situation, to sweep this night out the door with her, to let the seaside gales whisk the hours away onto the rocky beach, to see the remnants disappear into the water forever. Things that started out this good never ended well.

"Can't believe it's so late," he said.

"Late? More like early."

"I guess."

"Thanks for having me."

"Thanks for coming."

"All right."

"All right."

She opened the door, letting the morning in.

"Goodnight, Max."

"Goodnight, Julie."

When she had closed the door, Max stood on his tiptoes, watching her as she went. When he had returned to his normal altitude, he rested his forehead against the glass.

"Shit," he said to himself. "Holy shit."

Out the living room window, it had started to snow. He watched Julie making tracks and then disappearing. He shut the curtains. He took the wine-stained glasses and put them in the sink gently, treating them like relics. He went to his room, took off his jeans, and fell into his bed. He reached across it and opened the shoebox full of receipts on his bedside table. Inside, there was a little velvet box, containing the engagement ring from Peter.

He covered it back up and closed the drawer again.

"Shit."

He was very anxious and too excited to sleep.

# XIX.

**JULIE HAD ONLY JUST MADE IT** to the airport in Edinburgh. She hadn't packed until she had gotten home from Max's. She had been too excited to sleep at first, but when she'd awoken she was enormously crabby and couldn't shake the feeling that she'd end up regretting the previous night's events. She was anxious to get away from St Albas.

The taxi arrived at her house as she was fastening the straps inside her largest suitcase.

Caddy appeared groggily in the hallway.

"Need me to sit on that?"

Julie was struggling to close it.

"Yeah. Thanks."

"Where were you last night?"

"The cast party. Decided to go."

"Really? Until nine in the morning?"

"Yes. It was really fun. Can you sit without talking?"

"No."

Julie sighed.

"I should have known."

"And you're sure we're not backsliding with Harry?"

" 'We're?' What? No."

"Are you *sure*?"

"Yes. You know what, I don't think this is helping. Can you get off?"

"Somebody's testy."

"I'm sorry. I'm tired. And I just want to go home."

The taxi honked outside.

"No, I'm sorry. I'll go tell him you're coming."

"Thank you."

The ride to Edinburgh Airport was a nightmare. The roads were slippery. It seemed that the United Kingdom, for all its contributions and conquests throughout history, could not figure out how to remove snow from its own premises. *Two inches would never slow Chicago down*, thought Julie with contempt.

She was thankful to arrive at the gate just as they had begun boarding the plane. She held her boarding pass and passport in front of her, manically, exhausted. She could not lose it under any circumstances. This was her ticket to sanity, to a hug from her mother, her brother with his guitar, her father's whistling, and bedtime talks with her sisters.

She was determined not to tell her sisters about last night and Max though. It was nice, she kept telling herself. It was really incredible. But it could not happen again. The light of day and sobriety had restored her perspective: she could not touch Max with a ten-foot pole and a hazmat suit. Of course it would cause Peter to feel conflicted. Outraged, even, and betrayed. Why gamble the one reliable male relationship she had on this side of the Atlantic? She had already felt that she'd violated Peter's trust by sitting next to Max all night at that silly party. Now she had to pray that Catriona kept her mouth shut about it.

And of course there was the separate issue of Catriona. Apart from her being related to Peter, she was Max's girlfriend. Three years. Julie knew this. She would not inflict the depression and the hurt that Harry had inflicted upon her, and that she had inflicted upon herself, on another girl. Not any more than she would ever be one of those pathetic girls who wanted to get married at all costs rather than wanting to make a life for themselves. And she had, somehow, come dangerously close to becoming one in her four years at St Albas, never paying enough attention to who or what she wanted to be and chasing after boys instead. No more of that.

She had been repeating this pep talk to herself since she had woken up. As she packed her bags, as she said goodbye to Caddy, as she listened to the Christmas music the cab driver had on as they skidded all over the motorway. She was replaying it for the hundredth time as someone poked her on the shoulder at the boarding gate.

"Julie?"

She turned, and Ruth was there, holding hands with an attractive young man.

"Hello."

"Hi. This is—this is Clark."

"Oh," said Julie, trying to stop the shock from registering in her expression. She extended her arm tensely to shake his hand. *Fucking couples, man.* They were the worst. "Nice to meet you."

He smiled. Ruth said:

"I'm so sorry I missed your show last night."

"It's okay. You two must have had a lot to talk about."

"Yeah," she said, shaking her head and grinning. "So—you'll never guess what happened."

"Um, really? What?"

Ruth presented her left hand. It had grown something sparkly on the fourth finger.

"Can you believe it? Clark came over—all the way from Tennessee—yesterday night—and proposed."

Julie's face remained frozen in a stone-lipped smile.

"Wow!"

They both stood there, looking like those people in picture frames before you put a photo of your own in it. The kind you kind of wanted to punch: so young, happy-looking, meticulously groomed. And they clearly expected her to say something.

"Yeah! Wow! I guess that's a pretty good reason to skip the shitty play I was in! Congratulations."

She embraced Ruth.

"Congratulations, both of you."

"I just can't believe she said yes," said Clark. "I'm about the luckiest guy in the world."

He kissed Ruth tenderly on the hand. Julie looked forward to the barf bag that was sure to be in the seatback in front of her.

They were boarding the plane, making small talk as they waited in line until Ruth and Clark took their seats in first class.

"Have a good flight," she said, the crinkle of blatant falseness deepening in her nose. "And really, have a merry Christmas. Congratulations."

"It will be a blessed Christmas," said Ruth, looking into Clark's eyes. "Have a good trip home, Julie."

So there she sat, comically fussing over her seatbelt while Ruth buckled in up front in her spacious seat. The flight attendants began their rounds.

"And please be sure to turn off all electronic devices during takeoff. We will let you know when it is permissible to use these devices again."

It wasn't a bad idea. She clicked through her phonebook furiously.

Harry's number, along with the one Max had given her last night, both could use some deleting. She did so, turned the phone off, and hurled it into the depths of her purse with pure scorn.

She would not use it for another nine hours. Not until she was safely landed at O'Hare. And the boy on the other end—why, that would be a man, her father.

# PART TWO

"We're so different, you know:
she likes being good, and I like being happy."

—Edith Wharton, *The House of Mirth*

# I. CHRISTMAS

**EVERYWHERE, THE SNOW FELL. IT SETTLED** onto the curved steeple tops of Zurich. It battered the windows of Chicago, where Julie was sleeping through the night, snug in her flannel sheets as visions of sugarplums danced in her head. In St Albas, the golf course had frozen over, the bunkers and the greens frosted and the summer-crowded fairways now inhabited only by snowmen with seashell buttons.

In Lancashire, Catriona watched the flakes accumulating outside, blanketing the yellowed ground in a sheepskin of fluffy white. She was hanging ornaments on the tree in the crème-colored Christmas dress she had bought in town with her mother. It had long sleeves, a boat neck, a band of gold material under the chest. It was too tight in the stomach and suffocating in the shoulders. But they had both said it would do. Neither one had considered how uncomfortable it would make Catriona feel as she stretched her arms to the top of the tree, concerned about the welfare of the fabric.

She cursed Peter for deserting her this year. He and his parents were down at Warwick, staying with his girlfriend and her silly parents. They were all probably laughing and holding hands, walking through the country in their matching coats and getting on famously over crystal glasses filled with port. *Tra la la*, she thought spitefully.

Across the room, there was her grandmother, perched in the high-backed chair near the fire in her woolen suit and thick, grayish stockings. The large forehead and the pointed chin, with its fissured wrinkles and lack of smile lines, had been greatly affected by fifty years of marriage to the potato-faced man who talked more animatedly of livestock than he ever had of his wife. As if it were genetic, the same was happening, slowly, to her own mother. Catriona watched as Harriet Darlington-Welland passed her husband silently in the kitchen, reaching into the oven to bring out another batch of cookies. They were all the same freakishly calculated size. Her mother labored over such things for hours. Perhaps, Catriona thought, mutinously, it was because she would rather fret over cookies than over her husband's apathy. But this was what people did. They stayed together, no matter what.

She dipped her hand into the box of ornaments. They retained the smell of the dusty cardboard box in which they had been locked since the 6th of January last year. The red ones went on first, then the green, then silver. They must be placed evenly—they were all the same shape, and the tree's uneven branches must be accounted for. Her mother had ingrained the process in Catriona over the course of several years. Trimming the tree was a test of worth and obedience poorly disguised as a family tradition.

As she worked, she tried not to think of Max. Things had left off poorly, to say the least, before the holidays. The morning after the cast party and the terrible scene she had caused, she had met him at the Cathedral Café. There was a distinct disappointment in the way in which he looked at her over her tea, bordering on disgust. Neither brought up their argument. Max did not make promises about the future to reassure her, as she'd hoped he would. When he said goodbye to her at the bus station that night, he did not kiss her, and she supposed she deserved the unconvincing embrace she received in its place. When he did not call for three days after, she supposed she deserved the silence. When finally he called, she supposed she deserved the stilted, about-nothing conversation.

But that ended now. She deserved a Christmas gift and wishes for a happy Christmas. Boyfriends bought their girlfriends gifts. They called them to say happy Christmas, especially if they didn't come to visit. But he had not. He had not called this morning to say happy Christmas, and he had not given her a gift, though she had gone to the effort of giving him his in St Albas over breakfast in order to prompt him to do so in return. It had been excruciating, handing him the carefully selected watch and cologne and tie, when he had nothing to say to her and nothing to give in return.

Her grandmother and her mother had already asked what he had gotten for her. It was humiliating to tell them that it hadn't yet come, and the prospect of it never coming was too embarrassing to fathom. She wanted badly to get back to St Albas to sew Max and his shadow to her foot so they would stay there for good.

"Catriona," said her grandmother, "would you please come sit with me and not fuss with those ornaments."

"Of course," she said, putting a cock-eyed plaster Father Christmas down in the box.

"Well then," said the old woman, "how was the rest of your term?"

"It was lovely. Thank you for asking."

"Did you enjoy that stationery I sent you?"

"I did. Thank you."

"Such a sweet thank you note we got. And your handwriting is lovely."

Catriona nodded. She always tried with her penmanship when she wrote to her grandparents.

"Thank you, grandmother."

Her mother had come from the kitchen to finish Catriona's work. She was replacing ornaments, switching them to different positions, restringing lengths of popcorn.

"Such a pity Max couldn't join us for Christmas again," said her grandmother.

"It is," said Catriona. "He so wanted to come to see you and grandfather."

"I daresay, you'd better change whatever you're doing that's keeping him away."

She lowered her voice with great dignity.

"Young men, my girl, are greatly concerned with one thing and one thing only. I hope you haven't given up the one tool with which you might coerce him. It isn't natural for men to want to marry, you know. You've got to help him along."

"Yes, grandmother."

"I merely wish to impress upon you the importance of being able to—shall we say—*mold* a man's mind."

Catriona watched out of the corner of her eye as her mother disappeared back into the kitchen.

"Of course."

"For instance, do young girls these days even attempt the girdle?"

"I don't think so," said Catriona in a tiny voice.

"Still, I don't think it would hurt. You've got too thick a waist and too strong a chin. And that hair. Oughtn't you let it grow a bit?"

"Catriona," said her grandfather, who had just woken up on the sofa, "be a good girl, fetch your old granddad a coffee."

"I'll have a whisky while you're up," said her father, who had settled in his armchair near the fire. "Thank you, love."

"Pardon me, grandmother."

Up she went and across the burgundy rug into the kitchen. The radio was tuned to the Christmas station. She found the coffee tin where it always had been, sitting in alphabetical, imperial order with the baking powder to its left and the flour to its right. She watched her mother meticulously frosting the cookies in swirls of sugary green and red, not singing, not chatting. She did not look at Catriona when finally she spoke.

"Is your father wanting a whisky?"

"Yes."

"It's so early," she sighed.

"He wants one."

Mrs. Welland shrugged. What was there to be done when a man wanted a drink other than to fetch him one?

"Did you open that small parcel? Perhaps it's from Max."

"No," said Catriona. "Where is it?"

"On the writing desk."

Catriona quickly filled the coffee cup. She poured the whisky. After handing them to their recipients without their thanks, she scurried back into the kitchen. She was too excited to check the return address as she tore open the wrapping.

When she did, a copy of *Wuthering Heights* stared back at her. It was a hardcover, almost pocket sized. On the bound leather, a beautiful illustration of the Yorkshire moors. How Max could have found such a thing in Switzerland she did not know. What a relief to have such a nice gift. It wasn't very expensive, perhaps, but she was above thinking of that. The thoughtfulness of the gift soothed her. It was so pretty to look at. It wasn't jewelry. But it was pretty. It was pretty, at least.

With an eagerness for which her mother judged her harshly, she took the phone off the wall and dialed Max's number.

"Wilke, hallo," said a voice at the other end.

"Happy Christmas, Max."

"Happy Christmas."

"I've just got your gift here. I adore it."

He knew he'd forgotten something.

"What gift?"

"Oh, don't be silly! The book. *Wuthering Heights.*"

"I'm glad you like it," he said.

*But it wasn't from me*, he thought. *I would have given you* The Age of Innocence.

"I love it. Would you like to speak to mother or father?"

"Oh, I think we're just about to eat dinner."

Mrs. Darlington-Welland was huffing at the stove.

"All right. And Max—Happy Christmas. Thank you for the gift."

She clicked the phone back onto the wall. Mrs. Welland said:

"Are you quite all right now?"

"Yes. I think it's a lovely gift."

"I would have hoped for jewelry, if I was you. Poor thing."

Catriona left the kitchen to avoid saying something impertinent, placing the wrappings into the rubbish bin as she went.

In the trash, Simon's return address was crumpled on the packaging. When he never received thanks for the Christmas gift, he thought he had been too bold.

In Zurich, Max sat, relaxed near the fire with his parents. His mother sang a Christmas song, his father poured them all another glass of sparkling wine. Dinner, a goose and many peeled potatoes laid out like eggs, was still several hours away, though it was an hour later on the Continent.

Julie had just woken up.

# II. JANUARY

**SHE ARRIVED BACK IN ST ALBAS AT** the end of the first week of January. Trudging down Sea Street with her beaten-up suitcase wheeling behind her through the slush, Julie attempted to remember if she had ever felt so ready to leave a place at which she had just arrived. She did not recall that this was the exact same way she had felt twelve hours ago, waiting in the security line in Chicago and for the last few restless weeks at home.

At the house on the end of Fair Street, something smelled good in the kitchen.

"Hello," she said from the doorway.

"Hi. I'm in here."

"Smells delicious."

Julie peeled off her various layers of clothing, several of them new, and shed them onto the floor as Caddy peeled off various lids from containers of Thai food.

"Hey you," she said in her Southern accent, "give me some sugar!"

Julie embraced her, kissed her on the cheek.

"You made dinner."

"I ordered dinner and made the Thai guy bring it over here, if that's what you mean. I thought you'd be tired."

"You nailed it," said Julie as she washed her hands in the sink.

"I thought we could watch *The Sound of Music* and demolish the Thai until we pass out. Unless you're on a New Year's diet?"

"I decided not to fall for that this year. I don't care if a man sees me naked again for as long as I live."

"How was Christmas?"

"Nice. It was good to see my family. You?"

"A lark. My alive grandma got really drunk on eggnog. Now, why don't you run on upstairs and have a quick shower. I'll keep this all warm and get the DVD queued up."

"You're the best."

What Caddy hadn't mentioned was the very excellent Cabernet Sauvignon, which was also part of girls' night. While *The Sound of Music* played on in the background, the two friends talked over it, occasionally taking breaks from listening to one another for sipping and singing along.

"You want to know a secret?" said Caddy.

"What?" asked Julie, chewing with an open mouth and finishing her second glass of red.

"It's all kind of new."

"Okay."

"You remember that crew guy, Charles Maher? The one I went to *The Stroll* with?"

"Yeah."

"He kept calling over Christmas and said he'd been thinking a lot about me."

"I don't blame him. You're kind of the best."

Julie was happy for Caddy. She had never dated anyone in St Albas, at least not seriously. It was always a mystery to Julie as to why the boys didn't all want to date her: she was pretty, fun to be around, spontaneous, and loyal—in her own, charming, blunt way. It was nice to see someone getting what she deserved. It also made Julie feel irritated that she herself was alone, and it made the loneliness itch worse to know that there was Max and all the potentially wasted potential.

"You like him?" she asked Caddy.

"I think so."

"A lot?"

"A lot," said Caddy.

"You didn't tell me."

"You didn't ask. You were pretty busy at the end of last semester. With the show and everything."

"He's really hot, Caddy. I'm happy for you."

"You think so?"

"I think so. Oh, Caddy! Best part! 'You wait, little girl, on an empty stage, for fate to turn the light on.' "

" 'Your life, little girl, is an empty page, that men will want to write on.' "

They sighed in tandem.

"Such a shame, the whole turning-out-to-be-a-Nazi thing."

"I know, right?"

"Those German guys are hot, though."

"Yeah."

"Like that guy who directed your play. He was cute."

"You think he's cute?"

"Yeah."

"He's not German."

"He isn't?"

"No. He's Swiss."

"But he's cute. Swiss, huh?"

"Yeah. He is, isn't he? He's very cute."

She had been trying not to think that precise thought all through the holidays.

***

Julie woke up the next morning on the floor—her hand clutching an empty glass. The previous contents had spilled all over the floor. Caddy was snoring heavily on the sofa, her head bent backwards at a dangerous-looking angle over the armrest.

*Welcome back to St Albas*, she thought to herself.

She looked at her phone to find out what time it was and found a message from Max. Or, rather, a message from an unknown number that could only be Max's.

How were Julie's holidays? Had she heard the wonderful record he had gotten for Christmas? Would she like to come for a glass of wine in the next few days, or had she not yet recovered from the hangover she had likely experienced following the cast party? If not, he had tea.

Julie stared at her phone in utter disbelief. She didn't want to put it down, for fear she'd startle the message away. She looked over both her shoulders. Caddy was still asleep. The clock was still ticking on the wall. She could feel the floor, cold under her feet. It was actually happening. Max wanted to see her. He was asking to see her.

For three days, Julie vacillated between a joyful, nauseous feeling that Max was thinking about her and a horrific sense of foreboding that told her that having even the slightest, imaginary designs on another girl's boyfriend was bad juju.

She tried to take her mind off of the monkey swinging back and forth between these feelings in her brain, but it proved difficult even in the midst of planning a birthday night for Margot at the house. During her days of consideration, everyone but Peter had arrived back in town, wanting coffee dates and time to catch up before the onslaught of exams commenced. And of course, there was always research needing to be done for that dissertation that she had decided to write on 20th century Bildungsroman.

On the third day of her deliberations, she had firmly decided that no matter how much she would like to see Max, she must remain strong. He had a girlfriend. It was as plain as the chin on Catriona's plain face. She wasn't going to be That Girl. Although, in several weaker moments, she had found herself wondering why Max would choose someone with such an ugly chin when she had such a nice one.

For his part, Max had spent the plane ride back from Zurich attempting to draft a message to Julie in his mind. He sat there in his seat, armrests down, tray table in the fully upright and locked position, surprised to find his palms going increasingly sweaty as he attempted to remember how it was that one went about initiating contact with a girl. He was even more terrified when he realized that this was no girl. Julie was practically a woman. He had never dealt amorously with one of those before, and the prospect of attempting to sail smoothly back into her thoughts made him feel clumsier than ever.

Max hardly ever dreamt while asleep, but he had had several bizarre nightmares over the holidays, which had disturbed him. One of particular potency involved an emaciated Catriona burying him alive in a deep grave. Alongside her peculiar behavior at the cast party, this vision accounted for his wooden exchanges with her during the waking hours over the holiday.

In the terminal in Edinburgh, there was a painting of William Wallace, bravely charging on English troops along the airport corridor. Someone needed to push them back. Max did a third thing and a fourth: he sent both hers a text.

"Landed," read the one to Catriona.

"Hello! How were your holidays? Pretty standard in Zurich—got the new Cymbeline Fischer album. Heard it? If you aren't still hung over from cast party, maybe you can come over for a glass of wine soon. If not, I have tea," read the other.

Three days went by, and Julie did not reply. Max grew more and more despondent. He did not care to unpack his suitcase, thinking it would be defeat to recognize the fact that he must remain in St Albas for another five months, with all things being equal to last semester, to last year and to the year before it and to the year before that.

To make matters worse, Catriona had come back into town, bringing with her the copy of *Wuthering Heights* to which she had grown so attached. Max had never read the book, but he had Googled it, anticipating the questions she would no doubt ask him about the meaning of the gift. Since she had clearly and unquestionably considered it to be from him, he felt no reason to undeceive her. He felt a superiority over her and a slight revulsion at how pathetic it was that she could be so happy that he had thought to give her a Christmas gift.

Max had a rather good idea as to where the book had come from, and it was of little concern. Simon would never reveal himself. He valued Catriona's happiness too much, and he was evidently under the same impression that Peter and Catriona herself were: marrying Max would make her happy. A deep and whispering part of Max's heart wished that Simon would say something—that it would set off a chain reaction, that it would finally make Catriona realize that he, Max, was not a boy worth marrying, but that Simon was.

Poor Catriona. She had made it so that she thought she couldn't survive without him, specifically. And now she had no future unless he was in it. That was why Peter had given him the ring. To seal Catriona's future. God, that was a lot of pressure.

Max's mind was becoming as full as his still-packed suitcase, and not with categorical imperatives. He was comfortable with those but not with questions about morality and happiness as they pertained to his own existence and the existences of those around him.

And so on the fourth night, after Catriona had gone to bed, he decided to have a walk around town. To clear his head and attempt to reset it, to block the frustration and distraction that were making it impossible for him to work, let alone enjoy being around his girlfriend at an even rudimentary level. He put on the red cashmere scarf his mother had bought him and the hand-me-down jacket from his father. Knowing that they wouldn't keep out the cold, he slipped into the comfortable old walking shoes he had purchased during high school and headed outside anyway. He didn't like the expensive ones his mother had bought him over Christmas.

He felt especially tired and old as he wound his way down Sea Street where the restaurants were just shutting for the night. The smell of frozen sea air and the drifting wafts of frozen fish coming from the grill houses were pungent. The windows of student flats were glowing, and many parties were being had. Max imagined he was a solitary polar bear floating on an iceberg, not caring to eat although the sea was abundant beneath him (though he did not extend the metaphor too far).

He had no idea what had made him think that Julie would be remotely interested in being his friend. She probably had other friends. Well, of course she did. She was friends with Peter, and Peter always had friends. He had met some of them—Ashwin and Brett. They seemed incredibly decent. He was jealous of Julie; he wanted Julie; he felt ridiculously stupid for sending that rambling message to her. He reminded himself it had only been one night of talking.

Max missed Fern with a supreme ache. She had been obliged to remain up north in order to work in the pub right up until the start of exams. He would have given anything for her company. For the last few days, it was lonely and cold in the flat, even with Catriona hanging about incessantly during the afternoon and early evening hours.

He had now wound his way to the east end of Fair Street, where the road ended and the cobblestones became enormous, as if Jack's giant himself had laid them using his index finger and thumb.

There was a group of people huddled outside of a brightly lit house. Judging by the loud music coming from inside, there seemed to be yet another party going on. But the talking and singing were louder than the recorded music—the people at the party were good friends. As he got closer, three figures came into focus. There was a tallish girl leaning up against a dark-haired boy, both of them holding multiple cigarettes. Another girl was standing inside the doorway, shivering and sipping from a flask. All three were arguing about something, though he couldn't hear exactly what.

This was Ashwin, Caddy, and Julie. Having had too much to drink, Julie had broken down to ask for opinions about how to handle a particular, nameless, potential suitor and a texting situation.

"Who is it?" said Caddy. "I'm not going to tell anyone."

"It doesn't matter who. I want objective advice."

"So it's someone we know."

"No. It's just someone."

"Just be cool," said Ashwin. "Seriously. Don't give in to his text messages."

"He may be drunk," said Caddy. "But he has a point. At least wait a few more days. Guys love it when you torture them."

"Truth. She speaks the truth."

"I know you're right. Okay. I won't text him."

"Good girl," said Ashwin. "I'm going back in. Holy fuck, it's cold. Coming in, Caddy? Julie?"

"Yeah," said Caddy.

Ashwin was Indian, after all, and Caddy was Southern. No number of St Albas winters could make them amicable with the cold weather.

"I'm going to stay out here a minute," said Julie.

"Don't get melancholy," said Caddy, taking Julie's flask away. "Promise?"

"I won't, I won't."

"I'm going to go light the candles on Margot's cake. Three minutes, okay?"

"Three minutes," said Julie.

"Okay. Who is it?"

"You're the worst, Caddy."

The door opened and shut. Max watched as it lit Julie's face and closed again to leave it in darkness.

Great. There she was, standing ten steps in front of him. She had not bothered to answer his message. And now he must face her. He pulled up his hood. If he was lucky, she wouldn't notice him. Was it too late to turn around? Oh God, but she looked pretty. Her cheeks were red. The back of his neck felt hot.

"Max?" asked Julie as she peered intently in his direction, trying to make him out in the dark.

"Julie? That you?"

"Yeah, hi."

"Hi. I didn't see you there."

Julie's usual social talents abandoned her. She needed to think up some excuse—anything—as to why she hadn't texted him back. She couldn't very well say she was terrified of Catriona and terrified of

Peter or tell him that she found him incredibly handsome and interesting and wanted to kiss him as soon as humanly possible, if not sooner still. Max grew as pale as the snow, and she felt moths in her stomach.

"So," she said, "how was your holiday in Switzerland?"

"Good. America?"

"Good."

He made an "x" with his foot in the snow on the sidewalk. He began to panic. He thought of Catriona asleep in her bed.

"It's funny you just came by," Julie said after a tense moment.

Max looked down at her, though it felt like looking up.

"It is?"

"I was just about to respond to that text you sent me."

"Oh, that. Yeah, yeah."

"I've been so busy planning this party and everything...coming back...to tell you the truth, I haven't even unpacked my suitcase. I know I should be glad to be back here, but. Ha. I'm not. Sorry, that's not what I mean. I don't want to be a downer."

"You're not. I haven't unpacked either."

Holy shit, she was smiling at him. He had made her smile. He looked at the door behind her, at the glowing windows, at the people behind the thin curtains, to avoid letting her see how much was going on behind his eyes.

"Did you want to come in? You can, you know. There's plenty of booze. Everyone's flights got delayed, and we bought so much stuff."

"I'd like to, but I have plans."

"Oh, nice. Okay. Well, even for a moment?"

"I'd better get going, I think."

"Okay," she said.

He turned to go back the way he had come. Julie thought of something her grandmother had said to her over the holidays—about how worlds turned not on plans but on impulses. So she blurted out:

"Max, if the offer still stands, I'd really like to hang out. If you're not too busy."

Max stopped in his snow-hollowing tracks and revolved back around, a shy smile on his white cheeks.

"Would that be good, Max?"

"Definitely. Definitely."

Here was a teaspoon of sugary happiness mixing into the air.

"Tomorrow night?" he asked, as his heart pounded like several monkeys on a timpani.

"Yeah, that works."

"You remember where I live?"

"I think so."

"Okay. Cool."

"See you then. Eight?"

"Yep."

"Cool."

Julie went inside and smiled the rest of the night. Anyone would have thought it was her birthday rather than Margot's.

***

The next day, Max was buzzing with activity around the flat, attempting to make it habitable for an evening with Julie. Catriona was on the black leather sofa, warming her feet by the electric heater. *Wuthering Heights* was on her lap.

"I should have bought you drapes," she said, "ages ago. That draft is awful. I don't want you to catch cold at night."

"It's fine," he said. "I'm a big boy."

"You are," she said. "Is there something the matter?"

"No," he said, nodding as he walked into the kitchen for the broom. "Why?"

"What's all the tidying about?"

"Catriona, this is going to be a wonderful semester."

He kissed her on the hand, something he hadn't done in a very long time.

"I'm glad you think so," she said taken aback.

"I just feel like things are falling into place."

"I suppose that's true. You are going to do well on your exams, and I am going to do well on my exams. We're both going to graduate with top marks, if we don't do anything foolish."

"Exactly."

Catriona had never seen Max so energetic. It was slightly alarming, especially given recent events. He had been such a loose cannon over the holidays and was growing more unpredictable still. Even after the nice Christmas gift, he'd been rather depressive and slightly cold since they had arrived back in St Albas. Perhaps he hadn't completely forgiven her for the outburst at the cast party, and perhaps he was beginning to obsess over his exams and dissertation. That always made him draw inward. But if there was one thing Catriona understood, it was feeling the need to impress one's parents through academic achievement as best one could. Besides, the better Max did on his exams, the better it would be for her in the long run. She must remember that, unsettling behavior or no.

"You know," she said, "I think I'll leave you. I don't want to be underfoot. Unless you'd like some help, of course."

"No, thanks. I'll be fine."

"Shall we have dinner?"

"At yours?"

"All right."

"I'll bring dessert."

"All right."

She was putting on her snow boots, plucking each leather glove from the coat pocket where it stayed and fitting it snugly to the crevices of her palms. She put on her earmuffs and her coat with her usual precision.

As she closed the door to Max's flat, she told herself that no matter how much it felt to the contrary, things with him must be on the upswing once more.

She did not yet guess how relieved Max was to see her go.

***

Julie came around the decided-upon time of eight o'clock in the evening. Max had arrived back from Catriona's dinner only moments before, just in time to thaw himself out, break open his computer, and scatter a dozen or so library books around him. He sat waiting at the table in the living room, hunched over a pile of old notes.

The doorbell rang at ten past. Julie had wanted to look busy too.

"I'm so sorry I'm late," she said as she took off her elaborate red coat and hung it near the door. "I was out for a drink with a friend of mine, and we just lost track of the time."

"Sounds like fun."

"He's a riot."

"No problem. I was just finishing up some work myself. Lots to catch up on."

After several more moments of small talk, they settled in at the table. Max put his new album on and poured two glasses of red. Julie listened politely, trying to remember what she had said that led him to believe she was eager to hear it. Then she remembered lying about it at the cast party. Now, she was answering Max's very specific questions about Cymbeline Fischer with incredibly non-specific answers.

Perhaps this didn't have to turn into one of those awkward pseudo-romantic things. Maybe she could have him as a friend that was a boy. She had plenty of them. Even ones she knew were attractive. What could be the harm in adding another? Hadn't her friendships with Ashwin and Peter and Larry begun with wine or some other form of alcohol being heavily dispensed? Though, that was in the context of a party, a pub-crawl. And there was no absent question about an absent girlfriend hanging in the air. Max must know that she was friends with Peter. He must know she knew about Catriona.

But, looking across the table at Max, who was leaning closer and closer to her with every glass of wine he drank, she just couldn't believe he was thinking very much about Catriona or Peter. And indeed, the only relationship that mattered to Max at the moment was the compelling one between him and Julie. Catriona, tucked away in her bed on nearby Church Street, and Peter, the giver of that ring in his room, could not have been further from his mind.

"What do you want to do?" she asked.

"Me?" he asked unnecessarily, and then continued. "Well, I study political philosophy."

"And, what do you do with that? What are you going to be when you grow up?"

"I thought about going into politics for a while."

Julie smiled. "It's hard to imagine you doing that. That's a loud profession."

"I know," he said. "So I think it's going to be academia for me."

"What're you writing your dissertation on?"

"Kant."

"Excuse me?"

"Immanuel Kant. He's a philosopher."

"I don't know much about philosophy," said Julie. "I don't think my mind works that way. I tend to just do things and not think about them."

"I wish I was more like that," Max said.

"It's awful. I'm always saying things I shouldn't and doing things I shouldn't."

"Some people would call that living a moral life."

"What, being happy?"

"Yes."

"I'm not happy all the time."

Max took a sip of his wine.

"What did Immanuel Kant say, anyway," said Julie. "What's his shtick?"

"Well, the shtick I'm studying right now is called the categorical imperative."

"That sounds so boring," said Julie, with a huge smile.

"It sounds boring, but it's so interesting."

"What is it?"

"Basically, Kant says that when we think about whether or not an action is moral, we need to think about whether we'd want it to be the universal law across the board for everyone, everywhere, at all times."

"So, if I'm thinking about stealing a candy-bar from Tesco, I should consider whether I'd want everyone to do it all the time?"

"Something like that. You should consider what would *happen* if everyone did it."

"What about lying?"

"Yes. When you're thinking of lying, you should think about what the consequences would be if everyone did it, all the time. You'd never be able to trust anyone."

Julie thought back to first semester. Her heart sunk. Here she was again, with a boy with a girlfriend. And this time she explicitly knew about it. She couldn't make any excuses, no matter how innocent this visit was on the outside. She would never want to live in a world where the universal law dictated that it was all right for boyfriends to spend time at night alone with girls who had possible ulterior motives.

"What about you, Miss English Major? What are you going to be?"

"Everyone asks me that."

"You can do anything, I think."

"That's really nice of you to say."

"I believe it," said Max.

"My dad keeps telling me to go into business. I don't know what I want to do."

"Why? You're a good writer. Do that."

"I'm not," she said, quite defensively. "You don't know that."

"I've read some of your pieces in the *Martyr*."

She grinned. "I'm going to stop writing those. They're a bunch of amateurs over there."

"Yeah. But yours are good. Or what about being an actor? You were amazing in the show."

"I don't know. It feels fake. I want to do something that's going to matter. Julie Lovejoy: investigative journalist. Something. I don't know."

"Don't laugh it off. I could see it."

"Really?"

"Yeah. Just as long as you're not a war correspondent, or something like that. I hate to think of you dodging bullets. But hey, if you want to, you should. You'll think of something. You have so many talents."

Julie smiled and poured herself another glass of wine.

Several hours of conversation later, it was dawn again. Julie announced that it was officially Monday and that her exam review sessions were officially on. She even believed herself when she said it. Max's faith in her talents had inspired her.

"I need to go home and catch a nap before I hit the books."

"Good plan."

"Maybe I won't sleep. It'll just cause a hangover. And then my forehead will literally *hit* the books when I pass out in pain."

Max laughed. He liked puns. He ruffled his hair with his hand, which Julie loved to watch. She turned the handle of the door and felt Max's soft touch at her shoulder.

"Julie—that was fun."

"It was," she said, turning her face to him over her shoulder. "Goodnight."

After he had closed the door behind her, Max returned to his room, feeling the same potent triumph and exhilaration he had after the cast party. He couldn't believe his good fortune: she had come to his apartment, she had stayed for nearly eight hours, and she had appeared to enjoy herself. Perhaps, if he played it cool, she would want to do it again. He watched out his window as she walked down the street, and he was happy.

He decided that perhaps it was worth unpacking his suitcase after all. He began pairing his socks and folding his boxer shorts. When the pile began to slouch over, he opened up his top drawer to make room.

It was there that a little blue velvet box stared up at him. Half out of fright, he thought he might throw it out the window. But he knew with his luck Catriona herself would find it in the street. He opened the box. The sharp stare of the white diamond inside seemed to be boring into his forehead like a laser. He felt like he was staring into the eyes of every Darlington and Welland woman who had gone into making Catriona. Holy hell. What was he supposed to do with it? Maybe he could just give it back to Peter. But he couldn't face Peter. Peter might hit him or call him a coward or, worst of all, tell Julie that he had said he was going to marry Catriona. Not that he should be thinking about what Julie thought about the possibility of his marrying Catriona.

Frantically snapping the box shut, he searched for somewhere in his room to hide it from both himself and from Catriona. Somewhere neither of them would look.

His toolbox.

He reached up into the far corner of the closet, stowed the ring inside, and felt extremely relieved when it was back in its dark corner—though he could almost hear it beating there, like a tell-tale heart.

# III.

GRIND-ALTERING MUGS WAS A SMALL, NARROW café. The décor and the furniture gave the impression that the staff had whittled it between rushes and on breaks. This was the only café for thinking people in town and, due to the lack of thinking people in town, the only one necessary. Here, the humanities students, the socialists, the anarchists, and the feminists met over heavily contested games of Trivial Pursuit on the coffee-stained board, disagreeing with one another with as much ferocity as they supposed the rest of the world disagreed with them.

Peter was sitting there on a stool at the counter facing Sea Street. This was the least comfortable seat in the café, but it had the best view—one of Sea Street's only views of the Sea. It was a cloudy, icy day, and he had taken the afternoon off from studying to read a book for pleasure—he had done a lot of preparing over Christmas, anyway. *The Great Gatsby* was growing sweaty in his palm as the heater below his seat cranked and creaked. "In my younger and more vulnerable years," he read, "my father gave me some advice that I've been turning over in my mind ever since. 'Whenever you feel like criticizing any one,' he told me, 'just remember that all the people in this world haven't had the advantages that you've had.'"

Peter looked around the café: the girls with the nose rings, and the boys with the tattoos. This was a narrator with a clever father.

He looked outside into the Scottish day and felt content to be back in St Albas. He was further contented to see what looked like a friendly face through the foggy glass. Wiping away the thin sheet of steam from his side of the window proved him right. Julie was standing outside, crouched over as she tied her boots. She was wearing her academic robes, the emerald-colored felt garments donned for official, University-related events such as chapel, graduation, and, as today, for sitting exams.

He knocked on the glass emphatically. When Julie saw Peter, she smiled in spite of herself, forgetting the secret developing in her heart like a Polaroid photo.

"Hey! I know you," she said, coming in the door and embracing him. "Happy new year—in person, that is."

Julie had called to wish him a happy new year, though she was in the middle of dinner with her friends in America. He had not returned the call, and she had not been offended. Julie had long surmised that the girl in Warwick hadn't (as usual) welcomed her tidings, and she had refrained from calling Peter for the rest of the holidays.

She had not seen him since coming back to town. Peter had arrived at the last moment before the beginning of exams in order to spend as much time as possible with his girlfriend. As for Julie: partly she had been avoiding him, and partly she had become busy seeing Max every other night from ten o'clock in the evening to eight o'clock in the morning.

"You know it's going to be February in about a week, right?"

"It's almost exams. I've been busy, and you haven't been around."

"You've seen Ashwin and Brett."

"At Margot's party, which you were not in town for—"

"Ashwin said you met him for pool at the union."

"I happened to have some free time."

She had, in fact, made the date with Ashwin in order to make a public appearance. People would soon start to notice that she turned down evening invitations, and she certainly didn't want an intrepid friend finding out that she was seeing Max at night. Thankfully, Caddy had been engaged with her new boyfriend, who had a nice house to himself just outside of town, and she did not notice Julie's absence at home or in the pubs or at the parties. But this did not solve the problem of her other friends, who would rightly grow suspicious of her new insistence upon being a model student after nearly four years of torpid academics.

Julie's growing passion for schoolwork had something to do with the opportunity it provided to spend time with Max. Studying was much more fun when there was a handsome boy to keep your teacups hot. And he thought she was smart. He thought she had thoughts. He saw the substance in Julie where others saw only the ebullient froth. She couldn't very well explain all this to her friends.

"How many exams have you got?" said Peter.

"Two. One today, one Friday. And at some point I've got to start my dissertation research."

"What's it going to be?"

"Bildungsroman of the 20th century. With a focus on the women characters. What do you think?"

"Sounds interesting," he said, clearly not buying what he thought to be a façade of studiousness.

"What about you?" she said to change the subject.

"Two. What are you getting yourself into tonight?"

"Nothing," said Julie. "Are you not hearing me? Working. Studying."

"Surely you can spare an hour for a pint and an old friend."

Julie floundered. Peter said:

"The old friend is me, Juliana Lillian Lovejoy."

"Maybe you should have come back to town earlier when I was still in fucking-around mode."

"You can be a pain, can't you?"

"You know I'd love to hang out. I just can't tonight," she said.

*Because I'm seeing that boy you told me not to*, she thought.

"Tomorrow, then?"

"Maybe. I'll call you?"

"I'll call you. Count on it."

"I'm off to the library."

"Okay. Whatever you say."

Peter had missed Julie and was sad to watch her leave. Some defect (others would call it a strength) of upbringing and culture made it impossible for him to say so directly.

And so he stared after her path long after she'd gone out the door and passed by the window once again.

***

As Julie sat in the library frantically reading through her notes on Harris's interpretation of Woolf, she began to itch for contact with Max. She checked her phone. He hadn't called or messaged. She was looking forward to tonight. To being in his living room, to drinking wine and laughing and tracing the lines in his forehead with her eyes as he did.

*Stop it*, she thought. *You have to study for this exam. You have to concentrate. You have to go against your instincts. You have to breathe in all this Harris stuff, so you can blow it back out at him, so you can get a good degree, so you can make your own money and buy your own house and start your own magazine and make even more money, so you can take vacations from your own house and magazine and never have to share any of it with any man, not even of the handsome Swiss sort. You need to grow up. You need to think about you and not some achingly good-looking, Germanic gentle giant.*

"Shit," she whispered, opening her laptop. She tried to cover the speakers near the keyboard as it booted up, emitting the loud noise that made the computer sound as if it were transcending space and time in an orgasm of robot sounds. She always forgot to mute the settings when she was going to the library. A toolbar with comic-looking icons bounced at the bottom of the screen. *Goddamit*, she thought. *I don't want any software updates!* She clicked furiously out of the grey boxes and started the Internet. When finally she succeeded in logging in to Facebook, there was a little red box with the number one in it, suggesting triumphantly that she had received a message.

"Good luck on your exam today," it said. "It will be fun to see you later. I am putting together a playlist that is entirely devoid of punk rock. If this is not enough to entice you, please note: I have cake."

*Max.* Her heart fluttered around her chest in airy little pirouettes.

Julie wondered yet again what on Earth she was getting herself into, more acutely aware now that spending time with him was in fact the very thing that Peter had previously advised her against. His words sat fresh and cold as meat in a butcher's window: "Please, Julie, for my sake, I beg you—leave it alone. For once, just leave it alone."

Peter had been right, perhaps. He loved her and wanted to protect her. This was something she knew for sure. Then, a thought landed like a fly on her nose. Was Max really just like Harry? Courting her, with no intention of giving up his girlfriend, keeping her on the back burner, relegating her to being an object of variation and nothing more?

She hadn't really looked over the notes, and it was time to walk to her exam.

Julie was thankful when exams were over because it meant that at least there was one less thing she had to feel guilty about when staying and talking at Max's until breakfast.

# IV.

**ONE BRIGHT AFTERNOON, MAX WAS SITTING** across from Catriona at her kitchen table eating lunch. The soup in front of him was growing cold. Catriona had made a project of it. Her mother had given her a book for Christmas called *Skinny Soups for Two*. Though it was passively and rather hypocritically meant to suggest that Catriona should lose a bit of weight, Catriona took it to mean that her mother thought Max was getting a bit chubby (she had commented on several photos Catriona had shown at Christmas). This was Max's third straight meal of vegetable soup, which explained the regularity of the chocolate cake with Julie.

Despite her initial approval of Max's newfound habits of cleaning and eating well without any nagging, Catriona's suspicions were becoming aroused, and not simply because he didn't seem to be losing any weight. She and Max were spending fewer and fewer nights a week with one another, and now with exams done, she wondered why. Max blamed it on his dissertation, saying he preferred to be alone, at home, in the peace and quiet of his room as he read and wrote. He had always been like that: studying a lot and liking his quiet, but he had never minded her quiet company so much before. While at first she attempted to be understanding, and was in fact quite grateful for the time it allowed her to begin work on her own dissertation, there was now a distinctly hungover look in Max's eye when they met for their daily lunch that she found both irritating and increasingly worth investigating.

"This is delicious, Catriona. Thank you."

"I'm so glad."

They slurped in solemn silence, until Catriona said:

"Did you have a nice night? You look awfully tired."

"I'm fine. Slept well."

"I missed you."

"I know," he said, reaching across the table to pat her hand without taking his eyes off his spoon. "Everything will be better in a couple of weeks, when I've got a good foothold and an outline. And things can go back to the way they should be."

"You're right."

"You'll see," he said, taking his empty bowl to the sink. "There's nothing to worry about. Exam time and then the start of term is always like this—you know that."

"That's true."

"And you need time to plan your art show anyway. You're a busy girl."

"That's also true."

Catriona had recently been asked to put together an exhibition at the local art museum. Max could not have been more thrilled for himself.

He headed now toward the front hall, thinking of his good luck and putting on his shoes.

"Where are you going?"

"Studying to do."

"Max—can't I come over this evening? Perhaps I can help you?"

"Can we not talk about this now?"

Catriona bristled at the phrase. Max felt a sudden wave of guilt burning in his throat. Then he told Catriona some of the things he'd been thinking about, the ones intertwined with his frequent thoughts of Julie.

"I've been doing some thinking about next year," he said.

"You have? Really?"

"Yeah. I'm definitely going to apply for graduate programs next month."

"That's wonderful, Max!"

"I was thinking of Oxford and Cambridge, and LSE."

"Yes?"

"And possibly St Albas, as a backup."

"It would be so nice."

Catriona's mind rushed to think of the flat they could get if they were engaged, of how easy it would be to plan a wedding in Lancashire from Scotland.

"I was also thinking of Princeton. And New York University."

"I'm sorry?"

"Princeton, NYU."

"Oh. But—those are in America."

"They're the best schools in the world. Some of the best."

"Isn't Oxford better?"

"Britain's still an option. All right? Don't be upset. It may not even be America. Just a thought."

"All right."

"It's all going to work out. I just don't know about the details yet."

Catriona nodded. What else was there to do when a man wanted not to speak but to let him not speak? To remain silent and wait for his intention to change or to hope that it would. That's all a girl could do.

***

Vera Morgan, who was, after all, Catriona's flatmate, spent the night at Harry's. And because she did, Peter spent the night on Catriona's sofa, making sure her bedroom door stayed open.

Peter hardly slept. Neither did Catriona. Watching her hallow eyes eating porridge silently at the breakfast table was almost more than Peter could bear. When he'd arrived back at RMac, he called Max—from the landline in his flat, so that he would be sure to answer.

"Hello," said Max, who was wandering the local bookshop with his morning coffee.

"It's Peter. How are you?"

"Fine. Everything all right?"

Max immediately regretted answering the unrecognized number. This is why one should never, ever do that under any circumstances. He had been avoiding Peter religiously, hoping that maybe by ignoring his existence, and that of the ring, they would both simply disappear.

"Not really, Max. No."

"Anything the matter?"

"I don't know if you've noticed, and I don't want to pry, but Catriona doesn't seem to be all right lately."

"She's all right."

"Max—she's quite anxious about next year. About your applying to school in America," said Peter.

"She told you?"

"It wasn't a secret, was it?"

"No. It might be surprising, a little," said Max. "But it's a good thing. It's a good thing for both of us."

It was difficult to make Max impatient, but Peter was succeeding.

"If this is really about the engagement ring, or proposing—"

"I have to let you do it," said Peter.

"You have to let me do it," said Max, who wished he had the courage to tell Peter he couldn't.

***

Later that day, Catriona met Vera in the conservatory of the Watson Hotel. It had been built in the 1920s, after three of the last thatched-roof cottages in town had been bulldozed to make way for the stylish inn and restaurant. Catriona stopped in the entryway for a moment to admire the Tiffany glasswork in the foyer. It was well done. They must have brought craft workers up from England. That was the only way such a thing could be accomplished in Scotland.

Stepping inside the reception room, with its many high-backed chairs and fireplaces, she did her best to keep her chin in the air. According to Catriona, this was the posture—with the shoulders thrown back and the eyebrows tense—that made people believe you had money. Clearly, she had never seen Ashwin raising hell in Brooks Brothers.

Vera was waiting in the conservatory, sitting in a tight, taupe Ralph Lauren sweater dress, an *Hermès* scarf roped around her neck, a pair of Chanel tights attempting to find some fat to cling to, an iPhone in her hand, and a notebook on her lap in which she'd written notes from her French and Spanish lectures that day. Her legs were crossed at the thigh, and from the tip of her toe dangled a shiny, nude-except-for-the-bottom Louboutin, the partner of which was resting urbanely on the pretty, white rug beneath it. This outfit and everything surrounding it were bound to make Catriona feel frightfully underdressed. The cobblestones in modest heels, Catriona could take. But she could never manage to navigate the icy streets in stilettos like Vera.

Catriona entered the conservatory with its friendly portrait of Prince George and his golf club. The waiter came to take her jacket, which she squeezed her own sweatered-self out of with the mental promise that she would not eat any cakes this afternoon at tea. She would try to be calm and not think about Max applying to schools in America. And why not? This was her favorite room in St Albas: the glass-topped tables that were always immaculately free of fingerprints, the crystal lamps hanging from the ceiling, the light wood paneling cheerfully carved with cherubs, and, of course, the wide windows on two walls that gave impressive views of the Ancient Links, Flat Sands, and, in the distance, the Ancient Links Hotel.

"Hello, dolly," said Vera, rising in one impossibly fluid motion to give Catriona a kiss. "You look as if you haven't slept."

Catriona and Vera had met one another in first year, first in hall and then in general course lectures. Vera was exactly the sort of friend Catriona required: someone who she could try to imitate, a vision of what she herself wanted very badly to be. For all her uppity judgment, Catriona was from Axbury Town, and Vera was from London. Vera had gone to all the schools a step up from Catriona's, on both the tuition and social scales. She had taken all the slightly more extravagant holidays, been to all the influential fashion shows and parties and art auctions where she had rubbed elbows with ministers and royals and all kinds of old and new money.

Vera needed Catriona just as much as Catriona needed Vera: it was hard being both attractive and rich. No one wanted to be your friend really, unless they wanted something from you, and Vera found that with Catriona at least the admiration and the jealousy were transparent. There was something essential they understood about one another, and it stemmed from Catriona's being morally superior to everyone they knew and Vera having more beauty and money. It was lonely at the top, or so they both thought, and that is why they liked each other.

"I didn't sleep very well," Catriona conceded.

"How was lunch with Max yesterday?"

"Max?" said Catriona. "It was all right, I suppose. But odd. Very odd."

"What do you mean?"

"It's only—I suppose he's very tired, working on his exams and dissertation…"

"Of course he is. But tell me, what's really the matter?"

Catriona sighed, opening up the menu.

"Hadn't we better order tea before we dive into all of this? If we have to dive into it at all, I mean."

"I took the liberty of ordering tea for two. Is that all right? Rose tea for you, if I've remembered correctly."

"Yes."

"Good, that's settled, then. Now, about Max."

Catriona sighed.

"He's been so odd. There was the business about my—my outburst, at his cast party, and then the Christmas present, which you know I love, and lately he's been so weird. Truly weird. He's polite. At lunch, he's polite. But you must have noticed he's not around much at night these days."

"You sound suspicious. I'm surprised at you."

"Do I? I don't mean it, exactly."

"What on earth can you be thinking?"

"It's strange. In a way, it's all been lovely these past few weeks. We haven't been quarreling, it's not as if we've been—upset with one another. But whenever we're together, I have the feeling there's something I don't know about. He's looked so *smug.*"

"So?"

"Vera, he isn't thinking of me. Don't you understand? Yesterday afternoon, he practically told me he's planning on leaving me."

"He did not."

"He said something about graduate school. In America!"

"Oh, Catriona. It's nothing. When has he ever been serious about something like that before? It's a joke."

"It's not," she said. "Something is going on."

"Yes, it is. He's thinking about the future. He's planning for it. And talking to you about it. I don't know what you're on about, to be honest. This is what you've wanted, for Max to grow up and start doing things."

"Do you think he's seeing someone else?"

"Oh, Catriona."

"No, really, Vera, I'm serious."

The tea arrived on its silver tray, bringing the conversation to a halt. The waiter's white gloves matched the gentle white of the fine, painted bone china. When all of the little bits had been placed upon the table and the tea had been poured by the hands in the white gloves and the man attached to them had walked away, Vera inhaled into her little cup.

"I do love a nice cup of Earl Grey."

She looked across the table to see her roommate's frown.

"Catriona," she said, having taken English forthrightness from somewhere in the odor of the tea, "I'm going to tell you something that you'll need to keep a secret. It's important, for your own sake, that you keep it quiet."

"Is it about Max?"

Vera nodded as she sipped her tea.

"What is it?"

"I don't want to excite you. I didn't want to ruin the surprise. But it is in your best interest to know, if you're this paranoid."

"To know what?"

"He's going to propose to you."

"Who?"

"Max, of course."

"What!"

"Yes."

"Max Wilke?"

Catriona's eyes were as big as they had ever been or would scarcely ever be again. Her teacup had frozen a few inches from her mouth, apparently too shocked by the revelation to budge.

"How on *earth* would you know a thing like that?"

"I heard him talking about it this morning, in the book shop. Can you believe it?"

"No. As a matter of fact, I can't."

"I ducked in to buy the latest *Vogue* and all that. You know, since my sister's spread is in it this month?"

"Yes."

"And Max was on the phone, talking about an engagement ring."

"That doesn't mean he is going to propose to me."

"Not by itself, no. But he said it's a secret and a surprise and that he has to do it."

"Who could he have been talking to?"

"Does it matter? Why else would Max Wilke be talking about an engagement ring? Who else does he even talk to?"

"Did he say when?"

"Soon."

"I can't believe it," said Catriona. Instead of buoying her, however, this revelation brought a dull, overwhelming pain to her head as if it had turned into a bowling ball that had been dropped repeatedly and them placed back on her shoulders.

"Are you all right? This is supposed to be a happy thing, you know."

"Yes, I'm all right."

"Have a sip of your tea. There's a dear."

Catriona took a sip of tea but found no English stoutness in it.

She closed her eyes and opened them to her friend.

"Vera," she said, "are you quite sure?"

"I am," said Vera. "You should have heard his voice. He was more excited than I've ever heard him."

Still, Catriona thought it best not to tell her mother.

# V. FEBRUARY

**THE THICK ICICLES THAT HAD FIRMLY** fastened themselves to the tops of St Albas's ancient buildings were beginning to thaw. Streams of clear, cold water ran along the streets, not bothering to freeze. The permanent grey cloud that had hung in the sky, from horizon to zenith, from November 'til now, had gone by the morning of the first of February, replaced by a dome of blue and a sun so convincing that it made you think it a good idea to go outside without a scarf. Of course, this was wishful thinking. Spring was on its way, that was clear, but spring in St Albas was still what many people in more southern-lying longitudes would call "dead winter." Everything was enormously wet and windy as the sleeping, icy giant known as Scotland began to awake from his winter-long nap.

With exams over and term begun, the students began to take up their mischievous activities in full force once more. The pubs were full of revelers again, out of relief in the weeks following exams rather than out of denial in the weeks preceding them. Every group of students, it seemed, had something to celebrate: the first years congratulated themselves on surviving one term with as little studying as possible; the third years were similarly ecstatic to be done with their first upper-division courses; and the fourth and second years rejoiced in the fact that they had again avoided stepping on the cursed William MacGregor stones. The real panic would not, of course, set in until the weeks before second-term exams.

Max was more relaxed about his course load than he had ever been, despite what he told Catriona. His professors had always loved him; he was a genius when it came to theory and a genius when it came to the application of it. He felt confident that his dissertation would be a success and that he could get his applications for master's programs together in time to meet the deadlines. He thought of how silly it was that he hadn't started on his applications before. What had he thought he was going to do? He supposed he had thought he would go back to Zurich or Bern or move to Brussels for a year, doing more of the same type of research that he had in the summers. But somehow, that was no longer good enough. He needed to move forward. He needed to change. Graduate school had always been in his future. Now it was time to apply—to choose where to go and to go there.

Catriona, for her part, attempted to see the good in all this for her. After hearing the news of her pending engagement, she had started to tell herself that Max's idea of going to school in America was only a ruse to throw her off his trail. Of course, when they were engaged, she must insist on staying in Britain. She tried her best to build a mental house and to live in it, imagining how good it would feel to welcome her Cambridge-professor husband home, wearing oven mitts and serving shepherd's pie. Perhaps they would have to live in noisy Cambridgeshire for a few years, but that would be worth it considering the excellent real estate they would be able to afford in Lancashire thereafter. Max would be very busy, she supposed, but initially that would give her time to plan a wedding and then to furnish a home with lots of pretty things that would make all of her friends quite jealous.

For three or four days, the self-deception had worked. But it was when she ventured outside of the cozy delusions she had created for herself that she realized with stark, naked certainty that nothing, still, was for certain. In spite of wanting to make happiness out of the news about the ring, a little snake called fear was coiling inside her chest, feeding itself with pangs of doubt that it slurped quickly with precise movements of the tongue. Swallowing them whole, it digested them slowly. So close to her goal of engagement and marriage and babies and pleasing her family, she was terrified of losing it all.

Her newest hobby was to wander around Max's Facebook and email accounts. He could be forgetful with these things and had written down his passwords on a sticky note that he had fastened to the bottom of his laptop. She had noticed it a few days earlier at one of their *Skinny Soups* lunches and taken a photo of it with her phone while Max was in the kitchen. After absolutely no soul-searching, she logged on once he'd gone to class. First, to his Facebook and then to his email.

Like a hunting hound, Catriona sniffed Max out. She checked his messages for signs of other girls. She checked his inboxes for signs of other girls. She monitored what he wrote on other people's walls, though, with Max's dearth of friendships, these posts were mostly related to assignments. No one was safe from her inquiring eyes: the girls from hall in first year; the undergraduate secretary in the philosophy department; the woman who checked his books out at the library.

And so, after sweetly wishing Max a good rest of the day and watching him walk down Church Street, she decided to investigate his mysterious behavior once more. She made herself a cup of tea, wiped the kitchen table with antibacterial in a serious, clinical manner, and turned on her computer. When she tried to log onto Facebook using his username and password, she was greeted by a message informing her that she had used the incorrect information. Thinking she had made a typing or spelling mistake, she entered everything once again, quite deliberately. When the error appeared again and again, it became clear. Max had changed his password. He must know she was snooping.

This made it even more apparent; he most certainly had something to hide.

Catriona spent several minutes pacing around her kitchen, until Vera came in to pour herself a glass of orange juice.

"What are you up to?" she said. "Stop pacing."

Catriona sighed heavily and went to her room. She sat there on her bed, waiting for the steam to come out of her ears and thinking about legal ways to punish Max while also thinking of ways to punish herself. Max would be made furious by her betrayal of his trust. She must keep calm and not do anything silly. She should be very sneaky indeed from now on. She could always deny it. And perhaps he had changed the password at random. She mustn't assume guilt immediately.

Max did not call or email or text to tell her he had noticed that she'd been on his accounts. If he was angry, he was hiding it.

She must see for herself that he was actually alone when he was away from her. Yes. That was the solution. She would see to it that he was home, that he was alone, that he was actually studying. That would calm her nerves and keep her from obsessing each night over whether he was telling her the truth.

Catriona stewed in her own misery and anxiety for hours. She didn't wish to chance giving herself up, letting on to him that she was suspicious or anxious. She waited as long as she could and finally called Max at half past midnight.

"Are you home?" she asked.

"I am."

"Yes. Just calling to see if you needed anything."

"No."

"Are you sure?"

"It's all fine."

"All right, then. Goodnight."

"Goodnight."

"I love you."

She hung up the phone quickly. Saying "I love you" was an embarrassing affair these days. It seemed to her that he paused for too long a time before repeating it, so she usually ended calls immediately after uttering the phrase and avoided saying it in person.

After deliberating momentarily over which coat to wear—her crème trench would surely draw too much attention, and her Barbour was at the cleaners—she knocked on Vera's door. When she opened it, the lights were out. Harry was lying on her bed, the computer screen glowing, casting an exaggeratedly large and monstrous shape onto the leaf-papered wall behind him. *Where the wild things are, indeed*, thought Catriona.

"Hello," she said. "I didn't mean to interrupt."

"You all right?" said Vera.

"I'm nipping out for a moment, and I was wondering if I could borrow your jacket."

"What's the matter with yours? Mine will never fit you."

"I spilled something on it this morning. I've dropped it off at the cleaners, and I wondered if you would lend me yours."

Vera peeked her head into the hallway, where the coat tree stood, full of evidence to the contrary.

"Isn't that it?"

"Hmm?" Catriona's nose squinted, lifting her glasses several centimeters with it.

"Isn't that your trench?"

"Can I speak to you for a moment?" She indicated Harry on the bed.

"Just pretend I'm not here," he said.

Vera closed the door.

"It's about Max. I need to check up on something," said Catriona.

"Ca-tri-o-na!" said Vera, putting a stop between each of the four syllables. "Is this what you've been moping around for all evening? How many times must we go through this? Max is going to come after you with a cricket bat if he catches you sneaking around. He will never forgive you. And please, don't forget about the ring. You're nearly there."

"He changed his Facebook password."

"You don't know what for. Perhaps he doesn't want you to see something about the proposal. Don't be such a cow. He isn't seeing anyone."

"I'm going. Are you going to lend me your jacket or not?"

"Now?"

"Yes, now. I've just rung him, and he says he's home."

Vera knew when to accept defeat and nodded.

"You can have the jacket."

As she put her friend's coat on in the narrow hallway, Catriona heard Vera say to Harry:

"She's going to ruin everything."

"What?"

"She's going to Max's."

Catriona closed the big, blue door of the house behind her. The night was as foggy as the last scene of *Casablanca*. It sounded like it too—the Royal Air Force was practicing some of its night drills in the skies above. Feeling rather exhilarated to be participating in the great tradition of British detective work, though still disapproving of the pipes often associated with the Victorian brand of espionage, she moved through the cool, hazy air in Vera's jacket. Her excitement waxed and waned as she walked down Redfriars Street, past the hair salon and the handyman's shop. The storefronts at night looked like those commonly found in miniature, light-up Christmas Villages. She could see her breath. Winding down Church Street, a gust of salty wind blew the fog in her face. Her glasses steamed.

Down the street and up the stairs, Max and Julie were cozy and warm and settling in for the night. They sat at the living room table, Max's papers spread out before them. Max felt he had handled the surprise phone call well, especially given his current level of frustration with Catriona. He had known that she had been spying for the past few days and had been extraordinarily thankful that he'd had the foresight to delete all of Julie's messages.

He thought he should be angrier, but really he was disappointed. Something in him wanted to believe it wasn't true, to at least give Catriona some sort of credit after all the years together. To know she didn't think quite so badly of him. Besides, at this point he was less worried about Catriona catching him making plans with Julie and more anxious that if Catriona told Peter, it would mean that Julie would stop coming to see him in the evenings.

He put it all from his mind. Julie helped to soothe his nerves.

"Who was that?" asked Julie when he'd hung up.

"Wrong number," he lied.

"Not a prank call?"

"Not this time."

He smiled. Julie said:

"Where's Fern tonight?"

"Rehearsal, I guess."

Julie had been looking forward to an evening alone with Max all day. A lecture with Professor Harris on *A Portrait of the Artist as a Young Man* had made her feel like a particularly dim young woman. She had hoped perhaps there would be wine. Tonight, though, tea had been mandated. Max seemed very keen on getting at least a little work done. Julie had taken to following Max's lead when it came to studying and did not complain. There could be nothing to complain about when she was with Max.

Max smiled as he went into the kitchen.

"You want some olives?"

"Yes, I do."

"Okay, but when I get back, it's time to work. No goofing around."

"I have work to do too you know," she said, feigning offense. "Just because I'm not thinking about ethics doesn't mean it's not important. I'm just glad you have chocolate cake, or I wouldn't be here at all."

She smiled and buried herself in *Anna Karenina* as a means of disguising the true reason for her visit. She was getting to the end and could feel poor, crazy Anna's death chugging along to completion. She laughed as she realized that Max reminded her of Levin.

Momentarily, her cell phone buzzed. She picked it up from the table. To her surprise and dismay, there was a message from Harry. Though she had erased the number, she recognized it immediately from Dubai's +971 country code. Without acting as outraged and alarmed as she actually was (or at least she hoped it wasn't showing on her face), she read the following:

catriona on way to max's in case you're there. H

Without questioning the possible motives behind the warning, or immediately second-guessing the reason Harry should care about what happened to her, Julie began to pack her things. When Max came back from the kitchen, a teacup full of fleshy green olives in his hand, she was putting on her boots.

"Are you going?"

"You know, I was thinking maybe I should get home. I have so much work to do, and we both know it won't really get done here."

"Okay, if that's what you need to—"

"I'm sorry," she was struggling to get out the door quickly. She recalled feeling this way after particularly long sermons during childhood masses: that is, wiggly and nervous like someone was watching her. She leapt down Max's stairs and turned the corner on the sidewalk just in time to escape being caught in Catriona's eyesight. That was what the fog was for.

Upstairs, Max sat on the couch, puzzled by Julie's speedy exit. In the next half minute, the doorbell rang. The tune of Dixie filled the flat, flamboyant and uncalled for. Like an executioner climbing the gallows, he opened the door. There could be no mistake as to who it would be.

"What a surprise."

Catriona entered the flat without being invited to do so. Her plans had only extended as far as the doorway.

"Can I help you with something?" he said.

"Is there a *girl* here?"

She squeezed past him and the door and flipped on the lights in the hallway, in his room, in the bathroom, spinning around in a nauseating fashion like an unruly top.

"Just you. You're embarrassing yourself, Catriona."

"Why did you change your passwords?"

There went her brilliant plan of self-control. She advanced toward him, one finger pointed at his heart.

"What are you talking about? I changed them because you've been using them."

"That's ridiculous."

"Come on. Next time you stalk me on my own computer while I'm in the kitchen, why don't you try deleting the browser history after. Just a hint. And by the way, you just confessed."

Catriona's mouth was agape. Her thoughts pulled themselves deep inside like the ineffectual legs of a fat turtle.

"I didn't do anything wrong," she said in a small voice. "I love you. I was just making sure you were—"

"What?"

"Making sure you're being faithful to me."

Now she was near tears.

"Seriously?"

"Max," she pleaded. "I'm so sorry. Please, love me still. You've got to."

He didn't move. After a moment, he simply said, "Can you please go home so I can finish my work? I know Vera's probably missing her jacket."

Catriona stopped whimpering. She thought of Winston Churchill and would defend her island. She walked through the door, nearly tripping down the stairs when Max closed it quietly behind her.

*I've really done it now*, she thought. She'd ruined it all, and it had taken less than a minute.

Catriona began her sad and lonely walk back through the fog-filled street.

Walking home, Julie opened her phone to see if Max had rung.

He had not, and did not, through the rest of the night.

# VI.

AFTER THE PREVIOUS NIGHT'S STRANGE TURN of events and close call with Catriona, Julie decided to take a break from her nights with Max.

Besides, she had begun to crave the sparkle of social life outside Max's living room. So Julie did one of her favorite things, which was to take a near-scalding shower with a beer in her hand, then straighten her hair while watching *Star Wars*, don massive amounts of red lipstick and the royal blue wrap dress with the deep v-neck, and go have expensive drinks with her friends. She had not recently felt as beautiful as she did when she arrived at Fourteen Ten, the elegant cocktail lounge that took up the first floor of one of the boutique hotels on the Avenue.

The room was paneled in cherry wood, the ceiling inset and glowing from inside the crown molding. Enormous navy lampshades, with tiny star shapes cut out of them, contained enormous, dull bulbs that cast an uneven and mysterious light onto the groups of people seated below on upholstered chaise lounges and deep, red-cushioned chairs. French doors were opened into the cool, evening air, where people stood to French kiss and smoke and make phone calls and look out onto the back garden thinking about how nice it was to sit out there in the summer, though there were well-disguised heat lamps on full power to keep them warm alfresco even in the middle of the winter. Still, the smell of the heather and hydrangea was noticeably missing. Disappointingly, no amount of money could duplicate it.

Inside, Julie was progressing through the crowd of familiar faces to Margot, Neve, and Helen, all in gorgeous cocktail dresses.

"Hello," said Helen, giving Julie a gentle hug. "You look lovely."

"Thank you. So do you, as usual."

"We've missed you lately," said Neve as she put her drink on a passing waiter's brass tray. "Where have you been hiding?"

Julie kissed Margot lightly on the cheek, trying not to bump the swanky vodka drink in her hand.

"I've missed you ladies too. Just the dissertation catching up with me, I guess," she said evenly. "What's everyone drinking?"

Before any of them could ask more about her dissertation or her lack of a social life, Larry appeared at her shoulder, laying a quiet hand on it and smiling at them all kindly.

"Look who's back. Julie Lovejoy. We all thought you had fallen off the Castle Wall or something."

"Not quite. Just working on my dissertation. I don't know why it's so hard for everyone to believe. Do I come off as that much of an airhead?"

"Not remotely. I'm not friends with stupid girls."

Neve and Helen smiled. Larry continued:

"Boy, Julie, you look great."

"Oh, this old thing."

"Seriously, though. You do. All of you do."

"What, this old thing?" said Margot, nodding at Neve.

They all laughed, taking sips of their drinks.

"Julie," said Larry, his hand placing itself gently on her elbow. "Just an FYI that Harry's here."

"Yes," said Helen. "That's right. Would you like to leave? Or perhaps poison his drink?"

"It's fine," said Julie. "He's not worth it."

"He's not going to bother you," said Larry, excusing himself. "I'll keep him out of your hair."

Julie had seen Harry, standing in the corner, his arm around that girl, What's-Her-Name. *Vera.* There he was, in that crowd of supermodel people who always stuck together. Apparently, he had taken to ignoring all the people who had befriended him when he had no other friends in the cold little town besides poor Larry, who still clearly felt guilty about the entire situation.

She wasn't surprised that Harry wasn't speaking to any of them; they probably wouldn't have responded if he had tried. He wasn't stupid—clearly, he was the asshole in the situation and not Julie. And besides, it wasn't as if Harry Ommar had any notion of loyalty. But Julie wondered: if Harry was going to ignore Ashwin, who was standing right behind him, why should he feel the need to do something such as warn Julie of Catriona's impending arrival? And how could he know in the first place? It made no sense whatsoever.

She had partly come tonight hoping to get answers from him. But neither Larry's promise that Harry would leave her alone, nor Vera's presence, portended good things in terms of uncovering any more evidence.

The bar was busy. For all the waiters running about the room with their trays, people were eager to fight for their drinks at the overcrowded bar, and then they were eager to fight over who got to pay for them. She was standing in line when someone tapped her on the shoulder.

"Excuse me," said a pretty brunette with an English accent.

"Yeah?"

"That's quite a nice dress."

"Oh, thanks."

"I'm terribly sorry—do you mind if I ask where you got it?"

*Target*, thought Julie.

"I don't remember. Harvey Nicks?" she said.

"I'll have to remember that," said the girl, receiving a bottle of champagne. "Have a lovely evening."

The girl's glossy brown head glided back into the crowd. Julie saw her and her long legs take a seat next to the prince. That girl, again. So lucky, the way he put his arm around her, gripped her, did not let her go.

Julie waited for a bartender. The man at the piano was singing "Fly Me to the Moon." Finally, over him and the chatter, the clinking of champagne flutes and the clattering of heels on the wooden floor, the turning of the old rusty door handle, she said:

"I'll have a gin and tonic."

"And put it on my tab," slurred Brett from behind her.

"Hey," she said, as he kissed her hand. "Someone's a little drunk."

"You're the best," he said sloppily. "Where have you been?"

"Just—" It wasn't even worth it, to lie to him. "I've been thinking of shagging a boy with a girlfriend. That's all."

Brett laughed as if he thought she'd said the funniest thing in the world and pinched her waist.

"Seriously," she said to the bartender, "that's on me. And a beer for him."

"A Guinness. Both on *me*."

"Okay, a Guinness."

When she had handed the Guinness to Brett and collected her gin and tonic, Julie walked with him onto the balcony. It was darker there and less crowded and Harry occasionally smoked. Perhaps he would follow. Perhaps this was some sort of game to get her to talk to him.

"There you are," said Anastasia to Brett. "What are you drinking?"

"Guinness."

"Hello, Julie. Long time, no see, huh?"

"Long time."

They stood there awkwardly. Anastasia lit a cigarette. She was also very drunk. Brett had taken a seat next to her on the long, low, stone bench, his arm around her waist, his head pressed against her stomach. For a long time, they stayed like that. Brett was falling asleep; Anastasia was swaying. Julie stood there, though she couldn't stand the waiting. Harry was not taking her bait.

"He's useless," said Anastasia, mostly to herself.

"All boys are useless," said Julie. "One of us is worth twenty of them."

Anastasia laughed. "You're right. Ugh. I want another drink. And now I can't even reach his inside pocket for his wallet."

So she opened her purse for the little pills.

"Thank God! There are some left. Want one?"

Julie pretended not to hear as Anastasia swallowed one dry. Harry was still in the lounge. For all she could tell, he hadn't even noticed she was in the bar at all. Larry stood next to Harry, bless him, thinking he was helping Julie. A bulldog, a protector, gatekeeping. She had to distract Larry. And here, right next to her, was the bait: Anastasia. Brett sleeping. It was mean. Maybe just a little. But it would work.

"Will you excuse me?" asked Julie. She parted her way through the crowd, over to Larry and Harry. "Larry, I need your help. Can you come with me?"

"What's up?"

"Anastasia's about passed out, and she just took some pills. Brett's a mess. I hate to ask—could you drive them home? I think you're the only sober one here."

"I didn't bring my car," he said, with genuine concern, for Anastasia at least. "Is she okay? I'll call them a cab."

"I can drive them," said Harry. "Always useful, being the one with the car."

"No one would expect you to," said Vera. "They can get a cab."

"Oh, it's only ten minutes. And I've only had two drinks."

A big man. A hero.

"All right," said Vera. "Shall I come with you?" She eyed Julie.

"I can handle it, babe. Thanks."

"They're over here," said Julie, trying to sound perturbed but not believing her luck.

"Night, Vera, I love you," said Harry, kissing her.

"You're not coming back?"

He shook his head. "Come to mine after, yeah?"

Larry looked at Julie. "You okay?"

"Yeah," she said. "Fine. Just want to get them home."

"Sure?"

"I'm sure."

Harry collected Anastasia and Brett from the balcony, slinging Anastasia over his shoulder and urging Brett to hold onto him. Messily, they made it down the stairs, through the garden, and into the small parking lot off the street.

There, Harry pulled out his phone as Julie waited in steely silence. Clearly, Vera didn't realize who she was. The look she had received was far too mild. And besides, if she had realized, she wouldn't have let Harry come outside, in the dark, with her. Somehow, this made her more embarrassed and angrier with him.

"Who are you calling?" she asked.

"A cab."

"Aren't we driving them?"

"No. I know a good guy. Put them to bed. I'm not going all the way out to those apartments."

Julie rolled her eyes.

"I guess I might as well go back inside then. If I'm not needed to *haul* bodies or anything."

"You're coming home with me."

"No."

"Don't flatter yourself. Only for a chat, that's all."

"I came out tonight to see everyone, not to—"

"You came out tonight to see me. And I came to see you. You always loved Thursdays here."

That shut her up. She had a death grip on her clutch purse. Fuming, she sat down on the hood of Harry's car, listening to him making the phone call. He motioned for her to get off. Brett and Anastasia dozed in the back seat, their arms as limp as dolls' arms.

He hung up.

"Get off."

"No."

He folded his arms across his chest.

They were quiet until the cab came. Julie watched an old couple across the street get ready for bed through their lace curtains. She envied them.

When Anastasia and Brett had been loaded into the taxi to Anastasia's flat, and the taxi man had been paid indiscriminately—whatever bills were available, don't worry over the change, it's not worth the time it takes to count it—Julie got into the passenger seat of Harry's car, and they drove the two minutes to his house in silence.

Inside Harry and Larry's place again, she felt irritable and dirty. The old, thrilling memories seemed ugly, covered in shadows, weak imitations of the objectively tamer memories she had since formed with Max.

"You're lucky I care," he said, tossing his keys on the kitchen table and taking a seat there. "You could have been in big trouble. I don't even think it occurs to you how deep you're in."

"I'm lucky you care?"

Julie remained standing, her arms folded.

"Yes, lucky."

She was quiet.

"You could have been in a world of trouble last night. And so could Max."

"Even if that were true—"

"Yes?"

She stomped her foot.

"How would you even know?"

"Does it matter?"

"I guess not."

Harry scratched the bristle that was growing on his jaw.

"Does it even occur to you to thank me?"

"Oh, so you're the hero now. I get it. Funny," said Julie.

"If you tell me what's really happening, maybe I could even help you a little more."

"There's nothing to tell. Max and I are just friends."

"Just friends."

He laughed, shifted his weight in the chair.

"How did you know?" she asked.

"Know what?"

"That I would be there, at Max's?"

"Simple really—process of elimination. I said to myself, 'Harry, who else could it be?' Then I put two and two together. Max has a girlfriend...you're, you know, *you*...""

"Seriously. You're going to go down that road with me? I didn't know about Vera, Harry. You should have told me."

"You should have asked."

"That one's on you."

"It wouldn't have changed anything. We still would have done it," said Harry.

"I wouldn't."

"Oh really?"

"Really."

"What exactly is it that you're doing now, Julie?"

"Whatever it is, it's none of your business. You saw to that."

"I'm just trying to keep you out of trouble."

"You're trying to make yourself look like a good person. You're not actually being one," said Julie.

"Well, in any case, I'm being serious."

"You think you're so clever."

"Listen," said Harry. "Vera's living with Catriona. They're flatmates."

Julie felt her indignant sails deflating behind her.

"Oh."

"And he hasn't been staying over much lately."

"And?"

"And, other than people like me hearing things—"

"I understand."

"—maybe you should take more care when you bob back and forth between his flat and yours. No other students live in that house, you know. People, passersby. They could notice. Maybe they could even recognize your laugh through an open window. Poetic, huh?"

"Poetic justice, maybe. You remember my laugh?"

"Don't flatter yourself."

They were both still, each one angry with the other. The frustration was hazy and permeating, a gray cloud in the air between them. After a long moment, Harry spoke.

"Just stop being careless. I know you can be careful. I remember."

"Why do you have to bring us up?"

He hadn't meant to.

"I didn't mean to. It's just, this girl—she has some serious problems, Julie."

"We all have problems."

"This is different."

Harry had stopped by one evening to get his wallet, which he had left on Vera's bed. He had been in the hallway while Catriona was getting out of the shower. Hearing the rustle of the curtain and her wet steps smacking on the floor, he'd gone into Vera's room as quickly as possible. Finding the wallet there, he came out of the door just long enough to meet Catriona's backside in a towel. She'd turned with a gasp and then a sharp look of anger.

"Are you trying to frighten me to death?" she'd demanded.

"I'm sorry. Forgot my wallet. I come in peace."

He held it up as evidence.

"You could have called. You have no manners."

"I didn't mean to frighten you."

She had apparently realized all at once that she was standing in a bath towel, talking to a man she didn't like and didn't approve of. She scurried into her room, face turning red. Now she could only hope he hadn't noticed the backs of her legs.

But he had. His mother, the same, the scars.

"If she has problems," said Julie, "I'm sorry for her. But it has nothing to do with me. And it's not what you think it is with Max. We're just friends. Something you wouldn't understand, I guess."

"You think so, do you?"

She headed for the door, opened it, and left it swinging behind her as she walked down the stairs, into the alley, and on to the street.

*If I didn't understand, why would I have helped you?* he thought to himself and closed the door behind her, long gone to—he didn't know where.

# VII.

**MAX DIDN'T MUCH CARE FOR MUSEUMS.** In them, he felt stiff and stuffy, as if someone was moving him, in an unchanging stance of faux-thoughtfulness, from painting to painting. There was something false and awful about the art neatly hung and spaced on the white walls of the gallery. They probably would have been a delight to look at on a real wall in a real home or in the foyer of a theatre or above the fireplace of a queen or in a café full of Bohemians. But here, they were dead—unjustly exiled refugees from the imaginative world from which they had come.

Catriona had organized the evening and the show, which revolved around a series of Monet sketches that had been given to the University's Art Department by an alumna. Miss Darlington-Welland had been selected by her professors to execute the exhibit and the reception of its opening on the grounds that she was the most reliable art student they had ever worked with. A memo was passed around the department one afternoon not so long ago, asking for recommendations as to which fourth year should have the honor. Only one name came back on the forms when the secretary collected and tallied them. None of the other students in her year were surprised, which is why very few of them showed up.

Max progressed around the blocks of framed "artworks." That was the haughty, Catriona-approved-and-used terminology anyway. He was reminded, in viewing their taxonomical organization, of a board of pinned-through, categorized butterflies, all their uniqueness stripped from them among too many other similar, yet unique, things. Catriona had really killed it, he thought. She'd flogged order into it all.

She was standing next to him, and he knew very well she would not have had it been two years ago, when she was only a little more confident. Now, she clung to every moment she had with him.

He was thankful that talking in the gallery seemed to be almost against the rules, as if Monet himself moved through the display and one must pay tribute to him with silence.

Catriona minced her steps and her words. Though this was her moment and her night, a month of hard work and preparation coming to fruition, she felt it important to remain next to Max. Like some sort of floating statue, she hovered next to him as they went through the motions of looking and stopping and looking and stopping.

The last few days had been a challenge. Max was still upset about her snooping. She had apologized several times, and it seemed to have mildly worked. Max didn't go out of his way to reassure her, but Vera tried her best to remind Catriona that when a boy bought a ring he would never change his mind, especially not after three years of keeping her waiting. Max was feeling as if Catriona had betrayed his trust, so he was being distant, Vera reasoned. This was, of course, a more attractive scenario than the alternative, which was to believe that he no longer felt sympathetically toward her and was trying to shut her out of his life slowly, in the way that men did it. The way where they made you crazy and then accused you of being crazy and were gradually more and more mean to you hoping that you would leave them before they had to leave you.

Catriona was cautiously relieved he had come to support her. It was nice for the other arts students and her professors to think there was another side of her. Max was always polite, if quiet, which left it to the imaginations what sort of person he was, what he studied and did and wanted to do. Perhaps they would think better of him than he actually was (as she'd noticed many people did with Max), and this way no one would ever be able to guess that there were problems. They would just assume, at the very worst, that Catriona and Max were a bit pedestrian. But that was how she wanted people to think of them, anyway: just another couple that met and fell in love at St Albas, who would send their progeny and a reasonably-sized donation envelope back up to the sunny side of the Scottish coast so that more like-minded people might do the same.

Simon was there too. He had put in a request to Father Tom that his newly-enforced curfew might be extended until eleven, so that he might be able to spend as much time as possible comfortably hidden in the wake of friendship and as near to Catriona as possible.

Max was glad to see Simon, the only interesting object in the room, and said as much when they shook hands:

"Hello, Simon. Good to see you."

"How are you, Max?"

"Getting on."

"The show's marvelous, isn't it?"

"You think so?"

"It's well organized. She did an excellent job, really. Or at least, I think so. Not that I know much about Monet's sketches, in particular."

"I'm not terribly keen on him, myself."

"Are you not?"

Catriona, who had disappeared for the briefest moment to greet the head of the department, surfaced once more at his side. Max was irritated that a potentially interesting debate was cut short by her reappearance. He was not likely to have much good conversation tonight: Julie's sister Elizabeth was coming from America, and they were in Edinburgh having dinner. Well, by now, they must be on the bus back to St Albas…

As Simon and Catriona exchanged mind-numbingly temperate greetings, he thought about how Julie was. What she might tell her sister on the bus. Would she be wearing the perfume he had snuck a whiff of the last week? Looking over at Monet's sketch of the Cliffs of Étretat, he imagined what it would be like to be there with her. The colors filled in before his eyes. The thick brushstrokes became precise and direct. He could see the curves of her face against the blue water and white rock. Urgent, the feeling that he must take her someplace like that.

But there were places like that in St Albas. The cliffs, the old Castle, the beach. He had to get her there. He had to get her there tonight. She had been avoiding him since the night Catriona had come barging in. He knew it. He didn't blame her. He missed her. He could not let her slip away.

He could pass Catriona off on Simon. Make excuses—a headache, a toothache, an existential crisis. Well, perhaps not an existential crisis. That was too close to the truth.

He had to know how Julie felt. If seeing him was more important than being with her sister, he'd know. If she wanted to introduce him, he'd know. And what would it be like to kiss her? *No, too fast.* One shouldn't hope so much as all that too fast.

He could do this. He could very much do this. Max felt himself capable once again of something that did not have to do with books. Pleasure and courage and other poetic words filled his chest. Tonight, he would do something brave. He would take Julie in his arms, dip her back into the evening air with the cathedral ruins watching in the background, and—

"Max?"

"What?"

Catriona was standing there beside him. Her arms, which had been folded around her chest, the material at the upper arms claustrophobic against the flesh, were dropping to her side. She hooked one through his like a heavy steel tool.

"Would you care for another glass of wine?"

She thought she was being very Continental, didn't she? So suave. And so nice to him—two whole glasses of wine, he would be permitted to have. As if he should jump for joy.

"No, thank you."

"Simon and I were just going to have another. Would you like to come along?"

"Actually," he said, grimacing and gripping his side. "I'm not feeling so well."

"What's wrong?" asked Simon. "Do you need to sit down?"

"I just—my stomach's not feeling so well. I think I'll have to leave."

Catriona's face stretched hot and waxy across her head as she tried to conceal her exasperation and fear.

"Are you really that ill?"

"I am."

"I guess you'd better go, then."

"Yes," he put his arm around what waist he could find and attempted to kiss her dutifully. She swerved her head so that it landed on her cheek.

"Not appropriate," she mumbled. "But thank you."

"Right," he said, relieved. "Goodnight, Simon. Make sure she gets home, yeah?"

Simon nodded. Something was going on. Max was making it all too easy. Alone with Catriona and her art exhibit. He might as well have pushed them out to sea in a rowboat with a bottle of champagne and a harpist.

"I hope he feels better," Simon said after Max had gone.

"He will. It's all in his head."

"Well, would you care for another glass of wine?"

"I don't know if I feel like it so much now, but that's very kind."

"Your exhibition is beautiful, I have to say," he said.

"You think so?"

"I really, really do. It's brilliant."

"Simon," she said, "thank you."

"Not a bother. I was happy to be able to join you."

"I'm so glad you did. Would you care to take a walk around the room? Perhaps I could show you some of my favorite sketches."

"Brilliant. That would be brilliant."

And yet what a wonderful gift Max had given him, an evening spent alone with her. Or, as alone as they could be in a crowd of people. She stood close as she expressed her admiration for the sketches of the indoors, of the lace tablecloths and the ladies at rest. With the facility of the artist's hand in creating these beautiful images. Simon thanked the Great Artist too for the slippery slopes of chestnut feather, for the slippery slopes of her eyes and her feathery lashes, for the bit of plump wrist that squeezed against the large, cuff bracelet of silver lace around it. For the still life as she held her breath and let it out again.

"I like that one," she said. A sketch of a woman in a chair, reading. A man sitting in a chair, smoking a pipe. A baby on a tubed, wool rug, with the ends tied up.

"Me too. I like that you can see the garden outside."

"And the piano. You can imagine them all sitting around it. Singing. Happy. Can't you?"

"I can."

***

Several hours later, Simon was waiting at the coat check with their tickets. Catriona was saying goodbye to the remaining professors, receiving unsurprised thanks and congratulations for her hard work. He was glowing with pride of her, wishing he could put his arm around her and lead her home with him and rub her shoulders and kiss her head gently. But for now, helping her into her coat would have to suffice.

"Number 600," he said to the coat check. "And number 638."

"Right."

When he had the coat in his hands, he felt something in the

pocket. Catriona was turned away from him. Could it be? He checked to see that she wasn't looking and slowly pulled it out of the pocket. The gold-edged book cover revealed what he had suspected. She was reading the copy of *Wuthering Heights* he had bought—was carrying it around in her pocket. He felt a deep sensation of happiness, even down to his very leather-covered toes.

"Simon," she said, touching his arm, "are you ready?"

He turned to her, holding the book with a large grin on his face.

"Are you enjoying it?"

"I am."

"You haven't read it before?"

"No."

"I'm so glad. I didn't know you were reading it. You hadn't mentioned."

"I don't mention every book I read to you, do I?"

She smiled, a small smile, almost wry, almost interesting.

"Well, but this one. It's a gift, after all."

"Yes, from Max. How did you know? Did you help him choose it? I should have known."

"From Max?"

"Yes, for Christmas."

"No, I didn't help him choose it."

His heart sank. He wanted to hit Max. He really should have done so when the bastard was still here.

"He can be sweet, you know." There was something unconvinced and unconvincing in her tone.

"Of course. I didn't mean to suggest anything else. I'm glad that you're enjoying it."

He helped her on with her coat and escorted her to her front door, but no further.

***

It was an unseasonably warm night. BBC weather reported the temperature at 4 degrees Celsius or, for that matter, 40 degrees Fahrenheit. Julie and Elizabeth from America sat in silence in the house on Fair Street, flipping through magazines and drinking a bottle of red wine that the latter had purchased at the airport. For Julie, it was nice to have a friendly face from the Midwest here, sitting on her bed—to have feet dangling near her that had walked on native soil only half a day ago. Other than her mother, no one else said home to Julie like Elizabeth.

Having briefed her sister on what had come to be referred to as "The Situation" on many occasions over the phone, Julie was anxious that Elizabeth and Max should meet for the purposes of sisterly analysis. But that night, as Julie's phone rang, Elizabeth had already put her pajamas on and her curlers in.

"Well, answer it," said Elizabeth.

"Hello?" said Julie, glad to have caught the call.

"Hey," said Max. From the one word, she felt the relief in his voice as well. "Are you home? Can I come by?"

"Are you done already?"

"Exhibition was pretty boring."

"Great."

"Can I come over?"

"Can you come over now?" she said, making eye contact with Elizabeth, who shook her head in metallic protest. "Yeah. But my sister is here and she wants to sleep, so maybe we should go somewhere else. To yours, maybe?"

"Yeah, maybe a walk," he said. Fern was staying in. Though she knew how often Julie was in the flat, he didn't want to risk her getting fed up enough to yell something along the lines of "kiss her already" from her bedroom. "I'll come get you."

"Cool. See you then."

"Five minutes," he said, and then he hung up.

"Oh my *God*," said Elizabeth. "I am in curlers. I am not meeting him now."

"Come on! Who even wears curlers anymore?"

"Me. And I will absolutely not meet him now." She was firm, stacking the magazines on Julie's nightstand and plugging the wine closed with a satisfying rubber click. "Plus, I'm already in bed." She turned the lamp off. "Love you." She rolled under the covers gently resting her head on Julie's mountain of pillows.

Julie stood above her.

"Liz, you are being so unfair. You are, like, the only person who can meet him and see us together and tell me what you think because *you* are the only one who doesn't have to *live* in this stupid little town!"

"I know. Tough love."

"I am going to kill you."

"You might as well. I know too much already." From the darkness, she said, "Just make sure you bring a jacket. It's cold out there."

"It's not that cold."

But Julie took a wool sweater from her wardrobe. Without saying anything else, she shut her bedroom door behind her without any particular regard for the amount of noise it made as she did. As she descended the stairs to meet Max, she noticed the muddy shoe tracks (a relic from the age of Harry) that ascended them. Somehow, it all seemed an entire lifetime ago.

She was still shaken by the narrow escape she had made the previous week from Max's flat. When she was honest with herself, she couldn't imagine where things would be right now if Harry hadn't intervened, and she was thankful. She hadn't seen Max since, and it had been difficult. She missed him terribly. But he was only a friend, and it wasn't right to miss friends so much.

Elizabeth's words on the bus trip back from Edinburgh echoed in her mind. "He's a friend all right. A friend that likes to spend a lot of quality time alone with you in the evening hours."

But Max had never done anything that anyone could ever consider inappropriate. There wasn't the unspoken expectation, as there had been with Harry, that there would someday soon be the two of them, almost certainly without clothes on. The closest Max had ever gotten to her was as they were seated on his bed one night, alternately drinking tea and red wine, laughing and listening to John Denver. And, though she knew she wanted to be near him in a horizontal position, she did not feel from him the surging, incessant need that Harry had last semester. She had resolved not to feel any more for Max than he evidently did or did not for her. Tonight, with the moon and whatnot shining, she must remember that.

In the living room, Caddy was in her usual spot, the comfortable old couch with the lamp that hung above it like a moon that had been conjured by whatever Scottish grandmother lived here with her husband by the sea in the summers. She was reading *Peter Pan*.

"I hope that's not for class," said Julie, who was putting on her shoes. "Or we're really not getting our money's worth."

Caddy sat up. As she placed the book down next to her on the sofa, she rolled her shoulders back and then her neck.

"It's my favorite book."

"I didn't know that," said Julie, always surprised to learn something new about the person whose house she had shared for three years.

"My mother gave it to me for Christmas. A long time ago." She ran her hand gently across its front cover. The book was clearly well loved. Its cover, dark and slightly eerie with the exception of Big Ben's golden clock face, was not the perfect rectangle it had once been. The edges were rounded and wrinkled, the battle wounds of being thrown in book bags and suitcases and onto nightstands in endless succession over what could only recently be called the "last two decades." The pictures inside were still surprisingly colorful. Caddy had memorized the scenes they contained. The Georgian row houses of Kensington, looking stately and lonesome in the evening gaslight; a pea-green alligator swimming through reflectionless water, the clock locked deep in its belly calculating his speed toward Captain Hook; earthy watercolor depictions of the cozy, unkempt rabbit warren that housed the Lost Boys; people flying out of windows, leaving the shutters stark wide-eyed open to the chilly British air. Girls who told stories, and the boys who wouldn't grow up.

Caddy sighed a little.

"Where are you off to at this time of night?"

"Max is coming to get me."

Julie had, upon arriving home after her conversation with Harry, shared the identity of her suitor to Caddy, taking pains to swear her to secrecy and also being careful not to reveal his link to Peter. Still, Caddy had taken a hard line on the subject, even in her gagged state.

"Elizabeth isn't coming along?"

"She's asleep. I think you wore her out over dinner. And I don't need a chaperone."

"Julie," she said, in a warning tone. "You have to put an end to this. You're only going to get hurt. And what about his girlfriend?"

"Caddy, there is nothing going on. He's never tried anything. We're just friends."

"No, you're not just friends. Because you like him."

"All right, fine. I like him. But it's been, what, six weeks? And he's never tried anything. I highly doubt he feels the same way. So what's the harm? We'll all be out of here in June, and you know the only thing I want is to leave here and go home without any unnecessary boy drama. I am done. Believe me. I think we learned that lesson with Harry Ommar."

"Let's hope so," Caddy said. She was not unkind. "You'll forgive me though—six weeks, and he hasn't tried anything? So either he isn't interested in you and he's playing with your mind, or he is interested and has decided to lead you on while also screwing his girlfriend over, as I doubt she's aware of your nocturnal walks. Great catch, Julie."

Julie sighed heavily. Caddy continued:

"You know I just want you to be happy. And what you have here is a recipe for disaster. If he's not willing to see you in the light of day—"

At that precise moment, the doorbell rang. Caddy gave her flatmate a defeated look and returned to the adventures of Peter and Wendy, kicking her feet back onto the sofa and catching the electric moonbeams once more. Julie went to the door.

She shook the old crystal knob. Though its temperament usually left something to be desired in the way of functionality—one had to rattle at a very precise rate in order to squeeze it open—it was especially difficult tonight. It was as though the old wood had finally ceased to creak enough away from the lock to let her out. Outside, Max knocked again. Julie looked through the peephole, feeling Caddy's sense of superiority inflating on the sofa.

"I think the door is stuck," she said through the door.

"What?" asked Max.

"I think the door is trying to tell y'all something," said Caddy under her breath.

Julie marched past her roommate, going to the large window. Flinging open the shutters and lifting the heavy, splinter-bestowing wooden frame, she twisted her head into the flowerpots. She could make out a confused Max on the street.

"Pst," she said. "I'm over here."

He looked up to the second floor, where the window he imagined belonged to her bedroom was floating.

"I can't see you," he said, in this direction.

"To your left, in the bushes." Max turned to find Julie there, hanging out the window, her face a few inches over a pot of dying sunflowers that were struggling to keep body and soul together in the February chill, left there by Caddy who insisted in Southern stubbornness that it become spring already.

"Hi. I think your door isn't working."

"It's not. Do you mind if I just climb out here?"

"Be my guest," he said. "Can I help?"

"No, no, I'll only be a second." She pulled herself back into the house, taking her phone from the coffee table. "Guess I'm out the window," she said to Caddy.

"Always a lady."

"You're one to talk. Goodnight."

Julie pulled herself through the window. Door or no door, she was very happy to see Max. It showed on her face.

"I thought we'd head down to the Ancient Links. Yeah?"

"Sure," she said as they started in that direction. "How was the exhibition?"

The streets were slightly damp with freshly melted ice. The water, awake, ran downhill on Sea Street toward the Links, not knowing if it would wind up as part of the stream that ran under the old cobblestone bridge near the 16th hole or perhaps as a few drops more in the gyrating sea. Julie watched the streetlights playing games on the dewy curbs that skated downward in curves of smooth stone. The houses were mostly dark. Many of the students were out at the pubs.

Max was cheerful for the first time that day, matching his strides with Julie's as the two turned the corner and strolled down the narrow street that led downhill to the Ancient Links. In a small, rectangular window between the storefronts that faced each other in an eternal staring contest, the sea and the sky unfolded like a brilliantly embroidered tablecloth of navy water and air and gold speckled stars. The golf shops on both sides of the street were shut. The mannequins inside gave no testament to the passing pair's presence, other than to reflect them on their silvery surfaces. The lone man-made light came flooding into the street from a single pub full of students and tourists. The voices from the inside were muffled. The closer they walked toward the sea, the more blurred the noise became, masked by the sound of the water trickling slowly into the tributaries and tide pools and the restless waves racing onto the flat, sandy beach.

The beach by moonlight was otherworldly. Standing there, looking out at the cliffs and the endless expanse of water, one felt that this was what a Martian beach might look like. The plane of smooth sand stretched for miles to the left and right like an immaculate, undisrupted cut of satin, pulled tight and lit from above. From the hairy dunes made of sea birds' nests that marked the start of the beach, it was no short distance to the water. It took them several minutes to cross the sand. For a while, they stood at the edge of the sea, throwing stones into the water. Afterwards, they walked back to the Links, stumbling upon several incredible objects on their way—a gigantic log, craggy and angry after having been tossed onto this cold, dry shore by force, its red trunk naked-looking without the smaller vein-like branches it had of late lost; a fossil had clearly been home to a spiral-shaped creature that had also been hurled unexpectedly from the sea; and a smooth, lonely shell that Max gave to Julie without comment as they talked of other things.

The Ancient Links were a slightly dangerous spot for a nocturnal walk. The same variations in geography that confounded the best golfers were those that often led undergraduates to visit the emergency room at the community hospital. Perhaps the National Health Service would have done well to subsidize covers for the holes—many a student had experienced the uncomfortable and the embarrassing situation of having an ankle caught near the end of the 14th green while trying to pinch a pin. Evidently, The Ancient Links Foundation was not smart enough to collect the flags and store them in the field house at night. Thus, they were too often trophies in dormitories and residences, stood next to televisions and hung over fireplaces, inherited in academic families and given to girls the same way stuffed animals used to be won and given at carnivals. As usual, the leisurely interests of the upper class had won out over the socialist medical service, and, daylight disappearing at five o'clock when the golf was officially over for the evening, the Ancient Links was something of a hazard. Unfazed by these unpleasant possibilities, Julie and Max walked on.

The ground beneath their feet was spongy. Above, the full moon was stirring, obscured by the occasional cloud that passed quickly, illuminated like a thin veil of smoke under a flashlight. It made you wonder what was going on up there that you didn't know about.

Having crossed the Ancient Links without incident, they progressed down the Avenue, coming to a halt in front of the church. Across the street in the rectory, a curtain rustled at the sound of a familiar voice.

"Do you go to church?" asked Julie, staring up at the stained glass.
"No."

"Not even as a kid?"

"No. My parents never went in for that sort of thing, I guess."

Julie didn't know what made her say it:

"And your girlfriend?"

Max felt the collar of his jacket get a little tighter.

"She's a Catholic."

"Does she go here?"

"Yes. She does. I mean I think she does."

Julie evaded Max's eyes, which had become fastened onto her face like reinforced buttons of blue. In her most casual voice, she said:

"You know, I have been wanting to invite you to this thing I'm having at the Midway on the weekend. My sister Liz is here, you know, from America. And I know we haven't known each other for very long, but I think it'd be really nice if you guys could meet."

"You want me to come to the pub?"

"Yeah. There's a Facebook event and all. But. I didn't want to invite you there. In case—in case it gave you trouble with your girlfriend."

"Oh," he said, taken by surprise at Julie's caution on the matter. "No. I mean, I wouldn't worry about that. It's—fading out anyway."

"Oh. Okay."

They continued down the street.

Across the way, the disturbed curtain hung limp once more. Simon sat back in the chair that faced the church and the sea. In the daytime, the view was actually unrivaled in St Albas. Tonight, it seemed to have served a more sinister purpose. For the conversation looked much more intimate through the curtains: a boy and a girl caught in the complex mix of shadows from the moon and the streetlight, standing close to one another, talking in low voices, admiring the surroundings. Simon checked his watch. It was just past midnight. What was Max thinking? Lying to Catriona, leaving her at her exhibition. For this?

He dialed Catriona's phone number.

"Hello," said her voice at the other end.

"Hello, Catriona. How are you?"

"Fine. Are you all right? Did you leave something at the coat check?"

"I'm fine. And no, I didn't leave anything."

Silence.

"It's midnight."

"Oh, so it is."

"Is there something the matter?"

"No," he said. "I just couldn't sleep."

"I don't know that I can help you with that."

"No. I suppose not. Never mind. I'm sorry for disturbing you."

"You are behaving quite strangely."

"Am I? I'm sorry."

"Would you like me to come? Is it serious?"

"No, no. Don't. Can we—could we have coffee tomorrow?"

"Yes, if you'd like to. What time?"

"After mass?"

"I'll go to lunch with Max after mass, if he's feeling better, at the Cathedral Café. We could walk there from church."

"That's grand," said Simon, with every ounce of genuineness he could muster. He could think of no reason to press her about meeting alone.

"Goodnight," she said and hung up.

Catriona was sitting on her bed. Her teddy bear was next to her in a curled position, his head between his legs like an airplane passenger braced for an emergency landing. Catriona laid him down on the pillow next to her, readjusting the large, glossy book of *Cézanne* on her lap. How curious to get a phone call from Simon and after midnight. But she was glad he had called. She had been sitting up anxiously, wondering where Max was. She wasn't sleeping well these days. The paring knife had been coming out more and more often.

For their part, Max and Julie moved on to the Castle. Under any circumstances, it was an imposing sight: layer upon layer of gray stone, compounded with centuries of history and Scottish weather. In the moonlight, it was spectacularly ghostly. Remember, these ruins sat on the edge of a cliff: on one side, the shallow water and the brown rock; on the other, the soft bed of sand below the Castle. Having been burned at some point during the Reformation (what in this town had not? Several martyrs would surely attest to the many righteous bonfires that had consumed persons and places and things), the Castle as it stood now was nothing but four high walls, a few staircases without their landings, a courtyard, a well, and a tower that was curiously intact, standing like a straight, tall guard over the ruins and the town. Perhaps it was still anticipating, patiently as a dog waiting for the mailman, the Viking invasion its very existence predicted and promised.

It did one well to remember that students liked to die by hurling themselves from the Castle and onto the shallow rocks, which was devastating to hear about. One year, the generally bored police had gotten a budget surplus and had installed a rudimentary fence along the third side to prevent it from happening, or at least to give a person the chance to change their mind while getting to the tower. The fence was three feet tall and was comprised of long, sturdy wooden boards. You didn't have to be Huckleberry Finn to make it to the other side.

"I have never been inside the Castle," said Julie, staring at it. "Can you believe it?"

"Oh, come on. Let's go."

"I didn't mean we have to go!"

"We're going," said Max. "It's an adventure."

Julie was caught up in Max's enthusiasm.

"Okay," she said.

Julie and Max scrambled over the fence and walked around the courtyard in wide circles, their hands in their pockets and their faces tilted toward the starlight in the sky.

"I swear, I'm going to fall into the moat," said Julie.

"I could throw you in the moat."

Julie laughed. "I think there's just mud in there."

*If it gets your shirt wet,* thought Max to himself.

"You can swim, right?" he said, giving his companion a gentle shove.

"Hey," said Julie, trying her best to sound offended. She trotted in the direction of the tower, the outline of which was painted in black against the navy sky. Reaching the base of the tower, she searched with the light on her cell phone for a set of stairs. "Max," she whispered loudly. "Can we get up here?"

Max appeared next to her instantaneously.

"Yeah." He led the way around to a series of uneven bricks.

"How many times have you been here?"

"Just when my parents come," he said.

He had been here with Catriona that afternoon. He had taken photos of her in her emerald St Albas gown to put up in the gallery next to her biography at the start of the exhibit and in the program. What were a few photos, for the sake of peace, after all these years?

He was surprised at how detached he had become from Catriona. It made him wonder how he had ever been attached, if that was even what it was. When he thought about it, he had slid into the relationship. She was convincing. Never in a way that was too forward. It was the invitations to drink a cup of tea or to sit near her after dinner when someone awful was playing something on the baby grand piano in the lounge. He didn't like too many people. He was thinking coming to St Albas was a mistake, especially after Clara and her mysterious departure. And here was someone who thought he was funny. He resented himself for being too easily flattered, but in a way, he couldn't blame himself. Clara had been interesting—too interesting as a matter of fact—and Catriona was about as far from it as possible: her predictable, prescribed reactions to art, to culture, to everything. There was not an exciting thing about her, and he had thought that was what he wanted. It would be easy—ever so easy.

He thought back to that moment that he could barely remember, the scene when he told her he loved her. He recalled that he had tried to mean it, but that the truth was, he was lonely and missing Clara and resenting himself—and Catriona, well, she was there. Ripe for the picking and so willing. He wished he would have known then what the price would be.

As he had taken those pictures that afternoon, watching the lens snap up and down quickly, he began to realize what he had given up. A part of his youth. He thought of May Saving, of three of them gone by. He thought of the friends he might have made if he hadn't been lazily locked up for so many evenings being bored by Catriona and her lack of opinion, emotion, passion. It wasn't Catriona's fault, really. She had set the trap, of course, but he had watched her do it. "Put that stick there," he might as well have said. "And the net can hang here, under these leaves. I'll never see it." He had stuck his foot into it and thrust his whole weight upon it. No, he had no one to blame but himself.

But while a feeling of panic was building, so was the sense that here, with Julie, he was free. Here they were, climbing into castles, laughing, teasing. She was beautiful. She didn't know it or think it a possibility. She was too honest for that. Here was a girl who didn't hold back, who didn't care about rules, who made him feel his age.

He would always know what Julie thought because she would always say it. But if Julie wore her heart on her sleeve, why couldn't he tell what her feelings were for him?

This, all this, he realized, was Catriona's greatest fear. This delight, this danger, this uncertainty—this real, young love.

The tower had a small window overlooking the sands and, in the distance, the cathedral and the pier. It was large enough for two people to fit inside sitting cross-legged. The glassless window was barred vertically, but there was still enough room to fit most of an arm between the gaps.

Julie did something brave. She lay back on the cold stone. Staring up, she discovered that the tower's roof was gone. The clouds were beginning to depart. And here, in the small town where lights were not a competing force against the stars, Julie could pick out the pinpoints of needle-end light one by one. To her surprise, Max laid down next to her. Here they were, shoulder to shoulder, head to head. Here was the tension, as her legs, in the shape of a pyramid, swung slightly back and forth, touching the sides of his trousers. She left her hand open at her side. His hand brushed against hers. Every few minutes, it happened again. Was she meant to let him take hers?

His head came closer. It was almost on her shoulder. They lay there for a long time, just like that. The game of chess continued. Julie couldn't help but feel as if the universe was playing a cruel joke on her. Perhaps she had been transported back in time and was stuck in the middle of a Julie Austen novel, one in which she could never, ever accept this brushing hand that suggested something or didn't. She began to feel furious at Max. If he was going to take her hand, if that's what he wanted, what on earth could possibly deter him from just taking it? *But,* she remembered, *this is exactly what I'm not going to do. I will, at all costs, avoid desperation.*

"Maybe it's time to go home," she said, finally. She had cut him off in the middle of a conversation. Something having to do with telling the truth, and whether white lies were moral or not, something again about that philosopher Max loved.

"I guess it's getting late."

"I mean, it is like five in the morning."

"Really? How can you tell?"

"Look at the sun."

"Okay, Copernicus."

"I was a girl scout, you know." Julie brushed herself off and slid out of the window. "For ten years."

"Shows why you're so outdoorsy."

"Oh yeah." She was struggling less to find her way out the Castle's front door. The walk had worked wonders in the way of sobering up.

Max took her home. When they arrived on the doorstep, there was a note on the door. Caddy had fixed it. There was no need to come in through the window.

"Goodnight," said Julie.

"See you tomorrow?"

"Maybe," she said.

"I missed you, Julie," said Max.

"Okay. I know you did."

She went inside, locking the door behind her.

Max stood there for a moment, scratching his head in the inquisitive manner that was his trademark. After another few seconds of hesitation in which he thought the better of knocking on the door, he turned down the street and toward home. He had had such a lovely time that he had forgotten to ask Julie how she felt.

What they really talked about that night they never knew.

# VIII.

THE NEXT MORNING, CATRIONA WENT TO mass. Through the stained glass windows, the sun was shining with admirable vitality. The view from the cliffs was magnificent: the sky half full of watercolor clouds tinted in shades of salmon and gold. These colors were reflected in the placid water in the tide pools, looking as if God had gone to work with His pastel chalks, rubbing them onto the surface in an expertly blended palette that impressed even the more skeptical among His earthly critics.

A short while after the service, Catriona met Simon in front of the church. He had taken off his robes and was wearing a heavy cardigan of blue wool along with smart, recently ironed black trousers and a gray scarf. He looked restless. Simon had met with Father Tom that morning to indulge in the act of confession. Whether it was official or not, Simon never knew. Being friends with the priest, he did not mean to dampen their camaraderie by differentiating between the Lord's business and man-to-man advice. The two had been washing the gold chalices and bread bowls in the rectory sink:

"Father, I'm having a problem, and I'd really like to hear your thoughts about it."

"Of course," said Father Tom, who was much more personable in person than during mass. "Not sure who to bet on for the rugby, is it?"

"Not exactly. I've—I've been having thoughts about a young lady. A member of the congregation."

"Really? Who?"

Father Tom longed to be a part of the town gossip, and his tone suggested as much.

"Catriona Darlington-Welland, as a matter of fact."

"She seems to be a nice young lady."

He had recently heard her very boring confession. Catriona was certainly not Father Tom's type. He had always liked the ill-behaved girls himself.

"What's going on, then?"

"Other than my wanting to become a priest, of course?"

"Of course," said the priest, a little too quickly to be convincing.

"She has a boyfriend."

"That is a problem."

"And last night, as I was lying awake, I heard him talking to a girl in the street. I saw him. They looked awfully comfortable with each other. And so, I called Catriona to tell her."

The pair was silent for a moment. Father Tom considered the dilemma facing his young charge. He had, over the years, grown accustomed to hearing these types of concerns from young men trying their hardest to hide from their sexual urges. It was a difficult thing to do, like pulling an entire tree up from its roots and asking it to grow just as strong in a pot full of water rather than soil.

"Did you tell her?"

"No. I didn't."

"Perhaps that's for the best. Sometimes when we convince ourselves we're helping our friends, we are merely being selfish. Besides all that, even if it ends for the two of them, are you willing to break away from the path you've chosen? Can you be sure that she will return your affections after you agitate her scorn towards the other boy?" He sighed. "Perhaps I have limited experience in these matters, and maybe that is true compared to other men of my age. But I must tell you, as someone who has the best interests of your soul and heart in mind, that you must seriously consider the possible repercussions of telling this young lady what she most certainly does not want to hear."

"I wouldn't want to hear it, if I was her."

"It's tricky, isn't it? Thinking of how we impact others."

"Yes."

"But I know you well, Simon. And you are one of those rare people who do think about it."

"I'm going to meet them both this afternoon," he said.

"Well, then, you'll just have to pray about it, won't you? I can't tell you what happens in the end. I don't know." He clapped Simon on the shoulder in a show of brotherly affection. "Now, hadn't you better light some candles and sweep between the pews? You have to earn your keep, young man. That is, if you're still interested."

Simon tried to remember these friendly words of caution when he saw Catriona. A heavy collar obscured her neck, leaving it in darkness below her pink face. In the bundle of shadows, he could make out the little gold cross that settled on her throat. They strolled in the sunlight from the Avenue to the end of Sea Street, where the Cathedral Café was fixed on a spot near the town's only stoplight.

The outside of the café was painted a bright white, though the windows and the door were lined with a fire engine red. The color scheme made the place look as if the Swiss Army had acquired an outpost in Scotland. Inside, the boxy shape and hard wooden floors made for a great lot of noise, particularly because the Cathedral Café tended to employ rather robust women who were prone to accidental rearrangements of the furniture as they bustled through the tight lanes of chairs and tables.

Catriona and Simon had seated themselves at a table near the kitchen. The waitress with cotton candy hair came to take their order: two cappuccinos, a blueberry muffin, and a bagel with cream cheese and salmon.

"I thought Father Tom's sermon was lovely," said Catriona.

"Did you?"

"Particularly the theme of thinking of others instead of ourselves. Sometimes I feel as though he is speaking directly to me."

Simon tried to compose himself.

"It can certainly seem that way sometimes, can't it?"

He hailed the waitress, who lumbered her way through the room as quickly as possible.

"May we have some water, if you don't mind?" He turned to a pale Catriona. "You would like some water, wouldn't you?"

The waitress smiled and said she'd bring some. As she walked away, she moaned something about the English to herself.

"How are classes getting on?" asked Catriona. "Is your Greek seminar all right?"

"Catriona," said Simon, with the utmost caution, "I have to tell you something. I know I've been a bit strange today."

"Between last night and this morning, especially. You were quite yourself when you dropped me off at my door—and at the exhibition. And then that odd phone call. If there's something the matter, I wish you would tell me instead of making me anxious."

"I never mean to make you anxious."

"I know that," she said, gently. "So, please, tell me what's going on?"

Father Tom's words of caution were echoing in Simon's ears.

"You have to promise you won't be upset at me."

"I'll try."

Catriona was bewildered. Here she was, trying to make after-mass conversation in a coffee shop, and Simon did not seem to share her view that the topics discussed there should be of the kind not likely to cause an upset stomach.

"Did you see Max last night?"

"Excuse me?" Her tone of voice managed to suggest her suspicions toward both Simon and Max.

"Don't be upset. Please. I'd simply like to know."

"Why?"

She was so tense that Simon felt he needed to retreat. He was reminded of Napoleon at Waterloo—perhaps this gamble was not the wisest. Perhaps it was time to pack up camp and call it a day. Better exiled than dead. Better off course than sunk. The water came with the coffee, with the food, just in time.

Still, he thought of the book she'd been carrying around and said:

"Lately, I've thought that things weren't going quite right with Max. And you've seemed quite upset in the last few weeks, and, well, when I watch you in church praying like that, all I can think is maybe there's something wrong...and maybe I can help." He had no idea where the latter half of this speech had emerged. Perhaps he would be a priest yet.

"You aren't a priest yet," said Catriona, letting out a sigh of relief that Simon had no bad news to convey related to Max. "We're only friends, Simon. And until you're wearing a white collar, I'm afraid you'll have to go about helping me through the normal channels. For instance, inviting me to coffee."

She was warming again. Perhaps it was the muffin that'd just been placed before her.

"And if you'd like me to be honest, things might be better with Max. They have been better with Max."

"I'm sorry."

"However, I don't think there's anything to fuss over."

"You don't?"

"No," she said, lowering her shoulders, "Simon—Max is going to propose to me."

Simon stared at her catatonically.

"So, you see, don't worry so much." She gave a little laugh that he couldn't quite believe. There was an air of desperation about her as she shared this information. "There I was last night, worried about you, when you were worried about me. You really will make the most fantastic priest, Simon."

"Perhaps I shall."

He was glad not to have said anything about Max after all.

Then Max came through the door.

"Speak of the devil," said Simon.

Max smiled at them, hanging his jacket on the series of hooks near the front of the room and wiping his old, worn-out shoes on the rug. Arriving at the table, he took a seat next to Catriona, giving her a kiss on the cheek before burying himself in the menu.

"Have you eaten?" asked Catriona.

"No. I just woke up."

Simon couldn't quite resist:

"Up late last night, were you?"

"Yes," said Max. "And I couldn't sleep." In his mind's eye, he saw Julie, jumping down from the tower window. He hadn't slept. The frustration of having the best night of his life without accomplishing his goal of telling her how he felt had made him too ill to shut his eyes all night.

"That's too bad. Did you try taking a walk? Sometimes that helps me sleep."

"No," said Max, as casually as possible. "I listened to some music and tried to read a book. How was your night?"

"Very similar."

"What'd you get up to last night, Catriona?" Max said.

"I just went over some *Cézanne*, don't you remember? I told you."

Perhaps the farthest thing from Max's mind was what art book Catriona had spent the night with. But he was being made uncomfortable and was happy at least that after the fight about her snooping Catriona no longer asked him questions about where he had been.

"You're so odd sometimes," she said. "What a funny boy I've got."

"That's me," said Max.

There was an awkward silence.

"Excuse me, I'll be back in a moment," said Catriona, with a thin smile on her face as she made her way to the ladies' room.

When she had gone, Simon and Max sat without speaking. Max was the one to break the silence, preferring to play offense rather than defense.

"I hate to presume but is something the matter?"

Simon had not prepared himself for this direct line of questioning.

"I think you know what's the matter."

"Not with you, I don't."

"Catriona will be back any minute."

"What does it have to do with her?"

"I saw you last night."

Max felt the tectonic plates clicking out of place below him. Simon wasn't referring to the exhibition.

"What?"

"With that girl."

"Where?"

"Outside the rectory."

If Max knew one thing for certain, it was that Simon was not a liar. For this reason, he found protest, denial, and dishonesty impossible. He folded his hands on the table like a criminal who gives himself up before the interrogation has begun.

"I could tell you it's nothing."

"Is it?"

"No."

"Are you going to tell Catriona?" Simon asked.

"Yes, I promise."

"When?"

"Listen, Simon, it's complicated."

"You think I don't know that?"

Max sighed heavily and played with the edges of his napkin.

"Please don't say anything, Simon. I'll figure it all out."

"Listen, all I want is for Catriona to be happy. You're my friend, Max. You always have been. Despite our differences. Or similarities. Including this one."

"I know."

"Catriona thinks things are getting serious. And if you're only going to break up with her, then you need to do it sooner rather than later. I don't know how much longer I can keep my mouth shut. It's not fair of you to ask me."

Though this was not a satisfactory end to the conversation, it was ended out of necessity. Catriona had come back from the toilet.

"Simon," she said upon seeing his severe expression, "are you all right?"

Simon was relieved not to have said any more to either of them than he had. He took his scarf from the empty chair next to him and tied it around his neck. Placing a £10 note on the table, he stood.

"You'll have to excuse me."

"You aren't ill as well, are you?" said Catriona. "Maybe you've caught something from Max."

"Perhaps that's it. In any case, I think maybe I'll take a page out of Max's book and get some more sleep. I had to wake up early this morning." He smiled. "I hope you two have a lovely day. Catriona, that tenner should cover you as well. Breakfast is on me. Goodbye, Max."

Catriona turned to her boyfriend as Simon departed.

"He called me at midnight. Very strange."

"What did he say?"

"I'm not sure." She paused. Max looked pale. "What did you two talk about while I was in the toilet?"

"Nothing."

"Max," she said meekly, almost knowing his answer would be a lie, "where were you last night?"

"Home. Like I said." He took a bite of Simon's bagel. "Can we drop it?"

He felt as though he had told the truth.

# IX.

JULIE AWOKE THAT MORNING TO A blaring radio in the kitchen. From what it sounded like, Liz and Caddy were bonding over their mutual love for the radio program *Breakfast with the Beatles*. And so, to the opening notes of "It Won't Be Long," she opened the curtains, took a Tylenol, and went downstairs. The kitchen was flurrying with activity. Caddy was smoking out the window and stirring pancake batter simultaneously. Liz, in her jogging clothes, was unloading a bag from the farmer's market. Her hair was bouncy. The curlers had evidently served their purpose. Barrie, the gingery town cat, had jumped up on the window ledge and was resting there quite comfortably, stretching and purring luxuriantly. Perhaps he knew it was these behaviors Caddy found favorable in human and feline companions alike, or maybe she had simply conditioned him well with treats over the years.

"I know," Caddy was saying. "He's such a nice guy."

"He just looked so sad."

As Julie's presence in the room was noticed, the conversation immediately stopped. Julie thought little of it; the two had clearly been catching up on the latest town gossip.

This was Liz's fourth visit to St Albas. While sisters who were not so loyal might choose to travel somewhere warmer than home in the spring, Julie was lucky in that Liz never tired of Scotland or of her friends there. In fact, Liz and Caddy's liking for one another sometimes exceeded their collective liking of Julie.

"Look what the cat dragged in," said Liz, who had gone to work skinning a potato. Barrie gave a concurring purr.

"Hello, Barrie, my love. How was your run, Lizzy?" asked Julie.

"No one gives a shit," said Caddy. "I mean, no offense, Liz."

"None taken. I think we'd both rather hear how your night was."

"Guys, nothing happened. We had a little walk around town. You know—Flat Sands, Ancient Links, up the Avenue..." She crossed to the cupboard, taking out a box of fruity cereal.

"You're not eating cereal," said Caddy, who lifted the wooden spoon from the batter and pointed it in Julie's direction. Some of it fell onto Barrie, who licked it happily away. "What do you think I'm doing over here? Details. Or no pancakes."

"I second that," said Liz.

Julie broke down in a romantic sigh, resting her chin in her palms.

"We took this epic walk, and then we broke into the Castle. We sat in that big tower for a while. And at one point, I laid down. Just to see what he'd do."

"And?"

"And he laid down too. And I had my hand kind of like—hanging there at my side."

"Palm open, or closed?"

"Open. And he didn't hold it."

Caddy and Liz commenced to exchanging shifty glances. Julie felt like a kid called in to see the principal and vice principal at the same time.

"And nothing else happened?" asked Caddy.

"No. Although," she delighted in seeing them lean forward in anticipation, "I did stupidly invite him to the thing at the Midway. But, you know what? If he can't see me in the light of day, he doesn't deserve to see me at all."

"We're going to the Midway at night," said Caddy.

"Well. Metaphorically."

No one spoke for a minute. "Tell Me Why" was coming from the little radio. The potatoes were now frying on the hob. Liz and Caddy were both turned away from her now, laboring over the pancakes and the eggs and the hash browns.

"Well, what do you guys think?"

"I don't know," said Caddy. "He might be messing with your head. If he likes you, really, he would have taken your hand or taken some kind of action given the situation. Kissed you or something. You know?"

"But what about me? Did I do the right thing?"

"Hmm. I'm glad you didn't throw yourself at him," said Caddy.

"What a vote of confidence. Liz?"

"Listen, Julie, you have gotten into a lot of trouble this year. And

I hate to say it, but I don't think you could make a decision that was less wrong or more right than already laying there in the Castle with him."

"What do you mean?"

"I mean that he's already cheating on this girl. So it doesn't really matter if you are all kissing and holding hands and having sleepover parties or not."

"I wouldn't go that far." Julie set the table, laying the knives and forks and plates haphazardly. She never knew, and did not care to find out, the proper way. "But he did say something last night that was interesting. He told me not to worry about her. That it was fading out."

"I think that means he isn't worrying about her either," said Caddy. "All I'm saying is I don't want to see you go through what you did with Harry."

"I won't. It's different. If he even likes me at all. Which he may not." Julie was exasperated by the frequency of this conversation, both in her head and outside of it.

"Okay," said Caddy, who smoothed Julie's hair and gave her a quick, motherly kiss on the top of her had. "Let's eat."

The three girls sat down at the table. A lovely breakfast had been assembled, and Julie felt happy to be a girl. The strawberries, purchased at the farmer's market, laid in a bowl, split open, their middles shallow, wet, and sweet. Caddy was much more proficient with pancakes than her distracted cooking methods would suggest, and Liz's potatoes tasted good with the maple syrup she had brought from America. For quite a long time, they sat there, happily munching away, listening to the radio and not speaking very much. Eventually, the food was gone, and so was Julie, who went to Florians to buy sparkling wine for mimosas.

"Sorry about before," said Liz, who began clearing the plates. "I didn't want to talk about all this in front of Julie. She's got enough to worry about."

"What exactly did he say?"

"Okay, so we're standing at the strawberry stall at the farmer's market, and Peter sees me, and we say hello and all of that. 'Where's Julie?' he asks. 'Not that I'm not happy to see you. Next best thing.' I told him we both had a long day yesterday. 'I just haven't seen her in ages. It's funny, it almost feels as if she's avoiding me.' I was so surprised to be put on the spot like that—even though I'm sure it's not what he meant to do. But ugh—he looked so upset, and I didn't know what to say other than we'd see him at the Midway."

"That's probably for the best."

"But *is* she ignoring him?"

"She hasn't told you yet either?"

"No. Told me what?"

*Typical Julie*, thought Caddy. *Only part of the story.*

"About Catriona. Max's girlfriend?"

The wheels in Liz's head were turning.

"Peter's *cousin* Catriona? The crazy one? *That's* Max's girlfriend? Obviously, I knew he had one. But *her*?"

"Yeah. Peter's cousin. How do you know about her?"

"Julie's mentioned her a couple of times, over the years. Does Julie know? That Max and Catriona are a thing?"

"Probably, which is no doubt why she hasn't mentioned it. I mean, it's bad enough for her to be chasing another guy with a girlfriend. She doesn't want us to know that if she succeeds, it'll fuck Peter over in some way or another. Even I am not *about* to pry open that can of worms."

"Does Peter know that Julie's interested in Max?"

Caddy lit a cigarette.

"I don't know."

"But do you think—"

"I don't know! It stresses me out just thinking about it."

"Poor Julie."

"Yeah," said Caddy. "I would not want to be her. I wouldn't want to be any of them, to tell you the truth."

Caddy had turned to the window with a treat for Barrie, but he had already gone.

***

The next night, Julie gathered her friends at the Midway, and Elizabeth was the center of attention. She looked forward to her yearly visit to St Albas. No one ever changed there. She thought it was funny how none of them were ever aware of it—how they wouldn't realize how similar they all were as first years and fourth years until they looked at the pictures twenty years from now.

Julie was happy that the focus was off of her and wondered if Max would come. She certainly hoped he would, even in her frustration with his lack of action. She felt that in some way his coming would be proof that he liked her, and besides, it would be nice to see him in public, to have a drink together in the dusty, old Midway. And it would be good for Peter to see them together, as friends, in case Max did like her and in case things worked out eventually. She had even invited some members of the *Vojtech* cast so he wouldn't look so out of place, and she was happy when they showed. Only Fern had declined, saying she'd be staying in to catch up on fixing a few things in the flat.

The pub was hot. It was a busy night, and there were very few places to sit. A cloud of sweat and perfume drooped in the air. People hung around the bar, half sitting, half standing. Bodies pressed against one another both accidentally and on purpose. Elizabeth wiped a little bead of perspiration from her forehead. Here she was, sitting next to Julie, who was noticeably on edge. The excitement from the walk, obvious though her sister denied it, was clearly turning into anxiety. For all of her false stoicism, Elizabeth knew that Julie cared for this one. In fact, it was the relatively restrained manner in which she described him and the events surrounding him that set this situation apart from the others.

Peter had returned from the bar with a pint. He handed it to Liz without making eye contact. This, he felt, was a sign of familiarity. In turn, she didn't offer to pay for it. This too was a sign of familiarity.

"How is our Liz this year?"

"Good. Happy to be back."

"We're happy to have you back." They clinked their glasses together. "I'm sorry about this morning. Don't know what got me talking about—well—"

"How is—" Liz paused, avoiding this line of conversation at any cost. "I'm sorry, what's your girlfriend's name again?"

Before Peter could answer, Julie was upon them, a gin and tonic in her hand.

"Plotting against me, are you?"

Peter moved his chair closer to Liz, pulling another up beside them.

"As always," he said. "I was just about to ask Liz the details of your life of late. Some of us have been kept rather in the dark."

"Liz knows there's nothing to tell."

"Not anything I *would* tell, anyway."

She had meant it as a joke.

"Now that's a diplomatic statement," said Peter. "Knowing Julie as I once did, I am unwilling to believe there's not something behind it."

Julie fidgeted with the label of the empty bottle of Prosecco that Ashwin had abandoned on the table.

"You always think you know everything," she sighed. "I never expect that to change."

Peter put his arm around her and squeezed her shoulder good-naturedly.

"I can't *always* tell what's going on. You're just so good at giving yourself away."

Outside on Fair Street, Max and Catriona were walking in the direction of the Midway. Max had taken Catriona to the cinema, figuring it was a wonderful opportunity to not talk and perhaps an even better opportunity to throw her off—to give himself some time to think, to bide his time.

He resented himself for not just breaking up with her as they walked down the street. There was no reason not to. He should have been more frightened about Simon and their conversation in the Cathedral Café and his knowing about Julie and his loving Catriona. But somehow he felt it a help. If only Simon would man up and tell Catriona everything, so it would all end in a big bang instead of in this horrible, Chinese-water-torture way that ensured that Max himself must be the one to break things off. Besides, it would ease his conscience to know she was in good hands.

"I thought it was a bit violent," said Catriona of the movie. "But thank you for taking me. It was so lovely to go on a proper date. We haven't done in such a long time."

"You're welcome," said Max. "Is there a reason we're walking this way?"

He had just remembered Julie's invitation—and the location and time that went with it. Peter would be there, and Max had continued to avoid him like the plague. Besides, he couldn't imagine Julie's reaction to seeing Catriona and him together would be favorable, even if he didn't know it outright.

"I just wanted to take a walk."

"It's freezing. Let's turn around. I'll walk you home."

But they were already in front of the big, sweat-frosted windows of the Midway. Catriona saw that there, inside—yes, there was that

Julie Lovejoy. The girl who had spent the cast party talking to Max.
A feeling more potent than her insecurity over the current state of her
relationship with Max rose in Catriona, and it was injustice. If it weren't
for Julie, Catriona never would have exploded at Max during the
party, and perhaps things wouldn't be so strange between them now.

The nerve. She should make Julie suffer, the way she had
suffered. And here was Max on her arm, fresh from a date. She felt
a surge of courage. She didn't like the pub, no—not at all. But
something inside her (perhaps it was even her heart) told her to go
in, to talk to Julie. To flaunt Max before her. To let this Julie
Lovejoy character know that a vulgar girl like her would never get
the better of Catriona Darlington-Welland. Besides, Peter had been
avoiding this introduction for years. Always telling her that she and
Julie wouldn't get along. Perhaps he was right, but somehow it
irritated her, and it ended right now.

"Look," she said, stopping in front of the window and putting on
her sweetest peony-voice. "It's Peter."

She waved.

"We'd better go in."

"Go in? You haven't been inside a pub since—I don't think I've
ever seen you—"

But Catriona had already stepped inside.

Julie saw Catriona and felt the adrenaline rushing in her neck. The
thick, irrational, and hollow ball of hatred inflated in her stomach
and her head. There was another girl with Max. Julie felt as if she
were finding out that he had a girlfriend for the first time.

Catriona approached the table where Julie was sitting with Peter
and Elizabeth.

"Hello," Catriona said. "Good evening, Peter."

"Catriona!" said her cousin in a state of shock. "What on earth are
you doing in here?"

"Just passing by with Max, on our way home from the cinema. He
took me to see that new film—the one about this woman serial
killer. It was all right, but blood makes me rather faint. I never get
used to seeing it. So, I spent most of the film wrapped up under
Max's coat! Hiding into his shoulder—can you imagine?"

Peter was baffled by this monologue and slightly sick at what
she'd said about the blood.

"That's—wonderful," he said eventually. "Wouldn't you like to sit down? We can make room. Scoot along, there, Julie, won't you?"

Under the table, Julie grabbed Elizabeth's arm like the handlebar on a roller coaster. She couldn't move under Catriona's gaze.

"She's had a long weekend," said Elizabeth, staring at Max. "Julie, sweetheart, can you move a bit?"

She nodded. How was this happening? She was unable to meet Max's eyes. Just the other night they had been lying back in the tower, all alone, as if there were no other human beings in the entire world. Just them in a universe of their own creation, the beach, the Castle, the little green light at the end of the pier.

"You and Max remember each other, don't you?" said Peter to Julie.

"Yeah," she said, finally waking up. She stood and reached across the table to shake his hand. "It's nice to see you."

He nodded.

"And Catriona," said Peter. "Julie."

Catriona did not extend her hand, but nodded.

"Good to meet you after all this time, Julie."

"Yes."

"I saw you at the cast party."

"This is my sister, Elizabeth," said Julie in a hurry.

"A pleasure," said Catriona.

Max nodded.

"So, what movie did you say it was?"

"*Cut Queen*," said Max flatly.

"Sounds romantic," said Julie, her eyes sharp.

"You know, it sort of was," said Catriona. "Max was so protective. Stoic. He held my hand the entire time."

"You know, I'm really sorry, everyone. I think—I think it's time for me to go home," said Julie.

"You haven't even finished your pint," said Peter. "Are you feeling all right?"

"Yes. I'll be fine. I think maybe that Chinese from earlier was rotten or something. I gotta go."

"Should I come with?"

"Liz, no. Stay. Enjoy."

In this, Liz heard the command to report back.

"I'm very sorry. I just need to lie down."

Taking a £20 note out of her purse and putting it on the table, she said:

"Buy a round on me."

She went out into the street, not knowing where to go. It seemed that every indoor and outdoor space in town reminded her of one her mistakes. Every monument and pub, and several of the apartments, had a failed fling attached to it.

She should have guessed Max would take Catriona on a date instead of coming to see her at the Midway.

*** 

When Max arrived home an hour later after dropping Catriona at her door, Fern stood waiting for him in the living room.

"Hi," he said, planning on a quick escape to his room, where he had left his phone.

"I don't think so, mate," she said, shutting the door to the hallway and preventing his flight.

"What is this?"

"An intervention. Please, have a seat."

"I don't really have time for one of those right now. Especially if it's about Catriona. I've finally decided, Fern—"

"This is for your own good."

He sat.

"This is ridiculous."

"I'm going to have to ask you to remain quiet. You may ask all your questions at the end, when I am done—intervening. Now, answer me this."

She slid a little velvet box across the table.

"What are you doing with the One Ring, Frodo Baggins?"

The extent to which Max was embarrassed at this moment in time defied description for several decades to come. Eventually, he was able to say that he knew how armed robbers must feel when they turn on the television to see their license plates published on the six o'clock news.

"What?"

"I finally fixed that leaky faucet. I needed to borrow some tools to do it though."

"I can explain."

"Ah—no comments from you just now."

Fern dropped her head in her hands.

"Max, you're my best friend in the world, you know that?"

He nodded.

"I love you like a brother. I will do anything to help you. Do you believe me?"

He nodded again. Fern lifted her head and took his hands in hers.

"But you have got to let this go. Are you proud of yourself? No. I'm not proud of you either. And I'll tell you another thing. You're killing that poor lassie. You're not the one for her. So just sack her and let everyone get on with it. Please."

Max put his head down on top of the pile of hands that had formed on the table.

"Can I ask you a question, now?"

"Looks like you just did, but you're welcome to another."

"Would you be telling me this if there wasn't someone else?"

"Yes. It's time. It's been time for a long time. You know that. And while you know I'm no great fan of her, Catriona—she knows it too. Somewhere in her, she knows."

She took the box and put it in his hand.

"Now, I'm giving it back to you on the condition that you don't go putting it anywhere it doesn't belong."

She ruffled his hair affectionately and kissed him on the cheek.

"Don't ever tell anyone I did that. All right, you old curmudgeon. I'm going out for a fag. I'm going to smoke it for, oh, let's say, the next three hours. Do what you will with this empty flat to fix this mess."

***

Julie found herself walking down the Avenue. Tonight was colder than the last few, and the stinging salty air whipped at her cheeks. The displaced pieces of the sea mingled uneasily with the stream of teardrops that looked like a twig of glass laid on her cheeks and under her eyes. She had rarely felt so low as she strolled past the English Department, thinking of the many love stories gone awry that it would have been beneficial to have paid closer attention to from the very start of her time in St Albas.

The moon was gone. The only trace of light came from beyond the Western hills, where the twinkling kitchen lights and televisions in the holiday cottages there glowed. In front of her was the ruined Castle, which had been the site of so much happiness only forty-eight hours ago and now seemed only to hold that which just as easily could have been a dream. Neverland, indeed. Breaking into castles. Going out windows.

Julie had just found, in the strange presence of Catriona of all people, that she loved Max. The devastation she had felt in the pub was too great for it to be anything else. She had no other way by which to recognize real love. She had never felt it until tonight.

She walked all the way down to the pier, watching the boats bobbing up and down in the water, helpless to resist the currents that persuaded them in one direction or another. She possessed the wild urge to cut them all free, the small fishing boats, the yachts, the sailboats with their linens put to bed, to watch them clamber against one another on their way out to sea.

Sitting down on the pier's hard, chunky stone, her feet dangling over twenty feet of air and twenty feet of water, she realized: the time had come. She must offer him her feelings. Max, "stoic." Ha. How many times had she seen him laugh? How many times had she thought she saw the blueprint of a kiss in his eye?

The waiting was killing her. The next day, she and Elizabeth would embark upon a trip to the Highlands. While the prospect of not seeing Max for a few days tied knots of intestines around her stomach, the idea of having no sense of his thoughts on the matter of her was even more morbidly pernicious.

She must tell him.

Her phone rang. A shiver went through her as she answered it.

"Elizabeth?"

"Where are you?"

"Down on the pier."

"Good God, has it come to that?"

"Very funny."

"We're all at the union, sure you don't want to join us? Max and what's-her-face have been gone for a while now."

"I have to drive tomorrow."

"You want to be alone, or should I come down there?"

"I'll be fine."

"Caddy's here, she can take me home. Only if you're sure."

"Yeah."

"You gonna be all right?"

"Yeah. I promise. See you at home?"

"You bet. I love you, Julie."

"You too."

She hung up. The phone was still in her hand, counting mercilessly, the time on the front display. It was nearly midnight. She knew this must be the last day she dealt with the uncertainty. It was making her obsessive, self-absorbed. She had been losing track of the things that made her, her. She had been lying to and avoiding her best friends—worst of all, Peter. It made her stomach ache to think she might lose him, but Max. Max. Max was so important. Either he must be integrated into her life as it used to be or be lost completely.

In her palm, the phone began to jump again. She was not surprised to see who the caller was.

"Where are you?" said Max.

"I'm down at the pier."

"Can I meet you?"

"Yes."

Max raced down Sea Street. He passed the old cathedral ruins with the many gravestones beyond the iron fences, where the seagulls perched, sleeping with one foot under a wing. In the moonless night, the outline of the massive stone could be seen—or maybe it could be felt? Which was a legitimate question, his mind had been seeing and constructing it there in the fog, snow, sun, and rain for four whole years. But the old, familiar landmarks were taking on new meanings. He saw, he felt them transforming as he ran. The Castle was now the castle in which he had wanted to hold Julie's hand, the Flat Sands behind him the place where their first kiss might have happened. And now, as he tripped down the long, steep road to the harbor, he found himself following the green light at the end of the pier that he and Julie had admired only forty-eight hours ago.

As he approached, he found Julie's dark outline. She was facing out to the sea, at the very end of the pier. From the distance, she looked like a marble statue from antiquity—a bit rounder of hip and hair than was considered fashionable in this century, perhaps. Feeling his eyes on her silhouette, she turned.

"Hello," he said. "Having a rough night?"

"Max, I can't small talk with you."

"Okay."

"I have to tell you something, or I think I'm going to lose it."

"Anything."

"I'm sorry I didn't stay at the pub. I just couldn't stand it, you know? Seeing you sitting there with Catriona. I'm not stupid. I know she exists. I've known the whole time. But I just couldn't bring myself to stay in that chair, to shake your hand, and to pretend I don't know you. You have to know how I feel about you. For me," she laughed ruefully, "it really, really blows that you're dating someone."

"But I don't love her."

"What?"

"No. I don't."

"You what?"

"I don't love her."

It was the first time Max said it aloud. It felt like freedom when he did.

"Then—why didn't you—"

"I wasn't sure you'd want me."

They sat in equal shock.

"But I do," she said.

"So do I," he said.

"Really?"

He nodded.

"I knew it," she said, though she had not.

Max put his arms around Julie. He kissed her eyes and cheeks, and on her mouth he planted a luxurious, ecstatic kiss that bloomed into the sincerest smile he had ever seen on a just-kissed girl. Julie buried her hands in his hair, hoping she would never have other cause for them as long as she lived. After several breathless moments, they separated. Julie burrowed her face into Max's shoulder.

"Do you want to come over for a glass of wine?" he asked.

"I'm flattered that you think you have to ask."

Hand in hand, they walked to the flat on Sea Street.

"Are you sure we shouldn't walk a bit apart?" she asked, when they were back in the glow of the streetlights.

"Absolutely not," he replied.

Julie was chattering happily by the time they reached his front door. In her mind, everything was decided. She and Max would be very happy together, and poor Catriona would have to deal with it.

Max was filled with elation. It would all change now. He could break up with Catriona, now that he knew Julie cared.

"I can't believe you've been thinking of me like that," she said.

"All this time. Isn't that funny?"

"I don't see how it's funny. You're wonderful."

He indulged himself with another kiss on her mouth. It produced the desired effect of adding another flower to the garden of grins she was growing with each new experiment in kissing.

"Have a seat at the kitchen table, I'll get some glasses."

"Just like old times, huh," she said, taking off her coat and sweater.

"Haha! You bet. Except, much better."

There on the table, Julie noticed a little velvet jewelry box. She reached for it automatically, her stomach sinking when she found inside of it a diamond ring. Taking it out, the entire world in slow motion, she examined it carefully. When Max emerged with the wine, he found her sitting there, the diamond between her index finger and thumb, holding it out towards him in strict accusation. The love on her face had quickly turned to hate.

"I can explain," he said.

"Okay," said Julie.

*I would love to see you try,* she thought.

"I didn't say I was getting married. You assumed it."

"True. But forgive me if I don't often hang around young men who buy engagement rings, who *keep* spare engagement rings on hand and then not use them."

"I didn't buy it," he stammered. "I wasn't sure there was another way—"

"You said you don't love her."

"I don't."

"I understand," she said.

"You do?"

"You're a coward. And a jerk. I'm just glad I figured it out before I invested more than the last, what, twenty minutes, into whatever it is that we're doing."

"I'm going to end it."

"When? Now?"

She slid his cell phone toward him on the table. Max stared at it.

"Call her. Tell her. End it, then, if that's what you're going to do."

"Julie, it's complicated."

"What? What's complicated?"

"I need to tell her to her face."

"Why?"

"We've been together for three years. Over three years. I have to respect that."

"You think I'm going to believe you'll actually do it? Why should I?"

"Julie—"

But Julie thought of Harry.

"I know how this game is played, Max. I'm not an idiot. You're going to sleep with me, and I'm going to love you, and then you're not going to break up with Catriona."

"That's not how it will be. That's not how it is."

"Then call her, right now. Tell her."

Max looked at his phone. He looked at Julie. He thought of Catriona's face, and how it would look when he told her he could not be with her. It petrified him, but that is how it had to be done. Catriona deserved to know that way, as much as he hated to think of doing it. As much as it made him sick to his stomach. Something told him he would never feel quite right about being with Julie if he didn't do something right by Catriona, even if it was only the final thing.

"I can't call her. That wouldn't be right."

"That's what I thought," said Julie. "Boys. All talk, no action. You never grow up. And you're all the same—you just have different faces."

"Julie."

"I don't want to hear from you ever again," said Julie. "I can't wait to leave this fucking town. I hope you and Catriona are very happy together. Seems like you deserve one another. Cowards. Neither of you are ever going to get anything you want. Fucking fools."

Max followed her as far as Fair Street, until she screamed at him and the large Turkish men who worked in the kebab shop came out into the street to intervene. Luckily, they didn't speak much English and wouldn't tell anyone who knew anyone what they had heard.

# X. MARCH

**MAX AWOKE THE NEXT MORNING WITH** a dull, scraped-out head. The one thought that flew around it was an ugly black moth of a memory that, with every flap of its wings, disrupted any idea of getting out of bed. He had pulled the rare trick of waking before his alarm, which he had set the previous afternoon. He was to have breakfast with Catriona, Vera, and that boyfriend of hers—Harry. His entire body groaned as he sat up.

He showered, leaning his head against the glass and allowing the water to fall over him. The events of the previous evening came nearer and nearer as if he were driving towards them. As he relived them in all the painful detail, the events of the past four years came into focus as well. There were so many detours, even on the path of least resistance. He dearly wished he'd taken one.

Julie was probably lost forever. That was all. And he must face another day of Catriona, whom he could not even look at as a consolation prize, now. Not after that kiss. He would still end it. But who cared when, now? He might as well propose tonight, suffer the next few months in relative peace, and then move away after graduation and not take her with him.

He dressed automatically. When he had finished, he came into the living room. The ring was still lying out in the open on the kitchen table. He picked it up. It wasn't very pretty. Julie must have gotten a rotten impression of his taste. But no. That didn't matter. What the hell should he do with this fucking thing now? He thought of flushing it down the toilet or of leaving it on the beach. Instead, he put it in his pocket. He could always give it back to Peter at the end of term.

As he walked down Church Street towards Catriona's, he felt an almost magnetic pull towards the Highlands. He hoped Julie would be safe in the car, not too emotional behind the wheel. If anything happened to her, it would be his fault for upsetting her. And he could never forgive himself for that.

Catriona's kiss landed on him in a more confident way than in the last few weeks. She was apparently very proud of the ownership she had displayed last night in the pub. He wanted to thank her for pushing Julie over the edge. In an odd way, yes, she was to be thanked. At least he had Julie's kisses now. But the sight of her in her bright, dotted apron made him sick to his stomach. She was nothing more than a sugar substitute, a silk flower.

And then, of course, they sat there around the table. Vera and Catriona chattered stupidly. They were already thinking, he heard in some distant space, that Catriona should go shopping for a Commencement Ball gown soon. She would have to buy a matching tie for Max because he never thought of such things. He never thought about what he looked like. They laughed. Isn't that right, Max?

He ignored them.

For the first time, he had a good look at Harry. He wasn't listening to the conversation either. He was occupied with the business section of the *Guardian*, or at least he was pretending to be. Maybe Harry wasn't the worst fellow after all. Perhaps he had been stupid, avoiding a friendship with the only other person around this house who was sane. He had let his opinions on Harry be formed mostly on account of Catriona, who could barely stand the sight of him, and that was probably wrong.

Perhaps Harry had been thinking the girls were stupid too. He said to Max:

"You look like hell."

Max nodded. "I believe you."

"I think I know what's going on."

"I would be surprised," said Max.

Catriona and Vera, struck simultaneously by the unlikelihood of this conversation, had abruptly stopped talking. Like two lionesses spying two water buffalo, they stared with low, frozen heads.

"What did you say, Harry?"

"Max and I were just talking."

"About what?"

"...The paper."

"Oh," said Vera. "Well, carry on."

The two boys shifted their eyes toward one another, disinclined to carry on the discussion under the pierced, listening ears of their girlfriends.

Harry took a few more bites, then spoke again:

"Actually, darling, I was thinking I might take your recyclables. Perhaps Max would like to help."

Harry had stood. Max looked up at him.

"Would you like that?" asked Catriona, her eyes narrowing.

"I would."

"Wicked," said Harry. "Do you mind, Catriona? Maybe Max and I'll hang out."

"And do what?" asked Catriona as calmly as possible.

"Have a drive. Go for a pint. Man things."

"That sounds good," said Max.

There was nothing Catriona could say. Vera would tell them to have a splendid time, and she could not risk looking like a spoilsport.

"Have a splendid time," said Vera, as Harry kissed her goodbye.

"Thanks for breakfast, Catriona," said Harry. "Exquisite pancakes. I could almost taste the love."

Catriona ground her teeth.

"Will you be about tonight?" she asked after Max, who was leaving through the hall.

"He'll call you," said Harry.

Catriona stood to clear the table.

"Your boyfriend is the worst influence in the world on Max," she said to Vera.

"They're simply going to have some male bonding. You know how Harry likes to take some time alone. Maybe it would be good for you and Max too. Absence makes the heart grow fonder."

Outside, Max was saying:

"We're not really going to do the recyclables, are we?"

"No," said Harry. He was taking out his keys and getting into the car. He gestured for Max to do the same. "Where is Julie?"

Max stared.

"That's where you want to go, isn't it?"

"Yes. Yes, I do," said Max.

He buckled himself in.

"But how do you know that?"

"It's a long story."

Harry was adjusting the mirrors and snapping his fingers back in a series of medicinal clicks. They were still parked in the driveway.

"Max, I just have to ask you one thing."

"Yeah?"

"Do you love Julie? I mean, really, love her?"

Without hesitation, Max said:

"Yes."

"That's what I like to hear."

He hit the steering wheel enthusiastically, then said:

"So where is she exactly?"

"The Cullin."

"The Cullin is enormous. Think, Max."

"Someone's holiday house."

"Whose?"

"Brett Something."

"Brett Michaelson? I'll just call him for directions once we're on the road up north."

Brett would surely take a call from him if it was about Julie.

"Harry," said Max. "Why are you helping me?"

He switched on the turn signal at the end of Sea Street, which indicated the decision to head out of town.

"Have you ever felt badly about how you treated a girl?"

Max looked at Harry in amazement. Of course Harry must know that his relationship with Catriona was less than perfect. Max had heard his fair share of lovemaking sessions from across the hall. Harry surely must have noticed the absence of them coming from the opposite direction.

Harry took Max's silence as understanding.

"Let's just say, I have a lot to make up to Julie."

*Not to mention, I'm the one who fucked it up for you*, he thought.

***

The road was familiar. It wound up the east coast, from St Albas up to Dunglen and then to Aberforth. The landscape transformed gradually along this route, from low, rolling hills and white sands to frightening dragon-tooth-sharp cliffs.

Driving away from St Albas—watching the bell towers and church spires disappear in the mirror—was always just as therapeutic as seeing them reappear. Julie looked forward to this part of Liz's visit each year, when they set off for a few days to the Highlands, and she could leave all of the worries of the little town, and its current year, behind her. It only took two minutes on the motorway before you found yourself in the countryside, seeing sheep more frequently than people, then seeing sheep more than houses, then seeing sheep more than cars.

Julie was well acclimated to driving on the other side of the road. It was simply one of the little adjustments that must be made, living in Britain, along with embracing the vinegar, rain boots, and bad teeth. Most of the stereotypes were true. But the Highlands, being sparsely populated by anything other than shaggy cattle, bushes of rimy heather, and breathtaking, hoary mountains, did not follow the rules of any civilization that tried to conquer them and, therefore, were a perfect escape from society.

In spite of being relieved to be getting out of town, she also wanted to bang her head against the steering wheel. She wanted to jump off a cliff into the cold, Scottish sea that hugged and thrashed against the rigid walls, wanting attention, sympathy. Her anger at Max was violent and her disappointment in herself acute. She had been, maybe, too dramatic. She was only thankful that Elizabeth was here, chatting to her mildly about how pretty the cows were or if Julie remembered the time they had gotten lost together at Disney World as children.

Despite the talking, the great therapy of girls, Julie thought of Max. She had spent the whole night hoping she would wake to find him flown in her window or waiting desperately in the morning at the ancient city gate, halting traffic and her exit from town.

But that hadn't happened. Perhaps the worst part about it was that she must now accept the fact that she was apparently not the type of woman men wrote poems or songs about. She would never inspire someone to a heroic act. No one would ask her to lie very still so he could document the outline of her body in oil paints. Some women would inspire men, or other women, to do great things. Julie had always assumed that the force of her personality would secure her a place among them. But now she realized that she would be the one inspired, perhaps by herself alone. And the effort of coming to terms with this realization was almost as exhausting as the eventual performances of art and emotion it would spawn.

In a few hours, they arrived at a house at the foot of the great mountain. This area of the world was the Michaelson clan's ancestral home. Once they'd gone Australian, maintaining a residence there lent credence to their business dealings with the British. Brett's family had always been gracious enough to let his friends make use of it—Elizabeth had even come here in first year with Julie and Brett.

Julie knew that Elizabeth was always up for traveling anywhere with her sister, but she also knew of her fondness for the marble bathtub upstairs that looked out over the mountains. Julie had spent several evenings of her life alone in Brett's dad's chair in the den while Elizabeth soaked and read Agatha Christie. Each year, Brett briefed them half-jokingly on what to do if "someone who looked like they were from Inland Revenue" showed up. This year, there was a distinctly more serious note in his voice as he said it.

They made their way up the steps onto the front porch. Julie waited patiently as Elizabeth fussed with the key. She looked out across the beautiful Cullin, so old, settling eternally into the bedrock, locking itself into the crust. The deciduous trees looked like they were clambering onto an escalator going up the mountainside. In the hills, there were the neon-yellow flowers, looking as if God had taken a highlighter pen to the slope proclaiming, "Look what *I* can do!"

In the kitchen and the great hall, the large windows framed all the beauty and detail of the outdoors. Brett's mother's assistant had sent a large bouquet of begonias and tulips, an unnecessary gesture of wealthy over-hospitality. An enormous moose head, needlessly sent from the Michaelsons of Vancouver, hung in foreignness above the large stone fireplace. Elizabeth placed their backpacks in the lounge before returning to the great hall, where Julie had already laid down and put her feet up. As Julie kicked off her shoes, she let out a sigh so deep that it propelled Elizabeth to say:

"He loves you, you know."

"Yeah, right."

"You didn't see how miserable he looked last night. He loves you."

"You think he looked miserable?"

"Awful. And have you noticed Catriona's Jay Leno forehead? It won't last. No man wants to wake up next to a forehead like that for the rest of his life."

This raised Julie's spirits.

"I have a nicer forehead."

"You do."

"Still, I'm not doing this again," said Julie. "I am not doing this thing again where I date some boy who isn't ready to grow up and own up to things and do things and be a man. Can we have a drink now?"

"So dramatic."

"I hate when you say that."

"I hate when I have to," said Liz with a smile. "Don't worry. Everything will work itself out."

"Why hasn't he called then?"

"Could be because you told him you never wanted to see him again."

"So?"

"What do you want? Do you want him to come riding in on a white steed?"

"Yes."

"Do you have any idea how sick that would make you if it actually happened?"

Julie took the pillow out from under her head on the sofa. She put it on her face and screamed into it.

"Okay. You know what? No more boy talk. Unless it's your boy talk."

"Deal. But I still think he loves you."

Later that afternoon, Liz was soaking in the bath. Julie had situated herself, pajama-clad, in the big, comfy chair that smelled of cigar smoke, above the twin, black marks on the floor that had been imprinted there by the weight of Brett's father's and grandfather's and great-grandfather's boots. Each successive wife, and probably a fair share of mistresses, had scooted the chair up to hide the previous man's mark. Now, there just looked to be a trail from behind it to the front, as if the generations of men were playing a tricky game of leapfrog on the women and their domesticating intentions. *Boys will be boys,* thought Julie.

There was a glass of water in her hand. She had somewhat overdone it on the whisky earlier, and her better sensibilities had finally won out. She looked down at the expertly cut Waterford crystal and sighed, wishing dearly and praying earnestly that the only problem she had in life might be a potential visit from Inland Revenue.

Had she meant what she said? No. She wanted to see Max now, right this moment. But thinking of Harry, of all the meanness and bitterness that came along with how things had ended, she tried to make herself feel glad that she would never again be duped. How passionately she had hoped that Max would be different. Her faith had somehow gotten tied up in that hope and, like an invisible, untied shoelace, had tripped her up.

But he was different. But he was. But he was.

She started to cry. She would never be able to differentiate Max from any of the other boys she had tried to love or had tried to trick herself into loving. Even if he was the one, she had blown it.

There were steps on the front porch. She lifted her head from the armrest, disoriented. Perhaps she had spoken too soon about Inland Revenue. There was an urgent knock.

"I'm coming," she said, taking her time as she wiped her eyes, standing up and progressing toward the door, picking up a box of Kleenex on her way. With a sniffle, she opened it. And there was Harry Ommar.

"What?" She took in a deep breath of misunderstanding, exhaustion, and apprehension. "Why are you here?"

"Don't slam the door."

"Seriously? Right now? What do you want from me?"

"I wanted to talk to you."

"Harry," she said, "you know I—oh my God. Harry. Is that Max?"

"Where?"

"In your car!"

In the gravel driveway, in the back seat of the car, was Max, and he was looking in her direction.

"Perhaps."

"What is he doing there?"

"He's sitting there until I tell him he can come in the house. Handcuffed, actually. Wants to see you bad. But not until I'm done chatting to you."

"You are insane. Handcuffed?"

"Me and Vera."

"You're disgusting. Why would you say that to me?"

"I'm the worst, I know."

He guided her by the shoulders into the kitchen, and she sat down next to him at the kitchen table. From upstairs, Julie heard Elizabeth rustling around in the bathroom. She came to the door at the top of the stairs, opened it with a creak, and called down:

"Is there someone else in the house?"

"Yes."

"Oh. Who?"

"Harry. Ommar. You remember him. The asshole boy from *last* semester."

"Oh," she said. "Is everything okay?"

"He has Max in the back seat of his car. In handcuffs."

"Should I get back in the bath?"

Beat.

"That's...probably for the best."

The door shut.

"We drove all the way up here today."

"I realize that."

"I wanted to tell you something."

"Okay. What."

"I'm sorry."

Julie looked at him in disbelief. The nerve of him, telling her he was sorry. This proclamation spoke only to his unchanging vanity, and not to a change in him, as far as she was concerned.

"It doesn't matter. I don't care."

"You don't care that I'm sorry, or—"

"What does it change if you're sorry or not? I'm over it. I'm over you."

"You are?"

"Yes. Because you're an epic, remorseless, heartless asshole, and a waste of my time."

"You're not over me, Julie."

And he was very quiet and peaceful, sitting there across the way, his hands clasped together and his broad shoulders rounded. He looked softer to her than he ever had.

"Yes, I am over you. Don't tell me how I feel, especially about you. It should be apparent. You're an asshole. You made me look like a total idiot. Like a complete fool. In front of everyone. I believed you. Just for a minute, I thought maybe you cared about me. In a real way. And you didn't. Loudly, publicly, you didn't."

"I know."

"That's why I'm over you. What idiot girl doesn't forget a boy like you?"

"You haven't forgotten though."

She stood up.

"Get back in that car. Turn it around. I'd say 'have a nice life,' but I know I'll see you somewhere around those three streets sooner than I want—which is never."

"I can't do that."

"Why not?"

"Because Max loves you."

"It's just bizarre that you of all people would drag him up here with you."

"Julie, listen to me. You've got to hear this from me, or you'll never believe it when you're with Max."

"I'm not going to be with Max."

"Listen, Julie. Listen to me now. Listen to me for ten seconds."

This was the old, direct Harry she had thought she could possibly have loved but somehow softer still. Softer than the hands clasped together, his palms came to rest on the sides of her cheeks, a different, gentler spell of calm, entirely unsuspected and, she was surprised to learn, not unwelcome—not unwelcome, the smell of his wrists, not unwelcome, the dark hairs on the side of her face. She let them stay there.

"Listen to me," he said. She brought her hand to rest on top of his. She took a deep breath.

"He's not me," said Harry.

"But he—"

"Shh," he said, stroking her hair and pulling her close. "No. He's not me. He's not me. He's not me."

"But these things always end the same way. Just the way they did with you. All the wasted effort. With me the only one who cares, in the relationship all alone, by myself. Feeling like an idiot because everyone knew it was like that, being the last one to know it would never work."

"It's not like that this time. You have to give him a chance."

"I'm scared to."

"Of course you are. But you need to give him a chance. You have to at least give him a chance to fuck it up for himself. Properly. And can I tell you something else?"

"As long as you're at it."

"You aren't her, Julie. He doesn't love her."

"They've been dating long enough. I saw the ring he is going to give her."

"He probably just thought it would shut her up. You don't know this girl, Julie. She's bollocks. And she's got a lot of her own rubbish to sort through. Max just doesn't want her jumping off the Castle Wall or something."

"He doesn't love her?"

"He doesn't."

Harry held Julie for a few minutes, feeling her hurling breaths against his chest. He remembered, somewhere far off, what it had felt like, being with her. How urgent and passionate she was in everything. He had always felt that if he hadn't loved Vera, he would have loved Julie. If he didn't already, that was.

Julie sighed and looked up at him, saying nothing.

"Max loves you, Julie. He really does."

"I know," Julie said. Hearing it from Harry somehow made it true. "Can we go get him from the car?"

"Anything for you."

"And Harry," she said, putting her arms around him. "Thank you."

"For what?"

"For being a man. For today, at least."

***

Julie and Max stood at the top of the cliff. Below, the wistful, sugary-peach beach was blowing away in the wind. Even in the dullness of the cloud-beset sunset, these tiny pieces of Scotland shone cheerfully as they rose and fell. Harry and Elizabeth were back at the house, making dinner. All the right phone calls and excuses had been made.

At the moment, though, Max worried about none of it. He watched Julie watching the waves, Venus staring at the ever-changing scene of her birth, not able to return to the exact place she came from because it was in the place's nature to change, long blonde locks catching on themselves, blowing out erratically away from her ponytail, a stray thread or two loose above her right temple. The round, arched eyebrows, the tired eyes. Right hand resting on the center of her chest. He took Julie's other hand and they stared out to sea.

"Thanks for coming to get me," she said.

"If it wasn't for Harry—"

"It still would have worked out," said Julie. "It may have just taken longer."

"And it's going to work out," said Max. "I promise."

"You're right. Funny to think, how things work out."

She smiled at him. Her eyes had cleared of their tears. Max pulled her close to his side. Julie felt for the first time that she had a plan for the next sixty years. She felt it in her bones. She would love Max, and that would be enough not just for the next year but for all the years. That was the goodness of life and its goal.

"Things have already worked out," said Max. "I'm happy."

"I'm happy too. Right here. Right now. I wouldn't change a thing."

Max knew for sure he loved her when she said it.

And to him, it was youth.

And to Julie, it was growing up.

***

The next morning, the two of them lay in bed. Under normal circumstances, neither thought they were very original, but it sure felt that way this time. Julie's head fell on Max's shoulder easily and softly, almost like a child's rests upon her parent's while being carried upstairs to bed. Indeed, somehow it felt like they were children on Christmas Eve, although all the gifts that had been unwrapped and given that night were of a different sort. Still, bows had been untied, boxes shaken, things opened urgently and hastily before the cards were read.

In any event, she noticed that the sun had already set. Or not yet risen. It was too late or too early to know which, and so she contented herself with keeping time by the consistent beat of Max's pulse against her slightly damp cheek. Looking up at him from her perspective, she recalled the instructions she had been given during a scuba diving trip in Hawaii: if you're not sure whether you're facing up or down, blow bubbles and watch the direction in which they float. Julie felt that she was perhaps neither up nor down, but rather sideways. The advice did not seem to be of help on dry land, even in this bed where gravity seemed to have disappeared. Submerged, though, that was right word to describe it. It was like floating underwater—peaceful and dim. She closed her eyes, seeing the strange fish of new love dancing around them.

Max slept on. This was truly the most wonderful thing she had ever seen. His high, round cheekbones and the steep slope of his jaw where her fingers had, of late, been skiing up and down, shimmered slightly with light blond stubble. When he opened his eyes, Julie thought she saw what astronauts did when they looked at the earth from outer space after all those years of just seeing their planet in pictures:

"What happened?" he said groggily.

"You were sleeping. But you're here now."

He nuzzled his nose into her armpit.

"Mm. I should go wake Harry. We have to get back."

"Why?"

He laughed. "I don't know. Fern."

"You really think Fern, of all people, is going to care?"

"Catriona."

She was not going to accept it forever, Max going to Catriona. But the sun had now definitely started its climb in the sky, the seagulls had awoken and for the first time in her life, she did not find lines about nightingales and larks blatantly inauthentic. She loved Max, and Max would make it right.

"Okay."

He kissed her on the forehead. She curled into the shape of a croissant.

Max found his trousers. They had fallen at the foot of the bed, a trustworthy dog made out of corduroy. He pulled them on.

"I'm sorry that I have to go."

"I know."

"It makes me sad too."

Julie looked up into his face. It glowed with earnestness. She looked back down at the bed. His body had made an impression, the sheets were rippled in the shape of water that's receded from dry sand. He had held her teddy bear through the night, pressing the stuffed creature's nose into her stomach as he wrapped his arms possessively around both.

"Sure it does."

He was sorrier than he had ever been, looking at her there wrapped in the sheet like a leftover Roman goddess, with everything but the laurel behind her ear.

"I want to end this the right way," he said.

"I know, and I don't blame you."

He sat down on the bed. She was sitting up now, her legs apart. As he got back down onto the bed and curled between them, his head resting on one of her upper thighs, he thought with wonder about how wonderfully used to this he could get. It was terrifically exciting. She stroked the heavy, matted hairs on the back of his head. After a moment she bent down and kissed him passionately. Max felt faint.

"It's better this way. With Peter too. Let it all—marinate, for a week or two. And then, gradually, we can let people know we're together."

"Absolutely."

She nodded to herself, slowly at first. Then with more conviction. Max started to laugh.

"You need to convince yourself?"

"Max! It's going to be so difficult."

# XI.

**GOD CREATED THE DARKNESS, CATRIONA THOUGHT** as she spent the sleepless hours. And she must remember, God didn't make anything that He didn't intend to that wasn't good in its way.

Max had called, but that had been hours ago. Something about male bonding and pints and going home to sleep. Furious as Catriona was, Vera had convinced her that sometimes men needed their alone time, and women who didn't indulge this in their mates were under the distinct threat of not being missed during these male rampages of ego and testosterone. "Better let them have their night out in Dunglen," she had said all afternoon, evening, and then in the bathroom where they stood brushing their teeth before bed. "The worst thing that could happen is they end up taking a cab back to town instead of Harry's car."

The worst thing that could happen. Catriona had often thought in these terms—the worst that could happen: the failing grade, the failing relationship, the failure to keep one's little brother alive. Vera had an awfully interesting way of looking at things. Max a little drunk, perhaps—that was the worst that could happen. Not so, she wanted to say. He could be halfway inside some little hussy in some big, throbbing club in Dunglen, no thanks to Harry.

Or perhaps Vera was right, and it would come to nothing in the end. No one would buy a ring and then not give it. Especially not Max, who found things of this nature so entirely devoid of actual meaning. How hard could it be for him, when he didn't believe in sacraments? Surely even he could at least appreciate the embarrassment it would cause her socially, if he didn't propose by the end of the year. They had been together for so long, had both invested so much time in the relationship. Simon would never do this to a girl.

She found it even more troubling, as the light crept into her window on Church Street, that she should think of Simon, instead of how happy she and Max were going to be when the time came. Why, between counting the lines on the floor that the weak sunlight made as it fell through the blinds, did she wish Simon were here with her, lying next to her in the bed?

It dawned on her: she might have had him years ago. Why had she gone scheming after Max, trying to get him to notice her, riding on the coattails of his failed relationship with that terrible, cracked-out Clara?

Still, she had chosen Max, and it was unchangeable. Her mother and father, they had stayed together. Her grandparents and their parents. It was what people did. They didn't talk at the grocery store or over dinner, they didn't talk about politics or about books or even about the weather. They enjoyed their solitude, each during the day, man at work and woman at home, all in the same town, staring out their afternoon windows at opposite sides of the same hill, never comparing notes about the slant of the light or the color of the trees or how the grass changed every shade of green throughout the year. Just like her and Max. The same three streets—over and over and over—never a real conversation about it or about leaving it. It was never going to be different, and it was never meant to be.

Proudly, she had resisted the strong urge to call him and ask where he really was. Weakness of that nature must be avoided. If she could suspect Simon's feelings toward her, perhaps that meant Max might as well, and perhaps that meant she had leverage. Something to make him jealous. So she would let him wonder what *she* was doing and why *she* hadn't called. She had spent most of the night with the little paring knife that she kept in her sock drawer.

At some point, Vera knocked at the door.

"You all right in there?"

"Yes."

"Can I come in?"

"Yes."

Vera, in the silk dressing gown, looked like an old movie star. She had to tie the tie around her waist twice. Her long, thick hair fell in perfect waves on one side of her shoulder.

"You all right?"

"Yes. I am. What are you doing awake?"

"What are you doing awake? Not worried about Max, are you?"

"No. Not really."

"It's natural, you know, for him to go out. You're lucky he doesn't like it."

Catriona looked at Vera. Objectively speaking, she was probably the most attractive woman she had ever known, at least in the conventional, beauty-magazine way of looking at the world and women and their bodies. The perfect proportions, the long hips, the thighs without a trace of fat, except for at the very last moment—a type of suspense. The dark brown eyes and the light blonde hair, her eyebrows in perfect, oblique angles that made her Sphinx eyes more dramatic and seductive, a miracle conducted by nature and not by a technician in a beauty salon.

"How do you stand it, though?" she asked.

"With Harry being gone?"

"Yes. And not knowing where he is."

"You mean to ask how I can stand him cheating on me, don't you?"

Catriona had never meant to have this blunt a discussion on the subject. She hadn't known for sure that Harry cheated. She didn't want to think the word, let alone hear it or say it. If Vera repeated it a certain number of times, perhaps the bogeyman would come. But she set the word out into the air aloud once more, in spite of herself:

"I wouldn't know what to do if Max cheated on me."

"I know about Harry, Catriona. I'm not a child. I knew about it, even from Spain."

"How?"

"Because that's how he has always been. Not all the time. But something was clearly going on last term. I felt it. I heard it in his voice."

"And you knew?"

"Well eventually, I asked him."

"You did?"

"And he said, 'Yes. There is someone.' And I said, 'Are you sleeping with her?' And he said, 'Yes.' So I said, 'Are you being careful?' And he said he was. And he said he missed me and that he loved me."

She folded her lovely hands in her lovely lap, staring straight at Catriona, anticipating the next question but forcing her subject to ask it anyway.

"You weren't upset?"

"I was curious. And yes, I was upset. But, do you know, Harry always comes home to me. And that's what matters in the end, doesn't it?"

"Did you ever find out who this other girl was?"

"Yes. Julie Lovejoy. I saw them together at that fashion show. Him leaning over her and all that. I asked who she was. Who wouldn't?"

Catriona hadn't told Vera about Julie and Max, about the cast party. She'd been far too embarrassed that her boyfriend had been paying all that attention to another girl, and it had turned out to be the same girl Harry Ommar had paid too much attention to. St Albas never failed to surprise. Catriona admired Vera's courage in telling her and felt an even stronger distaste for Julie Lovejoy than she had even felt before.

"It must have hurt, though. I would have been furious with him."

"But he chose me. He chooses me every time. And do you know why?"

*Because you let him get away with it*, thought Catriona.

"Because he loves you?" she said.

"He does. And it's in the choice. Are you really so silly as to believe we only love one person? Come, Catriona. Not even you could believe that. Could you? Or am I wrong about someone called Simon?"

"You are wrong about that, yes."

"Always the voice of truth," said Vera, as she stood. "I hope I've helped rather than hurt you."

"Thank you," said Catriona.

"Are you going to just sit there until he calls?"

"Yes."

And maybe take out the paring knife.

"All right," Vera said, shaking her head. "Goodnight."

"The sun's almost up."

"I didn't say I wasn't going back to bed. Got to have my beauty sleep, haven't I?"

She closed the door.

Vera cried prettier and quieter than most people.

*** 

For the rest of the week, Catriona did not see Max. There were hardly even excuses.

"What do you think he's up to," she asked Vera one dreary

afternoon as she was ironing her clothes.

"It's getting late in term," she replied as she sat painting her nails on her bed. "He always spends a lot of time in the library this time of year."

"You think so? Every time I call him, he either doesn't answer or doesn't really talk to me."

"They always get that way before they propose. They're nervous."

Catriona paused.

"How would you know?"

Vera smiled.

"What, you think I've never been proposed to before? Trust me, you've only to leave him be for the rest of the week. You'll have a diamond on that finger before you know it."

Catriona felt slightly better, especially when Max called on Thursday afternoon to see if they could talk about something important on Saturday morning.

But again, she felt it best not to tell her mother.

# XII.

MAX AWOKE THAT SATURDAY MORNING WITH a sense of freedom he had not felt in years. It struck him as rather pathetic that this was all it took—so simple in the end—to make him feel the possibilities of life again. He was only twenty-two. What was it that turned him over like a coin in the street? Was it ridding himself of Catriona or was it simply Julie?

At the Cathedral Café, he treated himself to a coffee and the paper. He sat there for an hour, picking over the stack of black-and-white columns, lovingly folding them as he had watched his father do. He stretched in the hard, wooden chair, reaching his arms up to the sky, getting slightly dizzy with the good feelings. He smiled when the waitress brought him his check and tipped her an extra 10 percent although she didn't deserve it.

It was only on the walk to Catriona's that he began to feel nervous. He found himself searching the lining of his coat for the emergency cigarettes he kept there. Remembering that Catriona had long since disposed of his lighter, he briefly considered going to the newsstand to purchase another. But no, she would smell it. And that would make her more upset. *But, does it matter?* he asked himself. *Does it matter what initially makes her upset? Because at some point she would be, surely. Surely, she will get upset.* He had been broken up with before and broken up with others. Someone had even thrown a flowerpot at his head.

A part of him that he couldn't completely quiet told him that by breaking up with Catriona he was putting her in danger, maybe of losing her mind. Not because he thought she would be devastated in the long run by losing him—he knew better than anyone else how capable he was of making her miserable and, indeed, how long he had succeeded (whether purposefully or not) in playing the villain to Catriona's sainted maiden. He knew that she would feel as if she had lost, and that it would devastate her completely. He was ruining the only plans she had ever made, clinging to them no matter the cost to her sanity or her relationships. She felt she must marry him because they had been together. Whether it had been once or a thousand times would never have made a difference. She felt herself ruined for anyone else. For a moment, the attractive and the lazy charms of guilt set upon him.

He stood at her big front door. Though a pagan of sorts, he knew with Christian certainty how terrified Daniel must have been under similar circumstances. What would protect him, he wasn't sure. Only himself, he supposed. But was that true? No. He had Julie now. And it was because of her that he could do this—that he wanted to do this. No matter how unpleasant it may be, he'd had his chance to do it wrong, and it had nearly cost him Julie, and now he was going to do it right. He knocked firmly.

Momentarily, Catriona appeared at the door.

She looked prepared. She had gone through all the effort of doing her hair and makeup. She had put on the heart necklace Max had given her for their first anniversary and was wearing the dress she had bought in Zurich during their first trip to see his parents. It was what she thought she looked best in and was most representative of their togetherness. Despite this front Max had the sick feeling she knew exactly what he was going to do, what he was going to say.

"Well, come in," she said.

He obliged her.

"Is Vera home?"

"No. I don't think so. Why?"

"No reason."

"Come into the living room," she said, leading the way. He marveled at her confidence. Though the atmosphere of aching dread in the room was so strong he could smell it, she gave no outer hint, other than the lack of a kiss or embrace, that she knew what was about to hit her. Catriona sat on the sofa. When Max didn't get down on one knee, she said:

"You'd rather stand, then. Let's have it."

She looked pathetic and pale now, sitting there. Turning the same phlegmy color as the throw pillows.

"I need out. I'm sorry."

"Wait—what?"

"I can't be with you."

"You're joking?"

"No."

Her eyes were fixed on the window. She clenched the pillows on either side of her. A heavy, viscous despair was being siphoned into her lungs in place of air. A cold, cruel liquid raced into her heart's center and was pumped out again toward her legs and into her brain where it steamed against her anger-filled, red-hot brain.

"No, Max. Please, don't do this. Please."

"I'm sorry. I can't do it. I can't be with you. I don't want to be."

The world was dimming in front of her. So the effort was all for nothing. All these months, these years. All a waste. She must change his mind. He couldn't just change everything like this: rearrange it all in an instant. Not after all the nights spent in her bed, all the fingers in her hair, all the mornings by her side. It wasn't fair; it wasn't right. It wasn't just a picture; it wasn't a play; it was their life. What was she going to do now? What would next year be? Oh God. What would she tell her mother?

There must be something she could do to make him reconsider.

*No,* said a voice in her head. *There's nothing you can do.*

*But there must be!*

*No, there's not. I'm sorry.*

She felt the house falling away. The light living room walls, the couch, the pictures, the shrubs outside the window. It was all she could do to choke out the words:

"Max, I thought—I thought you were coming over here to ask me to marry you."

*Damn. How had she found out about the stupid ring?*

"No," he said finally. "That's not it. I'm sorry."

She was trying to keep her composure. But an icy, limitless anger was beginning to spread in her veins like frost spreads stealthily across bud-ridden branches in the manner of a lethal injection. Her voice turned suddenly vicious.

"Is it someone else?"

"No," he said because he was not as brave as all that.

She sighed. Max realized, astonished, that she trusted him. This was the thing she was going to choose to believe him about. After all of that.

"Then what? What have I not done?"

"It's not that. You've done everything."

"Max," Catriona said pleadingly, "please reconsider. You mean the world to me."

"We're not supposed to be together. I think you know that too."

"No. You're wrong."

"In time you'll see."

"No, I won't."

"Come on. I don't make you happy. Look at yourself."

"If you leave me, I will kill myself."

"No, you won't. Don't say that."

"You don't care if I die?"

"That's not a fair thing to say, Catriona."

She had never felt so purposeless and angry in her life.

"You're a liar, Max."

"I'm not."

"Yes, you are. You are completely worthless."

"If you really think that, then you're better off without me."

"You're going to hell. I hope you know that."

Max started for the door. Catriona called after him:

"Is there anything else you'd like to say before I ask you to leave my flat?"

"I'm already leaving," he said, then turned on his heel:

"I'm really done. It's over."

With that, he walked out the front door. When he was sure he was out of her sight, he hung his head, planting his entire hand over his face and running it from forehead to chin with frustration. He started to cry.

It felt like the right thing. And he'd thought it would be the right way. It was the better way, maybe. But not completely right. He should have ended it. Years ago, he should have ended it.

In his pocket, his phone buzzed. When he opened it, there was a text from Catriona.

Please, come back. We can talk. I love you.

He dropped the phone in a nearby rubbish bin, dried his eyes, and then he headed to Julie's. Even he was surprised about what a short time it had taken.

# XIII.

**IT WAS THE MIDDLE OF MARCH.**

"Goodnight," Julie was saying.

They were all standing outside the pub. The time was midnight.

"You don't want to come back with us? The real party starts after the pub," said Margot, who was waving her flask in Julie's direction.

"I'm good. Promise."

"Where are you off to so soon?" asked Peter, who came closer to her as the others shouted their farewells, throwing them carelessly and charmingly over their young, sharp shoulders, assuming they would fall where they were meant to land.

"Just going home. Little headache."

"D'you have time for just one more?"

She had told Max she would be at his flat shortly after midnight. But maybe he could wait, now that they had all the time in the world. It was a pleasant discovery that she had never made in previous relationships because never before had it been or seemed true that there were actually, definitely, several decades ahead in which to talk and behave well together and to give and to receive warmth. Peter, on the other hand—who knew how much longer they would be in the same vicinity? It would be harder next year. While she wasn't quite ready to reveal her secret about Max, she felt safe enough to have a pint with Peter. Now that Catriona and Max had been separated for two weeks, she could start creeping back into Peter's world. Slowly, but surely. And then she would tell him that they had started to see each other, and she hoped he would still love her.

And so she said:

"For you? I have all the time in the world."

He offered her his arm.

"Just like old times, then."

"Just like the old times. Where shall we go, sir?"

"How about the Burns?"

"Sounds about right."

"Will you drink a Scotch with me?"

"Of course. It only seems right."

The streets were slick with the rain that was in the business of seeping slowly through the old walls of the brick houses. They walked leisurely past the bustling Italian pizza restaurant, with the large, black and white photo on the wall of the 1950s pinups in the low-cut dresses, bending over onto enormous plates of pasta, their lips red from lipstick and sauce. To the left, the little fashion boutique where all the wealthy girls shopped, sometimes buying the small, medium, and large of a dress just to make positively sure that no one else in town could wear it. There was the little café too—the one that had those excellent chocolate chip cookies that they sold for fifty pence from nine o'clock 'til ten o'clock in the morning, which, accompanied by a cup of espresso, was the surest way to eliminate the possibility of a bad start to the day.

To call the Burns a pub was an insult to pubs: it lacked the size and the flurry of activity and the amount of brews on tap. To call it a hotel bar was, however, too great a boon to the institution of the hotel bar. The Burns was somewhere in between. The smell of spilled and stale beer on the rug and upholstery, the many bottles of liquor behind the counter, alternately guarded and pawned by the barman like a Shakespearean apothecary, the little antique reception desk of the bed and breakfast, likely worth a fortune if someone cared to have it appraised and sold. A fire roared in a cast iron frame. Pictures of hunting dogs and framed tartans lined the dark green walls.

When they had seated themselves and taken off their coats, Peter went to the bar with the order of two Taliskers. Julie pulled out her phone to send Max a message.

"Who were you texting?" he asked.

"Just Caddy," she lied, taking her drink. "Cheers."

"Prost," said, clinking his glass with hers.

"Why 'prost?' "

"It's German."

"It is," she had just learned the Swiss variation, *proscht*, from Max a few nights ago, in the name of initiating her into Swiss-ness. "You've just never said it before."

"Perhaps if you cared to pay a little attention to your poor, old, friend's comings and goings, you would know that I started taking German again this term."

"Really."

"Modern history. A good language to know, don't you think? It's a pity Catriona broke up with Max. I'd love to get some conversation in with him. Those Swiss speak so many languages. You remember Max, don't you?"

"I do," she said.

"Of course. He was in the pub when Elizabeth was here."

Julie stared into her drink as he continued. Perhaps Peter had forgotten that she'd mentioned her crush on Max, right at the start.

"He just broke up with Catriona, actually," he said, in such a way that made Julie believe he had. "If I'm a bit tired, it's because poor Catriona hasn't been taking it well. Lots of quality family time."

"I'm sorry to hear that," said Julie. "That she's not doing well. What happened?"

"Just burnt out, I suppose. Catriona doesn't seem to understand, exactly."

Peter found that he was relieved that Max hadn't proposed. He felt slightly embarrassed that he had been so forward with the ring, but that didn't matter now. Especially because he also had the overwhelming sense that the break up had perhaps saved Catriona from greater misery in the future. It was all over now. He had found the ring in his mailbox the day after Max had ended it with Catriona. He would never have to speak to Max again.

"I hope you aren't having to spend too much time with her," said Julie. "You do need to study."

He nodded vehemently, then, shook his head out of it into a shrug.

"She's family."

"I know. But—but anyway."

She was very glad when Peter paid their tab an hour later as the bar was closing.

"I suppose I'd better get back home to see what's left of my flat. Ashwin can do a lot of damage in an hour, as we know."

"Maybe you'd better just go to the police station now, and see if they can't give you a lift there. I'm sure they're on the way."

"Right—or the fire department." He smiled, helping her put her jacket on.

She felt a sudden rush of affection for Peter. He had cared for her all these years like a brother. Never asking anything in return. Enduring her moods, enduring her emotional vacillations, her highs and lows. Coming to every performance and ball and party, asking only that he be given the right to complain with her and talk with her because it made him feel happy.

And he was more thankful to her than she would ever realize. For, without Julie, his university days might very well have looked like Max's. Ashwin and Brett may have been only occasional amusements rather than boys he loved like brothers in spite of himself. He had needed Julie to really help him live. Yes, without her, his years in St Albas might have consisted of locking himself in his room, studying and waiting for his girlfriend to call—or, rather, waiting in his room to be called so he wouldn't be yelled at for being out elsewhere.

"Can I walk you home?" he asked.

"Don't bother," she said. "Seriously. It's not far, and you've got to get back."

"You don't want to come?"

"I think I'm growing up," she said. "Just a little bit. I actually do want to go to bed. Believe it or not."

He laughed.

"All right. I believe you."

It made her feel awful to keep looking over her shoulder the entire way down Sea Street to make sure he wasn't following her. When she arrived at Max's, Fern answered the door.

"You have no idea how happy I am it's you who keeps coming in that door," she said, swinging the door open and leaving it to Julie to close it behind her as she settled herself back on the couch where she was organizing rock samples.

"Hi, Fern," she said, peeling her boots off her feet haphazardly. "That looks like fun."

"They do say geology rocks."

"Is that a fossil?"

"Yeah. Cool bugger, isn't he?"

"Where did you find that?"

"Near Kingsbarns. But they're all over in Scotland. This guy was just lying on the beach."

"Incredible."

"It is, isn't it?" She was clearly trying to hide her enthusiasm that someone shared her enthusiasm for a piece of stone but did a poor job at it. "I mean, think about it. What the hell would this thing think, if it was alive today?"

"It would probably have no idea what to do with itself."

"Definitely not."

They smiled at one another like people do when they are in the beginning stages of a long friendship.

"I'll leave you to it. Max in his room?"

"Yes. And Julie—Please don't break up with him, ever. He can be an arse sometimes, but really, there's nothing much not to love."

Julie nodded and opened the door to the hallway. The door to Max's room was open slightly; dull light from the streetlamp spread out across the wooden floor. Max was sleeping, his hands folded together under his left cheek. Quietly, she put her bag down and undressed, throwing her mustard sweater across his desk, on top of a box of junk, and letting her jeans and underwear fall to the ground. Even in the spring, the floor was chilly. She jumped into bed and took off her bra, hanging it on one of the corners of Max's carved headboard. He stirred.

"I missed you," he said, throwing his arm over her middle and pulling her toward him. She was glad to feel his warmth radiating against her back. "Your feet are so cold."

"I'm sorry. I'll put socks on."

"No, no," he said, half awake and half asleep, "put them between my legs. That's it. Now they're warming up. I'm warming them up."

"Yes you are," she said.

"I don't ever, ever want you to have cold toes, you know."

"I know."

"I love you," he said, falling back to sleep.

It was the first time he had said it aloud, but she had known it for weeks. He had been looking at her, wide and starry in the eyes, saying "hello" at random and meaning "I love you."

She kissed the sleepy arm that was resting under her head.

"I know. I love you too."

***

The next morning, Max awoke to his alarm buzzing. His arm was nearly dead as he pulled it out from under Julie. They had both slept like rocks, like those little fossilized animals he had been asking Fern about before Julie had come in last night. Today was one he had not been looking forward to. A terse, tense email had made its way to him on Tuesday. It was from Catriona, asking if he might bring her things by this Sunday, at nine o'clock in the morning, before she went to church. Though he felt it ungenerously early, he also felt he had an obligation to be as nice as possible.

As much as Julie hated the idea of Max having to see Catriona, she knew it was a necessary evil. And always better to be cooperative and nice, even if it was only to help Peter.

"I don't want to go," Max had said. "She wasted three years of my life. And now she wants to ruin a perfectly good Sunday morning that I might spend in bed with you."

"I know," Julie had replied. "And I don't blame you for not wanting to go. But she is going through a tough time, so we just have to play along. Or you should play along. It's not going to take more than fifteen minutes and then you will be done with her forever."

"I don't know, but there's always just one last thing with her."

"It's over," said Julie, who was not in the business of hiding her feelings. "For a reason. But, she does deserve to have her belongings. And I'm sure there are things of yours over at her apartment too. You'll probably be surprised at what you get back."

Max had shrugged at the time and agreed, but he thought more deeply on Julie's words as he dressed quickly and picked up the box from his desk. He wondered what sorts of things he might have left at Catriona's flat. Nothing he had missed, that was for sure. He had always been very careful about leaving things, even in the early days. Toothbrushes and clothing items and books and movies were systematically packed away after he had stayed at Catriona's for the night. He had resisted, asking for his things back, and she had responded by clearing a drawer for him anyway, and filling it with toothbrushes and extra pajamas and books she thought he might enjoy. And, sheepishly, though it had not been offered, she asked one day in first year if she might have a little drawer in his room. He had said yes, not wanting to hurt her feelings or to explore the reason why saying yes made him like her less. Before he knew it, her things were everywhere. She was talking about buying curtains; she was ironing his shirts; she was framing pictures and arranging them among his books. There was no way to fight it. When he moved into the flat on Sea Street the next year, it was with the newly perennial box of Catriona's things that had annoyed Fern in the attic at the beginning of this year.

But as he looked around before leaving the room, he liked to see that a pile of Julie's dirty socks were collecting on the ground, in an undemanded corner of their own. That her earrings were rolled to the edge of his desk that sat on the slightly slanted floor. Julie did not stir. She was dead asleep and looking peaceful. He hoped for a moment that perhaps she would wake up, beg him to come to bed, and then this dreadful task might be put aside for another day. But that was one of the things he admired in Julie. She got things done if they had to be done, even if she didn't do them very well.

She had even helped him collect up Catriona's things. There was an advantage in having her assist him. He could no longer distinguish what was his from what was Catriona's, but Julie seemed to have an innate sensitivity to these things. Items that looked out of character. She knew about these things—how people felt and acted. It was a strange sort of intelligence that he appreciated, not having it himself.

The sky was only half-lit by the sun, casting a bluish, ghoulish glow on the town, most of which was still sleeping. Through the crusty, sleep-laden lashes that clumped together under Max's brow, everything looked like a cheap set to an old horror movie, flat and spray-painted. He felt as though he looked like he was walking in place in front of a movie screen, the image of the passing town being projected behind him, poorly and carelessly, an inaccurate portrayal of his actual surroundings.

He hadn't seen her. After the text she had sent him following the breakup, he had not heard from her, except for in the email asking him to please bring her things by. He knew it would have to happen eventually, but he had supposed more time would have passed, so she could show him how well she was doing without him.

Simon, he had seen. He and Julie had been out for a walk along the Avenue, retracing their steps from the night of the Castle. They were holding hands under the thick sleeves of their St Albas robes, which provided perfect camouflage under the dark, moonless night, though wide stripes of gaslight hit them under the passing lamps, another gothic scene. Max had decided he was going to drop off a book that he had promised to Simon.

"I just have to drop into the rectory a moment," said Max. "It won't take long."

"Should I wait out here?" Julie asked.

Max nodded apologetically.

"It's all right. I don't mind."

"You are the best."

He tried to kiss her.

"Ah, ah ah—not until we get inside somewhere. Remember."

She stepped close to the side of the high, wrought iron staircase with the golden-cross-topped banisters, unseen in the shadows. Max ascended the stairs and rang the doorbell. An "I've got it, Father," and then Simon's face, backlit warmly.

"Hi, Max."

"Hi."

Simon closed the door behind him, coming into the cool night air.

"Maybe it's best if you don't come in. Catriona's in the sitting room."

"Oh, all right. Well, I've just brought your book."

"Excellent. Thank you."

Max handed it to Simon.

"Listen," said the latter, "I've got to ask you something."

"Yes?"

"Did anything ever happen, with—you know. The other girl?"

"Simon—"

"Max, I'm worried about Catriona. Tell me you told her the truth."

"Would you have? Would you have told her?"

Simon stared out to the sea, to the gulls eating the remains of who-knows-what on the stretch of Flat Sands.

"I don't know."

"There's no reason for her to know. I'm handling it. I swear. And she'll never know you had an idea."

"I don't worry for me. I just worry about her. If someone finds out and tells her. That's all."

"I'm sure you and Peter have had a lot to deal with," Max stopped. "I'm sorry. I don't mean that how it sounded."

"Are you apologizing to me for breaking up with her?"

"No," said Max, perplexed by the lightness in Simon's voice. "I'm sorry."

"I'll take care of her, Max. I'm not an idiot, am I?"

"No," he said, heading back down the stairs.

"Just show some compassion."

"All right, Father Simon."

"Don't call me that."

Max waited around the corner for Julie.

"I wish it could have been different," said Julie.

"What do you mean?"

"I wish it was easy for you and Catriona."

"How so?"

"I just wish people could tell each other the truth. And not be so scared."

She could have said that again. *And again, and again…*he thought, marching down the street with his box. He and Catriona and Simon—yes, Simon too. Perhaps it had something to do with her being American, but Julie's face was readable from a mile away. She hadn't grown up like the rest of them, the stiff upper lip, the standoffishness—what was there to be guilty for? Existing? Loving? Being young? A priest feeling something in his trousers? An atheist feeling something in his soul?

Back in the present day, he did not need to ring the bell. Catriona was watching him from the front window. When she saw him coming, she came to the door.

"Hello," she said meekly.

She looked pale, the smile more wide and forced and looking ready to split at the seams of her face than it ever had before, if that was possible. The edges of her eyes seemed to be lifted toward the top of her forehead, as if invisible threads were pulling them there. Her eyes were intense, the brows had crept down at an uneasy angle, distinguishable lines forming between her tear glands and the shape of the brow itself. She did not look well.

"Hi," said Max. "Here are your things. I think it should all be there, I did a pretty thorough check."

"Wouldn't you like to come in?"

"It's not heavy, you can take it."

He stretched it out to her.

"How are your mother and father? Your grandmother?"

"They're fine. No news. Just your things."

"Have you told them yet—have you told them you've broken up with me?"

"I have."

"Oh."

"Yes."

"Aren't you going to come in?"

"I'm not."

"Come in. Don't be silly."

"I said no, Catriona."

Any concern he had felt for her quickly evaporated. She really thought she could still control him?

He felt the violent urge to scream at her. To throw her silly box at her. To be cruel to her, to make her feel badly. He wanted to demand his youth back, to ask for and receive every moment she had stolen from him with scenes like this that had made him believe that he was a bad person for not loving her. So many scenes like this over the years. Being vilified. Listening to her sneaky tricks of tone and manner that let her say mean, judgmental things about everyone else, all the while sounding and seeming as if there was no meanness in her words. And somehow, this person, this manipulative, miserable coward, willing to go to any lengths just to have a husband who wouldn't love her, had made him feel like a fraud. Had kept him from growing up and thinking about the future because it had been too scary to conceive of when she demanded it all. He had been a creeping plant, grown as full as he could in the little closet of his youth. He was finally transplanted in the open air, and though the growing pains hurt more now—taking time to get used to the sunlight, and all of that—he was better for it.

"You can at least bring the box inside, Max."

Slowly, he set the box down in front of him, on the threshold.

"That," he said, "is as far as I'm taking it."

"Don't be so sensitive," she said, folding her arms. "Just bring it inside, can't you?"

"I'm not coming into your house," he yelled.

She was startled.

"Please don't yell at me, Max. You're making a scene."

"I don't give a shit," he screamed, grabbing the tops of his long hair with his hands. "You have no idea how good it feels to be rid of all that crap."

Catriona backed down. She paused. They stared. She spoke.

"I've got your things too. I suppose you'll have to wait here while I get them, since you're apparently averse to coming inside."

Max waited, just to see what she could possibly have scrounged up that belonged to him. A few loose shaving hairs, perhaps? A glove he could have lost just as easily anywhere else?

She was standing there with a Tesco bag. Inside it, there was a Donald Duck comic book, several DVDs, receipts from the movie theatre, three pairs of neatly folded boxer shorts, two tins of the tea he liked that she always brought back from Lancashire, and his bowtie from the November Ball. The heart necklace and the pearl necklace and the sapphire necklace he'd given Catriona on their anniversaries. There had been good times. So there really had been things worth leaving, as well as not worth leaving, behind.

"Oh, and there's one more thing. Since you're really not coming in."

She went to the living room, opened one of the drawers in the writing desk there and came back to the front door with the copy of *Wuthering Heights*.

"It looked like it was worth something. I didn't feel right keeping it."

Max took it in his hands.

"Catriona, this isn't mine—"

"I'm giving it back. It's all right."

"No. I mean, I didn't give it to you. I forgot this year. About your Christmas gift."

"What?"

"I never sent it. I said I did."

"Oh."

Max met her eyes, for what he felt might be the last time.

"I think we both know who it's from," he said.

They were both quiet there for a moment, standing on their respective sides of the door. Catriona nodded to herself, and said, "yes" softly before turning her manipulation back on at full blast.

"Have a lovely Sunday afternoon."

She closed the door in his face.

Of course it was Simon. This was different from the previous gifts she had received from Max, the ones she'd suspected Simon had picked out. He had sent it himself. Every positive feeling she had felt from believing it to be Max's gift multiplied and multiplied now that she knew it was from Simon. Catriona was elated—there was hope. Simon must love her and perhaps had for a very long time. Any thought of Max, her sadness on seeing him, on his refusing to come in, melted away. She felt the urge to run to the rectory right this very moment, to kiss Simon with so much happiness that he would forget there was a priesthood at all.

But then the negativity came crashing in like a thunderstorm, out of nowhere, unpredictable. How stupid to think that Max could have picked something like that out for her—considering her taste, thinking in terms of what she liked—that was always too selfless for Max, whose gifts were kisses and hugs and odd books. She wondered what junk was in the box.

She picked up the box, which was heavier than Max had said, and put it down next to the couch. Then she sat down, slowly and carefully, exhausted, like an old woman. It was long and quite shallow. Immediately she recognized the shape of her perfume bottle, which Max had put inside a plastic Tesco bag, thinking that would protect it from the sharp edges of the large books of artworks that were tossed haphazardly into the box. There was the DVD of *The Importance of Being Earnest* that she'd made him watch a hundred times. And a sweater—a mustard-yellow sweater, argyle. This was not hers. Certainly not. She smelled it. There was perfume, and it wasn't hers. She checked the tag. A medium. Certainly, this normal-sized, perfumed sweater could not belong to Fern. She knew enough to know that. He really was a liar. There must be someone else. She had been right. But who. She stared at the objects, silently interrogating them. They must have seen something. All of them had been in his flat, in his room, looking and listening.

There was the program from *Vojtech* that he had signed for her. She picked it up carefully, handling it the way one was supposed to handle old artworks…gently, with the weight of history on one's shoulders. She opened it. No special thanks to her from Max, of course—nothing in the director's note to mention that she existed or that she had helped. She flipped through the program, the faces of the actors in their unprofessional headshots, several degrees of idiocy and self-importance evidenced. One photo, however, struck her. Peter's friend, who had flirted with him at the play. Harry's lover, the one who he had cheated on Vera with. The girl who sat next to Max through the cast party.

That Julie Lovejoy.

And wearing a mustard-yellow sweater.

***

She went there straight from mass.

"Max is dating your friend Julie, is he?" said Catriona Darlington-Welland. She walked into the Midway for the second time in her life. She still hated it. Probably because she did not want to get any more of whatever lurked on the floor on the brown leather boots her grandmother had sent up from Harrods, which she kept neatly paired beside her door, tugging up the edges before turning out her lights at eleven o'clock in the evening. In the gray, midday sunlight that blushed through the dusty windows of the pub, they looked the same as they might have at night with the light from the street lamp outside Catriona's window cast upon them. With the rest of her, they came to a halt in front of a table comprised of Brett, Ashwin, and Peter, who had come for an afternoon pint.

"Where did you hear that?" said Peter.

"It doesn't matter *where*. What matters is it's true."

Brett and Ashwin remained silent, sipping their dark ales and looking at the television. The barman looked amused as he wiped the counter. It never got old, girls and women barging into pubs to yell at boys.

"Let's have it," she said, "you must know. I can't believe you wouldn't tell me."

"Catriona," said Peter, "I would know. And I haven't heard anything, from her or anyone else. In fact, I just had a pint with her recently. She's not dating Max."

"I don't know. I wouldn't be so sure, seeing as they're both liars."

"Why don't you work on figuring this out with them instead of trying to crack us?" asked Brett, not unkindly. "Peter and I have no idea what you're talking about. Neither does Ashwin."

Ashwin nodded in agreement, eyes still on the television.

"I don't suppose it interests you that I found a girl's sweater in the box of what are supposed to be my things that he's brought to me."

"It doesn't. And even if it did, it could have been anyone's. Doesn't he live with that girl, Fern?"

"Yes. But *Fern* doesn't wear a *medium*."

He looked up at her slightly incredulously

"I really am concerned about you."

"Well. Let me ask you this: how often have you seen Julie this term?"

"I admit, not frequently."

"She doesn't go out nights, does she?"

"She's been studying."

"She seemed awfully social before. She's always out with you lot."

"Listen," he said. "I mean, really, listen to me. There are about seven thousand other men in this town she could conceivably be spending time with. You have absolutely no case. I'm sorry."

"We all know she gets around," said Catriona.

There was a collective intake of breath from the table below.

"Vera told me she slept with Harry first semester. And I know about Brett."

Brett frowned for the first time. Catriona continued.

"*And* she's been trying to get with you too, Peter, if you'd only notice. Ashwin—well, I don't know. You're probably the one who should be with her, for how silly you are. But the point is, I'm not a child. I know these things, Peter."

"I don't have anything else to say to you about this."

"I'm sorry to have disturbed you, then. Enjoy your pints," she said bitterly.

With that, she shook her boots, once each in turn, ridding them of the miniscule amount of liquid they had accumulated in the course of her brief and ill-advised foray into the pub. She was right when she said nothing good would ever come of her being in there.

The snow outside was dirty as she slipped through the tiny outer door of dark wood and stepped onto Fair Street. She took out the white woolen gloves that she had purchased with her father in the Highlands, put them on one by one, finger by finger. She applied her white beret in the same cautious fashion, and, tucking her Italian handbag under her left arm, she proceeded down the street with an even step.

It was impossible. They had only been broken up for such a short while. Try as she might, Catriona could not decide whether Julie's luck was incredible or awful, in dating Max. And determining whether she was more jealous or more disgusted was beyond her powers of contemplation at the moment. Walking down the slushy grey Scottish streets, she felt a hatred for everything north of Newcastle. A pang of longing struck her for Lancashire in the summer, with its vast, organized sheets of land: yellow and gold and green, all in perfect squares, a quilt of English countryside dotted by cottony sheep. Taking long walks through these fields, measuring the kilometers by counting her steps. Hearing the birds singing in straight diatonic scales and appraising round, low shrubs for their shape. Drinking tea with her mother in the garden, being sure not to eat too many cakes that might thicken her waistline and decrease the tiny puffs of small breasts that behaved themselves beneath omnipresent white camisoles. She longed to sit and watch the platforms at the Victorian train station, the conductors in their smart suits and hats, blowing whistles. Things going and coming on time and in turn, as they were supposed to do, and not jumping out of order in every which way.

How could he want to be with that vulgar, American slut? She was loud and obnoxious and there was something so fake about her. So dramatic. It couldn't be her personality he was drawn to. Boys didn't leave nice girls like her for crazy ones like Julie. No, they certainly didn't. Catriona wondered what it could be as she stomped off back to Church Street.

***

In the Midway, the boys continued drinking for several moments before Peter spoke.

"Julie hasn't been that weird," he said evenly. "She's just busy."

Ashwin and Brett were both silent.

"She hasn't been coming to too much stuff," said Brett, after they had all finished their pints. "I haven't seen you two talking alone together once since, like, December."

"There was that pub night here."

"When Elizabeth was visiting. And she left early."

"But she'd tell me. Right? We went for a pint the other night. She'd tell me."

Ashwin looked sideways at Brett.

"Listen man, I'm not going to get wrapped up in this. But—"

"What?"

"There have been rumors going around. And Harry has pretty much disappeared too. I'm just saying. They left Eighteen Ten together a while ago."

"And," said Brett, torn even as he was saying it between keeping what might be Julie's secrets and being honest with Peter, "Harry Ommar called me a few weeks ago, trying to find out where she was when the girls were up at the house."

"You think she's sleeping with Harry Ommar again?"

"Yeah," said Brett. "You know Julie. She likes to backslide."

"What do you think?" said Peter, turning to Ashwin.

"It makes sense, man. He was the last dude she was gung-ho on."

"Good God," said Peter. "Why didn't you speak up before? How can someone so clever be so dense when it comes to boys?"

He took his coat from off the hook near the door, put it on, and said:

"I'm going to go talk to her before she winds up barefoot and pregnant." He stormed out.

Ashwin and Brett were quiet for some time.

Finally, Brett said:

"It's not Harry, is it?"

"No," Ashwin lit a cigarette. The barman didn't mind. "I don't think it is."

Ashwin had, after all, seen Julie checking out at the grocery store with a tall blond boy he thought he recognized as Max.

"Who d'you think it is, then?"

"How many times do I have to tell you, sometimes it's better to pretend you don't know anything? Especially when you only have suspicions instead of facts."

With the Indian sage having spoken his final words for the next pint or two, their glances returned to the TV and the calmness of mutual understanding settled in between them.

# XIV.

JULIE AND MAX WERE STRETCHED OUT together on the couch in Julie's living room. Caddy had gone to Paris for the weekend, to ride around on fancy boats with her fancy boyfriend, and hopefully, Julie thought, to buy some fancy chocolates. Other than, perhaps a taste of these, Julie felt she could not possibly want anything else in the entire world. Max's long body cradled her from behind, making her feel much smaller and more delicate than she was. What she did not yet understand, and would not understand for many years, was how wonderful Max felt too. The flowery smell of her hair and skin, the warmth of her belly under the curve of his arm and hand, the movement of her legs settling in beneath the blanket.

And, on the television, *Some Like it Hot*, or something like that. Max's favorite. Though Julie was sure it was an excellent film, what with all the hijinks ensuing, she couldn't pay attention. Probably, it was because Max was here—distracting and handsome. She turned around, with no shortage of wiggling, to come face to face with him.

"This is the best part," he mumbled.

"Oh, I'll turn back around."

"I didn't mean the movie."

He kissed her.

"Max, do you think I'm boring? Because, if you want, we could go out to a party, or have a drink—"

"You? Boring?" He smiled slowly. "I don't think so. I happen to find you very, very interesting."

She smiled too.

"Yeah?"

"Yeah."

"Okay."

"There's plenty of time for other parties."

They were quite comfortable indeed when the doorbell rang several moments later.

"Max, someone's here," she said.

"I didn't hear anything. I can't hear anything. All I want to hear is—"

"Max, the doorbell rang."

"Oh, oh. Oh, shit."

They sat in silence.

"Maybe they'll go away," said Max in a hopeful whisper. Julie showed her support for this wish by keeping quiet, bending her head onto Max's shoulder.

And yet, the bell rang again, this time accompanied by a hard knock.

"I'd better get it," said Julie, climbing off the couch and away from Max, who was occupying himself with the sudden, uncomfortable business of making himself presentable in a conventional sense, always difficult with his wild hair. "Maybe you'd better go to the kitchen. I have no idea who this could be."

"I don't care who it is."

"Max."

Max remembered reluctantly his promise to be discreet, though he felt that, at this moment at least, it was becoming far too much of a burden. He ducked below the window and walked hastily to the kitchen, sitting at the table in the darkness. Julie opened the door.

"Pete," she said, at the top of her voice. "Hi."

*Fuck*, she thought.

"May I come in?"

"Sure."

He knew something, from the way he looked at her, and around the room. It seemed to Julie as if he was checking a crime scene without a warrant, not able to touch anything but wanting to pick through the visual evidence.

"What's up," she said in as unfazed a manner as she found possible.

"I wanted to check up on you is all." He moved over to the couch, sat down. "It's warm in here, huh? What have you been doing?"

"Just dozing in and out, you know. Watching the movie."

"It's a good one. Listen Julie, have a seat."

"Okay," she said, thinking she would rather be doing something else on the couch with someone else.

"I'm not going to be mad if he's here."

"What? What are you—no one is here except me. And you, I guess."

"Stop lying. I'm supposed to be your best friend. Right?"

Oh God, but this felt terrible. How could she have ignored Peter? And worse, how could she have lied to him? Shown him that kind of disrespect? Oh God, the guilt crept over her—an itchy sweater your grandmother knitted that you knew would break her heart if you took it off in front of her.

"You are. You *are*. It's just—don't you think some things are better kept—under wraps? For everyone's sake? Stiff upper lip, and all that?"

"Is he here right now?"

"Pete—"

"Is he? Just tell me. I'm not going to be upset. I just want to speak to him. Ashwin and Brett helped me to put two and two together. Can't believe I've been so thick."

They must have seen them in the street, where they had planned to run into each other. Julie had known it was a silly risk, but Max had been firm. He had wanted to shop for groceries together, and the only way to do it would be to run into each other on Fair Street. Acquaintances, both on their way to the supermarket. In tiny St Albas, what could be more commonplace? But perhaps Julie had underestimated how glowing and happy they must have appeared together. Brett and Ashwin had known her for years, and she had never, in all those years, been this happy. The spring in her step and the way she looked at Max (with more anticipation than any—than *all*—the French chocolates you could put in front of her) would be out of place, and therefore not just noticeable but, when exaggerated by Julie's inability to keep her emotions off her face, unmistakable.

And now Max was there, in the kitchen. It was a prisoner's dilemma. What could he be thinking back there? Was he nervous? Would he come out? This scenario had never been discussed—the one where they were directly confronted. So finally, she told the truth.

"You haven't been thick. You're right. We are seeing each other."

"I knew it," Pete said. "Is he here? Upstairs?"

"I don't think this is a good idea," Julie said.

"I just want to let him know what will happen to him if he treats you badly again."

"Again?"

"Embarrasses you, like that. Don't look so daft, old thing. Like at *The Stroll*."

"You mean Harry."

Her heart began pounding in her ears. *Tell him*, it said. *Tell him, tell him, tell him*, with a heavier emphasis on the first word, thumping and thumping.

"Who else would I mean?" he asked, rhetorically.

"It's Max," said Julie. "Peter, it's Max."

"Max?"

Max came out of the kitchen.

Peter looked at Max, then back at Julie. He looked at Max's pajama bottoms and at the top of his ruffled hair. Studiously, he worked through the visual problem. Peter felt stuck in one of those coloring book games where you try to guess the seven things that are different in two almost-identical drawings.

"You're here. With you," he said, indicating Julie. "What?"

"I can explain," said Julie.

"You're not Harry."

"He's not Harry," said Julie, eyebrows pressed together. "No."

"How long...?"

Max walked to Julie's side, taking her hand.

"I need a glass of water," Peter said, passing between them as he headed toward the kitchen. "Do you have any idea how irresponsible this is?"

Julie and Max followed him into the kitchen, seating themselves at the table like two children awaiting their punishment for eating all the cookies in the cookie jar.

"*You* might not," he continued, indicating Julie and coming to the table and taking a sip of the water. "But Max—you know better. Breaking up with Catriona—I knew there were problems. But this? It's going to kill her."

He was speaking softly and seriously, keeping perfect control now over his emotions. It was, after all, mostly a matter of business, with Catriona. The business of kinship, of protecting your own.

"Why do you think we haven't told you?" said Max.

"Because you're rightly ashamed of what you've done. I know both of you. Especially you, Julie. You want all the fun of everything and none of the responsibility. None of the consequences. You're children."

"You have to try to understand," said Julie. "We're not trying to hurt Catriona."

"You don't even know how bad it is, with her."

"I worry about her," said Max. "That's why Julie and I have been doing things this way. I wanted to let her down as easy as I could. She doesn't need to know. I worried about her."

"You don't worry about Catriona, Max. You never did. You are not a martyr. You're selfish," said Peter. "You could have waited. I can't believe you."

"Peter," said Julie. "I didn't want to hurt anyone. I just wanted to be with Max."

"You realize how you've lied to me, don't you? You sat there, the other night, knowing all of this and not telling me. Letting me buy you a drink and make small talk. Unbelievable."

This shut her up. There was a long stretch of silence, as wide and tense as Catriona's smile.

"I'm happy now," Julie said. "So is Max."

"At what cost to Catriona?"

"It was over," said Max. "I'm done with it. Julie's done. And Catriona is going to have to learn to accept it. She'll be better off for it."

"I thought you were decent, Max. Even if you weren't decent to Catriona, always. I wouldn't have let it get so far. But I thought better of both of you. I thought you were good people," said Peter.

"You think we like sneaking around?"

"Maybe you do. Is this the first time you've cheated, Max? We know it's not Julie's."

"Don't talk to her like that," said Max. "That isn't fair."

"It's all right Max. He's just upset."

"Upset doesn't begin to describe what I am. You've broken my heart. I have been nothing but kind and good to you, Juliana Lovejoy. I have been the truest friend you've had in your life. Never believing the rumors, helping you through every mistake, taking care of you on every occasion. You know it's true. And I'm done. You've lied to me. It's over. Don't expect me to take any of your calls when Max decides he's done with you too."

They were all very still. Peter started again.

"I asked you back in, what, December, to leave it alone. I even

322     LAUREN B. MANGIAFORTE

forgot—genuinely forgot, that you had mentioned Max. I put it completely out of my mind. I thought it wasn't even worth remembering, so I didn't. For you. Because I trusted you. Not to take care of yourself but at least not to lie to me. Because I love you. But I need to take care of my family. If I had kept my eyes open, I might have saved Catriona some of this pain."

"I'm your family too," said Julie.

"No. You're not."

"I'm the family you choose."

"You choose to treat me like crap. You choose Max, Julie. And you choose yourself."

"You can't make me choose between you and Max."

"You already have! And so have I. It's done."

Julie bit her lip angrily. She knew he was right, but she had hoped with all her considerable might that it would never come to this.

"I'm sorry, Peter." She went quietly into the other room and up the stairs.

Max came to the realization that this was his battle now. Julie couldn't do everything on her own. *And that's what I'm here for*, he thought. *I can do this.*

He said:

"I'm sorry about Catriona, Peter. I know how hard it has been for you, taking care of her."

"You don't know. You imagine."

"However you want to put it."

"She's family."

"Yeah."

"So we take care of each other."

"You take care of each other?"

"Yes."

"All right."

Peter stared deep at Max, hardly blinking. Perplexed that he could have the gall to suggest what he thought Max was suggesting.

"Let's have it."

"What?"

"What's it you mean to say? Really."

"Just. When is Catriona going to take care of you?"

"Watch yourself, Max."

Peter turned to the chair and snatched his coat, throwing it up over his shoulder with a violent, sloppy motion.

"Why? What does it matter now?"

"You never knew what was going on with her. Who do you think has been cleaning up after all your messes, Max?"

"I don't know what you mean."

"Really? Three years and you never noticed?"

"Noticed what?"

"The cuts on her legs? The disappearances during dinner? After dinner? What did you think she was doing?"

"I don't know. You're crazy."

"You're crazy," said Peter. Then he said:

"She never even told you, did she?"

"About?" asked Max.

"Never mind," said Peter. "You don't deserve to know."

Peter thought for a moment that he'd shake Max or hit him. He thought of telling Max that Catriona knew about Julie, that she'd been right in the Midway about the sweater. Then he thought he wanted them to have to keep sneaking around, or at least to wonder. That was what they deserved. That was much less than they deserved. So he said, very quietly and intensely:

"If giving you that ring had any part in making sure Catriona didn't end up your wife, I'm glad to have done it. You don't deserve her."

Max stared.

"And by the way," said Peter, "good luck with Julie. She's not perfect either," he said, raising his voice up the stairs. "You'll soon find out she's just as desperate for answers as that cousin of mine you found it so easy to leave. She'll take anything. Julie's got no idea what the hell she's after in life. No idea what to do with herself. Other than you, probably."

Peter opened the door boldly and widely, a gesture that said something along the lines of "frankly, my dear, I don't give a damn." In a moment, he was gone into the mist, coat draped over his shoulder, done.

He thought fleetingly, in some other corner of his mind, that Julie would have been proud of him for being so American about his exit.

# XV.

DAYS LATER, CATRIONA WAS LEAVING THE art building. Her little leather bag was perfectly packed up following a lecture on Gauguin, it swinging at her side tempered by her arm's weight over it.

Now came the hard part. Class—the lecture—well, that was easy. Going out into the real world was hard. As much as she hated Max, she also missed him awfully. Missed having someone to eat skinny soups with, someone to call before she went to bed, someone to tell her how wonderful and beautiful and perfect she was. It did not cross her mind that Max had not been that way or said those things for years, or that when he'd said or done them he had been patently insincere.

With regret, she considered how cold she had been in the last months. How calculating and jealous. If she would have shown more restraint and had kept those thoughts to herself—why, she could be engaged to Max right this moment. He may never have cheated in the first place. Yes, she'd be happy instead of wandering into the foyer of Connery Hall having very little understanding as to why she should do anything at all.

With the exception of mass and the Midway episode, she had rather shut herself up at home since she discovered Max's infidelity. While she had originally sought solace in Simon's friendship, she could not share this detail with him once she had discovered it. Surely, it would devalue her to him, to have been cheated on. It was painful, embarrassing.

Besides, it had become too confusing to sit with Simon in the evenings, wanting badly to hold his hand, wanting to know what it would be like to be warm and cherished. But why should she think she was good enough for Simon? A book was nice, but it didn't prove anything. He had never done anything wrong in his life. He was a perfect judge of character. Everyone loved him. Even if he decided not to go into the priesthood, he could have his pick of so many girls in St Albas. He was handsome, sweet, nurturing, pure. She had ruined herself for him; she was impure, and, in addition to this, she was now cheated on. There was no hope. Who would want such a girl? And so she had stopped seeing him, except for at mass. He was too gentlemanly to ask why, just as he'd been too gentlemanly to tell her about the gift.

That damned mustard sweater was still folded and sitting on her corner chair, the one she had recovered from a charity store and reupholstered (quite expertly, she had thought) in a heavy floral print. Catriona had no idea what to do with it, other than to occasionally stare at it in genuinely hateful condemnation.

As for the photos of Max still in her room, she hadn't the heart to pack them away. There was perhaps still a chance that he would see that he didn't want some American tramp. Although the tone of his voice, and the look in his eye had sort of said, "it's like I've been dating a dead fish for three years" and spoke more to the possibility that he wouldn't come back, no matter what happened with the American and certainly not with a diamond offering. Goddamn him for doing this to her. Even after he had left her, he still had to make everything a disappointment.

The little key was pulled from the white leather bag, and its ancient prongs stuck into the comfortable old keyhole. It turned, and Catriona was home. She walked up the stairs to her room, ignoring the noises coming from Vera's bedroom. Obviously, they had thought she wouldn't be home for another few hours—her second lecture of the day had been canceled. They had been spending most nights at Harry's, she supposed, and supposed that they didn't wish to irritate her with their happiness.

As Catriona unpacked her bag, her phone buzzed. As usual these last few days, it was Peter. He had been calling her roughly at the rate of one call per waking hour. Since he had refused to believe her in the Midway, she had adapted a policy of silence toward him. Here she was, in her darkest hour, and he wasn't even willing to consider the possibility that Max and Julie were together, had been together, for quite some time perhaps. The time had come to prove that she could get through anything, with or without Peter. She did not need or want his pity. Just her little paring knife.

She locked her door, jiggling the handle the correct number of times to make sure it was really locked. She took off her clothes and sat down on her bed and opened the drawer of the nightstand next to it. The knife was in its place below the long, low jewelry box that had always covered it. It became warm in her hand as she gripped it while her other hand found the little pouch of baby wipes and pulled one out. It was best to be sanitary in these situations if she possibly could. She lifted her right leg straight into the air, feeling the back of her leg for a fresh place to cut. When she felt a little stretch of unscarred skin, she drew a little line on the skin, surgically, evenly, with hands that didn't shake. First, she felt nothing, and then a hot white pain, and then a bit of a sting. And it felt good, for a moment.

The next buzz of her phone was accompanied by a loud pounding noise downstairs on the front door. All that effort and not even able to enjoy it. To look at it in the mirror when it had stopped bleeding, and to clean the knife in the bathroom. The blood began to run down her leg. She held the baby wipe to the wound as she looked out the window. She was unsurprised to see it was Peter there on the old rug outside. When the knocking didn't work, he switched to the doorbell.

Next door, Harry and Vera had stopped. "I'll get it," she heard Vera say.

Catriona rushed to pull her clothes on, to stop him in the doorway. By the time she opened the door of her room, Vera had let Peter into the foyer.

"Thank you for getting the door," said Catriona, halted halfway down the stairs, staring at Peter. "But he knows he shouldn't be here."

"We didn't know you were home," said Vera, who was in an outfit of messy hair and her silk bathrobe. She had avoided Catriona since the breakup. Perhaps she felt badly for making her think Max was going to propose. Catriona was too exhausted and egotistic to say it wasn't her fault. "I suppose I'll let you two get on with it, then."

Meeting Catriona's eyes halfway up the stairs, she said:

"Well he's here now, for Heaven's sake!"

And Vera floated up the stairs, back to Harry.

Peter said:

"Hello. Nice to see you."

"I don't care what you have to say," said Catriona. "You chose to

believe Julie Lovejoy was right instead of me. And you embarrassed
me in front of your friends. I must have looked like a blubbering
idiot, or something. But I have proof that it was her" —*sitting in my
room,* she thought—"and I am dealing with it on my own. No need
for my thoughtful and mature cousin Peter to come to the rescue.
Especially when I know you care more about that obnoxious, loud
American whore than your own flesh and blood. Me, namely."

She folded her arms, looking down on him as he stood in the entryway.

"That's fine," he said. "I understand."

"Good."

"But—" he struggled for the words. "May I come in, I mean,
really, sit, or something."

Catriona sighed as she came down the stairs. He followed her into
the living room, where they sat on the couch together.

"Can you talk now you're sitting?" said Catriona.

"Yes," said Peter. "I wanted to tell you that I know you're right."

"You mean you believe me?"

Peter nodded.

"I do."

"How? Why?"

"It's difficult, Catriona. I—you see, after that day in the Midway, I
thought maybe Julie was with that Harry fellow again. And so I
went to her house to check up on it."

"Max was there."

"Yes, he was."

Catriona let out a thick, short sigh. The proof.

"She's lied to you, Peter," she said with conviction and all the
weight of false pity. "She's really quite good at lying. I'm sorry you
were friends for so long with such a vile girl."

"The point is, I'm sorry. And I'm here for you now, Catriona. If
you'll let me help."

*I can't afford to fail you and lose her,* he thought.

"I accept your apology," said Catriona, who was glad to have been
proven right.

"Thank you," he stood, as did Catriona, who walked him to the
front door. "Would you like to come round for dinner tonight?"

"No thank you," said Catriona, who was no longer eating. "I'll
ring you tomorrow, though. Perhaps we can have tea, if you come
back here."

Peter embraced his cousin briefly. Pulling away, he headed toward the door. As she turned to go back up the stairs, he saw the little line of red expanding down her leg like the seam of a nylon, sloppily-sewn. He caught her by the arm, gently but seriously.

"You have to stop doing that," he said. "Find another way. I can't keep keeping this a secret."

Catriona pretended to ignore him. But she heard in his voice a grave ultimatum.

She continued upstairs where she tried the mustard sweater on. It fit everywhere but in the breasts. That was enough. She would make Max pay. He couldn't love Julie Lovejoy for her personality, after all. And oh, it would hurt him to see her, walking down the street with gorgeous, well-shaped breasts. There was no time to waste with the break in classes coming up.

# XVI.

**EVERY YEAR, THEY HAD A PICNIC** in the spring in the cathedral yard. It was a historically impromptu gathering. Each member of the group of friends would tap the grass with his or her foot whenever he or she passed by. And then, on the day when it was finally dry and the sun was shining enough for it to be no-jacket weather, the tree of communication was lit up with messages and phone calls to say that it was Picnic Day.

Usually, Ashwin had the luck. But this year, Julie was happy to receive the signal from Larry. He had had a rough year and deserved the honors.

"Julie, Picnic Day," she heard through the phone.

"Really," she said, putting down the copy of *Middlemarch* she had recently attempted reading once more.

"It is. See you when I see you."

Julie went to the kitchen of Max's flat, where he was putting bread in the oven for breakfast. As much as Julie loved his Germanic morning ritual of cheese and meat and rye, she loved Picnic Day even more.

"We're going to a picnic."

"Today?"

"Yep. As soon as we can, as a matter of fact."

"Where?"

"The cathedral."

He smiled.

"That sounds lovely."

"This is one of the best days of the year. Everyone brings what's in their fridge, and usually Ashwin brings a lot of champagne, and we hang out and play Frisbee and be happy that all the cold weather is probably over."

"So, is this a friends thing?"

"Yeah," she said. "I guess it is. And I think it's time you met them all."

"You mean we can go out together, in public?"

"Yes."

"And I can kiss you and hold your hand and make sure all the other boys don't steal you?"

"Yes."

"It won't upset Peter?"

It took all her courage to convince herself to speak it, but she said:

"He'll get over it. He'll be there. We do this every year."

They dressed without showering. With the warm bread and breakfast foods in their arms they crossed the street, walking down Sea Street and hopping over William MacGregor's WM.

Most of the group had already arrived. Several little blankets checkered the grass. Brett and Ashwin were uncorking a few bottles of champagne, and Julie was happy to see Anastasia and Larry tossing a Frisbee with Neve and Margot.

She was sheepish, introducing Max into the group. Most of them had heard a lot about him at this point, after the explosion with Peter. And she couldn't blame people for wondering how serious she could be about Max, when he had a girlfriend, especially after the whole mess with Harry. But perhaps she didn't give Max enough credit—it was only a matter of moments before he had successfully inserted himself in a conversation with Caddy and Helen. She excused herself to see Brett and Ashwin, who were setting up a grill.

"Happy Picnic Day, Julie," said Brett.

"You too."

"Hi," said Ashwin, hugging her tightly. "How are you getting on?"

"All right. You know. It's been an interesting few weeks."

"I'm glad to spend some more time with Max," said Ashwin.

"You've met him before?"

"Yeah," said Brett. "You know, a few years ago. We had dinner with them."

"Oh. Max and Catriona. That would make sense."

"Julie," said Brett, noticing her face dropping. "We never liked her."

"Really?"

"She's nuts," said Ashwin.

"Thanks. But it's okay. Really."

"We always thought he was a decent guy."

"Good," she said. "Speaking of which—any word on whether Peter's coming?"

"I don't think so," said Brett. "He said he had a lot of work to do."

"Oh," said Julie.

"But hey," said Brett. "We have spring break to look forward to. Are you and Max coming?"

# XVII. SPRING HOLIDAY

**JULIE STRETCHED HER HAND OUT TO** her side. She was amazed how healthy the arm attached to it looked, golden and, just maybe, more muscular than four weeks ago. She tilted her head up and down, playing with the sunglasses that reflected different shades of blue and white, depending on the angle of her nose. Looking down her body in the sunlight, she realized that she appreciated it more than ever before, now that she was with Max. Her breasts fell slightly to either side, her soft belly relaxed, her thighs were slack, her toes pointed in opposite directions. In the sunlight, she hardly recognized herself. And the sun-kissed hand, it held Max's.

She hadn't thought of her dissertation, or Catriona Darlington-Welland, in days.

"What are we doing here?" she asked him as she sat.

Out in the sea, two massive mounds of rock—possibly islands, possibly the other side of the bay—were at the long, lazy work of settling into the ocean floor. The surface of the water reflected them impressionistically. God's best pointillism was on display: on closer inspection, the sand was varying shades of white and black. On one of the rock masses, several housing structures indigenous to the area huddled together. Julie had never felt this far away from home, but she was amused to see how similar this place looked to Scotland, only in an entirely different color palette. The world was much smaller than she had realized.

"We're being very, very lucky," he said. "I can't believe you talked me into this."

Julie stood. Belly still soft, she put her hands on her hips.

"I know. But I'm so glad I did."

Brett came running down the beach, carrying Anastasia in his arms, finally landing in the water with her screaming and playfully smacking him on the back of the head.

"How did you get to be so beautiful?" said Max.

"It's not much of a beach body. More like a pub body. But I'm glad you like it."

He smiled. "Takes one to know one."

Julie counted her blessings and her friends. Caddy was there with her boyfriend, out in the bay in a long, thin boat. Neve and Helen were taking a walk along the shore with Margot, who was trying to keep a kite in the air, and Larry, who kicked a volleyball along in the sand. How much more could she ask for?

She could wish Peter was here. Not surprisingly under the circumstances, he had decided to go to Warwick for the holiday to see his girlfriend. She couldn't help but think that she was the reason why Peter and Heather hadn't simply joined them all for this trip—and not only because Catriona had likely reinforced her opinion that Julie was trouble.

Max had a talent for reading her face, and therefore, her mind. So he said to cheer her up:

"Should we go into the sea?"

Julie almost agreed, but:

"Dinner!" yelled Ashwin from the house.

"I guess not," said Max, turning around to collect his book from the sand. "What should we do tonight, Julie, my love?"

"Oh, I thought we'd have whatever ridiculous meal Ashwin's cook made, followed by whatever ridiculous dessert there is, while drinking whatever beer that wonderful little local man in the wonderful little motor boat has brought us, and then maybe we could swim 'til midnight and sit around the fire with everyone else."

"And then?"

Julie just smiled, watching them all in the water, on the beach. It struck her violently that they were wonderful people, and that she would miss them, and that this was almost the end. Her chest ached, thinking about it. How they would all be scattered around the world soon, how these were the good old days right now, happening. No amount of Max could fix the fact that her friends would not always be three streets or two streets or one street away. It was sad. And more than that, it was terrifying.

Max watched them all in the water, on the beach, and was very happy to be young.

***

Catriona considered her body in front of the mirror in the hospital bathroom. She had to admit, for once, the cuts, the tummy, and the tiny breasts were not the first things she saw. When she looked in the mirror now, she saw two incredibly dull, shallow eyes with circles of grey surrounding them. As she stood there with her arms at her sides, she focused on the issues at hand. They stared back at her helplessly, two little mounds of flesh, saying, "Why are you doing this to us? We love you."

She wanted to go home, but the only thing more embarrassing than telling her mother about the surgery had been asking her to drive her to the hospital. While her mother had upbraided her harshly in the past for buying silly DVDs or nail polishes or special trapper keepers with the kittens on them, somehow Harriet found it fitting that her daughter should want to be fitted with breast implants. It seemed to her a worthwhile investment, particularly after the failure with Max, and if Catriona wanted to spend her savings on a new pair of tasteful size 36C breasts, why should she be the one to stop her? She did stop short, however, of agreeing to bring Catriona to the hospital or to pick her up. In fact, they arranged together for the surgery to take place in a hospital in the Cotswolds, where Catriona might recuperate over the spring vacation without making her father uncomfortable. She would take a cab to and from the little cottage that served as her grandparents' holiday home. In regards to the rest of the family and especially the people of Axbury Town, she was not to discuss the procedure. And if people noticed, one must hope that they would be polite enough not to ask.

Catriona had gone to the doctor the day after Peter had apologized. Since she had scheduled the surgery, a voice in the deepest recesses of her heart had been pleading with her not to do it. *If you think you are ruined for Simon now—wait until he sees you after*, it said. But she had shut it up. There were more important tasks at hand, such as making sure Max was filled with regret. If this was what he wanted, this is what she'd get.

There was a knock at the door.

"Ready in there?" asked the nurse.

"Just a moment," Catriona said, slipping the hospital gown on backwards. She folded her skirt and her sweater. She threw the little bra into the garbage can in the corner and opened the door.

"It's natural to want to say goodbye, if you need another moment," said the kind nurse from outside.

"That's all right," said Catriona as she opened the door.

The nurse nodded. She led Catriona to a large, plain room full of glossy white industrial floors and many beeping things.

"Go ahead and have a lie down, if you would. You can hand your things to me, I'll keep them safe 'til after."

Catriona did as she was told. The hospital sheets were of poor quality—starchy and hard against her bare, carefully shaven legs. She stared up at the ceiling as the nurse completed some paperwork. Momentarily, another assistant entered the room, asking Catriona if she wouldn't mind signing a disclaimer.

"What does it say?" she asked.

"Just that there are certain risks associated with the procedure—such as swelling, bruising, nerve damage, et cetera. Quite a small chance, obviously, but there are risks with anesthesia."

"You mean death."

"Yes."

"Where do I sign?"

She pointed the sharp pen and traced the well-considered letters of her well-considered name perfectly above the dotted line. She folded her hands as the people fiddled about, thinking of very little. It did not bother or surprise her that she should be here alone. She did not expect anyone to come to save her, to try to stop her, to tell her how beautiful she was without any silly nonsense like this. She'd told Peter she was going to stay in Axbury for the week.

When the doctor had asked her why she wanted to do this, though, all she could think of was Julie and Max. How important it was to make them understand that she was a force to be reckoned with, that she was someone desirable. No one could see her scars on the street, but these, these perfect 36Cs, they would surely notice.

People were plugging her into machines. Some for blood pressure, some for drips of medicine, another to keep track of her heart rate, which she watched detachedly bobbing up and down. She watched it change as she thought of Julie. The doctor and nurses asked her to relax. It all seemed very elaborate and very according to plan, and eventually they wheeled her into the operating theatre, a term she was not quite comfortable with. They announced that they were starting her on the anesthesia, that she might begin to feel slightly "loopy" or "dizzy," as if she was a little child who had spent the day at a carnival eating cotton candy and going on spinning rides and must now endure the British motorway, in order to get home, with its many roundabouts and curves.

"Are you sure you want to do this?" she thought she heard someone say, though it was only her Self.

"Yes," she replied, either within or without, and until the end of her life the last thing she remembered thinking at this moment in time was, what is one more slice of me?

# XVIII.

**THE PHYSICAL PAIN THAT FOLLOWED THE** surgery was at least a departure and a distraction from the psychological pain she had felt before it. She took the recovery and its aches from as logical and realistic a perspective as she had undergone the procedure. She needed revenge. This was one way of accomplishing that end. And the week that followed, holed up in the cottage in the Cotswolds, not being able to carry more than a teacup or raise her arms over her head, was a part of making sure that Julie and Max paid.

Of course, her upper body was horribly swollen and red. It was difficult to sleep, and at night she often lay awake thinking of where Julie and Max were, what they were doing. Sometimes, she felt a cautious, unconscious flicker of pity for both of them. There was no way that two lying, cheating people would ever be happy together, would ever have a successful, whole, loving relationship. It just wasn't possible. Still, the fact that Max could be with another girl made her hot with an anger that rapidly depleted any feelings of mercy or sympathy for that evil American and her boyfriend. When she thought of how miserable they would eventually make each other, how it would all self-destruct—give it ten years, not even— she was finally able to fall asleep.

Catriona had gone straight back to St Albas on the train. She and her mother had agreed that her father shouldn't be bothered with the awkwardness of knowing what his daughter had gone through, and neither of them had been keen on letting the rest of the family know—and Peter as a chauffeur was out of the question. Her mother had thought it was due to the embarrassment, but Catriona knew that this counted as cutting, and that Peter had been serious when he'd threatened to tell on her if she didn't find another way. She would have to be careful to avoid his finding out.

Wheeling the suitcase behind her was agonizing. She trundled down Fair Street from the station, so close to being at her house after five hours on various trains and then the bus. Catriona had taken great pains to freshen up in every bathroom she passed. There was always the chance that Julie might see her on the street, and she wanted to look polished, made-up, and well dressed when she arrived in St Albas. What had been the point of all this if not to make Julie Lovejoy realize that she hadn't got the best of her.

Lost in these thoughts, the pain began to subside. Funny, how it worked like that.

She stopped into the pharmacy to buy some medicine. The initial painkillers had run out, and she needed to purchase some icepacks to keep the swelling down. She prayed that no one would see her as she loaded a basket with as much weight as she could stand. At the cash desk, she kept her head down and paid by credit card to get home as soon as humanly possible.

When she arrived at the house, the lights were on in the living room. Vera was watching a movie alone. *Thank you, God,* thought Catriona. *At least I don't have to worry about that Harry Ommar pig.*

"Hallo," said Vera. "You all right?"

"Yes," said Catriona. "How are you?"

"Good. Have a good holiday down South?"

"I did."

"Good."

"And yours?"

"Nice is nice," she giggled. "What's wrong? Have you got that suitcase?"

Despite her best efforts, Catriona had bent back in pain. Tears were welling up in her eyes.

"I'm all right, really."

"What's wrong?"

Vera leapt from the couch. Catriona found her concern annoying. She had not intended to tell Vera until the breasts were beautiful. But it was a stupid idea; she knew that now. Of course she would notice.

She allowed Vera to take the shopping bag, to put her suitcase upstairs for her on her bed as she sat on the couch.

"What's going on, you silly cow," Vera said upon returning.

In absolute spite of herself, Catriona laughed through the grimace on her face.

"I've had surgery."

"Surgery!"

"On my breasts. I've got them done up."

She turned her face to Vera, who looked at her with an incredible amount of compassion and understanding. So Harry's suspicions were right, Catriona had found out about Max and Julie.

"Well, you're in the right place, poor dear. Do you know how many of my friends have done it? Don't you worry, I'll take good care of you. As best I can."

This reluctantly relieved Catriona.

"I'm guessing that's ice packs and pain killers?"

She gestured toward the bag.

"Yes."

"Good. You're well on your way then. 'Had a nice holiday'—liar."

Vera smiled, patted Catriona gently on the knee.

"I have some good news for you. Don't worry, I've checked all my sources."

She had gone too far, joking about checking sources when she'd been the one to tell Catriona about the engagement that never happened. But Catriona was too tired to say anything about it.

"What?"

"There are some gorgeous roses waiting for you upstairs."

"Roses?"

"Don't look so shocked."

Her imagination flashed. Max?

"They're from Simon, you know," said Vera.

"How do you know that?"

"I snuck a peak at the card. Wouldn't you?"

Catriona had to admit that she would.

"I'm going to go up to see them," she said, resenting the sofa for attempting to trap her back in it gulping folds as she tried to stand.

"I can bring them down for you."

"It's all right. I'm going to change and unpack."

Vera wanted to tell her not to overdo it. But she knew enough about Catriona Darlington-Welland to know that she wanted to owe as little as possible to any other woman.

Catriona turned on the light in her room with a wince of pain. On her desk, there was a luscious, pristine group of white roses, in the perfect stage of blooming above their thick, strong stems and leaves. They were in a painted porcelain vase, the exact one that she had been admiring with Simon at the antique store on Church Street a few weeks ago. Around it, he had tied a red ribbon. Next to it, he had placed a card.

Dear Catriona,

Know that I think only of you,
and that I miss you terribly.
I do hope you will join me for a stroll on
the Braw Braes after mass this Sunday.

Simon McLean

She sat at her desk chair reading and re-reading it, thinking of the thought he had put into it all and thankful in a way she had never been for anything anyone else had ever done. Still, she was scared. This was a gesture meant for the girl she had not been for quite a long time. But how could she refuse him this walk and along with it a chance to express himself? Catriona resolved not to think of it, to think only of her pain. That was a simple thing to think about. Once she began putting away the things in her suitcase, bending and carrying all about the room, it wasn't a difficult task.

It was true that Simon had missed Catriona a great deal. He couldn't stand being rebuffed after mass, couldn't stand that she had turned to Peter instead of him, so suddenly. He'd been elated that she had chosen to come to him with her problems. Though it took great patience and restraint, he had listened to her vacillate aloud between her sadness and anger, the feeling that she had been swindled out of the life Max had made her believe was hers. The extent to which he cherished the quiet evenings alone, listening to her in the rectory over a few cups of tea, longing to hold her and protect her and keep her warm, he could not describe. All he wanted now was to give her the life that she wanted, the one that Max never could have given her.

When she had stopped talking to him, it had felt like the bottom fell out of the car he had been driving. He was left with his ass on the pavement, being run over by his own rear wheels. What was worse, he couldn't decide whether it was kinder to chase her or leave her be. Simon spent so many hours praying on what to do, that in the end, he did nothing at all.

He had not gone away from St Albas over the Spring Holiday. There was too much going on in the parish, which was preparing for Easter. But, on his way to buy eggs for the children to roll in the churchyard, he had seen the lights on in Catriona's house. His footsteps guided him there. He had rung the bell and been welcomed inside by Vera.

Simon was surprised by how helpful she was and by how concerned she seemed for Catriona. Catriona had described Vera many times as spoilt, morally bankrupt, and self-absorbed. But the few times he had met her, in short spurts of time, her behavior had not exactly substantiated Catriona's description. And this meeting was no different. He had accepted Vera's offer to take a cup of tea.

"There aren't many biscuits," she said, laying them out on a little plate. "I've just returned from holiday yesterday, and I'm afraid I've not been to Tesco."

"It's lovely. Thank you."

Vera crossed her legs at the ankles. She remembered Catriona saying that Simon was going to be a priest.

"How is Catriona?" Simon asked.

Vera was relieved that she wasn't the one to ask it.

"Not very well, I don't think. Though I don't believe she'd be too keen on my telling you that. If you wouldn't mind keeping it between us."

"Of course."

For a moment, neither one spoke, not knowing which lines they could cross, what information the other would be comfortable sharing.

Eventually, Vera said:

"Seems as if she's been spending some time with you. That's quite good, isn't it?"

He might as well be honest. Who knew if he would ever have the chance to speak with someone about Catriona this candidly again.

"That's the trouble. She hasn't been speaking with me. I didn't know—"

It was against his nature to pry. He took a sip of tea.

"You didn't know if you'd done something wrong."

"Precisely," he said, relieved.

"I don't think so. Not that I've heard, in any case."

Vera poured Simon some more tea.

He was unnerved by how nervous she looked now.

"My boyfriend used to be quite close to Julie Lovejoy."

She stopped. Simon nodded.

"I see you've heard. News travels, I suppose. But I didn't know it traveled as far as all that," she smiled. "Catriona took a turn for the worse before the holiday, you see. Wouldn't speak to anyone. Not to me, and not so much to Peter either, for all I could tell. Harry finally ventured to tell me that Max and Julie were together. I didn't tell her. I didn't wish to make her more embarrassed, but Harry guessed that Catriona must have found out. You must know how she can be—keeping up appearances. She was—probably worried about what you'd think."

He understood perfectly, in fact. Vera noticed, and continued:

"She'll be home tomorrow evening, I believe. I don't know that she'll want to see you. I know that must sting. But there's no telling. I'm sorry I don't have better news."

Simon's heart blubbered against his ribs. At least she was coming back. He hadn't been sure if she had left St Albas entirely.

"Would flowers be too much?"

Vera considered it for a moment.

"No. Flowers wouldn't be too much."

Simon stood, extending his hand to Vera.

"Thank you so much for the tea."

"You're welcome. I quite enjoyed it."

"So did I."

He collected his jacket from the chair near the door.

"I would be grateful if we could keep this conversation to ourselves."

"So would I," said Vera, leading him to the door. "Goodnight, Simon."

***

Catriona was wearing a light purple Easter dress with a small floral pattern. She had bought it before the surgery, guessing at the size. To her credit, she had done well. It fit perfectly. Its high neck and flared skirt distracted from her breasts. For her arms and shoulders, she had purchased a boxy yellow dress jacket.

She waited nervously in the patch of sunshine in the churchyard as Simon fulfilled his duties, helping Father Tom to hand out candies to the children and speaking with all the old ladies who would go home to an empty house for the rest of the day. Being one of them, Mrs. Leslie had been good enough to volunteer to clean the church after mass. Thanking her profusely and slinking away from Father Tom, Simon approached Catriona with a mixture of nerves and determination.

He couldn't explain the joy he felt upon seeing her there in her purple dress. Today was a blessed day, the most meaningful of his life. After all these years of patience and persistence, he would finally tell Catriona his feelings. He had rehearsed his speech a dozen times, and it was all he could do during mass not to burst out with his feelings before the entire parish.

"Happy Easter," he said, beaming at her. "You look lovely."

Catriona blushed.

"Thank you. Happy Easter."

"Shall we?"

He extended his arm to her once they had passed through one of the wynds, away from the Avenue and onto Redfriars Street. She had to remind herself that it was all right to take his arm. She took it and found it was stronger than she had ever imagined.

Redfriars Street led all the way to the tiny, iron-gated pass off Church Street that guarded the dusty, dirt path known as Braw Braes. Catriona had not been here in years, though it was her favorite part of town. She had discovered it in the first week of term, had loved taking walks and bike rides there. It reminded her of George, in a good way. But Max claimed to have allergies to the trees and once they began dating she thought it would have looked odd for her to take a walk by herself.

The path was densely wooded on either side, spreading out into the countryside for a few miles and then winding its way up a steep hill back to town. Birds were singing in the shrubs and the trees. Flowers were making courageous attempts at budding. Bugs of every shape and size were scurrying up and down the barks and branches, making whatever preparations for Easter luncheon British bugs are apt to make.

"It reminds me of Lancashire," Catriona found herself saying. "I use to love to be outside with all the wee creatures."

Simon liked to think of her happy and young like that.

"I didn't know you liked the outdoors."

"I did. Especially when I was a girl."

She stopped, remembering why she had turned indoors on so many occasions in her life. She thought of George again, in a sad way.

"I don't walk as much as I would like," she said.

Simon didn't press this topic any more, and Catriona was thankful. She was surprised to find how little her breasts were hurting. And this was decidedly the least she had thought of Max or Julie in a longer time than she would have been proud to recount.

They kept on the trail, passing a shallow stream where a large family of ducks had convened, kicking their bright orange paddling legs in the water, dipping under the water to eat a plant, tipping their cute duck bottoms into the air. They stopped at the worn wooden bridge above the ducks. Catriona laughed at them, pointing out her favorites to Simon. If it hadn't been the first time, neither of them would have noticed when Catriona took Simon's hand without thinking.

Each felt that the other's heart was racing, but they started again towards the clearing with the view of the magnificent hills outside of town without saying a word about it. Catriona and Simon were both enjoying the solitude, the possibility—ignoring the nerves or converting them, perhaps, slowly into something more like glee.

When the hills were before them, coming alive with new shades of green for the spring, Simon stopped Catriona.

"Shall we sit?"

Catriona nodded, backing up onto the stone bench on the path. They rested there, staring out ahead of them, still holding hands.

Simon sighed happily.

Then, Catriona spoke:

"It should have been you," she said. "It should have been you—"

Simon turned to her.

"Let me finish. I'm so sorry. I'm so sorry I chose Max. I didn't know I had a choice, you see. I don't know what I was thinking. But it was always supposed to be you. I know that. I know that now."

His heart skyrocketed. It soared up into the branches, dancing around, sending the birds flying as it whizzed off in all directions. He buried his head into her neck, relieved and ecstatic. There, he took a deep breath. She smelled so clean. He reached for her face, gently turning it to his, so close he could feel her breath on his mouth.

"Catriona, it can still be me," a smile spread across his face. "I love you."

"Love me?"

"I've loved you for years. Every day since I first saw you."

"Simon—"

"Quiet, Catriona. Be quiet."

He said it in such a loving way that she fell silent and even closed her eyes.

Though the poetics of romance dictate unchecked passion at a moment such as this, what Simon did next he had both the time and the ability to calculate. He placed his other hand at the side of her face, letting her feathery hair fall on top of it like a dying wing. Her skin was soft and cool and pale. This was just as he imagined. When he felt as though the imprint of his skin on hers was deep enough, he kissed the pink little mouth softly. It was certainly not the first time that Simon, with his good looks and kindness, had ever kissed a girl. But it was far and away the most exciting. For several turns of the head, they remained there, exploring one another's mouths.

*So that's what it feels like*, thought Catriona.

"You love me too," he said when they had separated.

"Yes, I do. I love you."

He pulled her close, pressing her to him. She involuntarily pulled away, in pain.

"I'm sorry," she said, standing. Walking several feet away.

"Did I hurt you?" he said, following her. He put a soft hand on her back.

She remembered that it couldn't be. Yes, she loved him. Yes, she wanted him badly. Even her swollen breasts told her so. But she had been with another man. She had been cheated on and ruined and scarred in so many places, and in so many ways, by it. Just as Max had found that Catriona wasn't a perfect person, so too would Simon. And the discovery would hurt so much more if she didn't speak up now, before it went a moment further, before he built her up any more than he might already have over the course of nearly four years.

"I have to tell you something, Simon. I'm afraid to tell you."

He did not like the sound of her voice.

"I'm not who you think I am, Simon."

"Of course you are."

"No. I'm not. It's going to sound very dramatic, I suppose."

"Catriona," he said, guessing at where this was heading. "I don't

346     LAUREN B. MANGIAFORTE

care that you've—been with Max."

"It's not just that." She lowered her voice. "He's cheated on me. I suppose that makes me damaged goods, or something."

"Not to me."

He wondered how these moments seemed to be falling apart. He panicked. He had to put them back together. She had to see.

"You're perfect," he demanded.

"I had my breasts done," she added. "I suppose that makes some sort of difference."

"I don't care," said Simon. "I don't care if you've got a tattoo of an elephant standing on a beach ball on your back."

This attempt at humor fell flat against the forest floor. Simon stood behind her, put his hands on her shoulders.

"Did you know I had a brother?"

"I'm sorry?"

"I had a brother. He's dead because of me."

"What?"

"When we were children. He was shot. It was an accident. I wasn't watching him."

"Catriona, I'm so sorry."

"I hurt myself, sometimes."

"There are no conditions," Simon said. "You can never frighten me. I don't understand why you're trying to."

"You're so selfless," she said. "You've always thought of me. I see that now. I—I've known about the book for some time, you know. *Wuthering Heights*. You must have wanted to tell me, didn't you? That it wasn't from Max."

"Of course. But you seemed so happy that he'd thought of it."

"That's what I mean. You're selfless. And I'm selfish. Horribly selfish."

This revelation fell over her like a ton of fish.

"No, you aren't."

"I really am. And if you don't become a priest. If you marry me instead—it will be such a waste."

"I'm not selfless," he said, flustered. "I'm not selfless at all. I could have told you about Max and Julie, you know. I could have saved you that pain."

"What?"

"But I didn't. I wanted you so badly. I knew all I had to do was wait, that eventually you would hear about it and you would finally see me, finally want me."

"You knew and didn't tell me?"

Catriona had never been angrier in all her life. Was no one above betraying her? Did no one care about her feelings? Was no one in the world interested in her happiness?

"I can explain—"

She threw her hand out behind her and brought it back hard against Simon's face, pushing him back down onto the bench.

Then she headed off into the distance on the path, disappearing bit by bit.

Simon sat with his head in his hands.

And there was no profit under the sun.

# XIX. APRIL

**IT WAS A DINNER GIVEN TO** the senior class by the administration. Or at least that's what they said. The price of the meal was included in the student fees for the year, but it made for an excellent publicity stunt on the part of the administration. It took place, always, in the University Towers, the building that was on the cover of every pamphlet the University had ever sent to a prospective student. It was the one that looked the most like Oxford or Cambridge, and therefore, the one that Oxford and Cambridge rejects would find the most comforting when they decided to choose St Albas instead of a school in London without such monumental arches and bell towers.

It was another occasion for a decadent meal and for another, slightly different set of decadent outfits and the accessories that went with them. Max was surprised to find that he was excited to go, and that it took no coaxing on Julie's part for him to feel the need to go to the tailor on Fair Street and purchase a proper suit jacket. He had even enlisted Julie's help in finding a shirt and tie. Though he still hated shopping and dress shirts and fancy dinners on principle, he found that things in general, and especially things he had thought he hated, were generally more pleasant when Julie was involved.

Together with Fern, they walked to the Towers. A member of the wait staff greeted them and took their coats and directed them to the staircase, which had been adorned with a thick, red carpet embedded with the St Albas crest. Banners displaying the University insignia hung from the ceiling, the chandeliers were lit to a beautiful middle setting that made everyone appear to have a golden glow that was impossible to achieve without the assistance of such artificial lighting or frequent trips to either Capri or the tanning beds at the Ancient Links Hotel.

In the hall, six long, wooden tables, three hundred years old at least, were set out. Heavy lace tablecloths with red and green tartan runners of wool lay across them, beautifully complemented one another and the large, wild floral arrangements set with heather and thistle in golden flower vases. The gold goblets and best china had been set out, along with the silver cutlery that had roses carved into the ends, each piece probably worth twice the value of the meal they would eat with it. They were seated at the end of the fourth table, in a cluster of seats near Margot, Neve, Ashwin, Brett, and the others. Peter was absent. Julie still felt distressed to have been the cause of his absence.

Ashwin promised her, as he had many times over the spring holiday, that Peter would calm down. Julie doubted this.

"And in the meantime, we have only a month left here. Let's enjoy it," he had said. "Don't feel like you shouldn't come to things just because Peter is being a little baby."

"He's not, though. He's completely right."

"You think you can be best friends with someone for that many years without doing a little bit of damage as well as good? Look around you. We've all hurt each other over the years, haven't we? He'll get over it, and in the meantime, no one has any intention of doing anything other than being friends with both of you."

His absence tonight was very keenly felt, though. And not just by Julie.

She found she had somehow managed to simultaneously greet everyone and take her place while churning these thoughts over in her head. The harp had stopped playing. Now an old man of some sort was giving a speech about hard economic times, how the graduates must take heart and plow into the new world, life after St Albas, and become the leaders of their generation. They were endowed with the wisdom and connections that would allow them to do so, it was their moral obligation to their families, to their teachers, to society, and—most importantly, the big finale—each other.

Across the hall, she could see Vera and Harry. Harry had his arm around Vera's chair, in the same fashion that he had had it around Julie's at the fashion show. It didn't bother her so much, but she couldn't help but wish that it didn't bother her at all. And beside Vera, there was Catriona. And she was sitting next to Peter. He had come after all. Julie could tell that her cheeks were going red. An invisible, hot hand gripped her stomach.

"Max," she whispered, "I think I'm going to slip to the ladies' for a minute."

He nodded, putting a hand on her hand.

"It's all right, you know."

"What is?"

"Peter. And Catriona," he said.

"All right?"

"All right."

"I'll be right back."

She stood up as inconspicuously as possible, shimmying down to the end of the table and walking out of the room and down the staircase again to the ladies' bathroom. As she sat down on the toilet, not having to pee but needing to sit by herself for a moment or two with her head in her hands, she heard another woman enter the bathroom. She felt the need to cut her alone time short. There was rarely ever such a thing as privacy in a woman's toilet. So, she stood up, flushed the toilet for good measure, and opened the door, wetting a paper towel and putting it on her neck. Looking up into the mirror, she saw that Vera was standing behind her, having come out of the other stall.

Immediately, her heart began to pound with an animal anger, an animal fear. And there too was human shame and human guilt. Her jawbone felt tight, more connected to her ears than she remembered them ever feeling, a buzzing electricity running through a tautly pulled line between them. Her mouth went dry.

"Vera," she said, trying to catch her breath as she turned around. "Hi."

"Hello."

She came to the sink and washed her hands. Julie passed her a paper towel. *Maybe,* she thought, *this is the universe giving me a sign. Maybe this is my one chance to talk to her alone, to try to make things as right as they can possibly be, perhaps even to pass on a message of some kind to Catriona. A woman-to-woman talk.*

"Can I—can I talk to you for a moment."

And for a moment, Vera seemed receptive, if tense, if tight-lipped. She seemed willing to listen, to try to listen without talking.

"You know who I am, don't you?"

"Yes," said Vera. "I know."

"Okay. Well. I want you to know—I'm sorry."

"I know you are."

"Okay," said Julie.

"I know you probably didn't mean it. You probably didn't even know."

"I didn't."

"Harry probably didn't even tell you about me. Did he?"

"That's because he loves you."

Vera nodded. Then she said:

"No one ever tells you how exciting it is, do they? To steal another girl's boyfriend?"

Julie was taken completely aback. Which was something that was hard to do.

"I don't know."

"You're not the first one who's done it, Julie. And you're not going to be the last."

"Okay."

"You're friends. That's how it always starts. You laugh at his jokes, he smiles at you, you get on so well. He tells his girlfriend she's mental for thinking that he could like you. If only you could hear the things he says about you—'She's not as pretty as you,' 'Her? You're insane.' But eventually he leaves his girlfriend for you. Because you're the new and exciting thing. Because he's a boy. Because they're all boys, whether they are men or not. And boys like to dress up like cowboys and Indians and do whatever they please."

Julie was surprised to find Vera had such substance, and that she was capable of disappointment. She supposed you couldn't judge a book by its cover or a model by the length of her legs for that matter.

"What are you saying?" Julie said.

"Don't get too comfortable with Max. Catriona made that mistake."

"I don't want to talk about Catriona."

"What you did to her was not all right."

"I didn't do anything."

"I'm not an idiot. You'd like us all to be, but we're not all idiots here."

Julie raised her eyebrows.

"Noted. Thanks."

She turned away. She needed to find Max to tell him it was time to go home.

## XX.

**WHAT HAPPENS WHEN YOU GIVE UP** your real dreams at a young age is that you replace them with more boring dreams. And when those dreams don't work out either, you are startled and dismayed. Because you settled for them in the first place. Then you settle for more boring dreams still, and more boring dreams still. And on and on and on. And many people will tell you that is growing up.

It isn't. But to Catriona, it was. And that, perhaps, is why she had rejected Simon. Not because of the breasts or her brother or Max or Julie or because Simon hadn't told her he'd known about them. But because Simon would have loved to see her love to roam and be outdoors, would have wanted to watch her disappear to her own Neverland, no matter what it was. But the better dream had long since died, and no amount of clapping or believing in fairies or thinking wonderful thoughts could ever bring it back.

Catriona had so long worked on the blueprint of the life she would have not *with* Max, but because of Max, that once it had been smudged and then shredded so he could build a different model there was nothing she could do but try to become a different model herself. She had breasts now because Julie had them. But they hadn't worked. And so she must do something else. But what? She remembered someone saying that the best revenge is success. All right, but what kind?

That is when Catriona backtracked. Not to the original dreams, of exploring the wilderness, of becoming an astronaut, of seeing the Northern Lights, or of sewing a tent of leaves to live in or at least dream about it. She progressed two degrees of dreams after those childhood fantasies. She brought back her high school dreams of being the girlfriend of a proper English boy. She would settle for no half-measure socialist Europeans this time. And Julie would notice and know she hadn't won, and Max would see that she was capable of finding another boy, and Simon would be punished for his lack of loyalty.

A helpful epiphany sprung up inside her one morning as she was looking through Vera's latest issue of *Vogue* in bed. Here was a gorgeous fashion spread. Brilliant, beautiful women in clothing inspired by London street fashions. *All these thin women,* she thought. She looked across the room to her mirror. *That's not me. Her face is so gaunt. Her hair is too long.*

It was then that she realized she was closer to looking like the women in the magazine than she had ever been before. Exhilarated, she jumped out of bed, pulled the scale out from under the bed, stepped on it. The little dial slung to its mark—nine and one-half stone. The thinnest she had ever been, and that was including the breasts. Quickly, she kicked the scale back under her bed and stripped down to her underwear and bra. She turned on all the lights in the room. It was true—she was still boxy, but now she was thin and boxy, a completely different matter. Two twin curves of light sat atop her breasts. Her hair was falling straight at her shoulders. She took her glasses off, stepping closer to the mirror to examine the new, sharp curves of her face. Thin.

Something must be done about this, right this very moment, while she was still thin. She jumped in the shower, dressed, and went out to Foxfields Dressing Company where she bought a new wool, camel-colored coat that flared down to her knees, a crisp, tight-fitting button down shirt, and a slim pair of dark jeans. She took the bus to Dunglen, where she bought new makeup and a fantastic pair of Dior sunglasses. On the bus coming back, she made an appointment to be fitted with contact lenses. When it dropped her off on Fair Street, she went into Boots for a box of tooth whitening strips and a bottle of tanning lotion.

When she came back through the front door, Vera asked her if she would have enough money to pay the rent what with all these purchases.

"It's called an emergency credit card for a reason," she said.

"I doubt your mum will be happy about it."

"I'll call my father and sort it," she said, which is exactly the sort of thing that the girls she finally looked like might have said, might be saying to their own flatmates at this very moment.

Vera went back to doing her abs exercises on the floor.

"I'm coming with you to watch the rugby from now on," Catriona said.

And it worked.

She picked him out at the very first match.

Not bad looking. Single. English. Rich.

Catriona was surprised that she still remembered how to do what she had done with Max. And at how much quicker it went when you were attached to a pair of 36Cs.

No one knew where he had come from, and no one seemed to have known him before. Where they had met was a mystery, though a mystery not pondered extensively by anyone but Julie—and, even so, she too had grown bored with the gossip after a week. From what anyone could gather merely by indulging in a perfunctory once-over, he was English, slouchy-faced, reasonably well-to-do, and just a little bit fat. These characteristics either resulted from or explained his favorite extracurricular activity, rugby.

"Harold is nothing like Max," Catriona said a few weeks later, sipping tea with Vera one Saturday afternoon. "And thank God for that."

Vera sipped too.

"He's got priorities. He's an adult."

"Isn't he a third year?"

Catriona cast a warning toward her friend as she put another scone on her plate.

"Yes. Did I tell you he went to Eton?"

"Did he."

"He did. His parents are going to love me. Don't you think?"

"I don't see why not."

"They come from Tonbridge. Didn't I tell you they came from Tonbridge? Nice, civilized. Cozy. You know. Tonbridge. It's delightful to visit Tonbridge. Everyone knows."

"Yes."

"He plays rugby. Max never was very much into sport."

For as incredible as Vera's imagination could be, she was also very perceptive of life as it progressed around her. She had been more privy to Catriona's habits than any other human being, including Max, over the last year. Therefore, it was easy for her to determine what might be said to cause offense and how best to avoid doing so. Of course, as it goes with human beings, this also meant she knew her friend's weakest points as well and could pin them down to painful effect.

"Catriona," she began, "may I ask you something?"

"They have money, if that's what you're getting it. I rather hoped I had made that clear with all that lot about Tonbridge Wells. My word, Vera."

"It's not that."

"Then what?"

"Have you spoken to Simon recently? I haven't heard you talk about him."

The question left Catriona momentarily speechless and cold. She wished it didn't bother her. She wished that the outward appearances were enough. She wished she could hate him more, that she didn't miss him. She had not spoken to him since that awful afternoon. When the anger subsided, she would feel embarrassed, perhaps, but for now the hurt burned strong. Her desire to punish him, to separate herself from him, was unquenchable, and she often confused it with her hatred for Max and Julie.

Neither Max nor Simon had given any indication of being bothered by her silence, nor by her new boyfriend. And apparently, they were making up with one another. In fact, she had recently seen Simon on the street shaking hands with Max. It was infuriating how boys could bury the hatchet like that.

"There's nothing to say. We aren't speaking."

"Do you think he's jealous of Harold?"

"Of course he is."

"Did anything ever happen?"

"What are you implying?"

"With you and Simon, I mean. Did anything happen."

"He's going to be a priest."

"I know that. But, even before you broke up, I thought—"

"I am not Max. I'm not like him. I'm a good and decent person, and I would never have cheated on him."

But though she didn't say it, she realized she really wished she had cheated on Max. Perhaps, the opportunity would have presented itself, had she been open to it. She could be living an entirely different life. She could be marrying Simon, buying a little house in a little country town. She could have a horse and walk on hills and get her hands dirty and buy a telescope. She could buy those books of paintings she liked so much, even if she didn't like them quite as much as the stars and go to Rome to visit them every now and again. But not so often that it appeared she wasn't happy in a little house in a little country village. Just enough to be the only husband and wife in it that went to Italy to see paintings and go to mass at the Vatican.

She could see it: the fresh daffodils on the table, Simon on his knees in the garden. Perhaps a couple of children and a tidy, grey, silver-caged bird.

# XXI.

JULIE ENTERED PROFESSOR HARRIS'S OFFICE FOR her dissertation review. She had submitted it a week before in a whirl of nerves. Being with Max had forced her to study more. She found she didn't mind it quite so much when she could read and take notes in bed while leaning her back against Max's wide, soft chest, when she could feel his arm around her belly. And it was much easier to read and think and learn and know when you weren't hung over or drunk quite so often.

"Do you think it's done?" she had asked Max nervously as they had walked to the drop box in Bard House to submit it.

"It'd better be," he said, gripping her hand tighter.

"Max!"

"It's wonderful, Julie."

"Thank you for proofreading it."

"I liked doing it."

"Well, when it comes to yours—I'm afraid I Kant."

"Oh Julie, that's the oldest one in the book."

Still, he laughed at her joke and kissed her and they released the envelope together.

She thought wonderful thoughts as she climbed towards Harris's office. She knocked, and opened the door to a "Come in." The large, arched window framed a beautiful shot of the top of the Castle—the crumbling coat of arms and the little Scottish flag that either flapped or floated or seized in the wind, depending on the weather. Today, it was rustling softly as the sky was a beautiful blue where fluffy, white clouds permitted it to peek through.

"Hello," she said as Harris stood at his desk and gestured for her to have a seat across him.

"Tea, Miss Lovejoy?"

"Yes, thank you."

He nodded and rose to go to his kettle.

They paused in an almost-comfortable silence as the kettle came to a boil, and Harris brought Julie a cup of tea before settling back behind his desk with a Lady Grey of his own.

"Well then. Miss Lovejoy, how did you feel about your dissertation?"

"I felt good about it, yeah. I thought I tackled the subject well, from a lot of different points of view. I learned a lot."

"You think that's what you did."

"Yes," she said, draining her teacup and putting it on his desk. "What did you think I did? With all due respect, of course."

"Of course."

Julie saw Professor Harris smile his old smile as he reached into his desk drawer and pulled out the envelope that held her dissertation and final grade. He handed it across the table.

"Open it."

Without trying to look as nervous as she was, Julie ripped open the top of the envelope.

"It's a distinction mark."

"It is," said Professor Harris.

"You've never given me a distinction before. Even when you were being easy on me."

"You've never earned one before."

"Fair," she said, breathless. "Thank you."

"Don't make me get sentimental," said Professor Harris. "I have no idea how you pulled it off. Especially when it seems as if you've had several extracurricular activities at the same time."

Julie lifted her eyes off the grade.

"What," said Harris, "you think my ears don't hear the town gossip as well?"

Julie laughed. Harris stood, and did what no British professor had done before. He embraced his student.

"Whatever you do," he said, "do it well. Whatever you're going to be, be it well."

"I will," said Julie.

"Get out of my office," said Harris. "I have things to do. And so do you."

# XXII.

**SHE HAD MADE A SPECIAL APPOINTMENT** with Father Tom, had circled it in her planner, the mark that said it was important to remember. Three things had happened that she simply could not accept.

It was in the middle of Fair Street that the first catastrophe happened. Harold was off somewhere, probably shooting at some type of animal, who knew what—and she had decided to take a walk. She put on her light, spring jacket and fastened the tie around her waist. She took the shopping bag in case she saw anything she should want to buy and headed out the back door, through the garden, and, closing the iron gate that led to Fair Street behind her, took off by herself. The sun was shining and there seemed to be quite a few tourists in town today. She even thought she heard some Lancashire accents, which gladdened her considerably or, at least, as considerably as possible when one was horrifically depressed— though Catriona did not believe in depression, only in punishment for sins.

Walking toward the little shop of necklaces and other trinkets near the student union, she stopped to peer in the window of the chocolate store. As she stared down at the little treats, she noticed the reflections of people passing by behind her in the glass. And there was Max and there was Julie, holding hands in the street behind her, dark against the glass, like shadows.

She turned around, unnoticed. They were walking close to one another on the sidewalk, never letting their hands drop. There was something so beautiful and simple about it. Before she knew what she was doing, she was following them, ten feet or so behind. She watched as Julie's head butted up against his shoulder when he made her laugh. She watched Max kiss her on the cheek. She watched them go into Max's apartment, up the stairs, hearing their chatter.

And she crossed the street, bitter as she watched the blinds in Max's room close a moment later.

Max loved Julie. Really, loved her.

None of it had worked. Not pulling Peter away from Julie. Not dating Harold. Not getting new breasts. Not any of it. No. None of it.

She remembered the second catastrophe too. One of those nerve-wracking, tense, and terrible moments one so often had in St Albas. The pressure of avoiding someone, and the inevitability of running into him anyway.

Not so long ago, she and Harold had been walking through one of the town's narrow lanes, holding hands. Simon had turned the corner at the far end of the lane. She smiled brightly, picking up the pace and tone of the conversation. He must see her remarkably happy. Harold stood daftly next to her, probably not hearing her from so great a height and so thick a head. He did not notice that Simon stared into Catriona with an unimpressed look, knowing she was lying, saying so with his face, feeling sorry for her. She wished Harold would play along. The smiles, the little nudges, perhaps an arm around her shoulder, protective. He was oblivious. A bubble of tension asserted itself between she and Simon as they passed, two seals leaning in the same direction on an enormous red ball, so tense with the weight that it might break. Please, a shout—a curse—anything. Anything but this merciful silence. She half expected him to make the sign of the cross. *Pax vobiscum.* But he did not.

None of it had worked at all.

And in addition to none of it working, Peter had told her mother about the cuts. About the eating. That was the third and final catastrophe. She had been wrong to think he'd be too embarrassed to say something about the breasts, even if he found out. And when he had told her mother, she had to beg her parents to let her stay in St Albas, to complete the term. She could not look them in the eye, now that they knew she was even less perfect than she had been when she was the child who had not been able to stop their other child from dying.

It was after she had hung up the phone with her mother that she realized what she must do. She made the decision as staunchly as she had every other decision in her life.

Catriona arrived at the church shortly after Father Tom had finished his supper. He did not like hearing confessions after he had just eaten. It affected his judgment—it was difficult to care about the problems of the human sitting across from you when your stomach was full and you had bad indigestion.

"Miss Darlington-Welland," he said.

She was standing in the back of the church. He had come through the door at the altar. Eight o'clock in the evening, and the sun was almost completely gone. A dying glow came through the stained glass, though they were probably brighter from the outside. Someone, probably Simon, had lit all the candles in the chapel. They were the only trace of him left.

"Father," she said.

He stood there, looking at her. Why should he waste his precious alone time hearing about how she had been snarky with her mother, how she hadn't washed behind her ears? All this, as the prime hours of television slipped by!

"Shall we?" he said, taking a creaking seat in the front pew, facing the crucifix above the altar instead of her.

Catriona stood in the back of the church.

"Wouldn't you like to—in the confessional?"

"You think that makes it better?" he said, turning.

"No, I don't mean that."

"You can't hide from God," he sighed, his favorite evasive euphemism in an arsenal of euphemisms, though he was sure Catriona Darlington-Welland was not one to hide from God so much as herself.

"I just thought—we've always sat in there, is all."

"Then a change is good. Come."

She progressed toward the front of the church, taking a tentative seat next to him, listening to the seagulls squawking relentlessly on the roof. Every suspicious sound frightened her, made her believe that Simon, or worse, God, was going to pull a string somewhere, a puppet show, a theatre, and the roof would come down on them.

"Simon isn't here," said Father Tom. "Don't worry."

"Where is he?"

"I think I know where this confession is going," said the priest, a tart note to his voice. "Well, let's have it, mm?"

Catriona didn't move for a moment. Then, something possessed her and she bent quickly onto the red satin kneeler, pulling it down with a military motion.

"Bless me, Father, for I have sinned—"

"Dispense with it. The show. Sit up. Speak to me."

She remained kneeling.

"It has been one month since my last confession."

Father Tom rubbed his temples.

" 'Name your sins, my Child,' " she said. "Your part. Anyway, it doesn't matter if you're not going to listen. It wouldn't surprise me if you didn't listen. I don't know why you would."

He looked down on her, realizing. He'd been at his share of deathbeds.

"The truth is, I don't know what I've done. So I'll just apologize for it all. For whatever it is. For not watching my little brother and letting him die, if that's it. I'm sorry. And there's only so sorry I can be. I'm sorry for not being whatever it was I was supposed to be. A perfect daughter. A girlfriend for Max. I'm sorry for sleeping with him. If that's the punishment, though. I don't know. I don't know what I've done."

Father Tom did not speak. Catriona burst out into a scream.

"But I'm not like her! What about her? When is she punished? When does she confess? Isn't there something about the wicked prospering and the righteous suffering? Or is that all complete crap?"

"It's not for us to judge her."

"Isn't it? She doesn't go to church. Have you seen her here, once? Once, in four years? No. Neither have I. She's committed adultery. She's stolen what wasn't hers. She doesn't think about other people. I always think about other people. I always do what's right. I always, always have. And I'm always punished for it. It's too painful," she sighed, exhausted. "It's too painful."

"It was painful for Christ to carry his cross too."

"Christ was the son of God."

"Yes."

"…I'm Catriona Darlington-Welland."

"He was mortal, Catriona."

"But he had a man to help him."

"Yes."

"It's a funny coincidence. Isn't it? The name."

"Yes."

Simon.

"Who are you angry at?"

She didn't reply.

Father Tom knew a hopeless case when he saw one. He had started, as a young priest, many years ago, in an asylum run by Catholic priests. Healing the body with a remedy for the soul, a useless, one-sided equation with too many variables to solve for. Negative numbers where positives were needed.

"I'm going to pray for you," he said.

"I know that. It's why I came. Not my best confession, I'm sure."

"It's going to get better. Surely you can remember a time when you felt better. You do, don't you?"

Max. That wonderful afternoon in the fall, all those years ago when everything seemed new. St Albas, the fresh feelings, the fresh sheets. But perhaps she had edited it to look that way, to feel that way.

Perhaps the last time she'd been happy had been the moment before George had died because that was the end of being a child.

"Goodnight, Father," she said, standing up.

"God bless you, Catriona. Please think about what I've said."

"Thank you, Father."

When he heard the iron hinges creaking behind him and the door close behind her, he did not feel like watching the television anymore. And the heartburn had gotten worse.

"Jesus," he said.

# XXIII.

JULIE WALKED BY THE STEAMY WINDOW of Grind-Altering Mugs, pausing to look at the advertisements in the window because they always made for interesting reading material: "girl seeking girl with a dragon tattoo—in paperback or human form." "Missing Wookie: Responds to name, 'Chewie.' " "Handcrafted hemp bracelets for sale." She hadn't had a good sit alone for a while and decided to step in for a cappuccino.

When it was ready at the end of the bar, she took her drink and sat in one of the low sofas near the tiny, round tin fireplace. Even this late in term, a little extra heat was never a bad thing. The girl working at the bar offered her a slice of Victoria sponge cake—"it's been sitting out all afternoon, perfectly good but we'll never get rid of it"—and Julie took it happily. This is what sometimes happened when you decide to give yourself a break, when you appreciated yourself.

She closed her eyes, letting the sugar rush to her head. When she opened them, Peter had come in the front door of the café, taking the total number of people in the room up to three. There was no way he could not see her there. After all, she was only sitting. Not reading or arguing or playing Scrabble or writing. A girl sitting in a café not doing anything always warranted a look.

Peter ordered an espresso. Definitely, he had seen her, wanted his caffeine fix and to get out as soon as possible. Julie understood, in a way. And in a way, it was noble of him—choosing Catriona. Perhaps she would have too.

Then she heard him say:

"Can I top you up at all?"

She looked to see if someone else had entered the café. Then she looked into her cup.

"It's pretty full. Thank you."

Peter came to sit down next to her.

"Hello," he said, and she knew it was difficult for him.

"Hi."

The waitress sensed what was going on, or thought she did, and went through the back to the toilet. Julie was very thankful to her.

"You know," he started, "just because I haven't talked to you in a long time doesn't mean I don't know about every thing since."

"I can believe that," she said, widening her eyes and taking a gulp of coffee.

"It is St Albas, after all."

"Yes."

"Julie—Catriona is a very sick girl."

"I know, Peter. And honestly, I understand. I understand why you've chosen her. She's family. I know. I get it. I just want you to know that I never would have made you choose. Even if I was her."

Peter ran his hand through his hair in frustration.

"I know you wouldn't."

"And please tell me you don't believe I did any of what I did out of spite. I did it out of love. And maybe when some time passes, you'll see that it's best for your cousin too. She's already dating that rugby star, What's-His-Name."

"It's not easy for me to tell you this, Julie. And you know it's hard for me to admit that I'm wrong about something."

"You're never wrong," she said gently.

"I'm actually not speaking with my cousin anymore."

"What? Why?"

The force with which she had asked the question startled her.

"I mean, you don't need to tell me. But you can't blame me for being curious."

"The truth is, I've done everything I could to help her. Not only with this—but with everything, for as long as I remember. I've invited her out hundreds of times since we've come to St Albas. I've given her a ride to and from Lancashire I don't know how many times. I've taken care of her when she was sick. And—she's always asked me to keep it a secret. And I have."

"Keep what a secret?"

"Never mind," said Peter. "Let's just say I've finally told her mother some things I was keeping to myself for Catriona's sake."

He stopped himself.

"There was nothing I could do to help her anymore. So, I told someone else. And when she found out, she was none too happy with me. Apparently, I am the worst person in the whole world, and I have no honor and no loyalty. Or something as puritanically phrased. I couldn't carry it around. Not anymore."

Julie said nothing.

"Anyway, I think when she gets home at the end of term it's going to be pretty miserable for her. But that's not important. She'll be safe now, and—"

He was lost for words.

"Peter," she said. "I'm so sorry."

He nodded.

"And if you're about to apologize to me at length, I don't think it's such a good idea."

"No?"

"Not as good of an idea as just dropping it all and enjoying the next few weeks and the Saving."

"The Saving. Good God, is that this weekend?"

# XXIV.

**SHE STOOD ON THE ANCIENT WALL,** far above the crowd that was gathering below on Castle Sands. She couldn't help thinking they were very naïve. She hoped some of them would see her flying off onto the rocks. Would she seem to fall in slow motion, she wondered? How many seconds would elapse between final step and last sleep? She could only hope the death would be immediate and painless. If there was a God after all, surely He would at least let her die quickly.

The wind whipped at the sides of her cheeks, creating two brush strokes of red there, a disturbing addition to her pallor, which was ghostly pale from fear and lack of sunshine despite the tanning lotion. Even at these last of moments, she had taken great pains to ensure that she would be found looking as neat as possible. Her nails were manicured, her eyebrows plucked, and she had made sure to wear her most modest underthings—the clothes might be returned to her parents in the end. She had even made some shepherds pie so that Vera would have something to feed people when they came by the house, though she had not made a large one because there was no knowing how many might or might not come. Perhaps no one. That Harry Ommar might eat it all alone.

She wondered who would find her. She had fantasies of Max discovering her there, with her heart torn out of her chest or with her head separated from her body. If he did, one could only hope he of all people would notice the implants. She thought of herself decomposing into nothing, with only the golden cross necklace and a pair of silicone shells remaining in her casket when she had turned into a tree or soil. Perhaps in a thousand years someone would crack open her grave, and these remnants would be placed in a museum, in a room with one of those humidity detectors on the wall.

With every moment that passed, the sun awoke a little more, still unseen, but almost there on the horizon. With every moment that it did, the chances of being caught, and stopped, became more likely. And she did not have the strength to bring herself up here again. Maybe that was a good enough reason not to do it for some, but Catriona thought it brave that she was performing a task that she could never do again. This was her window.

Her parents, her family, the small group of friends—they wouldn't really be sorry. Perhaps, some of her art professors would wonder if there was anything that could have been done. ("She was such a hardworking student, so polite," they would say, after struggling to remember who she was, exactly.) And perhaps, Simon would be hurt, and Vera, of course, would need to find someone to take the flat until August. Peter might be upset at himself, think it his fault for telling the family about her cutting, about everything. But he flattered himself if he thought so, and if he was sad because of it then she supposed he deserved the sadness.

It was perhaps a shame to have done so much studying over the last four years and to never complete her degree. But what had she done in this horrible little town that could not be considered an utter waste? It was rather fitting that things should end like this, hurling herself off the old Castle, which was revered for no other reason than that it was old, that it had always been there. That it was still there—broken and useless as it was.

The potential bathers and their fires flickered below. Perhaps she had missed something, she thought, looking at them. They were so young. If she had accepted more of Peter's invitations earlier on, she may have been a different person by now.

But no, that was silly to think. She allowed herself to believe their legends now. She'd stepped on the stones of WM. Her destiny was always going to be to wind up on this high, windy wall, alone.

*** 

The fire created shadows, disembodied against the brick wall of the Castle, as the students danced and sang, as they started fires and put them out, as they kissed and cursed and drank and smoked just as they always did.

The friends had arrived on the beach an hour before, earlier this year than the last as it was the last chance after all to run into the sea together. Ashwin had had a proper pyre of wood delivered and had paid two first years to guard it since it had been brought to the beach the previous morning. Julie looked around with satisfaction and sadness, a dull and an insistent ache in her chest building from within that seemed to sober her the more she drank. With every chorus of the University's anthem, the *Iuvenis Perpetuum*, she felt herself waking to the dawn of what they called real life, the break with Neverland that she could feel pulling at the dark horizon of youth, starting to fray callously the seams that had held the last four years with its attendant loves and heartbreaks and friendships together. It made her feel empty, even as Max held her hand in his. It made her feel scared, even as Peter smiled at her from across the fire, promising silently with his chin set at an angle to always be there to catch her when she fell, which she would inevitably do again and again and again.

"You all right?" said Max.

"Yeah."

"What are you thinking about?"

"I'm thinking how happy I am for you to get to do this."

"It's been a long time coming," said Max.

"It certainly has."

"Do you want to dance with me? I know I'm terrible."

"You're perfect. And I do. In a minute?"

"I love you so much," he said. "Do you know that? Do you really know?"

"I do," said Julie.

Max kissed her, and she knew again.

Julie leaned against the Castle Wall as she watched Max take Caddy's outstretched hand to join the circle of them skipping drunkenly and happily around the fire. Her rain boots sank into the cold sand, which she could feel icily through the thick rubber. It was so comforting to lean against something so old. She remembered the day she had first met Peter, when they had finally sobered up and taken a walk through the town. She had stopped dead in her tracks on the Avenue in front of the Castle and had said:

"It's so old."

Peter smiled.

"Yes."

"No, Peter—it is *so* old."

He nodded, and Julie smiled too.

"I guess you're used to things that are old," she said. "You probably grew up in a house older than my entire country."

"I did, in fact."

"That's incredible to me. God. Looking at it makes me feel so young."

"And insignificant."

"Yeah," she said. "I wonder if it's even possible to grow up in a place as old as this."

"I guess we'll see."

"I mean, possible to *feel* grown up. Even if we live to be one hundred, we're never going to see the stuff that Castle's seen."

"I don't know, Julie. People never change."

"You don't think so?"

"I don't know."

"Well I think so."

"The Castle has seen it all, hasn't it? Invasions and reformations and saints and martyrs," said Peter. "And you're looking at it, all the same, again, now."

"There's that stuff, yeah. But, like—I don't know, also, people loving each other and falling in love, and May Savings, and leaving each other, and jumping off the Castle Wall."

Julie paused, wondering if this was too dark a place to take a boy she had just met. Peter had turned to her, and said instead:

"Friends becoming friends?"

"Yeah. All the good things," Julie said. "All the good stories."

"All the growing-up things."

"All the growing-up things," said Julie with a sigh, though she remembered thinking it was an odd thing to say.

Julie felt the urge to climb up to the top of the Castle. To watch from afar, for once. She felt a sudden distaste for the May Saving. Every year she had done it. And where had it gotten her, this strange baptism? What did she know better or do better because of it? Every year, students in St Albas would do it. And for what reason? Wasn't it juvenile, to take off most of your clothes and to run into the North Sea like a pack of lemmings? To prove your youth? To do it because everyone else did it? Drinking all night didn't make you a better person. Neither did running into the sea. It proved nothing at all. Without a word to Peter or Max or anyone else, Julie turned her back on them and climbed the steps to the Castle, one by one. She felt the height of every step.

Really, Julie knew deep in her heart that if she ran into the sea, it would all be over. Real life would begin, from the second her head reemerged from the water. It was safer not to do it at all. And so she climbed and climbed.

It was quiet on the Avenue. It was quiet as she swung her foot over the fence and dropped into the central courtyard. But as she approached the Castle Wall, she could make out the tinny sounds of the students below, as well as the outline of a girl's body, her knees pulled tight to her chest by her arms, sitting very close to the edge.

"Catriona," she said.

"Julie."

Catriona was startled and nearly tipped forward. Then she turned.

"What are you doing?" said Julie.

"Nothing."

"What are you doing up here?"

"I don't believe this," said Catriona to someone that wasn't Julie. "You. Of all people."

Julie felt a terrible twist in every muscle of her body. A horrible sickness. There was no mistaking why she was up on the wall, when everyone else was down below. Had she put Catriona up there? No! Of course not, what a silly idea. Everyone made their own choices, especially choices of this nature, of this magnitude. What should she do? What *could* she do?

"You have to come down."

Catriona said nothing.

"I want to talk to you," said Julie. "Can I come up there with you?"

Catriona nodded.

Julie's head filled with hot air. Under her ears her jaw felt strange and tense, as if millions of concentrated bubbles of champagne were fizzing there. When she had climbed to the ledge, she said:

"Can I sit down?"

"Yes."

To Catriona's immense surprise, Julie swung her legs out over the edge too kicking them back and forward. Catriona thought her maddeningly relaxed, but Julie had never felt more frantic in her life. She had never been in a life-or-death situation before. She was scared she would fall. She was scared Catriona would take her down with her. She was scared she wouldn't know how to keep her from leaning forward, to keep her from falling.

"Look," said Julie, "Catriona, please don't do this."

"Seriously?"

"You can come down. We can figure something out."

"No, we can't. Don't pretend. I'm sure Peter must have told you—if I don't kill myself, my mum is going to make me *want* to kill myself this summer when I come home."

"I'm sure that's not true."

"What would you know about it?"

"I don't know. I just know—my God, Catriona, do you know how close you are to graduating? Please, just think. You have so much to look forward to."

"You're presuming an awful lot."

It struck Catriona that perhaps it had all, in some way, worked. Julie knew about the boyfriend. Knew how good she looked. Knew, probably, that she would graduate with top honors. But it was simply too late for it to matter.

"I'm not. I know I'm not. You can't throw your life away, Catriona. Look, look how beautiful it is down there on the beach. Come on."

"My life isn't good."

"That's not true."

"It's true."

"That's all the more reason not to freeze it here, then, right?"

Catriona looked down. It was an awfully long way.

"I'm here because I have to be. Because of you."

Julie could not process this amount of blame. And she could not believe that it was just her, or just Max, that would make Catriona kill herself if that's really what she was going to do. Somehow, she thought it wouldn't have surprised her if she'd heard Catriona had killed herself this exact way in second year or third or earlier in their fourth. She tried to remember the thousands of things she'd rehearsed to say to Catriona if she ever got to talk to her alone.

And Julie was right: Catriona was lying to herself—of course she was. It wasn't just because of Julie or Max or Simon or Peter or George. It was because of all the horrible little wrongs that had been done to her, that grew and grew over the years, never being forgotten or forgiven, only being stockpiled. It was the girls in kindergarten and grammar school and university who had never troubled to get to know her, who she had heard calling her fat on the playgrounds and a teacher's pet in the lunch hall and an overachiever in the art galleries. It was the boys who believed what the girls said. It was her mother, who never did anything to allay her daughter's belief that a man and a hearth were the only things that were worth having, who never troubled to explain why Catriona was not allowed a pass on the pressure to be Harriet Darlington-Welland all over again. It was all of them, together.

Julie sat patiently as Catriona thought.

Finally, Catriona said:

"What made you take Max from me?"

*It took this for you to ask me?* Julie thought.

Julie shrugged. She had the right to defend herself.

"I fell in love."

"But he was my boyfriend. Don't you understand that? Seriously, Julie. Just tell me the truth. You were moving in on my boyfriend."

"I didn't steal Max from you. I didn't even try. We were just, you know, hanging out, as friends."

"Don't you see that it wasn't proper? To go about with someone else's boyfriend during the middle of the night?"

"We were just hanging out."

"Is it seriously impossible for you? To tell me the truth? Right now? I'm already up here, aren't I?"

"Fine," said Julie. "I wanted your boyfriend."

"Thank you," said Catriona, who was relieved beyond words to hear someone telling her the truth, even if it was Julie Lovejoy.

"He loves me, though. Catriona. And I love him. That counts for something."

Catriona said:

"Max told me he wanted to marry me too."

Catriona was surprised that there was compassion in her voice. And, perhaps, a warning.

"I know," said Julie. "There was even a ring. I saw it."

Catriona looked at Julie with pure, unadulterated hatred. Julie was scared by what she saw in her eyes and what it meant. If Catriona had not been so paralyzed by her hatred, Julie believed for the rest of her life that Catriona would have pushed her off the wall at that very moment.

"I'm sorry I said that," said Julie. "That was unkind. I'm sorry."

Before she knew it, her hand was extending out toward Catriona, a gesture she had learned in church as a little girl—*pax vobiscum*, peace be with you.

"Don't touch me."

"Take my hand. We'll go down together."

"No."

*If that's the way it's going to be,* thought Julie. *I might as well tell her what I want to tell her.*

"It's not your fault. Max chose me."

Catriona had heard something like that, somewhere before. Julie continued:

"There's nothing you could have done better, Catriona."

"How *come* he chose you?"

"I don't know."

"How come the boys get to do the choosing?"

"I don't know."

"It just isn't right, what you did. It isn't proper. How can you not see that?"

Julie was struck by the tenseness in her voice, the desperation and urgency.

"Didn't you know that it was over?"

"It *wasn't* over. If I felt that way, I wouldn't be here."

They sat there for a moment in silence. The sun was going to come up any second.

"I think I'm going to go down to the beach. I suggest you do the same. Using the stairs, I mean. You can come to the party, if you want."

"No one wants me there."

"I want you there," said Julie in a gentle voice.

"Of course you don't, Julie," Catriona said quietly. "Go. If God didn't want me to be here, He wouldn't have sent you up here to confirm it. To show me how I can't get anything right."

"If you want to leap off the wall—I can't stop you. Especially if you've got it in your head that God thinks you're no good. But doesn't it hurt to know that we'll all be running into that sea in two minutes and no one will even notice you aren't there, that you've split your head open instead?"

Julie sighed. "Have you ever done the Saving?"

"No," said Catriona.

"Don't you even *want* a chance to change it? Because you can, Catriona. Maybe it doesn't feel like it. But you can. I did."

Julie couldn't take her eyes off Catriona. She was sorry for what she'd said about the forehead, about her being crazy. She was really quite beautiful, if you took a moment to think about it.

"Please," she said. "Think of Peter."

They sat there together for a moment. Catriona stared down. Did not cry. Did not speak. Julie was terrified to touch her. Any move she could make to take her down from the wall might lead to either or both of them falling in the direction of the rocks.

"You don't understand," Catriona finally said. "I have no future. No one loves me."

"There has to be one person. I know there must be."

Seeing the whole world expanding into a big, blue sky before her, Catriona reached over for Julie's hand, and held it, thinking of Simon. Thinking that Simon would forgive anyone, anything. For a moment, Julie and Catriona were sewn together in such a way that you couldn't tell which was the girl and which was the shadow. They were one across the feet between them—or the metres, if that was your sort of thing.

Seeing what she thought were glints of light on the horizon, reflecting off of the sea, Julie let Catriona's hand go. She had been silly to think she shouldn't do the Saving.

"All right," Julie said softly, as she came down from the wall and walked into the courtyard without looking back. She took ten steps, and then she said:

"You know, everyone down on the beach right now has thought of doing it too."

"You think so?" said Catriona.

"Yeah. But I think you're the only one who's ever wanted to do it today."

Catriona watched Julie walking through the drawing gate, slowly, and then urgently.

*Funny*, she thought. *It's like I know her.*

Down below, Julie's friends, hundreds of them, were dancing with heathen abandon around the fire, playing the guitar, kissing in the dark, cool, damp beach coves and searching for treasures among the rocks.

Some One struck a match in the sky. One of the boys on the beach noticed it and, with the fire reflected in his eye, ran into the roiling surf. Another one ran after him and another and another until they all were mercreatures, rocking in the frigid shallows.

# THE BOYS WHO WOULDN'T GROW UP
## A NOVEL

LAUREN B. MANGIAFORTE

A READING GROUP GUIDE

**BELOW ARE SUGGESTED QUESTIONS FOR BOOK** clubs and reading groups in their discussion of *The Boys Who Wouldn't Grow Up: A Novel.*

**1.** What do you think of the title? How does it impact your understanding of the story? How does it relate to the girls in the novel?

**2.** The book presents all of its main characters as both good and bad in their own ways. Who do you think the protagonist(s) and the antagonist(s) of the story are?

**3.** Some of the themes in the book include destiny and chance, the eternal and the fleeting, and of course: growing up. Which of these themes resonated with you personally? What symbols represented each theme?

**4.** How does socioeconomic status impact the behavior of the characters in the story?

**5.** Many of the characters in the story are highly smackable. Which character did you most want to hit upside the head or give a piece of your mind?

**6.** Catriona and Julie can be seen as representing traditional and contemporary expectations of womanhood. How does each girl deal with these expectations or shun them? Overall, what is the author saying about women's roles?

**7.** Similarly, the boys in the book run the spectrum of the highly sexual Harry to the knight-in-shining-armor Simon to the hapless, intellectual Max. What does the book seem to say about men's roles?

**8.** Names play a large part in our understanding of the characters. Which names did you think were the most appropriate? Which might hold clues as to the characters' personalities?

**9.** How do the main characters see themselves? Is this different than from how others see them? How do different perceptions affect the outcome of the story?

**10.** Which character, if any, changes the most profoundly throughout the course of the book? How?

**11.** How have your thoughts or views changed after reading this book?

**12.** Who was your favorite character in the supporting cast (i.e. Fern, Caddy, Ashwin, Brett) and why?

**13.** What do you think Catriona decides to do in the final moment of the story? Why?

**14.** Did you feel the ending was satisfying? How would you change it if not?

**15.** If you could ask the author one question, what would it be? (Good news: email bahnheur@gmail.com and you might get a response.)

# A BRIEF NOTE

**HILLARY MANGIAFORTE IS THE COVER DESIGNER** for *The Boys Who Wouldn't Grow Up: A Novel.* She is also the author of the series Violet Pearls. Find her online at: http://violetpearlsseries.com.

Lucy Ryden provided preliminary sketches for the cover. Visit her at www.rosytuesday.co.uk.

The fonts used in the design of *The Boys Who Wouldn't Grow Up: A Novel* are Festivo Letters No. 6 (title and chapter pages), Festivo Letters No. 17 (author name and header), and Garamond (body).

The trim size is an A5 and was printed and perfectly bound by Lulu (www.lulu.com). The layout, produced in Microsoft Word 2011, is self-published by Lauren B. Mangiaforte under the publishing house The Bahnheur Press.

Liked the book?

Want a friend to talk to about it?

Cut or tear off this page and pass it on!

42202175R00239

Made in the USA
Lexington, KY
12 June 2015